Praise for *T...*

RETURN TO TYRINGHAM PARK

ROSEMARY MCLOUGHLIN

POOLBEG

Published 2016
by Poolbeg Press Ltd
123 Grange Hill, Baldoyle
Dublin 13, Ireland
E-mail: poolbeg@poolbeg.com
www.poolbeg.com

1

A catalogue record for this book is available from the British Library.

ISBN 978-1-78199-909-7

www.facebook.com/poolbeg
@PoolbegBooks

Typeset by Poolbeg Press Ltd in Sabon
Printed and bound by CPI Group (UK) Ltd, Croydon, CR0 4YY

www.poolbeg.com

ABOUT THE AUTHOR

Rosemary McLoughlin, reared as Rosie Fahey in Australia, lives in Dublin with her husband.

ACKNOWLEDGEMENTS

Grateful thanks to my original family, the Faheys from Tyringham, Via Dorrigo, NSW, Australia, and to those who have helped me in various ways: Frances Berry, Gabrielle Bowe, Maria (Crean) Cope, Kiera Fahey, Peggy Farrell, Geraldine Gardiner, Helen Halley, Evelyn (O'Toole) King, Sheila Morris, Bid O'Connor, Dr Mary (Fleming) O'Connor, Nuala Ryan, Lorraine (Morris) Smith and, most especially, Gayle (Kelly) Roberts from Perth for her valued commentaries.

Special thanks to my present family – husband Kevin, son Cian, daughter Orla, daughter-in-law Eavan Meagher and son-in law Daire O'Flaherty, who continue to be my most inspiring and trusted advisors.

Finally, to Paula Campbell at Poolbeg for her understanding support and to Gaye Shortland for her meticulous editing.

To Sam and Finn

PROLOGUE

I should have followed you in, my pet.

Victoria, it's me. Charlotte. Your big sister.

Is it too late?

Will you come and talk to me?

I can feel your presence, Victoria . . .

Thank you for coming so quickly. You don't know how much it means to me that you are here. I was afraid you would turn away in disgust when you heard my voice. I'm sorry I sent you on that long cold journey on your own. I wish I'd had the courage to go with you then . . .

I've just killed that horrible Nurse Dixon. You probably already know that, seeing you're on the other side. I had to shut her up. She threatened to tell everyone what I did to you so that my Mary Anne would be taken away from me.

I deliberately pushed her over the banister outside the nursery. I could say her fall was an accident. I could say that pushing you into the river was an accident as well. Who could contradict me when there were no witnesses? Miss East and Manus would lie about Dixon for me, I know. They would swear that I was nowhere near Dixon when she went over. Would I have the right to ask the two of them to perjure themselves for me? Hardly, when I never came down to

1

see them and I couldn't even look either of them in the eye just now.

Goodbye, Mary Anne. You gave me such joy that I can only repay you by leaving you. Your Aunt Iseult will care for you beautifully until your daddy comes back, then he will marry Niamh who will be good and kind to you and you won't even remember that I ever existed while, all the time, unbeknown to you, I will be looking after you and keeping you from harm.

Goodbye, Lochlann. Thank you for the happiness you gave me at the expense of your own. I feel almost light-hearted at the prospect of setting you free.

Our mother can do without my good wishes. She never liked me. I didn't blame her for favouring you and Harcourt – she had her reasons which I'll tell you about when we meet – but she didn't have to make it so obvious. She'll be glad I've gone, thinking she'll be able to get her hands on Mary Anne. I'd like to see her face when she reads my will.

Can you see me from where you are, Victoria? I'm heading towards the Dark Waterhole. It's difficult to be sure exactly where I am. I won't be sure I'm at the Hole until I step off the ledge. I can't feel my feet and the water isn't all that clear. I'm not looking forward to that first inhalation of water. How long before I stop struggling to breathe? Will I sink to the bottom or rise to the surface straight away or later?

Will you have a word with God so that I don't end up in that other place with Dixon, where I belong? He'll listen to the request of an innocent child.

Soon I'll know exactly what you went through . . .

Your doll is securely tucked into my bag under my arm. I'll make sure not to lose it.

The time has come. Breathe out.

Guide me, Victoria, and when it's all over have your hand out ready to catch me so that I don't fly straight past you. I don't want to end up lost in space, searching for you for all eternity, with no hope of finding you amongst the multitudes.

Are you ready?

PART 1

MARY ANNE

IRELAND

CHAPTER 1

Tyringham Park, Ireland, 1943

Charlotte appeared to be lifeless by the time Manus located her in the Dark Waterhole. He had been looking for her to tell her that he intended to lie about the murder she had just committed. He was prepared to swear that the nanny's fatal fall was accidental and that Charlotte had been nowhere near the nursery wing at the time the death had occurred.

When he first saw the shape in the water heading upstream, he could not make out what it was, but after focusing on it he suddenly realised it was Charlotte, chest-deep in the river, staring back at him, and moving with purpose towards the deep Dark Waterhole. As he watched, she turned her face away from his horrified gaze and moved forward, a few moments later disappearing from view.

He ran to the river bank, threw off his boots and jacket, entered the water, dived down many times, found her finally in the depths, pulled her to the surface and drew her to a secluded section of the bank where he laid her on the grass.

She was not breathing.

His lengthy attempts to resuscitate her were futile.

Checking that there was no one around, he lifted her up from the bank and carried her through the double doors of the stables, across the courtyard and into his office where he placed her on the wooden floor before going back to close the double doors, securing a bar in place across the back of them to make certain that no one could enter.

Eight-year-old Toby Prendergast, the grandson of the gardener at Tyringham Park, pushed open the oak door and saw, lying on the quarry tiles at the bottom of three flights of stairs, a large object that hadn't been there the previous day when he had sneaked in to explore the deserted nursery wing. The object was covered with a red blanket and there was something red that looked like blood oozing out all over the floor, so he guessed that the heap must be a dead body. He wasn't frightened as he had seen a lot of dead fish, cats and dogs in his short life, and had even seen three dead fishermen down on the quays in Cobh, and he never felt the need to turn away from the sight of any of them. In fact he found them really interesting and stared at them for ages, especially at the fishermen, wondering how they felt just before they died and if they had expected to be saved from drowning at the last minute.

He lifted up the blanket and saw that all the blood was coming from the back of a woman's head. Her face looked peaceful. Her skin was creamy and her eyes were open.

Things were scattered over the floor. Some foreign money. A passport. He could read the name 'Elizabeth Dixon' opposite her photograph on an inside page of the passport. An open handbag turned upside down. Lots of papers. A leather pouch containing five pretty things. He took out one, a bundle of plain glass beads, and held them up to the light to get a better look at them. Each bead created rainbow colours on the wall opposite the window. He would keep them. The dead lady wouldn't be needing them ever again and his mother would like them. The matching bangle would be nice for his new baby sister when she grew old enough to wear it. The beads and earrings made of blue glass were also pretty, but he only needed the two presents, so returned the blue pieces to the pouch, and put the clear glass ones into his pocket.

Upstairs he discovered that the tapestry cushion cover and the redheaded doll, which he had found the day before and come back to collect, were both missing. Never mind, he said to himself in a phrase used often by his mother. The beads would make really good presents without anything else to go with them. He hoped that the ghost of Miss Victoria, who haunted the wing, had found the doll. She might have been watching from a secret place when he had first uncovered it and had waited until he left to claim it and was now playing with it at this very minute. That must be what had happened. He was pleased to think it was because of him she had found out about its existence.

When he went back to the walled garden with his empty canvas bag, he didn't mention the body to his grandfather, Reg, as he knew he would get into trouble for going to the nursery wing when he had been expressly forbidden to go near the place. He didn't want his mother receiving a bad report. She was keen that he would one day work alongside his grandfather at Tyringham Park because he was never going to become a fisherman like his father. If he even so much as stepped onto a fishing boat he would come out in a rash and his face would puff up and he would start vomiting. His father said he might grow out of the allergy and even get to like the smell of fish, but Toby had strong hopes that he would not.

Manus came back to where Charlotte lay and stared down at her, remembering her as she had been as a child. She had been born into the aristocratic Blackshaw family, destined to lead a life of privilege at Tyringham Park, and here she was stretched out dead at his feet at the age of only thirty-four. What could have possessed her to kill Dixon? What had possessed her to drown herself? She had seen him coming down the avenue, he was sure of that, and had purposely completed her journey to the Dark Waterhole and gone under. She must have breathed in water straight away as she did not rise to the surface, not even for a few seconds.

He could think of nothing that could have prompted such extreme behaviour. He remembered her as a good-natured, biddable child, and Dixon as a kind and considerate nanny. The hatred he had seen on Charlotte's face as she pushed Dixon into the void was inexplicable to him.

As he continued to stare his mind began to clear. Two dead bodies on the same estate on the one day? How to explain that without dragging Charlotte's good name into disrepute? There could be no ordinary solution to cover up these two extraordinary events.

He knew it was up to him to come up with an answer, and there was one beginning to take shape in his mind. With the help of Lily

East, a woman renowned for her truthfulness, who had already said she would lie just this one time to save the reputation of her dearly beloved Charlotte, he thought there was a good chance of success.

Shuddering with the cold, he took dry clothes out of a press and changed into them, all the while trying to work out what he would say to the doctor and the police when eventually he would have to notify them.

How to avoid telling the truth?

Use one's reputation as a truthful man to convince everyone to believe a complete fabrication, tamper with both crime scenes so that they would match his made-up story, and ensure that Lily backed him up. That is how he would do it.

He slipped off Charlotte's shoes, towel-dried them and put them close to the pot-bellied stove, but not so close that they would be scorched. He dried the outside of her bag, tipped out the contents, hid a cardigan, scarf, gloves and something wrapped in a tapestry cushion cover in a press, dried the inside of the bag, placed it near the stove, dried the small contents – coins, notes, ticket, compact – and put them back into the bag. All this was to make it look as if the shoes and bag had not been in the water, that Charlotte had divested herself of them before jumping in.

Now for the execution of his plan. He and Lily had been the only witnesses to Charlotte's pushing Nurse Dixon over the banisters, to fall to her death on the quarry tiles below. No one else would ever find out, if both he and Lily kept that knowledge to themselves and did not waver.

Manus filled up the barrow with manure, covered it with a couple of towels and a horse rug, and wheeled it in the direction of the nursery wing, hoping to arrive there unobserved.

It was a well-known fact among the servants working on the estate that Manus did not cross the invisible line between the stables and the Big House unless it was a matter of supreme importance, and here he was wheeling a barrow around the back of the house. And looking very worried into the bargain, Reg thought.

"Something's up," whispered Reg to Toby who had returned only ten minutes earlier from viewing a dead body.

As far as Reg could remember, the only other occasion Manus had crossed that line was the time little Miss Victoria went missing twenty-six years earlier and Manus had ridden up to the house like a madman to break the news and to tell everyone to start searching for her. So even though wheeling a barrow might look like an innocent activity to anyone who was not familiar with the customs of the Park, Reg assumed there had to be a very serious reason for Manus to break his rule.

"You all right there, Manus?" he called over to him, stepping out from the entrance to the walled garden where he had been standing. "Anything up?"

Manus visibly started at the sound of the voice.

"No, everything's fine, thanks, Reg," he called back, adding, "Just bringing up some manure for Lily's garden."

Manure for Lily's garden? I don't believe that for a minute, thought Reg. He made up that excuse on the spot.

Lily East regularly collected small amounts of manure from the stables herself, as it gave her an excuse to chat to everyone she met on her way there and back, particularly to Reg, as they were both enthusiastic about plants. Apart from that consideration, the load was suspiciously excessive for a small garden like Lily's.

He's definitely up to something, thought Reg. And why is there a horse rug covering the manure?

Manus did not drop the legs of the wheelbarrow on to the ground, but stood holding the handles to signal that he did not intend to linger for a chat.

"Come over here, Toby, and meet Manus, the most famous horseman in the whole island of Ireland. Manus, this is Toby, my Daisy's son. You remember Daisy, don't you?"

"Of course. A lively young one, but frightened of horses if you remember, so I didn't get to see that much of her."

"Well, this lad isn't frightened of anything, are you, Toby? He's up from Cobh on his first visit to help me out." Reg winked at Manus. "Daisy has just given birth to a little girl, so that's why Toby's come to help – to get away from all the fussing. He's already got his name down to work with me when he grows up, haven't you, Toby?"

"That shouldn't be too long judging by the look of you, fine big lad that you are." Manus let go of one of the handles to shake the boy's hand, but still did not rest the barrow on the ground. "You have a resemblance to your mother all right, now that I come to look at you.

9

Let's see what I've got here for you and your new little sister." Manus put his hand in his pocket and brought out an assortment of coins which he handed to Toby. "You must get your grandfather to bring you down to have a look around the stables after everyone gets back, Toby. You never know, you could end up working there instead of in the gardens."

"That's a kind offer, Manus. Say 'thank you', Toby."

"Thank you," said Toby, who thought riding horses would definitely be more exciting than gardening. He put the coins into his pocket and heard them clink against the glass beads already there, and thought of the pleasure his mother would get when he showed her all these riches. He hoped the two men hadn't heard the clinking sound but he reckoned they hadn't as Reg was talking on while Manus stood as if ready to take off, still holding the wheelbarrow's legs up off the ground. Toby didn't want to be asked what it was he already had in his pocket. Often he couldn't make up stories quickly enough to get himself out of trouble, and he didn't have a story ready now and couldn't think of one.

"Come on, Toby, we'll let Manus off about his business," said Reg at last.

Manus was already moving off. "Good luck, Toby. Nice to meet you. See you around, Reg. Can't keep Lily waiting."

The two watched Manus pushing the barrow along the path and then turning the corner.

"Something's definitely up," repeated Reg, "but it's none of my business. Keep your nose out of other people's business, I always say, and you'll never get into trouble, young Toby. Along with obeying my two rules, of course."

Boys will be boys, and you can't go against nature, Reg believed, but after you gave them a long rope you had to make sure the rope wasn't so long that they would hang themselves with it. Freedom wasn't licence, after all, and that was why he had given Toby two simple rules to follow while he was under his care.

A minute later Toby slipped out of the walled garden while his grandfather was occupied and headed in the direction he had seen Manus taking.

Damn and blast, thought Manus. What bad luck. He hadn't expected to run into anyone. With the Blackshaw family, all the stable lads and a load of servants at present in Killarney at the races, and other servants taking their annual break to coincide with their absence, he'd thought he might be able to move Dixon's body unobserved. He should have known better. With the house the size of a castle, and the grounds the size of a parish, there was bound to be someone looking out of a window or someone peering over a hedge.

It had been his intention to tip out the manure and collect Dixon's body in the barrow and bring it, covered by the horse rug, down to his office to lay it beside the corpse of Charlotte that was already there. Now that he had been spotted by Reg and Toby, he had no option but to leave the body where it was for a while longer and bide his time. There was little fear that anyone would come across it where it lay, as the nursery wing had been closed, and supposedly haunted, for twenty-five years and most of the servants would not enter it even if you paid them to do so. Moving the body out of there into the open was where the risk escalated. By the look of that boy Toby's bright eyes and alert expression, you wouldn't be able to get away with anything secret with him around the place.

Manus positioned the wheelbarrow beside Lily's front gate, with the manure and rug still in place. He saw Lily beckoning him from her front window. He had thought she was still in the nursery wing watching over Dixon's body.

"Did you manage to find Charlotte?" she asked as soon as she opened the door to him.

"I did."

"Thank God for that. Where is she?"

"At the stables. Let us sit down for a minute and I'll tell you all about her."

"As you can see, I deserted my post in the nursery – straight after you left," she said as she led him to the two armchairs on either side the fireplace. "Too many memories in that wing. I picked up her bag to check the contents to find out if she has any next of kin but I thought I heard her speak and I dropped it out of fright – her things went all over the place and I took off back here as fast as my old legs would carry me without even picking anything up. I'm sorry. I shouldn't have left."

"Never mind that now." He leaned towards her and enclosed her old, gnarled hands in his strong, suntanned ones before saying, "I'm afraid I have some very bad news for you."

11

CHAPTER 2

Toby remained out of sight until he saw Manus going into the old woman's house. As soon as the door closed behind the pair he slipped into the nursery wing and took up a position on the third-floor landing, looking down at the red blanket covering the dead body on the ground floor. He wondered if Manus would turn up and take the body away in the wheelbarrow, or if the body was going to be left where it was to rot and, if it was left, how long it would be before the maggots turned up.

While he waited, he wondered what his grandfather would do to him if he found out he was disobeying his first and most important rule. Not send him back home, he hoped. He wanted to spend the whole of the summer at the Park to avoid having to listen to his mother's clucking over the boring new baby.

"Don't go near the nursery wing, disturbing the ghost that lives there," Reg had said to him the previous day. "That's the first rule you have to obey while you're staying with me."

"A real ghost?"

"Of course it's real – otherwise I wouldn't be warning you."

"What kind of a ghost?"

"A little girl ghost. Miss Victoria went missing twenty-six years ago when she wasn't yet three years of age. It was a terrible day that I'll never forget. Disappeared off the face of the earth, she did."

"Does she play tricks on boys?"

"Not if they do as they're told. You'll be glad to know you'll be as free as a bird while you're here with me – except for my two rules. Not disturbing the ghost is the main one."

"Have you seen it, Granddad?"

"No, but I've heard from those who have seen it at night looking through the third-floor windows. I have enough sense to stay away from the place and so will you or you'll have me to answer to. That's rule number one. Second and last rule: you are not allowed to speak to Master William when he gets back from the races."

"Why can't I?"

"Because Master William will inherit the Park one day when he grows up and will be your master when you come to work here, so you have to show him a bit of respect even though he's younger than you are. Is that all clear?"

"Yes, Granddad."

"Good. Now, apart from those two simple rules you can stay outdoors all summer long. I won't be breathing down your neck. Here, come and give me a hand with this."

Toby remembered what his granddad had said to his mother on his last visit to Cobh. They hadn't noticed he was listening. They never did.

"You can't keep a boy of that age cooped up inside the house," his granddad had said. "There's no such thing as a bad child, I always say – only a bored one. I'll make a catapult for him so that he can go out and hit a few magpies, and I'll teach him how to snare rabbits. Natural hunters, boys. Town life cramps their style. Leave him to me and don't you worry. We'll get on like a house on fire."

"I hope so," his mother had answered, not sounding convinced by her father's confidence.

Manus said as gently as he could that there was no time for mourning if they were to save Charlotte's good name. He hoped Lily would agree to tell even more lies than the ones they had already agreed on.

"You shouldn't even have to ask. You know I would do anything

13

for Charlotte. I promise you I won't break down. Do what you have to do now, and tell me later what I am to say."

"I'll wait here for a bit in case Reg's grandson is roaming about. He was a little too interested in the wheelbarrow for my liking and might have followed me. Can't afford to run into him. I'll wait here long enough for him to get bored and go off. Have you met him yet? Bright as a button. Wouldn't miss a trick by the look of him."

Twenty minutes passed before Manus, staring out of Lily's front window and seeing no one, judged it safe enough to carry on with his plan. Reg must have given Toby a job to do. All was quiet except for Lily's muffled weeping in the background.

Manus left the cottage and tipped the manure in the wheelbarrow out beside Lily's garden. He placed the horse rug back into the barrow and then made his way to the nursery wing, without encountering anyone. He entered it, bolted the oak door behind him and felt safe from observation for the time being.

He put the horse rug and the pair of towels on the floor, and said a prayer apologising to Nurse Dixon for what he was about to do.

Because of the unevenness of the floor, blood from the dead woman's wound had pooled around her head before flowing behind her, leaving her clothing free from stains.

He lifted her body. There was a sucking sound as her head was pulled away from the tiles. The wound leaked fresh blood through her matted hair. He placed her in the wheelbarrow, folding her legs up, and placed the horse rug so that it covered her entire body. Using the towels and the red blanket, he wiped the drying blood off the quarry tiles then tucked the blood-sodden towels and blanket back under the rug, which he shaped so that it didn't look as if there was a body underneath it.

He picked up the strewn objects from the floor and replaced them in Dixon's handbag which he hid in the cupboard under the stairs. Her hat he placed in beside her. As a final detail, he scraped up a handful of dust from a corner and sprinkled it over the surface he had just cleaned so that, as soon as it dried, it would match the rest of the unswept floor.

He went outside to check that there was no one around. If he could leave the wing without being seen, he was confident he would make it the rest of the way safely by changing his route. Aware of the principle that one was more likely to get away with doing something out of the ordinary than following an expected course, he wheeled the barrow along the gravel in front of the house on the way back to the stables – conduct unthinkable if the Blackshaw family had been in residence – instead of around the back where the servants, particularly Reg, were more likely to see him.

"Ah, I thought that might be you by the sound of it," said Reg, his head popping out from behind a myrtle bush. He stood up from where he had been weeding a border underneath a front window of the house and came closer.

"Did Lily not want the manure?" he asked, indicating the barrow. "You can drop it here if you like. Can always do with it."

"No. Yes, yes, she was glad of it. This is topsoil. Fair exchange. Compost. Lily's finest. Sunny spot against the wall. A few plants." Manus held on to one handle while with his free hand he wiped his face with a handkerchief.

"You only have to ask – I can get any amount of topsoil for you at any time. Never picked you as a man with green fingers."

"That remains to be seen."

Reg, lifting up his spade, placed it on the gravel and leaned on it. "I forgot to ask you. Had any winners yet?"

Manus held on tightly to the two handles. "Not that I've heard. I missed the results on the wireless last night."

"Me, too," said Reg. "I had a couple of bob each way on Bourbon Prince after what you said about him being a sure thing."

Toby appeared at Reg's side. Where had he come from, wondered Manus who hadn't seen him approaching.

"You can be sure I didn't say that, Reg. There's no such beast as a sure thing." He made as if to move off.

"How was Lily?"

"In good form," said Manus, pausing out of courtesy.

Toby, his head cocked on one side, looked at the horse rug intently for a few seconds before looking back up at Manus.

"I might pop over later and ask her if she wants any help with her garden," said Reg. "I could fork in the manure for her."

"I wouldn't go today. Her rheumatics are at her and she had a bad night last night. She was heading off to lie down when I left her. She's not as young as she used to be."

"You're looking a bit off colour yourself, Manus. Hope you're not coming down with anything. Can't be good for you going around with damp hair."

Manus lifted up a hand to feel his hair which was nearly dry by now. "It was sticking up so I had to wet it to get it to lie down. I'm feeling fine, but I must be off." He couldn't bear to delay for one more second. Unable to think of any reason for why he might be in a hurry, he merely said, "Cheers, Reg. Cheers, Toby," and hoped it didn't sound too abrupt.

The two answered him and stayed watching him as he headed towards the stables.

Along the rest of the way Manus kept a lookout but noticed nothing more worrying than the fluttering of shadows in the trees beside the path.

It was a relief to go through the double doors and close them behind him. The sound the bar made as it slotted into place along the back of the doors was so satisfying that his heart rate slowed within seconds. The most nerve-wracking part was over. From now on he would not be interrupted as he carried out his plan.

He was tempted to submerge Dixon's body in the horse trough in the courtyard, but imagined the water in it turning red when the congealed blood in her hair and the fresh blood from her wound dissolved in it. It was easier to lay her on the ground and saturate her with water from a bucket. He tried to be as respectful as he could be under the circumstances and prayed for her soul all the time he was doing it.

If he had glanced up quickly, he would have seen Toby's head poking over the roof of the stable lads' quarters that overlooked the courtyard.

Manus lifted Dixon's body off the ground and carried it into his office where he placed it beside the corpse of Charlotte.

He then retrieved the blood-soaked towels and red blanket, pushed them into the centre of the stove, put in two pieces of wood to cover them and fastened the door quickly to prevent the smell of blood permeating the room. He hoped the smoke from the chimney would rise to a height and be quickly dispersed into the upper air.

He then went out and placed Charlotte's almost-dry shoes and bag in random positions beside the river bank and kicked a clump of earth into the water before saddling up to ride into Ballybrian to report a double accident to Inspector Declan Doyle, his friend, who wouldn't think to question the truthfulness of the account he would be hearing.

Toby waited until he saw Manus crossing the bridge before slithering down a drainpipe into the courtyard and crossing over to Manus's office. The door was locked. He looked through the window and saw the body of the woman from the nursery lying on the floor and beside it a second dead body: one of a younger woman about the same age as his mother. Where did that body come from?

He would wait around and see if he could find out.

Inspector Declan Doyle questioned only Manus. Young Toby slid up to stand beside the policeman during the questioning, staring admiringly up at him and checking what he was writing down on his notepad. Toby had the kind of presence that one didn't notice after a while because he could stay motionless for long periods of time, looking inoffensive. The Inspector shooed him away twice, but Toby sidled back again after a few minutes each time and no one seemed to take any notice of him after that.

Manus explained what must have occurred in such a way that Declan said the whole case was cut and dried; anyone could see that. Manus said he had seen the two women standing on the edge of the bank where it was rumoured that Charlotte's sister, little Victoria Blackshaw, might have gone in twenty-six years earlier. They looked as if they were praying so Manus left them and went back into the courtyard to give them their privacy. The rest was a logical reconstruction of what had happened.

Toby's face was alive with interest, but neither man noticed as each was concentrating on the story and Declan was writing in his notebook.

The earth had given way under Dixon's weight – see the clod missing? – and she had fallen into the water, Manus went on. He assumed she was the one who fell in as she was still wearing her shoes. Charlotte, knowing the old nanny was terrified of water because of what had happened to her in the orphanage – the way the warders held her head under in the bathtub as a punishment – had pulled off her shoes – see them there? – and jumped in to save her, and must have been dragged under by the frantic Dixon. He had found the two bodies downstream at the weir, Dixon with her head jammed up against it, still with her arm around Charlotte's neck, ironically protecting her former charge's head from damage. He had shouted for help before trying to resuscitate them both, but there was no one around to hear him. He had worked on Charlotte first, but it turned out to be too late for both of them.

There had been quite a lapse of time between leaving them praying and coming back out to ask them if they would like to come into his office to have a cup of tea. Manus told Declan the last bit as he picked up the shoes and bag – not quite dry – and, making sure Declan had noted them, took them in to place them beside Charlotte on the wet floor of the office so they would soak up more water, helping to disguise their original dampness.

"She looks familiar," said Declan, looking at Dixon's face.

"She should. You questioned her when little Victoria went missing and rumour had it you took a fancy to her."

"Ahh, so I did. I remember it well, now that you come to mention it. She left soon after that, for whatever reason. What a pity to see her in this state, and what a pity her head was damaged by the weir. She was a fine-looking young woman then." He studied her face for a long time, watched by Toby, before continuing to write in his notebook.

Manus stayed close to him and then to the doctor after he arrived, retelling his story with conviction. There was no reason for either man to disbelieve him.

After the policeman and the doctor had left and an ambulance had removed the two bodies, Manus sat alone in his office. The sense of clarity he had experienced for the last couple of hours left his mind, and he wondered how he had thought of doing what he had done and how he had achieved it – how he had dared set up a false scene for the authorities. 'Perverting the course of justice' was what he had done, and he was not sorry. In fact, he felt proud that he had been able to do it.

The only thing he had to ensure now was that the lies would be believed forever, especially by Charlotte's husband and later the little girl when she grew old enough to ask questions about her mother.

Lily had to steel herself to collect Dixon's handbag from the nursery wing, seeing Manus could not be seen carrying such a feminine object. She retrieved it from under the stairs, placed it on her arm as if it were her own, and took it to her cottage where, in the privacy of her kitchen, she could go through the contents undisturbed. What she was looking for were the letters mentioned by Dixon when she had visited her cottage earlier, containing allegations that Charlotte had deliberately pushed her little sister, Victoria, into the river and drowned her. She didn't want such information getting into the hands of the police, who then might view the afternoon's double drowning in a different light. And she certainly didn't want Manus to find out that the Charlotte he thought so highly of when she was a child was the person responsible for the death of little Victoria, the child he loved.

There were no letters. Charlotte must have seized them all before she ran off. Please God she had torn them up before she went into the river or at least taken them with her and let them float away, the water causing the ink to run so they would be unreadable if anyone happened to find them. Manus hadn't mentioned anything about them, which was a good sign.

She picked up Dixon's passport and flicked through it, noting the Australian stamps and Dixon's recent return to Ireland. At the back there was a space for the name of the next of kin, to be notified in case of an emergency. The entry read, '*No next of kin. Do not notify anyone*', confirming that Dixon considered herself alone in the world, as she had told Lily earlier.

There was a receipt in the name of 'Beth Hall' signed by Mrs O'Mahoney from the boarding house in the village, which made Lily suspect that Dixon had used an alias for her stay there. In a leather pouch was a sapphire necklace and matching earrings that Lily recognised as the ones that had been stolen from Lady Edwina Blackshaw twenty-five years earlier.

She must have sold the diamonds, thought Lily, imagining that Dixon had come upon hard times at some period during her exile. A pity for the Blackshaws to lose an heirloom as valuable as those, but at least the sapphires were safe. She would think of some way of getting them back into the house without anybody's noticing.

In case Dixon had left behind more letters, Lily asked Manus to visit Mrs O'Mahoney and retrieve Dixon's belongings so that she, rather than the authorities, could sort through them first.

Manus was worried that if someone from Charlotte's husband's family travelled to the Park to question Lily, she wouldn't be able to conceal the truth when she had no practice in lying convincingly, no matter how much she believed she could manage it. After he handed Dixon's one suitcase over to Lily, he wrote to her stepdaughter in Inchicore in Dublin and asked her to come down and take Lily back home with her after the funeral to look after her while she recovered from the shock of the two deaths. It would get her out of the way of those keen to hear details about the drownings, and curious to hear about the past lives of the two women, both better known to Lily than anyone else at the Park. Manus hoped that no one would ask Lily any questions at the funeral before she left. He would stay close by her during it, to fend off any enquiries addressed to her.

It wasn't until the next day that he remembered the clothing and the wrapped object he had taken from Charlotte's bag and shoved out of sight in his office. He retrieved them to lay them out to dry so that he could replace them in Charlotte's bag, which he would later send up to the house so the family could claim it. He unrolled the tapestry cover and looked inside. His hand stayed suspended. A glimpse of red hair. He thought it might sear his fingers to touch it. He slid the object out of its wrapping onto his desk.

It was without a doubt little Victoria's redheaded doll, damp but well preserved. How had Charlotte come to be in possession of it, when the last time it had been seen it was in the arms of little Victoria? And he presumed it had stayed there, wherever she had ended up.

CHAPTER 3

Edwina seethed at being wrong-footed by every aspect of her daughter's death. Charlotte hadn't even informed her that she was travelling to Tyringham Park, let alone that she had left Mary Anne behind in the care of Iseult Farrelly, her husband's sister, rather than leaving her in the Blackshaw's Dublin townhouse in the care of the servants. As a result she was made to look foolish when two policemen were admitted to her rooms to break the news to her that her daughter had drowned at Tyringham Park. Not that she cared about the opinions of policemen, but she didn't want them to conclude that she didn't know what was going on in her own family.

So it falls to Iseult Farrelly to be the one to tell Mary Anne, Edwina thought sourly, no doubt talking about heaven, angels and harps. If I had been the one to do it, which by rights I should have been, I would have said: 'Your mother has died. She won't be coming back, so there's no point in making a fuss.' A two-and-a-half-year-old of Mary Anne's intelligence would have no trouble accepting that plain statement of fact.

Iseult was the one to tell her, as sensitively as she could in words that a young child could understand, and it was Iseult, heavily pregnant, who decided not to travel to the funeral, but to remain in Dublin to care for Mary Anne while it was on, judging that a funeral service was no place for a young child.

The grounds around the small private church, which had been built in the grounds of Tyringham Park three centuries earlier, were crowded with villagers and ex-tenants by the time Edwina and her husband Lord Waldron Blackshaw arrived. Those beside the path stepped back, murmuring with sympathy, as a manservant wheeled Edwina, and a soldier-valet supported Waldron into the church. The pews were already packed, except for the front row which had been left vacant for the chief mourners to occupy.

Local newsmen hovered in the background. Because of Waldron's fame and notoriety, added to the disappearance of his daughter Victoria and the heroic death of his son Harcourt in the war, the drowning of his last surviving offspring had made the national news.

Charlotte might not have lived well but she had made up for it by dying well, thought Edwina, sitting motionless in her wheelchair in the aisle, her face covered by a black veil to prevent curious eyes from checking to see whether or not she was crying. She never cried in public – that was a discipline subscribed to by her class and taken for granted by her – but people might be surprised if they knew she did not cry in private either.

The Cork Blackshaws filled the second, third and fourth rows. The Carmodys, Charlotte's in-laws, were on the opposite side halfway down the church. The usher had not known who they were so they were not invited to sit closer to the front.

After the service, Waldron, taking sips of whiskey from his favourite hipflask which had once been used by royalty, was able to stand supported by the soldier-valet beside the open grave, listening to the vicar and nodding his approval at intervals, though not always at the appropriate moments.

"Miss Charlotte, as we knew and loved her when she lived here as a little girl," the vicar said, raising the pitch of his voice and elongating his vowels, "was a woman who had everything to live for: a fine husband, Dr Lochlann Carmody, serving in the Medical Corps of the British Army and sadly not able to be with us today to say farewell to his beloved wife, and her infant daughter Mary Anne who has been cruelly robbed of the presence of a loving mother."

Sounds of weeping came from many sections of the large crowd of mourners.

Waldron began to sway. Edwina hissed something to the soldier-valet, who took Waldron's arm, held on tightly, turned him around and guided him past the mourners who moved aside to make room. Twice he lost his footing but his minder was able to take the weight and keep him upright.

"Poor man, burying his last child," whispered one of the mourners who had stood back to let him pass.

"No wonder he's overcome," said another.

"Overcome, my eye," said a third. "Did you come down in the last shower or what?"

The vicar waited until Waldron, now hiccupping, had been led away and the murmuring stopped before beginning to speak again.

It's time he stopped talking, Edwina thought. He's trying to impress the Catholics, now that he has them captive. It's chilly out here in the wind. Thank goodness I had the foresight to wear my mink.

She wanted to talk to Manus. She couldn't see him. She thought he would have made it his business to stand in close because of his link to her in the past and his devotion to Charlotte. At the back of the crowd, on a rise, she could see that old witch, East, or whatever she called herself these days, being supported by a hairy man. She had no intention of speaking to her old housekeeper if she could avoid it.

As soon as the vicar stopped talking she would look out for Manus. Did he still think badly of her for doing that inexcusable thing to nine-year-old Charlotte, forcing her to ride a mount she could not control?

Even if he did presently, she would win him around in the end. She had always been able to do that. She would need to have him on her side if Mary Anne were to be turned into a champion horsewoman, a destiny that was her heritage as a Blackshaw, which she was by blood if not by name.

The ritual was finally over. Edwina stayed where she was while the crowds filed past to offer her their condolences. Waldron hadn't returned. He had probably gone up to the house and stayed there.

There were so many soft, musical Cork accents alternating with the penetrating tones of the gentry that she became confused, especially as she felt no obligation to tilt her head and was consequently seeing everyone at chest level.

Lochlann's parents, Dr Grace and Dr Rory Carmody, made themselves known as they took their turn in the queue to sympathise. They hadn't seen Edwina since the morning of the wedding. They were sorry to be heading back to Dublin straight away, the father said, but they couldn't afford to miss the next train as he was on early call in the morning. They were effusive in their praise of Charlotte. A group of Lochlann's school and medical friends offered their sympathies and then followed his parents away from the church.

The line of sympathisers moved on and the East woman, shaking with nerves, appeared next and bent down to mumble something incomprehensible between sobs. Has she lost every modicum of self-control, Edwina wondered. If it weren't for the hairy man holding on to her, the overwrought woman might have toppled over onto Edwina's lap. The hairy man's voice sounded familiar. Must be one of the tenants from my time, she thought. He, whoever he was, didn't bend down to her level so all she noticed was an impression of hair and a firm handshake. As with all the others in the queue, she thanked him for coming.

Afterwards, the crowd of villagers made their way along the path and out through the main gates, turning left towards Ballybrian, while the invited gentry from the surrounding Big Houses were ferried up to the house for refreshments.

During the funeral repast Edwina mentioned to her husband's sister-in-law Harriet, the present chatelaine of Tyringham Park, that Manus must have been the only villager who didn't attend the funeral.

"But he was there," said Harriet.

"And he didn't come to speak to me?" Edwina couldn't believe the strength of the lurch of excitement in her stomach at the thought of his being so close, and the depth of the disappointment that he had not made himself known to her.

"I saw him in the line so he must have. He kept Lily East standing throughout it all. I hear she's taken the whole thing frightfully badly and is still in a state of bewilderment."

"Was that Manus with her? All hairy?" For the first time all day, Edwina almost lost her composure but controlled herself for fear of letting herself down in front of Harriet.

"That would be Manus, though I wouldn't describe him as 'hairy'. Bearded, definitely, but not what one would call 'hairy'."

"I didn't recognise him. I thought it was some tenant or other from the past. Well, actually, I didn't see him properly. Manus was clean-shaven when I knew him."

"Was he really? I can hardly remember back that far. I should have sent that poor woman out a chair. Rather remiss of me. Not used to women attending funerals, and not used to a crowd as large as that one. A great compliment to your Charlotte, I have to say."

"Yes, it was rather."

"Now, here are my great-grandchildren. Nanny has brought them in specifically to meet you. You're probably all confused at this stage about who belongs to whom, there's so many of us here all living under the one roof."

And so few of us, Edwina thought. Is she gloating?

"These are Giles's and Georgina's children. Giles is the son of Nicholas, who is the son of Charles."

"I know who they are, Harriet. I'm not in my dotage yet."

"Of course not, but even I get the generations mixed up at times. This little girl is Jane, the same age as your Mary Anne – this is Nigel, the handsome one – and this is William, who is the heir after Waldron, Charles, Nicholas and Giles. There, I think I've made that clear. Of course if Harcourt hadn't given his life so heroically, we would all be out renting somewhere else by now."

At least she realises it, thought Edwina.

"Such a pity for Waldron you had no other male heir. William is aged seven, off to prep school in England next year. Thank you, Nanny. That will be all. You can take them away now."

Edwina felt too overwrought to speak. Harriet was lording it over her. If Harcourt hadn't given up his life so heroically for his country, unlike Giles who had been discharged with only one foot missing, he would be the heir and he could have fathered three splendid children superior in every way to the three ordinary children who had just

25

been paraded in front of her. She also felt cheated that Mary Anne wasn't here with her on this day so that she could be introduced, eclipsing her cousins with her excellence and putting Harriet in her place.

Harriet noted the cross look on Edwina's face and changed the subject, asking who would be looking after Mary Anne until her father returned from the war.

"Mary Anne has lived in the townhouse ever since the family arrived home from Australia and I see no reason why she should be moved," said Edwina. "Queenie is used to the child and she can manage until I hire an energetic young nanny to help her. Actually today would be a perfect time to put out the word while everyone's assembled. You could mention it, and say it is a matter of urgency. Under the circumstances everyone will understand."

"Of course. It's the least I can do. It's nice to be able to do something practical."

"I would be most grateful. So if the doctor doesn't return from the war, Mary Anne will be safely ensconced in the townhouse and will live there under my supervision."

"And if the doctor does return?"

With a bit of luck, he won't, thought Edwina. He is the only one who has the right to take Mary Anne away from me. Aloud she said, "Then he can come back to live in the townhouse with his daughter. He already lived in Charlotte's apartment there for the week after he returned from Australia and before he went to war, so it would be expected that he return there."

"That would be nice for you." Harriet looked around the room at the guests, who were drinking tea and eating sandwiches. "Would you look at all the grey heads? Ours included, of course. None of us is getting any younger. If I were you, Edwina dear, I wouldn't bother putting that fur back in storage when you return to Dublin. By the look of Waldron, I think it will be needed again quite shortly."

"Yes, they'll be dropping like flies soon," said Edwina, mentally placing Harriet and her husband Charles, Waldron's younger brother, just behind Waldron in the requiem stakes. They were all in their early eighties, years ahead of her, a child by comparison at only fifty-six. It gave her satisfaction to think of it. There was something to be said for marrying a man thirty years older than oneself.

While the mourners were congregating in the drawing room, Lily East passed through the familiar servants' quarters to the main hall where, with difficulty, she lifted up the lid of the black-oak monk's seat which was piled with coats, dropped the sapphire jewellery into its dark interior and left the way she had come. It would probably be years before they were found, as the seat was stuffed with objects, but at least Lily didn't have to worry about them any more.

CHAPTER 4

The following day the ex-nanny Elizabeth Dixon was buried on the periphery of the Park graveyard. Charles Blackshaw paid for the coffin and the services of the vicar. Only Charles, the vicar and Inspector Declan Doyle were in attendance at the graveside. Manus stood back under the first row of trees with his head bowed. Reg and his grandson Toby waited a respectable distance away, ready to fill in the grave after the dignitaries left.

Toby kept staring at Manus and then at Inspector Declan Doyle with a look of puzzled concentration, shifting his focus, backwards and forwards, from one to the other.

"When I grow up I don't want to be a fisherman or a gardener or a horse trainer. I want to be a policeman," Toby said to his grandfather after the funeral was over and the three important people had left, but not before the policeman had gone over to exchange friendly words with Manus. "A detective policeman."

"And why not?" said Reg. "It shouldn't be any problem for a smart young lad like you, though I must say I hoped you would work here alongside me, carrying on a long family tradition."

"I only want to be a detective policeman," Toby repeated.

"Have it your own way. You have plenty of time to change your mind. In any event you'll have to stick to your books, mind. No slacking. Ah, there you are, Manus. Sad business."

Manus agreed that it was.

"Strange how two women drowned, don't you think, Manus, when they weren't out of their depth?" asked Reg, leaning on his spade as if settling in for a long conversation. "I've been meaning to say it to you. It's not as if they were anywhere near the Dark Waterhole. They could have just stood up and waded to the bank."

"Strange all right," said Manus, "but not uncommon, apparently. Declan Doyle asked the experts on the Water Safety Board in Dublin if they could explain the incident. They've seen more than a few drownings in shallow water, so it seems."

Manus had noticed how Toby's head had jerked up to stare at him when the words, 'two women drowned' were said, and how his stare continued to bore into him.

"They said," he continued, "that people who can't swim can get into a panic and be unable to right themselves and they thrash about in a horizontal position unable to regain their footing until they finally breathe in water and sink. And anyone who comes in to rescue them has to be careful not to be pulled under. A drowning person has great strength and no sense."

"There you have it, then. That explains it. Toby, you'll be able to solve cases like that when your time comes." He winked at Manus. "Did I tell you Toby here wants to be a detective when he grows up? What do you think of that?"

"I think it would suit him down to the ground," said Manus. "I'd say that your bright eyes don't miss much, do they, Toby?" As he spoke he studied Toby's face, searching for some indication of what the boy might be thinking. Toby looked steadily back at him. "Reg, why don't you send Toby down to the stables? Not just to look, but to learn. If you can spare him, of course. He can join the Blackshaw children for riding lessons from eight until ten every weekday during the summer. Would you like that, Toby?"

"Will I be allowed to talk to them?"

"Of course you will."

"Granddad said I can't, didn't you, Granddad?"

"I did, and I still say it when you're with me. But Manus is his own boss and when you're with him you do what he says."

"You can't say fairer than that," said Manus. "We don't stand on ceremony down there. The horses are the only kings in that place."

Toby's lids flickered as if he were finding it difficult to maintain his unblinking stare.

"So I'll see you in the morning then, Toby?"

"Thanks, Manus," said Reg. "That's very kind of you. I'll definitely take you up on the offer. He gets restless around the gardening. You'll be there, won't you, Toby?"

Toby nodded.

"I think working with horses might be just the thing for him," said Manus to Reg.

While his grandfather talked, Toby kept looking at Manus, finding it difficult to believe that a man like him, a man with a kind face and a friendly manner, had told the policeman at the scene of the drowning a whole pack of lies – lies which he had just repeated to Reg. He wondered if, when he was grown up and on duty as a policeman, he would be able to tell if someone was lying to him, or would he be fooled as easily as Inspector Declan Doyle had been fooled by Manus?

Manus closed the gate behind the stable lads, who were heading for the gallops to ride out the two-year-olds and turned to see Toby standing in the middle of the courtyard, watching the departing riders, his face bright with interest.

He could be my younger self, thought Manus. "So you came," he said. "I'm glad."

Toby fixed Manus with an open, fearless look.

"I have just the pony for you. It needs a lot of extra handling before it goes to its new owner. I would be glad to take you on as an apprentice. We'll start off with a week's trial to see how you get on. Does that suit you?" Manus used the word 'apprentice' deliberately, so that it was clear from the outset that no payment would be expected for the lessons he would be giving to the boy.

Toby chewed at his lips to try to contain his excited smile.

"What's that around your neck?" asked Manus. "A catapult by any chance? Here, let me have a look."

Toby took the catapult off over his head and handed it to Manus.

"Did Reg make this? It's a work of art." Manus held the base of the forked stick and stretched the rubber attachments. He smiled with pleasure. "This takes me back, though I can't say I ever had one as well made as this one. Let's go out and get some pebbles and have a few shots. Wait until William and Nigel see this. They'll have Reg pestered to make one each for them. I might even get him to make one for me for old time's sake. It sure takes me back. Ah, here they are."

The three Blackshaw children ran into the courtyard. They looked surprised and curious to see Toby there. They had noticed him around the estate in the distance but hadn't as yet spoken to him.

"Children, this is Toby," Manus said. "He will be in charge of Jester from now on. Now come and have a go at this little weapon and see who can hit the silver birch on the far bank. If that's all right with you, Toby?"

In Dublin on the same day Mary Anne's Aunt Iseult left a note for Edwina at the townhouse asking if she could call over at four o'clock to collect some clothes and toys for Mary Anne, whose intended two-day visit had stretched to a week. Edwina sent back a message with a servant to say that a visit from her would be most timely as she had a particular wish to speak to her. "*I presume you will be bringing Mary Anne with you. Queenie will look after her while we clarify some family matters.*"

Edwina remembered how she had felt an involuntary rush of relief when she first heard that her daughter was dead. No more of that sullen presence in the room. No more displays of maternal affection intended to taunt, the favourite one consisting of lifting Mary Anne up to snuggle with joy into her neck, all the while looking over the child's shoulder at Edwina, with what Edwina interpreted as an expression of both triumph and hatred as if to say: 'This love will never be yours, Mother. You want it desperately, but you can't have it. It's mine. You had your chance with a child – me – and you treated it with contempt. Don't think I have any intention of giving you a second chance after that.'

And here she was getting that second chance. How satisfying to look forward to unimpeded access to Mary Anne now that Charlotte's possessive, gloating presence was gone.

Edwina had put out word at the funeral that she needed a nanny, and one was soon found. It wasn't difficult. A lot of nannies were eager to leave the countryside and take up positions in the city.

Edwina waited impatiently to see Mary Anne for the first time in a week.

She would soon be here – that perfect little person with her prettiness, her miraculous skin, clear eyes, trusting nature, affectionate touch, animated warmth and musical voice. Was there ever such a child? How could Charlotte possibly fool herself into thinking for one minute that she had ever equalled the level of superiority in her early life that her daughter was exhibiting in hers, and that she should have elicited the same amount of admiration?

As the time for the visit grew closer Edwina's heart began to beat as if she were young again and about to meet up with a sweetheart. How satisfying to be able to inform Iseult Farrelly that a nanny had already been appointed and, as soon as the woman was installed, Mary Anne could leave the Farrellys' household and come back to live permanently in the townhouse where she belonged.

She heard the bell, and then there was a long wait as the slow footsteps of Queenie went to answer it. The front door was opened. There were words of greeting punctuated by Queenie's loud exclamations of welcome.

Don't delay her, Queenie.

The little footsteps were running.

She's keen to see me. She's running. The adults are calling her back. Don't stop her. Let her run! Quickly, Mary Anne.

Mary Anne, filled with explosive expectation, rushed across the hall, past Edwina's door, up two flights of stairs and down along the corridor in the direction of Charlotte's rooms on the third floor, calling, "Mummy, Mummy," over and over. She was beside herself with excitement by the time she reached the door, and danced with impatience waiting for Queenie to catch up with her and open it to let her in.

Iseult advanced more slowly, hanging her head so that her niece wouldn't see her tears. She was already feeling the devastation that Mary Anne would suffer when she discovered that Charlotte was not in her rooms. It was understandable that a child of that age had no real concept of the reality of death. Mary Anne had been told that her mother was in heaven, that she would not be coming back, but now, in her home surroundings, she expected her to be there. Iseult wished she had distracted the child instead of standing talking to Queenie, giving Mary Anne time to run too far ahead of her to be diverted.

It was too soon to return to the home full of the presence of Charlotte, who had not intended leaving it forever when she last closed the door behind her.

Please God, help me control myself, Iseult prayed. Don't let me sob. I don't want to alarm the child with my visible grief that I must keep for my private lamentations.

She could feel the child's longing for its mother, the swelling of an expectation soon to be cruelly dashed, the pain of abandonment.

"Your mummy is not in there," choked Iseult. "Let's come back another day."

"No. Mummy here. Mummy, Mummy." Mary Anne was reaching up, trying to turn the stiff door handle.

Queenie, also crying, looked to Iseult for guidance.

"Open it," said Iseult.

"Good afternoon, Your Ladyship. I'm sorry I'm late," said Iseult, who was still feeling weak from having witnessed Mary Anne's heartbreaking sorrow when she failed to find her mother. It had taken a long time to calm her down.

This was the first time the two women had seen each other since Charlotte and Lochlann's wedding and the first time Iseult had visited Edwina's rooms. It was Queenie who had given her directions.

"Good afternoon, Mrs Farrelly," Edwina said, noting that Iseult was heavily pregnant. "You are thirty minutes late. Punctuality is the courtesy of kings, but obviously not of housewives. Where is Mary Anne?"

"Queenie has taken her down to the kitchen while we discuss the family matters you referred to earlier."

"That won't take long. I would like to ask a favour of you. Would you be so kind as to keep Mary Anne with you for a few more days until the nanny I have hired is in place? I fear Queenie is not up to the task on her own, though she will be an invaluable back-up to the nanny."

Iseult looked uncomfortable and couldn't think what to say.

"Have I asked too much? Would that not be convenient for you in your condition?"

"No, no – of course it is convenient."

"Then why the hesitancy?"

"I think there has been a misunderstanding, Your Ladyship. Charlotte expected me and my husband, if anything happened to her, to provide a home for Mary Anne until Lochlann returns to decide on her future."

"And when did she inform you of that, might I be so bold as to ask?" Edwina's voice was full of vinegar.

"A week before she went to Tyringham Park."

"She must have meant for a couple of days and you misunderstood her."

"No, she said until Lochlann returned from the war and, if he didn't return, Mary Anne was to stay with me permanently."

"With you? Instead of me?"

"Yes."

"*I don't believe you!* You must have misheard her. A maternal grandmother would always take precedence over paternal grandparents. A paternal aunt would not even be considered." Edwina's face had reddened and she put her hands on the arms of the wheelchair as if to lift herself out. Her reaction was such that Iseult wouldn't have been surprised if Edwina had actually shot up into a standing position.

"I didn't mishear her, Your Ladyship."

"Do you expect me to believe that Charlotte entrusted Mary Anne to you? She didn't know she was going to drown when she went to the Park. She left the child with you for a day and a night, not for the rest of its life."

Iseult could hardly bear to look at Edwina's tortured face. "I'm sorry, Your Ladyship, but what I say is true."

"I have only your word for that. You think you can pass off any story as true now that Charlotte isn't here to verify it. It looks to me as if you have hatched a plot behind my back. You want to keep her in your Papist fold. I know how your Church can't tolerate the loss of any of its members, especially the children."

"I will ignore your unfortunate choice of words and repeat that I am truly sorry, Your Ladyship. I didn't want to be the one to tell you but, seeing you won't take my word for it, I will tell you. Charlotte wrote it all down in her will. It's all legally binding."

"Her will? I heard nothing about a will. When did she make her will?"

"A week before she died."

"Are you telling me she knew she was going to die when she went to the Park?"

"No, of course she didn't. How could she? It was because she had volunteered to become a Special Operator that she made it. She told me the average life expectancy of an agent in France is three months. She told me that Colonel Hardcastle had recruited her when he came over to explain how Harcourt had lasted less than a month before he was captured."

"And tortured and shot. I know all that. I don't need you to tell me my son's fate or my family's business. I was here when the colonel gave us the details. If my memory serves me correctly, and it's as clear as ever it was, she told the colonel she would not join. That her first duty was to Mary Anne. And you're telling me she changed her mind?"

"Yes, she thought about it and changed her mind. She was afraid she might not return alive from France and that is why she made her will."

Edwina asked with a nasty edge to her voice, "Were you a witness to the will by any chance, and Cook the other one? Was it an unofficial will? A homemade effort? Done under this roof?"

"No. I did not witness it. Charlotte went to Mr Dunwoody's rooms and had it witnessed there."

"Dunwoody drew it up?"

"He'll be reading it in public at some stage and then you'll be able to hear it for yourself."

"Don't give me any smart answers, Mrs Farrelly." Edwina's eyes were full of dislike. "Do you think for one minute I'll give up Mary Anne without a fight? I will contest the will. Charlotte was obviously unhinged when she wrote it. She had forgotten who she was and where she came from. She must have pulled the wool over Mr Dunwoody's eyes, which wouldn't be too difficult seeing he's an old bachelor who specialises in conveyancing. He wouldn't know the first thing about devious women or else he would have had more sense than to write down such an impossible directive."

So many insults in one outburst. Iseult was finding it difficult to stay calm. If it weren't for Edwina's age and disability, and pity for the losses she had suffered, she might not have been able to hold her tongue.

Charlotte had said with satisfaction at the time she spoke to Iseult that she would love to see her mother's face when she heard the will being read – if that was how things turned out. "Keep your eye on her," she had said, "and watch her reaction. Don't feel any sympathy for her and don't under any circumstances give in to her. Don't let her take advantage of your good nature. If she gets her hands on Mary Anne, you can be certain she will ruin her life in the way she nearly ruined mine. It was the kindness of servants that saved me from despair." Charlotte had paused here to take a long breath before continuing. "It's not that I expected my mother to look after me personally. She would never lower herself to do so menial a task as that. But she should have kept an eye out. What she did in fact was leave me at the mercy of a cruel stranger. I did tell her once that Nurse Dixon hurt me. My mother passed that information back to Nurse Dixon in an amused way, and Dixon said that if I ever told tales again she would pull out a chunk of my hair by the roots at the back where it wouldn't be seen. Needless to say, I didn't tell my mother about that." Charlotte fixed her sister-in-law with a pleading look. "So promise me, Iseult, that my mother will never become Mary Anne's custodian."

"I promise," Iseult had replied.

Mr Dunwoody's quavering voice read out Charlotte's will a few days later.

"*In the event of my death,*" the will stated, "*my mother Edwina, Lady Blackshaw, is to have no hand, act nor part in the rearing of Mary Anne Carmody. Mary Anne's aunt, Iseult Farrelly (née Carmody), is to be her guardian until Dr Lochlann Carmody returns and, if he does not return, Iseult Farrelly (née Carmody) is to retain guardianship until the child reaches her majority.*"

The nurse standing beside the wheelchair searched in her bag for sal volatile and held it out to Edwina, who pushed the hand holding it aside.

Queenie, who had been sent to wait outside the door but had been listening, sidled into the room, staring at Edwina and, while she stared, heard that she, Cormac Delany, Lily (East) Cooper and

Manus were each to inherit five thousand pounds. Queenie's knees began to shake and she was forced to sit down.

Edwina glared at the solicitor. "Charlotte was not of sound mind when she wrote that will, and you should be ashamed of yourself, Mr Dunwoody, for allowing her to make it."

Mr Dunwoody flushed.

"I will contest it," Edwina pronounced in her most hectoring tones. "I'm sure you were informed at many stages that my daughter was never of sound mind. There is a wealth of evidence to prove it. She deliberately caused my accident and left me a cripple, she refused to attend school and was tutored by a mad bohemian chosen by my husband, she never had a friend, she shut herself away for three years and ate herself into the size of an elephant, she turned down a peer to marry a Papist from the common orders, she had a doctor smuggled into the house to attend to her when she was having one of her hysterical outbursts a few days before she died and then she finished her life by drowning in shallow water. If these aren't the actions of a deranged woman, I don't know what are. I am sure there are more instances that I can't bring to mind at the moment, but I will correlate them and present them to you, Mr Dunwoody." There was froth in the corners of Edwina's mouth. "This will cannot stand."

"Your Ladyship," said Mr Dunwoody, looking over his half-moon glasses at Edwina and straightening out the papers in front of him, "we will await your –"

"Don't interrupt. I haven't finished yet. Mrs Farrelly is about to give birth to her second child, which no doubt will be followed by many more as is the custom of her kind. Her house has only three bedrooms. My granddaughter will be deprived of attention as well as privacy. As you know, Mr Dunwoody, the townhouse is spacious, and I have already hired a superior nanny whose sole responsibility will be the care of Mary Anne, without the distractions of household tasks or the demands of a husband and other children. She will be under my supervision at all times. Charlotte's will was written purely to spite me, Mr Dunwoody, for some little difference of opinion we had years ago, when her only concern should have been Mary Anne's welfare."

Mr Dunwoody's rheumy eyes looked over at a furious, heavily pregnant Iseult before he sighed deeply and left the room.

CHAPTER 5

Lochlann's first thought when he received a letter at his military base from his father to say that Charlotte was dead was that he would have to give the child back. He felt there was no justification for keeping her now that Charlotte was dead. He had stolen the baby for her, not for himself, and now had no alternative but to return it personally the very minute he had four months to spare. Australia was a long way away; it would take at least four months to get there and back by ship, plus having to make the trip up the coast from Sydney by train to complete the journey. He would make all the arrangements just as soon as he returned home.

The birth of Iseult's second child was difficult, and she was ordered to take plenty of bed rest during the following months. Her husband put off picking up Mary Anne from the townhouse after a visit to Lady Edwina and then decided to leave her there until Iseult regained her strength. He sent their own firstborn, Matthew, to be looked after by his sister.

A solicitor's letter was delivered to Farrellys' during this time but was mislaid in the middle of the domestic chaos. By the time it was found it was too late to appeal the ruling that Mary Anne was to move to the townhouse. It stated that the Farrellys would have access to her while the nanny was off duty for only a half day each week.

"I haven't the strength to fight it even if I thought we had a chance," Iseult said to her husband after she read the letter. "They're all of a clique. I might have known Edwina would win. But at least it's only temporary. Lochlann will claim her back as soon as he returns. He will always have prior claim on her, thank God."

By the time Lochlann was brought home to Dublin, six months had passed since Charlotte's death. By this time Iseult was in the early stages of pregnancy with her third child and Mary Anne was settled in the townhouse.

Grace and Rory Carmody barely recognised their bearded son who couldn't make eye contact with them and who could only grimace when he tried to smile.

"He's not as bad as he looks," said the soldier delivering him to their door. "Nothing wrong with him that a month of sleep and a few pounds of good steak won't fix."

"Here, give him to me," said Rory, trying to hide his alarm at Lochlann's unfocused eyes, slack jaw and emaciated frame.

The two men between them manoeuvred Lochlann up the stairs and laid him on his old bed. Grace settled him and checked his blood pressure and pulse while Rory accompanied the soldier back downstairs, to hear that Lochlann seemed to have lost the ability to sleep, talk or eat and had physically collapsed by the time they picked him up.

"Overwork, pure and simple," explained the soldier. "Complete exhaustion. He's been running on empty for months, apparently. It was the death of his wife, you know . . . well, of course you know . . . that put the tin hat on it. When we first saw him he kept asking when she would be coming back from Uganda. Thought she was still alive, poor blighter. Obviously the news hadn't sunk in properly. Still don't know if it has or not."

"Thanks for filling us in. At least we'll know what to expect," said Rory.

"Hope you've got some sedation to knock him out. We ran out of all forms of it coming over here. Haven't had a chance to stock up yet."

The soldier couldn't delay. He checked that he hadn't forgotten to hand over Lochlann's kitbag, and left.

Rory went back upstairs and didn't tell Grace that Lochlann had been asking for his old love Niamh McCarthy, and not Charlotte, during a period of delirium.

Lochlann felt his arm being prepared for an injection and tried once again to speak, but couldn't close his jaw or shape his mouth.

"When you wake, Mary Anne will be here," Grace said. "She's the most beautiful and good-natured child you could ever hope to meet."

Lochlann's eyes registered pleasure. He was glad he would be handing over a beautiful, good-natured child and not a little weasel.

He remained asleep for seventeen hours. During the last few he was tormented by nightmares, where images of the war-wounded he had treated and the orphaned babies he had heard crying for their mothers were mixed up into one swirling, scarlet mass.

A curly-headed child peeped around the door and for a minute Lochlann thought he was back in Australia being scrutinised by a young Hogan.

"Hullo," he whispered, unsure of his voice.

The head disappeared and he heard giggling and whispering.

Iseult emerged, holding the hand of the child who hung back and looked shyly at him from under her fringe.

"Say hullo to your daddy," Iseult said to the child. She smiled at her brother. "She has looked in on you many times. She didn't think you were real."

"She might be right. What a little pet. Don't come too close, Mary Anne. God knows what infections I have. Just let me have a good look at you." He hadn't seen her for nearly two years. Poor motherless little dote, how appealing she looked. His initial intention to return her to Australia seemed to him, in his state at this moment, to be impractical and undesirable.

Mary Anne shook her head and cuddled in closer to her aunt.

"I'll give you a shave and a haircut later," said Iseult, "and you can put on a new shirt so you'll look more human, and then Mary Anne might be able to recognise you from your old photos. Right now you look so wild you'd put the fear of the Lord into an adult, let alone a little girl."

Later, after Iseult had dropped Mary Anne back to the townhouse and returned alone to sit beside his bed to keep him company, Lochlann asked her in what he hoped was a neutral tone of voice if she had heard any news of Niamh McCarthy.

"Yes, she's back from Uganda and has gone to London to work for the duration of the war."

"Is she well?"

"She's lost a lot of weight. We all suspected malaria, but she says she's fine."

"That's good to hear," said Lochlann, closing his eyes. "I'm glad she's back and that she didn't contract malaria."

CHAPTER 6

After some of his vitality returned during his sixth week of convalescence, the first trip Lochlann undertook was one to Tyringham Park to talk to Manus about Charlotte's death. Manus repeated his lies convincingly. Lochlann was particularly keen to meet Lily East to thank her for her past kindness to Charlotte. Manus told him Lily had gone to live with her stepdaughter who had recently moved house and he was sorry to say he had mislaid her address. Lily would not be returning to the Park. She was due to vacate the cottage in January, anyway, so her non-return wasn't as unfortunate as it sounded. Her belongings had been stored in the nursery wing, ready for collection at any time, and her cottage had been taken over a few months earlier than planned, by a young workman with a family.

Lochlann had no reason to disbelieve anything Manus said about the drowning or the lost address.

The second thing Lochlann did when he returned to Dublin was to retrieve the film he had hidden in the bottom of his kitbag and drive to a chemist's on the north side of the city to have it developed. When he went back to collect it the chemist said there was a note to say that only four photographs had come out and the film must have been rewound accidentally.

Lochlann had known there would be only four photographs on the film as it was he who had rewound it deliberately and removed it from the camera so that Charlotte would not find it, have it developed and see photographs she was never meant to see.

He waited until he was out on the street before he looked at the snaps. They were even more incriminating than he had imagined they could be. There was the newborn baby, Alison Hogan, and there in the group was a girl, whom he remembered as Hanna, looking like a carbon copy of Mary Anne as she looked now, which wasn't surprising seeing she was her sister. The family resemblance was strong, even among the boys. Unfortunately the eldest girl, Zita, was away at school so did not feature. He would have liked to compare her, as well as Hanna, to Mary Anne. The second photograph was a close-up of Nell holding Alison, the third was one of him and Dan on horseback, and the fourth was a view of the homestead surrounded by trees.

He was moved at the sight of them, flicking through them many times before putting them in his inner breast pocket, and later hiding them on the top shelf of his parents' bookshelves in an out-of-date textbook on anatomy that had come in a job lot and that no one would ever open.

The images stayed with him. The realisation of the enormity of his crime, which he could sometimes put to the back of his mind, hit him with its full implications. He was a man in a position of trust who had stolen a child. He could construct as many plausible arguments as he liked to minimise his guilt, but the fact remained that that was what he had done.

That night, in an attempt to quieten his conscience, he sat up alone in his parents' sitting room until two in the morning and drank whiskey until he passed out.

Lochlann was grateful that he could blame the war for his not having to make any decisions about Mary Anne's immediate future.

Sometimes, in the initial stages of inebriation, which were now becoming more frequent, he allowed himself to imagine driving up to the Hogan farm in New South Wales, leaving Mary Anne asleep in the back seat of the hired car. She would not be frightened waking up alone in strange surroundings because he would have described the farm in detail and explained to her many times on the trip on the way over that

43

they were going to this particular farm to meet her real mother and father and lots of brothers and sisters. "Look at them in these photographs. Don't you think you look like them?" He would tell her that, back with her real family, she would be able to ride horses, just like she would soon be riding ponies at Tyringham Park, except that it would be more exciting as she would also be able to chase kangaroos.

He would walk along the path to the door with the tied-up dogs barking so loudly he would worry that they would wake up the child before he was ready to introduce her. "Anyone at home?" he would call out, as people in those parts did, and Nell would come to the door, wiping her hands on her flour-splattered apron, and he would say, "I have something to tell you and I have someone I would like you to meet. She's asleep in the car at the moment." And he would follow Nell into the kitchen and, after she had put on the kettle and taken the biscuit jar out of the cupboard, he would say, "First I need to tell you what happened when I was last here. Is Dan at home or nearby?"

Or would he wake the child up and have her standing beside him when he called out? Nell would look down at her and say, "Alison, what have you done to your hair?" or "Alison, where did you get that dress?" and then she would look up at him and come over all shy and say, "Dr Carmody! I didn't think we would ever see you again. Please come in," and she would be all flustered, wondering if they had enough food to feed an extra person for tea. And when Dan joined them and they sat down to drink tea, he would say, "Dan and Nell, I've come all the way back from Ireland to tell you there was an unfortunate mix-up when Alison was born. I took the wrong baby by mistake." Nell would say, "But we have Alison," and he would say, "I don't mean her. I mean her twin, Dolores." Dan would say, "Dolores? But she's dead," and he would say, "That baby was Charlotte's child," and at that moment Mary Anne would choose to come in through the open door and he would jump up in time to catch Nell sliding towards the floor in a dead faint.

There would be no need to confess it was deliberate. What good would that do? Why burden them with information that might make them want to rail at the sorrow they had suffered unnecessarily? Why make matters worse? One more lie couldn't blacken his soul any more than it had already been blackened.

"Alison's twin didn't die. Here she is."

But then, of course, he would not turn up unexpectedly like that, but would write beforehand. "*Dear Nell and Dan, I have come to an extraordinary realisation that the child Charlotte and I brought home must belong to you as she looks like a Hogan. There must have been a mix-up on the day the babies were born.*"

The questions and answers would go back and forth across the twelve thousand miles that separated them.

"*Why did it take you so long to discover it?*"

"*I was away at the war. I left a week after we got back when the baby was only ten weeks old. It was after I came back that I saw the resemblance. It was unmistakable. She was a Hogan. My wife couldn't have known as she never went to the farm.*"

"*And what did poor Mrs Carmody say when you told her?*"

"*That's the thing, you see. Poor Charlotte is dead.*"

They would be shaken by the news. "*She was a good woman. Everyone recognised that. The whole town was delighted when she gave birth to a live baby, and now you're telling me Mary Anne wasn't hers, but ours? That your wife had a second dead child?*"

In a few of the scenarios he summoned up, his revelations were met with a punch in the face from Dan for putting Nell through so much grief, a punch he accepted with resignation. In another he escaped the expected punch because of the respect Dan had for him as a doctor. The Hogans were humble people and they humbly accepted his mistake as an innocent one, feeling sorrier for him than they felt for themselves, and at the end of each scene they begged him to keep Mary Anne for her sake, to take advantage of the privileged life she was leading.

At the end of these sessions he always ended up by opting to leave things as they were, and felt a sense of peace that lasted for hours before his conscience started tormenting him again. But, when his eight-week convalescence was up, he would be heading back to England to rejoin the Medical Corps, destined this time for mainland Europe at last, so that, even if he wanted to, he would not have the time to take her back to Australia.

While he was in London, he would love to call into the hospital where Niamh was working and see her and talk to her. From what his classmates had told him, she was still unattached and it saddened him to hear it. His one dread was that he had ruined her life, a much sadder outcome than having ruined his own by allowing himself to be parted from her five years earlier by being obliged to marry Charlotte. He wouldn't telegraph that he was calling for fear she might absent herself deliberately to avoid him.

She had not tried to contact him since before his wedding. Could he indulge his shredded heart by seeing her for a few minutes for one last time before he was shipped across to Europe? What effect could one little inconsequential visit possibly have on the fortunes of the planet Earth which was bleeding and shuddering on its axis during this mighty conflict?

He thought of the hundreds of men's lives he had saved during the last two years, the thousands who were beyond saving, and the millions in the rest of the conflict who had been shot, blown up, gassed, starved, frozen, bombed, incinerated, drowned, executed, mutilated, tortured, burnt, orphaned, bereaved, displaced and dehumanised, and was confounded that the one face that often insinuated itself, among the many others that haunted him in his delirium and his dreams, was that of Nell Hogan's at the moment he lied by telling her that one of her twins was dead.

Lochlann made one courtesy call to Edwina in the townhouse, and visited Mary Anne in the nursery while he was there, but made no further attempt to see her.

"She's happy," he justified himself to Iseult. "It's not as if she even knows who I am. I've been away too long and I'll soon be gone again. It's not as if she'll miss me. She's in good hands. The nanny is no Nurse Dixon, so stop fretting."

Secretly he feared that if he saw a lot of Mary Anne he might become too attached to her, and then find it more difficult to return her to Australia after the war was over.

That is, if he did return from Europe, which in many ways he hoped he wouldn't. How much simpler life would be if he could bury his guilt in a grave somewhere on the Continent – preferably France – rather than carrying it around with him to haunt his days and nights for the rest of his life.

The amount he was drinking didn't worry him. It was only a temporary measure to help dull his conscience and to pass the time between one part of the war and the next. He was confident he did not have the addictive personality of an alcoholic.

CHAPTER 7

London, May, 1944

Niamh McCarthy saw Lochlann through the glass inset in the wooden door as she walked down the long corridor, but he didn't see her. He was in uniform at the front desk of the hospital talking to the receptionist, and Niamh had continued to approach after spotting him, keeping him in her sights, wondering if it really was Lochlann or someone who looked like him, and how could she be sure from this distance after five years of not seeing him?

Now she was right up against the glass inset and, standing motionless in order to concentrate more intensely, she identified that dear profile with certainty. It was Lochlann without a doubt.

Lochlann here in London?

She leaned against the wall for support. An elderly porter came up behind her and touched her arm to gain her attention. She turned her head towards him to see what he wanted. He was speaking to her but she couldn't make out what he was saying as, in the instant that she had identified Lochlann, her ears were filled with a loud, pulsing throb. The porter's face, fading in and out of focus, looked concerned. She pressed her hand to her chest as she felt a tightness there that prevented her from breathing evenly. Her legs weakened and the porter's arms held her up. She noted that the concern on his face had turned to alarm.

"Will I get you a doctor, Doctor?" she heard him saying through an echoing tunnel. "Or a chair? Or a glass of water?"

Five years. She put a hand out to hold on to the porter's shoulder and was able to breathe again.

"No, thank you," she said. "I don't need any of those."

Niamh was seized with a fear that Lochlann might not have come to see her, but someone else entirely, and might soon disappear down a different corridor or, worse still, go out the front entrance and walk away and never know that she had ever been there in the hospital on the other side of the glass door looking out at him.

He was writing something. He was handing the receptionist a note. He was saying something to the receptionist. He was turning to leave.

"Porter, run and tell that man leaving the desk not to go away without seeing me."

The porter looked out into the reception area, then back at her, unsure. He stayed holding on to her and didn't move.

"Quickly," she said. "This is important. Life and death. That man there is the love of my life and if he leaves now I may never see him again. Quickly. Stop him and then bring him around the back way to my office. Don't tell him what I just said. Dr Niamh McCarthy, second floor. Ask at reception. Go. I'll be fine. His name is Lochlann. I'll never forget you for this. God bless you."

The porter released his grip on her and she pressed herself hard against the wall so that she wouldn't slide down onto the linoleum-covered floor. He pushed open the door, looked back through the glass to check that she was still standing, and then began walking across the foyer as quickly as his stiff legs would allow. Lochlann had pulled back the first set of blackout curtains and passed through them into the space beyond while the porter was still only halfway across the floor.

Hurry, old man, for the love of God, or you'll lose him. You'll have no way of seeing which way he turns with your old eyes if you let him escape out there into the darkness.

"*Lochlann!*" roared the old man, exploding the silence and startling the receptionist.

Lochlann reappeared and looked to see who had shouted his name. He saw the old porter waving at him and waited for him to cross to the curtains, then bent his head to hear what he had to say. He nodded and looked around but did not see her.

He shook the porter's hand, and motioned for him to lead on.

Niamh had often wondered how she would react if she ever saw him face to face again, and now she knew. She would not denounce him or turn coldly away from him, as most of her friends had urged her to do, but would sit quietly and give him a chance to speak. That's if she could keep control of her mind and her movements long enough to make it back to her office.

She bumped into the walls along the corridor three times before her legs had recovered sufficient strength to keep her walking in a straight line. The meeting with him was now only minutes away. She reached the sanctuary of her office where she leaned over to grasp the edge of her desk before falling into her chair.

She decided . . . deep breath . . . she would hold out her hand to Lochlann as soon as he came in so there would be no awkward moment in case . . . deep breath . . . he thought he was expected to kiss her on the cheek. It might seem unfriendly, sitting in her chair, stretching her arm across her desk, but it would be safer that way, saving her from the horror of feeling her legs giving way at the moment of reunion if she took the risk of standing up.

After she made that decision she heard the familiar knock on the door that she recognised as Lochlann's. Five years later, he used the same knock and she remembered it.

By the time the handle turned she was sitting in a vacuum of stillness, already feeling the falseness of her stationary pose, wanting to leap up and rush over to embrace him, but restraining herself, remaining in her chair as she had decided.

He looked at her when he first came in and it was as if he were looking into the sun, disorientating himself. She held out her hand and kept holding it out until he saw it and took it in his.

"Thank you for coming," she said. "I think I gave that poor porter a fright."

"Not at all. He was glad to be your messenger."

Niamh withdrew her hand, and Lochlann sat down at her invitation.

"What did he say?" Please God he didn't tell you that you are the love of my life, she thought. I said it without thinking. I had to say something forceful to get the man to move.

"He said a Dr McCarthy wanted to see me in her office. He said you had spotted me and wanted to talk to me. An old friend, you said."

Wise and tactful porter, thought Niamh. He shall be rewarded. "As you truly are," she said. "Despite everything. I didn't want to go up to you in the foyer with the receptionist looking on. That's why I sent the porter." She paused, then said, "Why are you here?"

"To see you, of course."

"Who told you I was here?"

"Iseult – plus Pearse and Liam and Colm from school and Sam and Seb and Malachy from college and about ten other people after they heard I was passing through London." He was smiling as he spoke.

He's changed, she thought. Sadder, despite the smile. How could he be otherwise?

She's changed, he thought. Sadder, despite the smile. I did that to her.

They were facing each other across the desk. Lochlann didn't break the eye contact, but Niamh was forced to look away at intervals because the charge was too intense for her to bear.

"I'm only passing through. We're getting our orders tomorrow. The woman at reception said you weren't on duty today and I was just about to head off. It was lucky for me you saw me."

"I'm covering for someone. I wasn't meant to be here." Luck is on my side.

"You look wonderful. Iseult said you had lost a lot of weight and everyone was worried you might have contracted malaria in Uganda."

"Nothing as sinister as that. The tropical heat didn't agree with me, that's all. It sapped all my energy. I don't know how I put up with it for two years. Never again. But now I feel great. Back to my old self." As if that could ever be. "I was sorry to hear about Charlotte."

"Thank you. Yes, that was a bad business. Harcourt gone as well. Difficult to believe one family could have so much misfortune."

"And you have a little girl."

"Yes, Mary Anne. A sweet little thing."

"How old is she now?"

"Almost three."

"That's a nice age. I've heard she's a lovely child and the image of you."

"She's lovely all right, but I wouldn't go so far as to say she looks like me."

Now I can tell her everything, now that the subject of the child has come up, and then she can be horrified and go and forget all about me and think what a lucky escape she has had.

But now is not the time. Why say anything when there's a possibility I might not survive the invasion and she might not survive if there are more bombings? Why weigh her down with knowledge that will haunt her, especially if I don't return and she's the only one in possession of it? Why am I even thinking of telling her anything? I lost the right to confide in her years ago.

They talked about their classmates and what they were doing and about her family and his family.

"I was going to write to you," said Lochlann.

"Were you?" asked Niamh, hoping she didn't sound too eager.

"Yes, but what I have to say I couldn't commit to paper. I had to see you in person. I didn't want to go away without telling you that I never stopped loving you, not that that's any help to us now. I don't want to talk about Charlotte, God rest her soul, but I want to say to you, and to no one else, that I never grew to love her. Everyone knew I didn't love her when I married her, that I felt only a great pity for her because of the sad life she had led. Let her rest in peace. And I don't want to make excuses for myself. All I want to say is that I still love you and would like to continue where we left off, but I don't think it's possible. I'm not the man I was and I have done some wicked things, and I don't expect you to forgive me for the business with Charlotte and I expect your feelings for me have changed anyway." Dear God, why am I sitting here mouthing words? Why is she sitting there and me here? What wouldn't I give to hear her throaty laugh instead of having to look at the stricken expression on her face? Why don't I stand up and go around to the other side of the desk and hold her in my arms one last time?

"I have forgiven you about Charlotte, but I don't want to talk about that now. I don't believe you are capable of deliberately doing anything wicked, Lochlann." But Charlotte did a wicked thing deliberately, and I'll never forgive her for that. Never. "I know terrible things happen in life and especially in wartime but that's the nature of war. You have to obey orders."

"That's not what I meant." He paused. "I would love to marry you . . ."

Niamh looked away from him.

". . . but I can't marry you or anyone else."

Niamh looked back at him and shivered. "Why? What's the matter?" Her immediate thought was that he must have suffered an intimate injury in the conflict.

"I can't say. It's not really my secret to betray. I'm sorry."

"Oh."

"I had to tell you that. You will meet some other lucky man if you haven't already. I've heard that our old friend Malachy is still holding a candle for you. One of nature's gentlemen. I thought you and he might have teamed up while I was away. You could do a lot worse."

But a lot better, thought Niamh, watching with longing as he stood up to leave, wanting to physically hold on to him to prevent his departure.

"I can't delay, unfortunately. I'm under orders and I've a lot of miles to travel tonight."

"I'll come with you to the door." Why didn't you come looking for me yesterday? We could have had a day and a night together. Why have you offered such a small scrap of food to a starving dog?

She stood up and came around to the front of the desk, confident now that she could remain steady. He held open the door for her and their eyes met as she went through. He's like the Knight of the Sorrowful Countenance, she thought.

He took her arm and tucked it into his and closed a hand over her trapped one.

This is how we used to link each other when we walked down Grafton Street as students, she thought, and people used to trip over themselves when they saw him, staring at him and thinking he must be a film star. She let out an involuntary sound as the image of their old, happy, innocent selves projected itself on to her mind.

"Are you all right?" he asked, tightening the grip on her hand.

"Yes," she said. "I'm fine."

They walked the length of the corridor. When they reached the black-out curtains past reception Lochlann put his arms around her and kissed her on the top of her head. He held her tightly before releasing her and slipping out of sight behind the curtains.

CHAPTER 8

Ireland, 1944

Edwina thought her 'funeral' mink was in danger of being worn out. As she had predicted, the elderly were dropping like flies. Her older sister, Verity, was the first to go, closely followed by Lord Waldron, dying of cirrhosis of the liver at the age of eighty-five. She missed her sister more than she missed her husband.

Waldron's body was taken from Dublin to Tyringham Park to be interred in the family plot beside Charlotte. It was a year to the day since she had been buried there.

Edwina did not wear a veil this time as she wanted to show the villagers how to conduct oneself at a funeral. There was far too much weeping at Charlotte's. She thought and hoped, owing to her good example, there would be none at Waldron's.

Her example was wasted as no villagers or former tenants stood outside the little church on the estate to pay their respects to him. Memories in this part of the county were long, and the particular hatred in which Waldron was held, since he had done that unforgivable thing by recommending that the leaders of the Easter Rising be shot, had not lessened over the years. Those who expected a crowd as large as the one that had attended Charlotte's funeral were disappointed. Only some of the gentry and a few army personnel were present at the service.

"Frightfully poor turnout," said one of the local gentry, looking around in disbelief. "You'd think a man of his standing could do better than this."

"If it wasn't for the army representatives pushing up the numbers it would look like a pauper's funeral," said another.

"That's a bit of an exaggeration, but I take your point," said Lady Beatrice who had disliked Waldron since they were children growing up in neighbouring estates. "I can't say I'm surprised. Why should the villagers care for a landlord who only came here to check that the rents were collected and to lead out the occasional hunt, and was drunk the whole time he was here and never did anything for anybody?"

"So you're not worried about speaking ill of the dead?"

"If I could think of anything good to say about him I would say it," said Beatrice.

"It was the shock of Charlotte's death that killed him in the end," said a mourner standing in a group beside Beatrice.

"Don't talk such sentimental rubbish. It was drink. Though he might have died sooner if whiskey hadn't preserved parts of him while it was claiming his liver."

"Would you look at Lady Edwina? Isn't she an example to us all? The stiff upper lip is very admirable."

"And very convenient," answered her friend.

Lord Charles inherited his older brother's title as well as the estate of Tyringham Park, which he had been renting since Waldron relocated to the townhouse in Dublin all those years earlier. The day after the burial he called over the soldier-valet who had tended Waldron for years and was now wandering around in a disorientated state, gave him a ten-pound note and told him to bugger off, saying they could do without his sort around the place.

Edwina's long-term plan was for Mary Anne to marry her cousin William Blackshaw, the future heir to Tyringham Park. William would bring a title and an estate to the marriage and Mary Anne would bring money, an age-old solution to an often-recurring problem. William would inherit the Park with its depleted acreage.

Mary Anne would inherit her mother's fortune, the Dublin townhouse and the investments that had allowed Waldron to live a life of such extravagance in India and London. Between them they could become the most powerful couple in the country.

Marrying Mary Anne would save William from having to find a rich American bride, which often caused more trouble than it was worth if the bride was homesick or unwilling to fill the circumscribed role assigned to her or, worse still, had no interest in horses.

Who knows, thought Edwina, I might be still around to see the day. She calculated that she need hold on for only eighteen more years, which shouldn't be difficult seeing she was not yet sixty years of age. Most girls announced their engagements on their twenty-first birthdays. That would be worth living for: knowing Mary Anne had lost that hateful name of Carmody and was an official Blackshaw at last.

CHAPTER 9

Tyringham Park, 1945

When Mary Anne was four, Edwina took her to Tyringham Park for the summer so that Manus could introduce her to a life in the saddle. Learning good habits from the beginning was vital, and the age of four was a perfect time to begin. The nanny wouldn't leave Mary Anne's side the whole time they were there, so she would be well looked after. It would be good for the Cork Blackshaws, especially William, to get to know their only Dublin cousin. Then, come the autumn, Mary Anne, grounded in the good habits instilled by Manus, would have her own pony on the three acres Edwina had purchased on the outskirts of Dublin.

Edwina felt a wave of nostalgia and happiness as she was driven past the stables, knowing that she would have access to them and to Manus for the next three months. Later in the afternoon she would meet Manus face to face, and this time she would know who he was, bearded or clean-shaven. How would he receive her when they were unobserved? With deference, in accordance with her status as opposed to his? With sympathy, mindful of her disability? With affection, in memory of their past associations?

Giles Blackshaw became the heir to Tyringham Park at an early age following the untimely death of his father Nicholas from cancer a month before the incumbent Lord Charles Blackshaw died of old age. It was he who came forward to welcome Edwina and her large entourage. For the sake of Mary Anne, Edwina had decided to be pleasant to the young owner and his wife, Georgina, but would not go so far as to show gratitude for their hospitality, which she expected as her right.

Giles said that, unfortunately, Georgina was indisposed at the moment, but was looking forward to seeing her at dinner, and that the children would be back from their daily walk with their nanny by the time the visitors were settled into their rooms.

Edwina paid particular attention to her hair and outfit before being wheeled by a manservant down to the stables.

Giles had sent word to Manus that Mary Anne, accompanied by her grandmother, would be joining her cousins William, Nigel and Jane, for their two-hour daily lesson which was to be conducted exclusively by Manus, and was not to be passed on to any of the stable lads, no matter how competent they were judged to be.

Mary Anne, with her straight back and her beautiful smiling face framed by dark curls, walked beside the wheelchair. Manus was probably expecting to see a plump, plain, sour, waddling, mousey-haired replica of the young Charlotte. Edwina couldn't wait to witness his amazement when he first spotted this magical child who was, gratifyingly, now holding her hand.

The double doors were open. Manus, now clean-shaven, looked like his earlier self, except for some grey in his hair and an added gravitas in his bearing. He was talking to a striking, laughing boy, wild-haired and badly dressed, mounted on an impressive colt. Edwina noted in an instant that the boy had a naturally elegant seat on a horse. It took only one glance to notice something like that. William, Nigel and Jane Blackshaw were waiting on their ponies in the background, looking competent but ordinary.

Manus saw the pair outside the archway – the manservant had been dismissed – and came towards them. Edwina flushed in anticipation of his welcome.

"Good morning, ma'am," said Manus, standing out of handshaking range.

His expression looked cold. Even hostile. It must be a trick of the light, thought Edwina, with shadows emphasising the downward-sloping creases in his sixty-year-old face.

"So this is Charlotte's daughter," he said, turning towards Mary Anne with a kindly, loving smile. "What a beautiful little girl you are. You are as beautiful as your mother was at your age, and she was very special."

What a load of Irish blarney, Edwina thought.

Manus faced her again, and the cold expression returned. "Miss Mary Anne's pony is ready for her, as Lord Blackshaw requested, ma'am."

"Thank you, Manus," said Edwina. "Who is that boy on the colt?"

"That is Toby Prendergast."

"I wasn't enquiring about his name. I want to know who he is."

"A friend of the children's."

"But who *is* he?" Edwina repeated, looking past Manus at the young boy who was now joking with William.

"You'll have to excuse me, ma'am. I need to get back. Will you come with me, Mary Anne, to meet your very own pony? He's waiting in his stall for you to give him a name."

Mary Anne took Manus's hand and skipped off with him, leaving Edwina to suffer arrows of humiliation at the reality of Manus's unfriendliness.

She entered the stables and before long Manus led Mary Anne from the stall on a chestnut pony.

"Keep your hands lower down," Edwina called out to Mary Anne.

"I'll call him Chestnut," Mary Anne said, too preoccupied to hear what Edwina was saying.

"That's a great name," said Manus. "It's the best name he could possibly have. Now keep your back nice and straight while we do a circle."

"Jolly well done," said William.

"You must have done this before," said Toby.

"Manus, you have to lengthen the stirrups by at least an inch," Edwina called out.

"Come on, team, let's go into the paddock," said Manus, as if he hadn't heard her, leading Mary Anne through the gate that was on the opposite side of the courtyard to the archway.

He mustn't have heard me, thought Edwina. I'll mention it again when they return.

Manus, on seeing Edwina at Charlotte's funeral after a break of many years, had felt nothing in relation to their old friendship. The exuberance of their nine years of working and intimacy had been cancelled out, and for good reason, he believed.

The day after the accident at the hunt that had left Edwina crippled for life, he had returned early to the fallen Mandrake with a Clydesdale draught horse to drag the corpse back to the horses' graveyard beside the stables. The three stable lads were already in the process of digging the grave.

When Manus rolled the gelding over onto the slide that was hooked up to the Clydesdale, he saw gouges on the offside flank. The hide was torn and portions of flesh were bulging out.

He searched and found Edwina's riding crop in the whitethorn bush over the wall. He wouldn't have noticed it if he hadn't been looking for it. And there, pressed into the soft leather folds at the end of the crop were, as he had suspected, a dozen long, sharp tacks encrusted with dried blood and hide.

Lady Beatrice, who had died recently, God rest her beautiful soul, had not believed Edwina's assertion that Charlotte had caused her accident and had questioned the stable lads, Charlotte herself and many huntsmen until she could reconstruct the incident clearly. She passed on to Manus her conclusion that Edwina had been the cause of her own fall. Motivated by jealousy, she had forced Charlotte to ride a mongrel of a hunter that could not be controlled, while she claimed the perfectly trained Mandrake who had reacted to the ill-treatment Edwina inflicted on him – the tearing of his hide and flesh by tacks in Edwina's riding crop – by jumping too soon before the hedge and having his forelegs clipped by the mongrel hunter. Edwina blamed the nine-year-old Charlotte for the catastrophic aftermath when, in fact, her daughter was innocent.

Finding this out had caused Beatrice great pain. She had befriended Edwina when Waldron had brought her as a young bride to Tyringham Park (before promptly deserting her to travel back to India) and had always tried to think well of her. In this instance, however, there was no justification for what Edwina had done, and Beatrice's sympathies lay with the plain Charlotte who was always trying to please.

On hearing Beatrice's evidence, the bond that had tied Manus to Edwina had snapped and was never likely to be joined together again.

If sentiments of forgiveness surfaced when he thought of Edwina, all he had to do to banish them was to think of the magnificent Mandrake, looking sorrowfully at him while he, the gelding's trainer and master, shot him straight between the eyes after the drunken Waldron had aimed at that spot and missed.

At the end of the introductory lesson, Manus told Edwina in his gentle voice that he would prefer if she did not oversee the rest of the course, as he knew from past experience that they had different methods of training and he didn't want his system to be undermined by criticisms that she might make later to Mary Anne.

Edwina took his words as a challenge, ignored his request, and turned up the next day and the day after that. She was confident that memories of the old days would come back to him and he would change his mind and look forward to seeing her on a daily basis.

On the fourth day of Mary Anne's lessons, Georgina, mother of William, Nigel and Jane, asked Edwina in a sad voice if she would mind dreadfully if the nanny accompanied Mary Anne to the stables from now on instead of her.

"On whose request?"

"The children's, I'm afraid."

"Which children?"

"William was the spokesman. He didn't say which ones."

"It couldn't have been Mary Anne. Was it that boy Toby?"

"As I said, William didn't specify."

"I bet it was that boy. Who is he, if I might be so bold as to ask? Manus wouldn't give me a straight answer."

"He's the grandson of the gardener, Reg, whom you might remember. Toby's father is a fisherman from Cobh. Toby spends the summers here with his grandfather who is training him to take over from him one day. Our children think the world of him."

"So I've noticed. If he's going to be a gardener, why is he wasting

Manus's time teaching him to ride?"

"It was Manus's idea. The children are all such good friends he didn't want to side-line Toby, whom he refers to as his apprentice."

"Is Manus giving the orders around here now? What do you and Giles have to say about it?"

"Very little, as it so happens. Since so much acreage was sold off to the tenants, we have no cattle or deer or sheep any more. Or any rents, for that matter. Only the horses. They are keeping the Park afloat, and all credit is due to Manus for gaining us a nationwide reputation for breeding and training both children's ponies and racehorses."

Credit that would have gone to me instead of him if I hadn't been forced to move to Dublin for medical reasons after my accident. Edwina ground her teeth to think of her unacknowledged, unused expertise.

"As for the riding lessons," Georgina continued, "what difference does one extra child make, especially if he is as keen as Toby? The boy is setting my three a good example."

"There's something not right about having him around the place. I have enough trouble with the common side of Mary Anne's family in Dublin without having a common stranger thrust on me down here where I thought I was safe. I would be worried about the influence that boy might have on Mary Anne as she gets older."

"From what I've seen of him, his influence can only be for the good. William says that he is particularly kind to Mary Anne because she is motherless. You have to admit that that's the sign of a nice disposition."

Edwina snorted. "A regular little charmer all round by the sound of it. He doesn't need to patronise Mary Anne – she has no shortage of people who want to look after her. Is he paying for his lessons?"

"Edwina! I'll pretend I didn't hear that question. It's time to ring for tea. Will you have blackberry jam or honey with your scones?"

CHAPTER 10

Dublin, 1945

In June, a month after the war in Europe was over, Lochlann had returned from the Continent in the same state of exhaustion he had been in when he returned from Africa. The first question he asked his sister when she called in was if Niamh McCarthy was safe. Iseult told him she was. He smiled and sank into a long, natural, peaceful sleep.

Lochlann didn't visit Mary Anne at the Park where she was spending the summer in the care of Edwina. Instead, within two weeks of returning home he secured a place in the casualty department of the Mater Hospital on the recommendation of one of his old tutors who reckoned that Lochlann's war experience was a good training for such a position.

Lochlann worked long hours, sometimes sleeping in the hospital at night, but most times driving home to stay in his parents' house where he drank large quantities of whiskey to quieten the accusatory voices in his head. Now that the war was over, he no longer had an excuse for not resolving the two main problems in his life: how to live with Mary Anne and how to live without Niamh McCarthy.

At the end of August, Lochlann woke on the sitting-room couch to find four-year-old Mary Anne, newly returned to Dublin, staring right into his face. What a beautiful, entrancing child she is, he marvelled through the mist of his hangover.

Mary Anne ran off to tell her grandmother that her daddy was awake, and to bring him in the tea.

Grace came in with a tray a few minutes later. Mary Anne was helping her by carrying in a plate of soda bread to go with the tea.

"Tell your daddy where you went for the summer." Grace's voice was falsely bright for the sake of the child. She had seen Lochlann in this hung-over state too often recently to be sympathetic.

"Went to the Park with Weena."

"Who's Weena?"

"That's the name she has for Edwina," Grace answered for her. "She's the only one allowed to use it."

"That's because you're special," said Lochlann. "Did you like the Park?"

"Yes."

"Did you ride a pony?"

"I rode Chestnut. He's my very own pony. Weena gave him to me."

"That's good. You're a very lucky girl."

"Tell your daddy who you like best in the whole world," Grace prompted.

"Toby," said Mary Anne.

Grace smiled at Lochlann over Mary Anne's head.

"Who's he?" Lochlann asked.

"He's my friend."

"Where does he live?"

"In the Park."

"What do you like about him?"

"He's funny. He makes things and plays pirates."

"Now you sit here, Mary Anne, like a good girl," said Grace, "and tell your daddy everything you did since he went away and I'll go and see if your nanny has arrived yet to take you back to the townhouse." And I hope your daughter's chattering makes your head ache, Lochlann, even more than it's aching now, and I hope it teaches you a lesson.

Grace wondered how long Lochlann could go on the way he was going before his work began to suffer. He showed no interest in anyone outside the hospital except his daughter, and even that was in a limited way. He blamed his unsociable working hours for seeing so little of her.

Grace assumed that his uncharacteristic behaviour was a direct result of his experiences during the war, but her fear was that if he did not revert to the social drinker he had once been, he might slide into the abyss of alcoholism and become a lost soul.

When she and Iseult pointed out that he could now claim his daughter back from Edwina, thinking this might give him a focus in life and distract him from the drink, he said she was happy where she was and he had no home to offer her, so why not leave things as they were?

Lochlann knew he could not risk living in the townhouse. Edwina would have the servants spying on him. Between his long hours of working and long hours of drinking, she would build a case that he was not a fit father and would apply to have her guardianship made permanent. With her influence she would probably succeed. Hiring a nanny to care for the child in his parents' home was not ideal, with Grace, Rory and himself all working long hours. The nanny would be unsupervised in the house for periods of ten hours or more on most days. If he bought a house of his own, the results would be the same. Edwina would compare that lack of supervision to the constant presence of herself, Queenie, the nanny and the cook, not to mention all the other servants, in the townhouse. Iseult, with her expanding family and diminishing space, had already been ruled out.

After less than a year, Edwina hired a new nanny and dismissed the original one, saying she turned out to be unsuitable. The real reason she wanted to be rid of her was that Mary Anne had become too fond of her, holding her hand, hugging her, and wanting to be in her company all the time. Edwina thought someone like Nurse Dixon would be more desirable.

CHAPTER 11

Dublin, 1946

Before going off duty at two in the morning, Lochlann called in to see the young man whose chest had been gouged by the point of a paling when he had slipped while climbing a fence. Lochlann had patched him up early the previous day. The boy was asleep. His colour was good and his face relaxed. He would make a full recovery and be left with only a scar to remind him of his misadventure.

Which was a better outcome than Lochlann expected for himself.

While he looked down at the face of the untroubled young man, he allowed himself to remember how seven years earlier he had despaired after he lost Niamh by being obligated to marry the pregnant Charlotte. He felt at the time as if a cannonball had been fired at his chest while he was standing barefooted and coatless on the Arctic ice in a chill wind facing an endless winter. The ball had gone right through his body, leaving a gaping hole. At the time the only thing he wanted was to have Niamh press her dear hand against his wound so that for a moment he could forget his future which was painted in various shades of black.

The gaping hole was still there and there was no Niamh nearby to place her hand over it and heal it.

He had not expected to survive the war and that was why he had allowed himself to visit Niamh in London the week before D-Day and confess to her that he still loved her. But he had survived, and now wished he had never told her.

"To keep a secret you must tell no one, not even your nearest and dearest who one day might turn out not to be your nearest and dearest any more, but instead your deadliest enemy armed with the knowledge you have given them to destroy you." That sentence had struck him when he first read it in a novel, and the truth of it had been reinforced when his father was telling him about being asked to perform an abortion on a girl who had been raped. Refusing a termination to that distraught woman had been one of the most difficult things he had ever had to do during his career, but refuse he did, even though he was tempted out of compassion to do it and call it by another name. Being struck off for doing such a thing was too high a price to pay. Even knowing that the woman would have to seek out an inferior, even dangerous alternative, he had remained resolute and hardened his heart. He said that if he had carried out the procedure, the woman, at a later stage, would tell someone, most likely a woman in a similar predicament, frantic for help. How could that woman not pass on the name of the kind doctor who had helped her out, thus starting off a chain reaction?

Lochlann's common sense informed him, even if anecdotal evidence hadn't already convinced him, that secrets didn't stay secrets forever. How many times had he heard someone say to a shocked gathering, "Oh, was that meant to be a secret? I thought everyone knew that," revealing, for example, that someone's father had left behind his first family to take on a new wife. And even if it wasn't as overt as that, people gave themselves away by inappropriate responses or silences, facial tics, inability to dissemble, compulsion to confess, a need to dramatise, a desire to wound and, inescapably, by becoming indiscreet under the influence of alcohol.

"Never confess your sins to a priest who drinks," one of Lochlann's uncles had warned him years earlier.

It had come as a shock to Lochlann to hear such a thing, having been reared to believe that the seal of confession was inviolable even under threat of imprisonment or pain of death. Was it possible that the effects of alcohol were so powerful that they could override the conscience and loosen the tongue of a man who had taken a sacred vow never to reveal what he had heard in confession?

Lochlann knew only too well the power alcohol had to dismantle one's inhibitions, having fathered two children under its influence. Nevertheless, he didn't think he would go so far as to break the rule of patient confidentiality, so deeply ingrained was it in his mind, but how could he be certain when he suffered memory loss in the aftermath of heavy bouts of alcohol consumption?

He ended up by convincing himself that staying single and drinking alone were necessary to ensure that he would never confess to anyone that Mary Anne was a stolen child that he was passing off as his own. He cited his erratic roster when asked out to social events by his old friends, and continued to drink quietly in the dark in his parents' sitting room, confident that only in that way would his secret remain safe.

His friends gave up on him one by one as he continued to turn down their invitations.

He did not attempt to contact Niamh. The most favourable outcome he could hope for her was that she would finally give in and marry Malachy Glynn, the only bachelor left in their year, the faithful friend who, along with Lochlann and many others, had loved Niamh since their student days.

CHAPTER 12

1946

After her first week of school Mary Anne said that she was the only one in her class who didn't have a mummy and who didn't live with her daddy or granddaddy. She asked her Aunt Iseult, recently back home from hospital with her fourth child, if she could call her 'Mummy' and if Lochlann could come and live in the townhouse with her instead of living with Grandma and Granddad Carmody.

"Of course you can't call me 'Mummy'," said Iseult, her voice sharper than she had intended. She pitied the motherless child with the ineffective father. "I'm your aunt. I can't be your mother as well. And your daddy can't go to live in the townhouse."

"Why can't he?"

Because it might interfere with his drinking, Iseult thought to herself. Aloud she said, "He's waiting until he can afford to buy a house that he and you can live in together."

"Will Nanny still mind me then?" asked Mary Anne, referring to her new nanny Ivy Golding.

"We'll have to wait and see."

"I want her to come."

"Do you like her?"

"Yes."

"How much?"

"This much," said Mary Anne, extending her arms out fully.

"That's good," said Iseult. "You know I would love to have you stay with me. Grandma and Granddad Carmody want you too, but Weena was the lucky one. She had first pick because she is your mother's mother. We all want you. Everyone loves you because you are such a special person."

"Was my mummy special?"

"Yes, very special. She loved you more than anything in the world. Now, I'll move this little dote into his crib while you take off your shoes and then you can hop into bed beside me and I'll tell you lots of stories about your lovely mother."

Mary Anne was full of chat about 'Weena' and 'Nanny Golding' during the few hours she spent on weekdays at the Farrellys' house. Weena did this, Weena did that, Weena said this and that, Weena bought her this, Weena promised her that. And most thrilling of all, Weena's Yorkshire terrier was due to have pups.

It was later in the month that Iseult was startled to hear Mary Anne calling out the word 'Mummy', and even more startled when she heard Nanny Golding answering the call. At first Iseult thought that she had misheard Mary Anne, or that the child had made a slip of the tongue when she called Ivy Golding 'Mummy', but during the following weeks she heard her use the word openly and naturally, and Ivy Golding did not correct her.

It was easy to see why the child liked her new nanny so much. She was playful and amusing and was able to make Mary Anne do as she was told by coaxing rather than demanding, in the same way Iseult was able to do when she was on top of things and in the whole of her health, which wasn't very often these days with four children under five.

Edwina had miscalculated for the second time, thought Iseult, choosing another nanny Mary Anne had become fond of.

Iseult wished Lochlann would pull himself together, stop drinking, buy a house of his own, find Niamh McCarthy and marry her if she wasn't already married, and set up a household where Mary Anne could have a mummy and a daddy living in the same house.

Over the telephone Edwina broached the idea of Mary Anne's going to boarding school when she turned eight. It would be necessary to secure her a place well in advance as the school was so popular.

Lochlann listened to her without interruption.

It would be good for the child to be trained for the life she was destined to lead, was Edwina's main argument. "I went to the particular school I have in mind and it made me the woman I am today, so it would be ideal for Mary Anne."

What she didn't say was that she wanted to rid Mary Anne of her Dublin accent, educated though it was, of her Catholicism, of her attachment to all the Carmodys, her talent for making her nannies love her, her delight in her local school friends, and her lack of discernment – it was not seemly to be friendly to everyone one met.

Lochlann said if that was the case he would leave it up to Edwina to make the necessary arrangements.

"Wise decision," said Edwina who did not realise she was talking to a man who was very drunk.

Lochlann forgot the conversation as soon as it was over.

CHAPTER 13

"Lochlann seems to have broken off contact with all his friends."

Malachy Glynn was sitting at the kitchen table in the house of Iseult Farrelly.

"I know," said Iseult, who had written to him, asking him to come to see her the next time he was in Dublin as she wanted to speak to him about Lochlann. "He's opted out in more ways than one."

"Is he suffering from shell shock?"

"Something like that, we presume. War nerves of one kind or another, anyway. We know he was present when one of the concentration camps was opened. That would be enough to push anyone over the brink, if you ask me. He doesn't talk about that or anything else he went through. We're worried that he'll slide further downhill and end up jeopardising his career. If that goes he'll be finished off altogether."

"It won't come to that. He's too conscientious a doctor to do anything stupid."

"I wish I had your confidence. God knows his work is the one thing that has sustained him throughout everything." She looked at Malachy with gratitude. "I can't tell you how glad I am to see you, Malachy. A good friend from the past. You might be just the one to get through to

71

him and make him see sense. When did you last see him?"

"Just now, actually, at your parents' house on my way here. Couldn't resist dropping in on the off-chance. Just like the old days. Before that I hadn't seen him since he returned from North Africa. He seemed all right then."

"He was. The big change came later. How did you find him?"

"I hardly recognised him. He looks middle-aged. Couldn't believe he was jarred at eleven o'clock in the morning. Footless, in fact, and barely able to speak. It's not like him. He used to love a good night out like the rest of us, but this is worrying. You said in your letter that I can help. I can't think that I would be much use to him while I'm up there in Sligo."

"I want you to engineer a face-to-face meeting between him and Niamh McCarthy."

Malachy visibly reacted to the name. "Niamh McCarthy?" he asked, blushing. "I would have to hurry up, so, as she's planning to emigrate to Canada."

Malachy went on to say that it was no secret that he had loved Niamh since their first year at college, but he knew he didn't have a chance with her while Lochlann was around, and so it proved. He had tried to talk her into settling for him without loving him – he would marry her under any circumstances – but she could not be persuaded. He knew she was going to Canada because she had given up hope of Lochlann's contacting her.

"Did she ever think of contacting him?"

"Not after what he said to her in London just before D-Day."

Iseult did not know the two had met then.

"He told her that he could never marry her or anyone else. That he had done something too wicked. Have you any idea what he was talking about?"

"No. No idea."

"Nor has Niamh."

"I know I'm an interfering sister and Lochlann might never speak to me again if he finds out I wrote to you, but I think it's worth a try."

"I'm with you there. What's the worst that can happen? If they don't hit it off, Niamh will go to Canada as planned and Lochlann will keep drinking."

Malachy turned as Ivy Golding came in through the french doors, carrying one child and surrounded by four others. She had come to drop off Mary Anne for her weekly visit and the Farrelly children were clamouring for her to stay. She seemed to be glowing, back-lit from the sun coming through the open doors.

Iseult introduced the nanny, her four children, and Mary Anne, whom Malachy looked at with interest.

"Now I'd best be off," he said then. "I'm meeting my brother in Ranelagh for lunch. I'm heading back to Sligo tomorrow so I might give Lochlann another try later."

"Don't bother your head," Iseult said. "He'll only be worse. You have to catch him just before he goes to work or immediately afterwards or you're wasting your time. We'll talk again."

Malachy and Ivy Golding moved off together, talking, and forty minutes later they were still talking out the front beside Malachy's car.

Niamh McCarthy's father believed *Dracula* could have been written only in Ireland, where Bram Stoker, confined to bed as a child, had been fed stories of heartless landlords who were regarded by the tenants they mistreated as bloodsuckers, and he was not slow in passing on his beliefs to his children.

Her great-grandparents, along with all the other tenants on an estate in County Donegal, had been evicted during the Famine by a landlord who didn't want the expense of feeding them after the potato crop failed. To prevent their return, bailiffs dismantled the roofs and tore out the doors and windows of their small dwellings – hovels, some might say.

Niamh's great-grandfather, aged thirty at the time, already worn out from hard work and hunger, was one of the million people who starved to death while wagonloads of corn were being delivered to warehouses all over the country. The London government forbade giving any of it to the starving populace in case it upset the market. Exports of beef and grain continued to flow from Ireland to Britain, and imports of wheat came into Ireland to make bread that the poor couldn't afford to buy.

Niamh's great-grandmother made it as far as her brother's house in Bellmullet, County Mayo, with her four-year-old son. She suspected her husband had given any little food he scavenged to her and their son and had kept none for himself. After his death from starvation the mother, in her weakened state, couldn't rally even in her brother's house and died soon afterwards of typhus.

The uncle raised the boy to be a fisherman like himself, and the boy, when a man, sent his son to be a doctor, and that doctor was Niamh's father.

Iseult had heard this story from Lochlann who had heard it from Niamh when Harcourt Blackshaw had first invited the young woman to the townhouse and she had balked at the idea of having anything to do with "that lot". Niamh told Lochlann why she had this reaction, but said nothing to Harcourt. In the end she gave in and became a regular visitor to Harcourt's rooms, as she had grown to like and admire him when she got to know him.

There was no danger that Niamh would grow to like and admire Lady Edwina the more she got to know her, thought Iseult. There was more likely to be open warfare than a friendly regard as time went on. There were many serious reasons Iseult wanted Lochlann and Niamh to be reunited, but the extra bonus for her would be seeing Edwina pitted against a strong adversary like Niamh.

Meanwhile, all she had to do was wait until Malachy – unselfish, faithful Malachy – could inveigle Niamh on some pretext or another to travel with him to Dublin.

CHAPTER 14

"I got a good one today for Chuck Murray," said Father Crowley, sitting at the Carmodys' dinner table.

Lochlann was making a rare appearance at the evening meal, having just arrived in from the hospital.

"That's good," said Rory. Father Crowley had been a school friend of his.

"A bit unusual, but there you are."

"What are we talking about?" asked Lochlann, wishing his father would offer him a drink.

"A baby," said Rory. "Chuck Murray from Marblehead. Originally from Stamullen in County Meath. You might remember my speaking of him. He and his wife have been looking for a baby for over a year now."

"They're mad for Irish babies over there and I told him I'd keep my eye out for a good one for him and Colleen," said Father Crowley. "And today I found one."

"This is the first I've heard about this," said Lochlann, watching his father hand a second whiskey to the priest. "Are you talking about the United States?"

"Yes, the Catholic Irish-Americans want Irish babies and of course we want Catholic Irish-American parents so everybody's happy."

"What's the unusual bit?"

"The mother is married. She has nine children already and just gave birth to twins, and asked the midwife if she could take one of them as she's in financial straits, and the midwife contacted me."

Lochlann felt himself go cold all over.

"It happens all the time to me," said Grace. "Especially in the tenements. The mothers beg me to take the newly born child. When there's serious deprivation, and the mother already has a large brood at home and is worn out, sentiment goes out the window. Twins can often be the last straw."

"How do you arrange it?" Lochlann asked, concentrating on tracing a pattern on the tablecloth with a fork.

"The midwife who's there – well, not a trained midwife, but a neighbour who attends – tries to get a relative to take it," said Grace. "There's a lot of fostering goes on, especially with grandparents and aunts. But a lot of the mothers beg me personally to take the child to get it out of the slum areas and give it a good start in life. Sometimes when the mother regains her strength she changes her mind. But if she doesn't and the family is already overstretched, the midwife informs the local nuns who take it in alongside the babies of unmarried mothers to await adoption. A mother can be grateful if her child is sent to America where she thinks it will have a bright future."

"Is it legal to hand over a child just like that?"

"There's no law against it," said Father Crowley. "There is talk of the State legalising adoptions, but it hasn't happened yet. Until it does, the State is happy to leave it in the hands of religious bodies, both Catholic and Protestant, and secular priests like us."

"Does money change hands?"

"Not in my case, it doesn't. Providing a good Catholic home for an unwanted child is payment enough."

Lochlann wondered why he felt lighter. If other people did what he had done, could that mean his guilt was less? It certainly felt as if it were. The three at the table treated the transferring of babies so matter-of-factly that it gave him hope.

There was one big difference, though. In all the cases discussed the mothers had signed documents giving their consent, whereas when he had stolen Mary Anne the mother had no idea that a theft had taken place.

It didn't look as if his father was going to offer him a drink, so Lochlann, tracked by three pairs of eyes, was forced to stand up from the table to pour one for himself.

CHAPTER 15

When Niamh had not heard from Lochlann by Christmas 1946, she finally gave up hope of his ever seeking her out. She made plans to emigrate to Canada, where she could wrap herself up warm in the winter and stand facing the icy wilderness, where she could howl into the wind with grief and no one would hear her. She did not want to settle for a life without children, but neither did she want to settle for a man she did not love in order to have them. She thought that a change of country, especially a snow-swept country, might jolt her out of her constant obsessing about Lochlann, leaving her free to fall in love with a Mountie or a lumberjack, or any other sort of Canadian who did not remind her of him. She knew very little about the country and no one living there and that was part of its attraction.

How easy life would be if only she could find some way to fall in love with the honourable, kindly Malachy.

Malachy offered to drive Niamh to the Canadian Embassy for her interview. He had a few bits of business to attend to in the capital, he told her, and he would appreciate the company. She was happy to accept.

When they reached Dublin, he said he had just had an idea.

Would she mind if they called in to see Iseult for a few seconds? They were in plenty of time and it would be a good chance to find out how Lochlann was. Malachy had deliberately not mentioned Lochlann's name until this final part of the journey.

"Is there something the matter with him?" Niamh asked in immediate alarm, turning to look out the car window in case Malachy checked to see how she was reacting to his mentioning of that name. "I didn't hear anything from anyone."

In a way she was hoping there was something wrong with him, to explain why he hadn't contacted her in the time he had been back from the war. She could not forget the affecting declaration of love he had made to her in the London hospital just before D-Day.

Malachy had not told her about his earlier visit to Iseult. "I've heard rumours," he said. "That's why I want to check with Iseult first to see how much truth there is in them before I contact Lochlann himself. I don't want to put my foot in it."

No matter how many ways Niamh reworded her questions about Lochlann's health, Malachy was not able to give her any details.

Niamh had not seen Iseult for seven years. They had been close at the time and had looked forward to becoming sisters-in-law.

"Why don't you drop me off at the Embassy first and we can meet in Bewley's later and you can fill me in on what Iseult tells you?"

Malachy noticed that Niamh was twisting the strap of her handbag around her fingers in an agitated fashion.

"Too much of a waste of time for me to go there and back," he answered. "This will only take a minute seeing it's not far out of our way."

"I don't want to put you out. Perhaps you could drop me off at a bus stop."

"I couldn't do that. I promise I'll only be a minute."

"All right then. As long as I stay in the car." Niamh looked around. "This area looks familiar."

"It should. Iseult lives only a couple of streets away from her family home."

The fingers on Niamh's right hand were white from the constriction of the handbag strap.

"We'll be passing it on our way later. Ah, here we are. Iseult's street."

"Park out of view of the house, then, and I'll stay here and wait for you."

Malachy pulled over to the curb and switched off the engine. Continuing to look straight ahead, he argued that, seeing she was leaving for Canada soon, this would be an ideal opportunity to say goodbye to Iseult, with whom she had once shared a warm friendship, and through her she could pass on her best wishes to Lochlann.

"It will be painless way to close a chapter," he said. "A few minutes. No ceremony. No awkwardness. I'll do most of the talking if you don't feel up to it. We won't even have tea if we're asked. Trust me."

"I do trust you," said Niamh.

"Come on, then."

Iseult, flinging open the front door of her house as soon as the doorbell rang, greeted Niamh with affection.

She is not surprised to see me, was Niamh's first thought.

A look passed between Iseult and Malachy.

The two of them are in cahoots, Niamh realised. I have walked into a trap.

Iseult brought her into the sitting room where the front gate could be viewed through the bay window.

"Is Lochlann unwell?" asked Niamh.

Iseult looked down at her wristwatch. "You can ask him yourself. He'll be here in a minute."

Niamh turned pale and looked accusingly at Malachy. "Is all this a trick?" she asked.

"I'm afraid it is."

"I thought you said I could trust you."

"You can, when it comes to having your best interests at heart. I hope you won't waste all our effort and planning by making a bolt for it."

"I let Lochlann think I was ill when I rang to ask him to call," said Iseult. "Wicked of me, I know, but he wouldn't come otherwise. I have to go over to Palmerston Park to see how Ivy Golding is coping with my wild brood. She's doing me a favour."

"I'll come with you," said Malachy eagerly. "I'll be back in an hour to collect you, Niamh."

"I'll leave the door on the latch," said Iseult, leaving quickly. She imagined that if she stayed and had to pass between Niamh and Lochlann, she might be felled by the force of the electric charge that she was certain still existed between them.

Niamh watched the pair leaving. Her eyes were wide with a delicious fear. Memories came back to her of viewing Lochlann from a distance in the hospital in London, and how her legs would have given way beneath her if the porter hadn't come upon her and given his arm as support, and here she was again unable to move even if she had wanted to.

Just as before, she saw him before he saw her. He was walking along the road and then opening the gate, and walking up the path.

She heard his footsteps pause at the front door, the door opening, a well-remembered voice softly calling Iseult's name, and then the door to the sitting room opening and there he was – a man who had the shape of Lochlann but the look of an old man in despair. If she didn't already love the spirit and the bones of him, she might have pulled back. If she didn't believe he still loved her, she believed it now when she saw the wonder and joy on his face as he looked at her. Without hesitation she fell into his open arms, and let him take her left hand and press it against his exploding chest.

CHAPTER 16

1947

Edwina had a dream that she was dressed in armour, riding astride, pointing a jousting pole at Charlotte, who was galloping towards her, riding bareback, wearing a white dress, and holding Victoria in front of her as a shield. Just at the moment the point of Edwina's pole smashed into Victoria's chest, she woke and screamed out to the night nurse to go and fetch Dr Carmody this instant.

"I can't breathe," she shouted.

Lochlann might have been less patient at being summoned to her side for the third time in a month if he didn't suffer from nightmares himself. He knew too well how daytime rationalisations had no power against the terrors of the night.

"You must come and live here after you get married," Edwina said, still holding his hand after she had become calm. "Knowing you are in the house will give me peace of mind. You know you will have your own entrance and complete privacy, so I can't see how there can be any objections."

"That's a very kind offer."

"You can choose which of the four entrances you prefer, facing whichever of the four streets you like best. There is plenty of room for a surgery and waiting rooms and whatever else doctors need, and you already know how comfortable and spacious your living area would be."

"Yes, I remember."

"Mary Anne is already so happily settled in the townhouse. That should be an added incentive for you to move in. It would be a shame to uproot her."

"I see your point," said Lochlann.

Niamh didn't after he relayed Edwina's request to her.

Two months after their reunion, Lochlann and Niamh discussed plans for their forthcoming wedding. The ceremony was to be held in the Rathmines church, followed by a reception for one hundred and twenty people in the Shelbourne Hotel.

"Don't hold back," Lochlann had encouraged Niamh. "Go for all the trimmings. It might be my second time, but you have to take into account that it's your first."

"Just what my father said. He is so excited. Poor man probably thought he would never get me off his hands at my age." She looked into Lochlann's suddenly serious face. "What is it?"

"I was just thinking. I would like to ask Malachy to be my best man. Do you think that would be a tactless thing to do?"

"Because of me, you mean? No. I think he's over all that, thank goodness. There's nothing like a new love to drive out an old one."

"What are you saying?"

"I think Malachy has finally found his true love."

"In that short space of time after all these years?"

"It was love at first sight, apparently, for both of them."

"Well, don't keep me in suspense. Who is it? Anyone we know?"

"You know her well. It's Ivy Golding."

"Mary Anne's nanny?" Lochlann shook his head in disbelief and pleasure. "Well, well. Who would have believed it?"

"Iseult, for one. She saw the effect they had on one another at first hand. They apparently hit it off from their first meeting and talked outside for ages."

"Well, isn't that a good one? And here was I thinking he was still pining for you. Now I can go ahead and ask him to be my best man without any worries. My best man and a better one as well," he added with sincerity.

After the wedding Lochlann and Niamh bought a Georgian terraced house, consisting of six bedrooms and four reception rooms, not far from the townhouse and around the corner from Iseult's much smaller place. The pair intended to have a large family, and rooms would be needed for a surgery and waiting room on one of the floors. Lochlann took on a long-term mortgage to save his having to dip into Charlotte's legacy.

The house was compact and warm compared to the townhouse which rambled over a vast area with numerous rooms connected by chilly corridors.

Edwina's face contorted when Lochlann called in to thank her once again for her kind offer and to tell her that he and Niamh had bought a house of their own.

"You must be planning to follow the Catholic tradition of having a large family," she said when she heard the number of bedrooms.

"Not too large. Probably five," answered Lochlann, radiating health and optimism. "Blessed is the man whose quiver is full, as the bible says." And blessed is the man lucky enough to be married to Niamh McCarthy, he added to himself.

"And where will that leave Mary Anne?"

It had finally been established that Mary Anne was to live with her father, who only had to make his intentions known to claim his legal rights.

"As the honoured big sister. Niamh is already devoted to her. We will come to collect her and her things as soon as the house sale is finalised."

"Devoted to her, you say? So she will have led you to believe." Edwina's eyes narrowed. "I have it on good authority that stepmothers only pretend to like their stepchildren."

Edwina made that spiteful pronouncement deliberately, to get her own back at Niamh who, she presumed, had been the one to outlaw the idea of living in the townhouse.

"They do it to curry favour with the husband," she continued, "and then later when they have children of their own they freeze out the stepchild, some not even bothering to put on a show for the husband, citing the child's naughtiness as the reason for its being in bad favour."

"I don't think you need to worry about that, ma'am. You have obviously never met anyone as generous-hearted as Niamh or you wouldn't feel the need to pass on that dubious observation. She doesn't have a mean bone in her body."

"So you say now. Wait and see if I'm not right. I was thinking of the welfare of the child. Mary Anne would be much better off here where she has the undivided attention of us all rather than being pushed into the background by two busy people intent on rearing a large family."

Lochlan tried to think of something comforting to say to the old woman who, he knew, was genuinely devoted to Mary Anne, but found himself only mouthing platitudes.

Mary Anne was six years old when she went to live permanently with her father and stepmother, having spent a month moving between the townhouse and the new house so that the transition was not too abrupt. She continued to spend periods of time with Edwina, watched over by the newly engaged Ivy Golding, and Sunday afternoons with all the Carmodys in the parental home.

She'll be ours again in two years' time, Edwina consoled herself on the final official day of her guardianship before she handed over the child to Lochlann. After she turns eight, ten years of boarding school added to the summers at Tyringham Park should be enough to eradicate all that native Irish influence.

CHAPTER 17

1948

In early January Manus received a letter from Lily's stepdaughter, Catherine Cooper, living in Inchicore in Dublin. Contrary to what he had told Lochlann to ensure that the doctor couldn't contact Lily, she had not changed her address since the time she had left Tyringham Park.

Dear Manus, it read,

Thank you for the letters you keep writing to Lily. She reads them over and over. But I notice she has stopped answering them. I am writing to tell you why. Her mind isn't as clear as it used to be, though she's not aware of it. She talks about the past all the time as if it was yesterday. I hear nothing but Charlotte, Charlotte, and Manus, Manus, all day long. It's just as well I'm not the jealous type. She is praying a lot. She is worried about the state of her soul. She doesn't know what she will say to God on Judgment Day. She keeps catching the bus to the local Garda Station. She tells them a lot of unbelievable stories. They contact me as soon as she arrives now to come and fetch her. They say she has read too many mystery stories. I am only telling you this in case she is posting letters to you on the sly and you are worried about what's going on. Please continue to write to her even if she doesn't answer. Your letters buck her up no end. *Perhaps you will make the trip to visit her one day. I wouldn't leave it too long.*

I hope this year will be calmer for her than the last one.
Yours sincerely,
Catherine

Iseult looked around the Carmody New Year gathering and couldn't believe what a difference a year had made. Niamh had fitted so seamlessly into the family circle that it was difficult to imagine life without her. Lochlann was back to his full health, thanks no doubt to the influence of Niamh and the happiness of their marriage. Mary Anne was flourishing.

"You have more mothers than anyone I know," Iseult said to Mary Anne after the meal was over. "And they all love you. You have your mother up in heaven, me, Edwina and Grace who are grannies but act as if they're mothers, Ivy Golding, Queenie and now you have Niamh." She counted them out on her fingers. "Seven! Seven mothers! How lucky can you be?"

Iseult often emphasised the devotion enjoyed by Mary Anne as a way of counteracting, in some small measure, the heartbreak of the young girl's motherlessness. She had noticed but had not commented on the fact that Mary Anne now called Niamh 'Mummy' and addressed Ivy Golding as 'Nanny'. No doubt after Malachy married the nanny she would be addressed as 'Aunt', as was the custom in their circle.

Lochlann looked on. Add another mother to make eight, he thought. I wonder how they would react if I told them there was yet another one, more important in some ways than any of those that Iseult has mentioned? Her biological mother, Nell Hogan, living twelve thousand miles away and as unaware of Mary Anne's existence as all of you here are of hers.

"We all wanted you to live with us," Iseult continued, hugging the child, "but your father is your father and he finally got to pick. He and Niamh want you most of all so we all have to give in." She did some dramatic fake crying, and Mary Anne laughed and hugged her back.

Later Mary Anne went to sit beside Niamh and leaned into her. Niamh put her arm around her and welcomed her with affection.

Iseult smiled across at her brother and he nodded to acknowledge her look of approval.

So this is what it was meant to be like, Lochlann said to himself in wonder. How could he have known the married state could be so joyful, so right, so satisfying?

How could one person be so kind, giving, happy, intelligent, understanding, passionate and tender? How could he ever feel worthy of her regard?

No more having to take a deep breath and brace himself each time he came in through the front door after work – no more being forced to hide his feelings behind a mask as he had been obliged to do when he had been married to poor, unfortunate Charlotte whose personality had felt so alien to him. He did not want to continue making comparisons between that parched desert of a marriage, if it could be called a marriage, and the fertile garden in which he now found himself, and tried to wipe the memory of his first marriage from his mind. True to his earlier decision, he did not speak negatively about Charlotte. That was not so difficult as he did not speak of her at all unless someone asked him a direct question about her and he was obliged to answer.

And to think that if it hadn't been for the intervention – some might say interference – of Iseult and Malachy, he would have lost Niamh and never experienced his present happiness. Wise sister. And selfless friend who had received his reward without looking for or expecting one.

Lochlann had resolved to abstain from drink the minute he had seen Niamh again. It was not for love of her, though that could have been a secondary consideration, nor for the love of his profession. It was to ensure that his tongue was never loosened under the influence of alcohol during intimate moments shared with Niamh.

He had decided not to confess. To make up for his sin, he intended to live a life of sobriety and to be a good husband to Niamh and become a proper father to Mary Anne, and hoped that that would be enough to keep silent the accusing voice in his head.

He did not fear detection. Dan and Nell Hogan would never be able to afford to travel to Europe even if they had wanted to, which he knew they didn't. Some of their children might make the journey later on, after they had risen to wealth and success through education, but they would have no reason to look him up. He would be an uninteresting memory to those he had met, and no memory at all to the younger ones.

There were only two things that could contribute to his undoing if anyone did come looking for him. Firstly, for professional reasons his name and address appeared in the phone book for the convenience of his patients, and that was never likely to change. Secondly, and more importantly, anyone who knew Alison Hogan could not doubt for a second that Mary Anne was her twin if that person happened to spot Mary Anne. What a pity the two girls were identical rather than fraternal twins who would look no more like each other than any other siblings, a likeness that would not necessarily be noticed, especially with their Celtic features so like the millions of other Celts living in Ireland.

But no one would come looking for him. Why would they?

CHAPTER 18

Manus remained courteous but distant to Edwina when she visited the Park. She hadn't been able to win him over. She was now positive it was he, not the children backed by Georgina, who had banned her from the stables. To put him in his place she continued to turn up at the stables during the summer lessons, and continued to call out instructions to Mary Anne whenever she noticed Manus was giving her the wrong advice.

Georgina and Giles kept saying, "While you're a guest in this house you are to treat it as your home," accentuating the word *guest*.

A sharper thorn in her side than Manus, Georgina and Giles put together, continued to be that gifted young horseman, Toby Prendergast, now thirteen years of age to Mary Anne's seven. Even after four years away at boarding school, William still treated Toby as a friend when they were reunited at the Park for the summer vacation, and continued to follow his lead, as did Nigel, Jane and Mary Anne who remained in thrall to him. If the children had treated him as a type of court jester, Edwina would have understood, but they seemed to hang on his every word and fall in with his plans which they seemed to find irresistible.

Instead of making fun of Toby's accent, Toby and the Blackshaws good-naturedly imitated each other's accents and spent entire days concentrating on one particular one before changing to another the following day. William, a lively mimic, was particularly good at reproducing the Cork lilt, in imitation of Toby, and sometimes when Lady Edwina was nearby, he and Toby exaggerated its distinctive intonations to annoy her. Edwina invariably turned her pained, unamused face away from them and pretended she hadn't heard what they were saying.

It was Toby who had them tearing around on their mounts after lessons, playing Cowboys and Indians, messing around on the river pretending to be pirates, tying ropes on trees and swinging over ditches, jumping from the roofs of the outhouses, putting on costumes and funny accents and acting out plays they made up as they went along.

There was only one thing the Blackshaws did that Toby didn't do, and that was return to the main house to eat and sleep. Toby went back to his grandparents' cottage, even if he had been invited by his friends to stay with them.

On her last visit Edwina had instructed Manus to stop teaching Toby and to send him off to help his grandfather with the garden.

Manus had looked sadly at her and said, "Reg is happy for him to be here at the stables as he would like him to work at the Park when he leaves school, and if gardens don't suit him the horses will."

"Reg is happy? Who cares whether Reg is happy or not? I'm not happy, and that is what counts. I think he is a bad influence on Mary Anne."

"I don't know how you can say that, ma'am. I can't find fault with him."

"I wouldn't put you down as a good judge of character. You couldn't see any fault in Charlotte either."

Manus looked pityingly at Edwina. "You will have to take up the matter with Lord Giles and Lady Georgina Blackshaw," he had said. "They are fully in agreement with the present arrangement."

Edwina knew there was no point in talking to Giles and Georgina, who were admirers of Toby, so was forced to keep her chagrin to herself.

"Which boy do you like better?" Edwina asked Mary Anne on their way back to Dublin after the summer at the Park.

"Toby," Mary Anne answered.

"He doesn't count. Who do you like better out of your cousins?"

"Nigel."

"That will have to change. It's William you are going to marry so you can stay at the Park permanently."

"That's all right," said Mary Anne. "As long as Toby and Nigel stay at the Park, too. And Jane as well. I want them all to stay. And I'll buy them all a big boat each so we can play pirates on the river and sail all the way to Cobh."

There was another woman wanting to claim Mary Anne and that was William's mother, Georgina. She and Edwina were of one mind on the subject of a marriage between William and Mary Anne.

Georgina, for her part, spoke often to William about the Park and how worthwhile it would be to restore the house to its original magnificence. It would be an honour and a privilege to act as its custodian during his lifetime and, after his death, to pass it on in an improved state to the next generation. She brought him around with her, pointing out artefacts that had been in the family for four hundred years, lamenting the possibility that some of them might have to be sold to pay for refurbishments that could not be put off for too much longer. The 18,000 acres that had been sold to the tenants, with the subsequent loss of rents, would never be bought back.

"Mary Anne will help you restore the Park, so you must marry her when the time comes," Georgina told the twelve-year-old William. "She will bring a lot of energy to the project."

Georgina was too well-bred to use the word 'money', so used 'energy' instead.

Mary Anne's good looks would be a nice little added bonus to enhance the Blackshaw line when the merger happened, Georgina calculated. All she had to do until that time, apart from encouraging William, was grit her teeth and welcome Edwina to the Park every summer.

CHAPTER 19

Tyringham Park, 1949

Each time Mary Anne visited the townhouse Edwina talked to her about the desirability of going to boarding school. "You will make friends from all over the world. They will all be wealthy and important and come from high-born families like the Blackshaws. All of the girls there will marry powerful men who will run the countries they live in. You will learn how to behave correctly, how to speak and dress correctly, and how to set a table and do floral arrangements."

Mary Anne listened solemnly, not understanding all that her grandmother was saying, but aware that it was important.

Edwina emphasised the superior grounding the school provided so that one was never in doubt for the rest of one's life about what constituted proper behaviour.

"Did my mother like boarding school?"

"Yes, she did," lied Edwina.

"What was Mother like?" 'Mummy' was the term Mary Anne used for Niamh, 'Mother' for Charlotte.

"She was very plain." Edwina was miffed at the way Charlotte's reputation continued to grow, and was quick to give a realistic judgment. "Frightfully so, actually." As stories about Charlotte passed from one person to another, she became more skilled as a horsewoman, more likable, more heroic and even better looking, whereas everyone seemed to have forgotten about Edwina's early beauty.

"Oh."

"She was not pretty like you. You look like my other daughter, little Victoria, who was the image of me except for the dark curls. Has anyone told you about little Victoria yet?"

"Yes, Aunty Iseult has."

"Well, she shouldn't have. She has no right. It's none of her business. She should have left it to me." Her voice softened. "Victoria was such a good child."

"Was Mother good too?" Mary Anne asked, repeating the question she had often asked her aunt and hoping for a similar answer.

"No, she was not. She was always trying to curry favour with Manus and, when she was just a little older than you, she caused my accident and left me crippled for life and would never admit she was in the wrong."

Mary Anne's face slowly crumpled before she exploded into tears.

"There's no point in making a fuss. Tears can't alter the past. Now dry your eyes and act like the lady you are going to be one day soon. A lady never shows her feelings."

Queenie, sitting by the window, invisible to Edwina in the way of all good servants, quietly let her knitting rest on her lap and closed her eyes as if she were dozing.

After tea that night Queenie went to Lochlann's house to report to him what Edwina had said and what Mary Anne's reaction had been. Lochlann was not at home so she told Niamh, who had been wondering why Mary Anne had been so downcast since returning from the townhouse that afternoon. Queenie's loyalty had always been to Charlotte and Mary Anne and not to Edwina.

Niamh went straight around to tell Edwina that if she ever said anything derogatory again about Charlotte to Mary Anne, Mary Anne's visits to the townhouse would be curtailed and supervised, and there was no point in complaining to Lochlann, as he would back her one hundred per cent in any decision she made.

Later that night Niamh asked Lochlann if he would talk about

Charlotte to Mary Anne, stressing how admirable she had been, how joyful about giving birth, and how tender in her ministrations. It was important for Mary Anne's happiness to have a positive image of her mother.

Lochlann said he would do his best.

Edwina, assuming that it was Queenie who had told tales about her, dismissed her with immediate effect.

Queenie would have found herself homeless and disorientated if it hadn't been for the legacy Charlotte had left her. After a tearful leave-taking of Mary Anne, she found a place in a retirement home for gentlefolk where she could look forward to being waited on like a lady for the rest of her life. It would make a nice change.

Edwina sent over a trunk packed with the uniforms and sports kit from her old school, Borderline, a prestigious Prep boarding school for upper-class Protestant girls in England. She hadn't mentioned to anyone how miserable she had been there, having been sent over from India at the age of four, to remain until she was eighteen, seeing her parents only twice in that time when they came back to England on leave.

So far she had managed to restrain herself from telling Mary Anne that Charlotte had been expelled from the establishment after only one term, for violent conduct. That might be handy to trot out at a later date.

With the trunk was a letter from Edwina to Lochlann, saying she had already paid the fees for the initial year and would continue to pay for the following nine years.

Lochlann, puzzled, read the letter. He had no memory of having given his consent, but he must have agreed to it years earlier when he was in a state of inebriation. That was the only explanation he could come up with.

A pity, really. He would be sorry to see Mary Anne go, but presumed she must if she were to take her place in that other world that she would be part of. A world that still remained closed to him, which was no great loss as it didn't appeal to him anyway. He would miss her lively, happy presence around the house – he had grown extremely attached to her since she had come to live with him and Niamh.

One thing he would not countenance was Edwina's paying the hefty fees. He would take out a loan rather than allow that to happen.

He wondered what Niamh would say when she came home and saw the trunk.

She said a lot, beginning with the sentiment that Lochlann must not let his daughter go away.

"But I have given my word."

"Then break it. Mary Anne's happiness is more important than your word."

"Perhaps she needs to go to prepare for the life Edwina is training her for."

"You must not let her go, Lochlann. At the age of twelve I might be able to countenance it, but *eight*? She's too young. It's not as if we live out in the country. We're surrounded by good day schools. You know Charlotte would never have agreed to it."

"I know that. She was definitely set against sending her away."

"And so am I. Mary Anne will become detached from us. She will be moulded by strangers to become one of them. And if she's unhappy we'll never hear about it as it will be drilled into her that it costs a fortune to send her there, and it's a great privilege to be there and it would be ungrateful and cowardly to complain. She might be picked on and have no one to turn to. Her accent will change. It has already changed from her trips to Tyringham Park and her time in the townhouse. She'll lose touch with her local friends."

"She will make new ones."

"But they will be spread all over the world and she probably would never see them again after they leave. If she stays here, her friends will be her friends for life and she will stay close to her cousins. What about your agreement with Edwina that Mary Anne goes to Tyringham Park for the summer? Would that still stand?"

"It would. I have already agreed to it."

"That means we would see Mary Anne for only a couple of weeks at Christmas and a couple at Easter. To all intents and purposes, she would be abandoned by us. Bad enough for an ordinary child, but for one who has lost her mother it would have serious psychological effects on her."

"I'll take the trunk back," said Lochlann, kissing Niamh's

impassioned face. "You have convinced me."

Edwina was not happy when Lochlann returned the trunk, thanking her at the same time for her kind offer.

"You have gone back on your word," she said.

"I have, but things are different now. At that time nothing was sorted out, but now Mary Anne is living permanently with Niamh and me and is happily settled. I wouldn't want to uproot her at this stage."

"That's an ungentlemanly about-face if ever I saw one," said Edwina who was convinced that Lochlann would have given in to her if it weren't for that republican wife of his who seemed to be thwarting her at every turn.

"I'm sorry I did not tell you earlier," said Lochlann who did not see any need to admit to her that he had no doubt been drunk at the time he had agreed.

"It's an unedifying sight to see a man like you under petticoat government," said Edwina.

"Is that what you call it?" Lochlann laughed.

His response to her insult visibly annoyed her.

"If only the whole world were under Niamh's government," he said. "It would be in a better shape than it is in now."

CHAPTER 20

Edwina's theory about stepmothers was not proven or disproven, because Niamh failed to conceive. Tests were done and procedures initiated, but month followed month and there was no positive outcome. It was a great sorrow for Niamh and for Lochlann, who blamed himself – God's punishment for his sin? To her, it was evident that it wasn't his fault, with Mary Anne there as living proof of his fertility. He probably blamed himself to make her feel better, but she wished he wouldn't as it was illogical and made her feel worse.

With no child of her own to care for, Niamh had already put Mary Anne centre stage in her life. Afraid that the young girl might be lonely, separated from her cousins and from Ivy Golding, who had married Malachy and gone to live in Sligo, she operated an open-house policy, welcoming relatives and friends whenever they wished to appear. Mary Anne's best friends, Patricia and Jo, who lived nearby, stayed overnight so often they were given their own beds. It wasn't as if the Carmody house was short of bedrooms.

Niamh worked from nine until one in a joint general practice, and had no trouble juggling her responsibilities because of the help of Mrs Kaye, an older, friendly woman who came daily to keep house.

After Niamh accepted her childless state, she was left with only one other problem. She had to acknowledge that Lochlann was not the man he had once been, just as he had warned her before their marriage. He was still loving and thoughtful. If truth be told, she could not fault him, except for the times when he seemed to mentally leave her and drift away from her. An expression of sorrow would come over his face. If she left him undisturbed, the phase could last as long as an hour. If she intruded and spoke to him, he would make a visible effort to give her his attention.

"What's the matter?" she would ask.

"Nothing," he would reply. "I was deep in thought."

"That was obvious. What were you thinking about?"

"The war," he always answered.

The war was the answer to everything that was wrong. She couldn't question him any further as she hadn't been in the conflict, and so couldn't shape a question with any authenticity to it. The problem was she didn't think the war had anything to do with his lapses. She thought they went further back and originated in Australia where they were connected in some way to Charlotte.

Whenever she asked him about his time there he gave evasive answers and changed the subject.

"Do you ever hear from anyone out there? What about that farming family Iseult said you were so fond of? Do you ever hear from them?"

"No, I don't hear from anyone. I wasn't out there long enough to form any solid friendships."

She didn't mention Charlotte's name as he had requested that they wouldn't discuss her in a personal way between themselves.

Despite what he had told her, Niamh began to suspect that he had fallen in love with Charlotte after the marriage. The stillbirth of the first child, Benedict, and the birth of Mary Anne must have produced a bond of some kind. She would like to have questioned Iseult about it, but thought that approaching her would be an act of disloyalty to Lochlann.

CHAPTER 21

1953

At the age of twelve Mary Anne herself decided not to go to boarding school, as all her friends from the local primary school were moving on to the Sacred Heart Convent secondary day school and she didn't want to be parted from them. Mary Anne's home continued to be a meeting place where a large group of girls would gather for tea and biscuits and lots of chattering after school before making their ways back to their own homes.

Lochlann couldn't imagine cherishing any biological daughter of his more than he already cherished Mary Anne. She was everything anyone could want in a daughter, and he wondered how he could have ever entertained the idea of returning her to Australia or even sending her away to school.

Mary Anne continued to spend her summers in Tyringham Park, even though she was invited by school friends to accompany them and their families to the coastal counties of Galway, Donegal, Sligo, Wexford, Waterford, Kerry and Clare. She would have liked to have invited her friends to Tyringham Park, but Edwina was adamant that none of them would take away any of Mary Anne's time that was allocated to the Blackshaws.

While Mary Anne was away, Lochlann, along with other medical volunteers, spent, in what became an annual event, a month each year in Africa. At first they went to the mission hospital where Niamh had once worked – the nuns had contacted her asking for help – but later they were able to service other parts of Uganda as well. Most doctors and dentists contributed five years of their expertise before dropping out, usually for family reasons, making sure before they left that there were others to take their places, but Lochlann continued on, not missing a year, and ending up as head co-ordinator of the operation.

Niamh did not travel. She could not face the tropical heat again and did not feel an obligation to, having done her duty for charity by giving two years of her life earlier on. Instead she worked full days while she had the chance, filling in for her colleagues who, in turn, took their annual summer leave.

Niamh noticed that each time Lochlann returned from Africa he was in a tranquil state, like a penitent who had expiated his sins through suffering. The tranquil state didn't last long, however. Within a few weeks the sorrowful withdrawals would return.

There was a rumour that he was to be nominated for an award in recognition of his charity work. On hearing that, his mood darkened rather than lightened, Niamh noticed.

CHAPTER 22

Tyringham Park, 1953

Even without having seen them before, Toby knew that the two tall, broad-shouldered men who came into the courtyard were detectives, and before they opened their mouths he knew they would be looking for Manus. It has taken them long enough, he thought. Ten years to be precise.

"Detectives," he whispered to Mary Anne and the three young Blackshaws who had finished their morning exercises and were standing around talking.

Manus, leading a yearling into the yard, stopped dead when he saw the two men in their beige trench coats, looking as if they had just stepped off the cover of a detective novel. He was immediately transported back to events that had happened at the Park ten years earlier and the parts that he and Lily East had played in them.

Lily must have convinced them she was telling the truth, was his first apprehensive thought at the sight of the two men. Her stepdaughter must have got it wrong, saying the gardaí didn't believe her.

He had often feared that Lily might crack, possessed as she was of an over-sensitive conscience.

"Take him for me, will you please?" he asked, distractedly handing the reins of the yearling to Toby, waiting for the men to approach.

Please, dear God, help me stick to my story and lie convincingly. Please don't let me crack as well, he prayed.

"Can I help you?" Manus asked the men who were so alike they could have passed for an older and a younger brother.

Detective Inspector Dan Quirke introduced the younger man, Ronan Walsh, and then himself. They were from the Special Detective Unit in Dublin and they were looking for a man called Manus.

The three older stable lads stared with interest at the two strangers, before deciding to make themselves scarce by mounting their charges and heading out to the paddock to do some sprints. They presumed the visit would have something to do with Manus's membership of the Irish Republican Brotherhood during his youth. Some new revelation must have surfaced with the recent increase in rebel activities. It was rumoured that Manus had held a position of such authority in the IRB that it was he who had saved Tyringham Park from being burnt to the ground during the War of Independence.

Manus identified himself and the older man asked if there was anywhere they could speak in private.

"My office," said Manus. "Just over here. Toby, will you make sure we're not disturbed?"

Toby, noting the sickly pallor on the face of Manus, said he would.

"The rest of you, will you go home and come back later?"

The three Blackshaws went off, talking excitedly. Mary Anne, sensitive to the suppressed unease in Toby's manner, remained where she was.

Halfway up the hill, William turned around to say something to Mary Anne only to find she wasn't in their company. He was not surprised. She stayed by Toby's side whenever she had the chance.

The two men followed Manus into the office and closed the door behind them.

"Take over here, will you, Mary Anne?" asked Toby, handing the reins of the yearling to her. "I'm going to listen in to see what's up. Don't give me away, and don't come anywhere near the office yourself. I'll fill you in later."

He meant for her to put the yearling in his stall, take off the saddle and bridle and rub the animal down, but Mary Anne stood immobile in the courtyard where he had left her, holding on to the reins.

Toby walked casually out through the double doors, then ran around the outside stable walls until he was directly behind the office. He slid over the wall and stood among the weeds in the narrow space between the wall and the office, to one side of the window, and listened intently. The window was open and he had no trouble hearing the clear, baritone voice of DI Quirke who was speaking to Manus in a friendly manner. Toby made a mental note of the tone that the detective was using so that he would be able to reference it when his time came to question suspects. Up until now, going by the films he had seen, he thought detectives asked tough questions in raspy voices before provoking a fist fight which they invariably won.

"We were in the vicinity and thought we'd drop in and ask you a few questions, Manus. No one has charged you with anything, but a matter has been brought to our attention by a Mrs Cooper who said you would remember her as Lily East."

"I remember her well. We were good friends until we lost touch after she retired and left the estate."

"So she told us. She made a formal statement at her local Garda Station in Dublin and we had no option but to check it out with you because of the seriousness of her allegations. It's about the deaths of . . ." DI Quirke looked down at the open file, ". . . Charlotte Carmody, née Blackshaw, daughter of Lord Waldron and Lady Edwina Blackshaw, and her ex-nanny, Elizabeth Dixon, that took place on this estate ten years ago. It says here that the cause of death for both women was accidental drowning."

"So it was. A sad business," said Manus, trying to concentrate and keep his voice steady.

"We have a copy of the report made out by Inspector Declan Doyle at the time. I believe he was a friend of yours."

"He was and he still is," said Manus. "A sound man."

"So we've been informed. We will interview him later. The report states that you were the only person at the scene."

"I was. I didn't actually see the accident, but I arrived afterwards and found the two bodies downstream, jammed up against the weir. As it turned out, they were both dead by the time I pulled them out. I shouted for help but there was no one around. I immediately tried to resuscitate Miss Charlotte, but it was too late, and I didn't even try with Nurse Dixon – that's what we used to call her – as she had a large wound on the back of her head and was clearly lifeless by the time I got to her."

"Would you be able to go through the events again from beginning? We have a copy of your sworn statement here, but we would like to hear it in your own words if you can remember back that far."

"I can remember everything clearly. As if I could ever forget."

Manus went on to tell his well-rehearsed story that he could still recite word for word, long after he had first made it up.

He said that the last time he had seen the two women alive, they were standing on the spot where it was thought by many that little Victoria Blackshaw, Charlotte's younger sister, had fallen into the river years earlier.

He had gone back into the stables to allow the two women some privacy. They hadn't met each other for twenty-five years and were obviously pleased about being reunited. By the time he took leave of them they were in a sombre mood, thinking of the lost child, and preparing to say prayers for her. When he returned some time later – he didn't know how long exactly – they were both in the water at the weir with Dixon's arm tight around Charlotte's throat.

"So you deduced, it says here, that it was Elizabeth Dixon who went too close to the edge and fell in first."

"Yes. She still had her shoes and coat on when I found her. My reconstruction is in my statement. She must have been unaware that there was an overhang at the edge of the bank. She stood on it, it gave way, and she fell into the water. The broken-off clod of earth was visible on the river bed when I went to check the scene later."

He remembered kicking off the overhang himself, making sure to leave no heel prints, and watching it sink to the bottom of the river and settle there, to be noted later by Inspector Declan Doyle.

"She wasn't out of her depth at that spot, apparently."

"No. It was about shoulder height on the day. She could have waded out if she had kept her head but she had a well-known fear of water. The warders in the orphanage where she was reared used to hold her head under in the bath until she stopped struggling, to punish her, apparently." Manus was affected by this information, even though he had made it up when he had first been questioned by Inspector Declan Doyle.

"Poor woman. No wonder she couldn't think straight. There's a long description here of how a person in a state of panic can drown in shallow water and can constitute a danger to anyone trying to rescue them, which seems to be the case with Charlotte Carmody. We'll take that as read, especially after what you've just told us, and move on. How come you were the only one here at the time?"

"The Blackshaw family and the three stable lads and a few servants were at the Killarney races. I'm getting too old for that sort of thing. The young people love it, so I let them off and stay here to keep an eye on things."

"No one passing up or down the avenue?"

"No, not a soul. There usually isn't at that time of the afternoon, even during the busy times. As I said, I called out but there was no answer."

"Mmm. All of that tallies with Inspector Declan Doyle's report, all written down here. Perfectly straightforward. The only trouble is Mrs Lily Cooper said that not one word of the report is true. She said that no accidental drownings occurred on that day. She said that she saw with her own eyes Charlotte Carmody murdering Elizabeth Dixon by pushing her over the third-floor bannisters in the nursery wing. And that you were a witness to that as well as to Mrs Carmody deliberately drowning herself in the Dark Waterhole, but that you couldn't get to her in time to save her. What do you say to that?"

Manus was prepared to hear the accusation, but he had underestimated the effect it had on him when it was put into words. He felt nauseous and was aware that his face was flushed with heat.

DI Quirke was looking at him, and DI Walsh was looking at the file.

"I'm shocked. I can't believe Lily would make up a story like that. I'm flabbergasted, to put it mildly. I would say poor Lily has read one too many detective stories and has let her imagination run away with her. Or else she has become senile."

I'm sorry for blackening your good name, Lily, my dear old friend.

I understand your need to clear your conscience before you die, but I must stick to our original agreement for the sake of Mary Anne.

"That's what we thought in the beginning," said DI Quirke, "but she was so lucid and so clear on the details on the day we questioned her that we began to think she might have a case."

"She doesn't do things by halves, coming up with a mad story like that," said Manus with a convincing show of disbelief. "Turning an accident into a murder? That's a shocking thing to say. Why would Miss Charlotte do something as unthinkable as murder?"

"To silence Elizabeth Dixon. Apparently she knew what had happened to the missing child. She had found out from a former servant now living abroad . . ."

A servant living abroad. Teresa Kelly? Has to be her. Who else could it be? Emigrated to Australia. She knew. How? Why didn't she tell us? When did she tell Dixon?

". . . and she threatened to tell everyone here. She had told Mrs Cooper only a little while earlier."

Lily found out and didn't tell me?

Manus stood up suddenly and walked to the front window to hide his face from the men.

This is too hard to bear. Lily knew that I was still looking for Victoria. That I didn't believe the little pet had drowned. For God's sake tell me what she said and put me out of my misery.

He felt weak and sick by the time he had taken those few steps. He held on to the sill for support. Despite his effort to speak normally, his voice choked as he asked, "What cracked story did she come up with?"

"Mrs Cooper said she never wanted you to find out."

"What difference can it make to me thirty-five years after the event? You might as well tell me what she said, seeing it's probably as far-fetched as her murder story. If her accusations weren't about such tragic events, they would be laughable."

"We thought this part was a bit far-fetched all right. According to Dixon, Charlotte lifted her little sister – asleep at the time – out of the pram while you and Lady Edwina Blackshaw were tending to a wounded filly. She took her down to the river, pushed her into the water and drowned her."

Manus felt himself swaying and thought he was about to vomit.

107

So she's dead. And here was I still clinging to the hope that I might see her darling face again before I die.

He couldn't trust himself to speak again. To give himself time he opened the door of his office and walked unsteadily over to Mary Anne who was still standing at the other end of the courtyard holding the reins of the yearling.

"Where's Toby?" he asked.

"He left," Mary Anne said.

That was out of character for Toby, Manus thought. He had specifically asked him to stand guard. And it was odd that he had left Mary Anne alone.

"Deal with the yearling," he told her, "and then go on up to the house and join the others, there's a good girl. I might be a while."

Mary Anne led off the yearling.

Manus appeared to be watching Mary Anne, but what he was seeing was not in front of him but was in his mind's eye. It was the vision of a redheaded doll he had found in Charlotte's bag on the day she drowned. He had not made a connection then between Charlotte's being in possession of it and Victoria's death, and here he was being told that it was a direct one. As far as he had known at the time, Charlotte had not been anywhere near the river on that afternoon.

"Sorry," he said to the detectives when he returned, concentrating on appearing calm. "That girl I was just speaking to is the daughter of Charlotte Carmody. I know she was a long way off, but you never know with these young ones and their perfect hearing what they might pick up. It would kill her if she heard those things said about her mother."

"It will be out of our hands, I'm afraid, if we can prove that what Lily Cooper said is true."

"True? Charlotte pushing little Victoria into the river? Lily has definitely lost her marbles, coming up with a load of rubbish like that. Charlotte was a good child. She would never have done a thing like that."

"Exactly what the old woman believes. She said Charlotte wasn't capable of doing such a wicked thing. She said that the little girl must have fallen in accidentally and Charlotte was too afraid to tell anyone about it. But Dixon had a warped estimate of the child's character, according to Mrs Cooper, and would have assumed that it was deliberate."

DI Walsh read through Lily's evidence about what Teresa Kelly had seen, and why there was no reason to report anything and how Dixon had put the pieces together and jumped to conclusions. The wrong ones, according to Lily. But what could not be contested was that Charlotte had murdered Dixon, and that Lily and Manus had witnessed the act.

"The woman is rambling," said Manus with what he hoped was conviction.

"That's what her stepdaughter thought and paid no attention to her. Lost patience with her. In the end the old woman had to keep catching a bus to the local station to keep telling her story while her stepdaughter was out of the house. Because of the fame of the Blackshaws and the seriousness of the accusations, the station called us in. We couldn't shake her story. That's why we're here."

"Why is she only reporting it now?"

"She feels she's not long for this world, and she wants to make things right."

"Lily never told a lie in her life and she wouldn't be lying now if she was in her right mind. She must be ninety by now if she's a day."

"Eighty-eight, according to her. She said that you reconstructed the scene and falsified the evidence and made up a whole false story."

"Why would I do that?"

"To protect Charlotte's name for the sake of her daughter. You can see our dilemma, Manus. Lily Cooper's story and yours can't both be true. It's a pity there wasn't anyone else around that day to witness what actually happened."

There was a scuffling noise at the back of the office building. The three men inside stopped talking and listened. Footsteps along the side, then fumbling at the door handle, and then the door opening, and Toby standing silhouetted in the doorway.

"But there was," he said. "I was there. I saw what happened with my own two eyes, and I'm here to tell you everything."

That's the end of me now, thought Manus. I'll be sent to prison. My marriage will fall apart and Sinéad will curse the day I put the Blackshaws' interests before hers. Our family will be shamed.

With his head bowed Manus held the back of the chair to steady himself and then sank onto the seat.

So your bright eyes saw it all. I often wondered but couldn't ask.

The younger detective was taking down Toby's name and particulars.

Say what you have to say, Toby, and get it over with.

Manus kept his head bowed. He did not want to look at Toby in case the detectives interpreted the expression on his face as threatening or, even worse than that, pleading.

"Can you repeat that, Toby?" Manus heard when the whirring and pulsing sound between his ears had eased off. "It's very important, so choose your words carefully."

"I can't say it any plainer. Everything Manus said is true. I saw one lady falling into the river and thrashing about, and the other lady taking off her shoes and jumping in and both of them drowning."

"Why didn't you shout out for help?"

"There was no one around except Manus. I was up a tree stealing birds' eggs. Manus didn't know I was there. I wasn't supposed to be there. I had ducked out. My grandfather would have killed me if he'd found out. I was supposed to be helping him in the walled garden. By the time I climbed down Manus was pulling the ladies out of the water."

"You didn't think to run for help?"

"It didn't occur to me. It wasn't until a few years later that I thought perhaps I should have – though it wouldn't have done any good as it turned out. As an eight-year-old I thought Manus could handle anything."

"So it seems," said the older detective.

"Luckily for Manus you saw everything," said the younger one.

"Yes, it was," said Toby, his eyes bright with emotion. "Imagine what would happen to him if I hadn't been there."

When the young people ran up to the house with the exciting news that two detectives had turned up asking for Manus, Edwina told them to wheel her down to the stables immediately. She didn't trust Manus to put forward a case as decisively and forcefully as she could.

She assumed they had come about the scam. The previous month Rough Silk had been substituted for Blue Diamond in a handicap at a race meeting and had won by a length at 20/1. The bookmakers had paid out. It was only when a stable lad in the neighbouring stall drew attention to the fact that the blaze on the winner had been enlarged with paint to match the size of the blaze of the slower horse that was supposed to have run that the fraud was made public. The owner of the horse that ran second was suing for the prize money and for the payment of bets. The newspapers had taken up the story. Rough Silk had been bred and trained at the Park but had been bought two weeks prior to the scam, obviously with the substitution already planned. There was no way the Park was responsible for the blatant wrongdoings of the new owner. That fact had to be stressed to the detectives.

"He's not responsible," said Edwina, parked at the entrance to the stables, flanked by four young people.

The two detectives, hearing the accent and seeing the wheelchair, knew who she was from the description given to them by Lily Cooper. They introduced themselves.

"I can't say we've had the pleasure, ma'am," said DI Quirke.

"There's no pleasure to be had. It's not that I care about the reputation of Manus, who has grown too big for his boots recently, but I do care about the reputation of the bloodstock of the Park which this young man will one day inherit." She indicated William with a wave of her hand.

"You have nothing to worry about, m'am," said DI Quirke. "Its reputation is secure. Everything has been explained to our satisfaction." He nodded towards Toby who was standing behind him, alert. "And who are these fine youngsters?" He was keen to get a good look at Mary Anne Carmody, thinking of how close she had come to having her life destroyed.

He asked them their names and ages, and they answered in turn.

"William Blackshaw, sixteen."

"Nigel Blacksaw, fourteen."

"Jane Blackshaw, twelve."

"Mary Anne Carmody, twelve."

"Twins?" joked DI Quirke.

"No." Mary Anne smiled back. "Cousins."

Toby came to stand beside her, and she turned to him with pleasure to include him in the smile and moved closer to him.

"So that's the girl those two are lying through their back teeth to protect."

"You can hardly blame them. Such a sweet, trusting little face she has, and what a sunny smile. Reminds me of my Róisín. It would be a crime to take away all that innocence. It's not as if any good will come of fingering her dead mother."

"Well, what did you make of 'the divine Manus'?" asked DI Walsh, quoting Lily Cooper.

"Impressive style of a man. I wouldn't know about the 'divine' bit. He was doing a good job of lying until the fate of the lost child came up and then it was a different story. Did you see his face? He genuinely didn't know that she had drowned."

"Poor man. To hear it from us under these circumstances. Not ideal."

"At least he can now stop looking for her. I was relieved you didn't give away the fact that we knew he was its father – well, according to Lily Cooper."

"Credit me with some sensitivity. I'm sure he wouldn't want Toby to know that."

"Or the girl. Or anyone else for that matter. And what about the oul' one in the wheelchair? I have to say my faith in Lily Cooper's story wobbled at the sight of her, not to mention the sound of her. Difficult to believe she and Manus ever got together. One I could understand – accidents happen – but two children? The boy too? Can't understand it unless Manus was under orders."

"Ah, don't forget they had youth on their side, then. Makes up for a lot. And what about the young Toby? Isn't he something else? We'll have to keep our eye out for him when he joins the force. He's going to go far."

"You can say that again."

The men had reached their car. They stood looking around at the ancient trees and the castle-like building on the top of the hill.

DI Quirke threw the files onto the back seat.

"It looks as if we can shelve this report. No point in wasting our time looking at the scenes of the crime or checking facts with Doyle. No one is going to take the word of an eighty-eight-year-old against that of a reputable man and a bright seventeen-year-old backing up his every word. Lucky for Manus."

Lily took the bus to the Garda Station one more time to ask if the matter at Tyringham Park had been resolved.

The local constable came out to the desk to invite her into a private room to give her the results of the detectives' enquiries. He told her they had conducted a thorough investigation into the affair and that she was not to worry any more and she could leave the station with a clear conscience. Manus had been dealt with.

"I hope they didn't do anything bad to him. He's basically a good man."

"They didn't say, but when the Special Branch men say they have dealt with someone, you can take my word for it that they have. They said they were grateful to you for alerting them." He said all this in a loud, clear voice as if she were deaf and not quite the full shilling.

"I never wanted to get Manus into trouble, but I couldn't have his lies on my conscience."

"Completely understandable, Mrs Cooper," said the constable, nodding to impress on her the sincerity of his understanding.

"He was always a good friend."

"And still is. He sent you his warmest regards."

When she arrived back home her stepdaughter told her to stop bothering the guards. "They are very busy men. They might lock you up for wasting police time one day if you're not careful."

"It's all right, dear," said Lily. "I don't need to go back. It has all been dealt with by those very nice men and now I can die in peace."

"As long as it's not too soon, Ma," said the stepdaughter, kissing her cheek, remembering the loving care in which she had been raised. "I for one would dearly love to see you reach the hundred."

CHAPTER 23

"Did your father ring?" Niamh asked as she deposited the groceries on the kitchen table.

Mary Anne, back from Tyringham Park only the day before, lifted her head from the book she was reading and stared distractedly at her stepmother.

"What?" she asked.

Niamh usually chose her words carefully when speaking to Mary Anne during her first week back in Dublin, but said before she had time to think, "Please don't say 'What?' to me, Mary Anne. It sounds rude."

"Oh, does it? Weena says it is the correct thing to say when one wants someone to repeat something."

"I know she does. I've heard her use it often enough, even when she's obviously heard what has been said."

Each September Mary Anne returned to Dublin after the three months spent in Tyringham Park to face teasing from her friends because of her altered accent and vocabulary. She laughed along with them and soon reverted to her pre-summer way of speaking.

Mary Anne spoke and acted the way Edwina instructed her to while she was in her company. Arguing any point with the old woman was a useless exercise, as Edwina, owing to her aristocratic background, considered herself to be always in the right, and she was intent on inculcating Mary Anne with her certainties.

"But Weena can't tolerate the word 'Pardon'. It is common, she says."

"I didn't say you should say 'Pardon', but saying 'What?' sounds blunt and hostile to my ears. I know Lady Edwina doesn't agree with me as she follows a different tradition but, to please me, could you say instead of 'What?' something like 'I'm sorry, I didn't hear you,' or 'Would you mind repeating that?'"

"But that takes a long time to say."

"I know it does, but it's worth it, especially if you say it in a nice tone of voice. So, what else besides 'Pardon?' am I not allowed to say?" Niamh kept any hint of sarcasm out of her voice.

"She pounces on anyone who says 'serviette' or 'perfume'. She corrects them on the spot, no matter who they are."

"Two French words, I notice. I wouldn't be surprised if Lady Edwina was still feeling aggrieved about the loss of Normandy."

"We haven't done that part of history in school yet, so I can't say. Weena says as well that there are certain pronunciations we must use."

Niamh rolled her eyes. "You can tell me about them another time. At the moment it's more important for me to know when your father is due home so I can judge what time to put on the roast."

"He telephoned earlier. He told me to tell you he would be delayed. Apparently Weena lawst the pen I gave her for Christmas and he has gawn awf to buy a replica in the hope that I won't notice the difference."

"How frightfully naughty of him to tell you that and spoil her ladyship's subterfuge," said Niamh, smiling.

"What?" laughed Mary Anne, putting down her book and jumping up to hug her stepmother.

CHAPTER 24

At the age of eighteen, after finishing secondary school and working for a year fulltime in the stables at the Park, Toby joined the Garda Síochána.

"What was the point of all that training with Manus, and all that experience, then?" asked Reg, after he heard that Toby's application had been accepted. He had long ago given up hope that Toby would take an interest in gardening, but had consoled himself by thinking he would continue working at the stables and would one day take over the running of them when the time came for Manus to retire. "It's all gone to waste."

"I've only ever wanted to be one thing, Granddad, and that is a detective. Remember I told you?"

"I thought that was only kids' stuff, like wanting to be a fireman or a train driver."

"No, it was serious."

The desire had come from the strange behaviour he had witnessed when he saw Manus putting a dead body in a barrow and wheeling it down to the stables to be doused with water and laid beside another dead body. Wouldn't that make anyone want to know the reason why? He had got his answers when the two detectives from

Dublin had questioned Manus, but the desire by then had been so deeply implanted he could not change it.

"Why are you so set on it?" asked Reg.

"I want to find out why good people do bad things."

"That's a million-dollar question. Fair dues to you if you find the answer to that one. And what will you do if you do find out, just as a matter of interest?"

"I'll look out for them."

Reg laughed. "I thought your job would be to arrest them and lock them up, not look out for them. Are you sure you know what you're letting yourself in for?"

Rathmines in Dublin was Toby's first posting after training. The bedsitter he was lucky to find near the station was in walking distance of the Carmody house, so he was able to keep in touch with Mary Anne without its looking too obvious that he was impatiently waiting for her to grow up so that he could ask her to marry him. He had felt an exclusive, strong, protective attachment to her ever since he first met her and realised she was the daughter of the drowned woman he had seen stretched out on the floor of Manus's office. His compassion for the motherless child had turned to love as the years went by and her endearing qualities caused her to be loved, not only by him, but everyone she came into contact with. She shimmered with a warm vitality that drew everyone to her.

At the house he often met William Blackshaw who was a student in Trinity College.

Mary Anne's large group of friends, who spent most of their free time at the Carmodys' house, swooned over the two older visitors and found it difficult to decide which one they preferred.

Mary Anne and William were often invited to the townhouse where, in front of Edwina, William pretended to be particularly fond of his young cousin. Mary Anne thought it was a mean trick to play on the old woman. William said that she would find out soon enough that she had been fooled, and, besides, it served her right as she refused to invite Toby to the house even when they asked specifically if he could sometimes be included. Edwina had kept to her resolve of never speaking one word to the fisherman's son who had wormed his way into the life of Tyringham Park, mainly due to the patronage of Manus.

Toby had decided to ask Mary Anne to marry him when she turned eighteen. He was worried that after she left the all-girls school and went to university to study medicine, which was her plan, she would be snapped up by a desirable medical student on her first day of term.

CHAPTER 25

Edwina wanted to mark Mary Anne's eighteenth birthday with the most extravagant ball the Park had ever seen, eclipsing anything the Cork Blackshaws had put on during their time there, but Mary Anne said the ball could wait for her twenty-first birthday. The thing she would like most of all was to see an exhibition of her mother's paintings mounted in the ballroom of Tyringham Park. Not an amateurish exhibition, hung in a haphazard fashion on existing hooks wherever they happened to be placed, but one organised professionally by the Academician, David Slane, who had offered to curate and oversee the hanging of one fifteen years earlier. That enterprise had been cancelled at the time because of Charlotte's death.

The artist Cormac Delaney was pleased to hear it was being held at last. He often mentioned in letters to David that he would travel over from Paris if it ever went ahead so that he could take satisfaction in seeing his talented former pupil getting public recognition at last.

Mary Anne was keen to have the event in Cork rather than Dublin for two reasons. Firstly she wanted to make sure that Toby's grandfather Reg could attend. He was suffering from emphysema and could not be expected to travel and she didn't want him to miss the occasion. Secondly, and more importantly, she wanted to put flowers on her mother's grave on the day. She had no memories of Charlotte, but had built up a composite picture of her from what she had been told by Lochlann, Niamh, Iseult and the Carmody grandparents, and it gave her a warm feeling to think about her. From what they had said, she was a remarkable woman that Mary Anne could be unconditionally proud of. There was a faint memory of Weena saying something mean about her, but it was so indistinct she presumed she had merely dreamt it.

Toby asked Mary Anne to marry him and she accepted joyfully and without hesitation.

Both sets of parents, as expected, agreed that the two were well suited. Lochlann's only reservation was that he did not want Mary Anne to sacrifice her studies for an early marriage.

"I'll graduate before we marry," she reassured him. "It will be a long engagement. Toby wants to apply to join the Special Detective Unit in a few years' time, so we both have things to do before the day. There's no rush."

Toby's father decided he would not attend the banquet that was to follow the exhibition. He would make sure he was fishing many miles out at sea while it was taking place. He had a good mind to miss the wedding as well and wondered if engine failure might supply him with an excuse when the time came. It was not that he had anything personal against Mary Anne, a sweet-natured, thoughtful young woman, but he couldn't see himself dressed up to the nines trying to make conversation with the gentry or, worse still, having to listen to them. Life would have been much simpler if Toby had chosen to marry a fisherman's daughter from Cobh.

Toby's mother Daisy wondered how she would be able to carry off being the mother of the intended bridegroom. What would she say? What would she wear? How would she act? She was relieved her husband wouldn't be attending as he was bound to say the wrong thing and not even be aware of it. That, at least, was one less worry.

Even though she had been reared in the gardener's cottage on the estate she had never seen the inside of the house. The thought of entering it as a servant would have been intimidating enough, but to enter as a guest made her feel decidedly anxious.

Daisy went into her bedroom, crouched down beside her bed and pulled out a box from under it. Inside the box, wrapped in soft cloth, was the glass necklace that Toby had given her when he was a young boy. She had never had an occasion to wear it until now. Toby hadn't mentioned it since that day he had bought it from a charity stall with a few shillings that Manus had given him, and she wondered if he had forgotten about it. She wouldn't mention it to him. He would be touched and surprised when he saw her turning up at the banquet wearing it, looking so splendid he would not feel in the slightest bit ashamed of her.

Apart from Toby, she would like to do her best for Mary Anne, that gem of a young woman who unbelievably would one day become her daughter-in-law. It wasn't as if she thought Mary Anne was too good for Toby – no one was too good for Toby in her eyes – but Mary Anne could have had her pick of the highest in the land. It said a lot about her strength of character that she had chosen Toby over all others

"You will do brilliantly," Toby had encouraged his mother when she told him how nervous she felt. "You are a lady in the true sense of the word and you don't have to defer to anyone. The banquet is only a dinner with a fancy name in a fancy place. Mary Anne and I will be right beside you, so you have nothing to fear. What is the worst thing that could happen?"

PART 2

ALISON

AUSTRALIA

CHAPTER 26

New South Wales, 1941

The new baby was not thriving. Dan put it down to the fact that it was probably carrying the same defect that had resulted in the stillbirth of its twin. He didn't hold out much hope for this one's survival, either, judging by the look of it, and wondered how Nell would be able to bear the loss of a second child. The seven older children in the family had been robust from the beginning, so the contrast with this thin, sickly little one was obvious even to him, who normally didn't notice babies all that much, leaving the care of them exclusively to Nell.

It was a visiting neighbour, Cheryl, who pointed out that the child was starving.

Nell kept forgetting to feed it and as a result the supply of her milk was drying up.

"Are there any bottles around the place?"

Cheryl's tone when she asked the question was so urgent that three of the children immediately jumped up from the table and started searching in the cupboards.

"We need to get some milk into the baby fast. Nell, do you know if there are any bottles around?"

"I don't know," said Nell in a dull voice. "I normally don't use them. You could try the shed."

"Why would there be one in the shed?"

"I don't know," said Nell. "That's where I always look."

"Stevie, try the shed," said Dan to the nine-year-old. Most lost things turned up in the shed if they turned up at all.

Five-year-old Jack, affected by the panic in the air, flew out the door. "Bottle for the baby, bottle for the baby," he repeated, running past the shed over to the dairy to fetch the dirt-encrusted oversized bottle with the matching teat that was used for feeding the poddy-calves.

No baby's bottle was found in the kitchen cupboards or the shed.

"I'll go home and get one," said Cheryl. "The teats would probably be perished by now anyways, even if you did find one. I'll be back in a jiffy."

Dan felt inept as well as guilty as he went off to search in the marital bedroom as a last resort. It hadn't occurred to him that Nell wasn't feeding Alison. Nell was so modest, even around him, that she fed the baby in the bedroom, alone and with the door closed. He had taken Alison's lack of crying as a sign that she was full and satisfied, whereas all the time she had been getting weaker and losing the strength to cry.

Jack located the bottle in the dairy, ran back with it, poured milk into it from the jug without spilling very much, and was able to manoeuvre the teat back on. He was barely tall enough to reach over the side of the pram and aim the teat at Alison's mouth. The hole in the teat was so large that the milk poured out all over the baby's face, making her gasp for a breath as if she were in the initial stages of drowning. Her clothing and bedding were saturated. Nell, seated beside the pram, looked on but did not intervene.

Cheryl, who lived only a half mile up the road, had driven to her house and back within a few minutes. She and Dan talked in whispers outside before coming back into the kitchen together where they saw Jack trying to force the huge teat of the now empty bottle into Alison's tiny mouth.

"Jack, give me that," Dan said, snatching the bottle from the little boy's hand.

Jack backed away and burst into tears.

"Don't be such a girl, Jack, crying for nothing," said Cheryl. "Stop acting like a big sissy baby."

Jack ran to his mother and buried his face in her lap. Nell rubbed the back of his head without looking down at him.

Dan felt out of his depth with all these female concerns going on around him.

"Make yourself useful, Dan, and boil them bottles for five minutes to sterilise them." Cheryl handed him two bottles and two teats and he put them in a saucepan of water on the stove. "I'll have to change everything. Where are the clean clothes kept?"

Dan and the three empty-handed boys looked blankly at her. Nell said they were in the washhouse.

Cheryl undressed Alison, took out the soggy bedding and wiped around the interior of the pram. Then she carried the baby out the back to the washhouse and saw dirty clothes and nappies piled up as high as the window and giving off an awful stench. At least Nell had managed to bring the soiled items to the right place and had not left them lying on the floors all over the house, so that was something to be grateful for.

Cheryl poked her head back into the kitchen to say, "There's a mountain of dirty clothes in the washhouse – no point in asking youse how long it's all been there as youse wouldn't know. Light the copper, Dan, and I'll give everything a good scalding." She was enjoying herself, bossing Dan around. She had been in awe of him and his strong principles ever since she had married a local man and come to live in the district. She hoped her two children would turn out as brainy and as sensible as the Hogans. Her older boy was giving trouble at school, but she put it down to the fact that his teacher didn't know how to handle him properly. "Do you think you can hang the clothes out on the line after I've washed them and then bring them in when they're dry?"

"I think you can trust me to do that much."

"I was beginning to wonder. Nell spoilt youse all – that's your trouble. Thank heavens it's a good drying day. Plenty of wind. I'll have to make do until then."

Cheryl wiped Alison clean with a warm flannel, used a tea towel for a nappy, swaddled her in a shawl, and held her on her hip while she quarter-filled a sterilised bottle with warm milk to which she added a dessertspoon of sugar. "That should do the trick," she said, referring to the sugar. "Watch me, Larry," she said to the ten-year-old. "Then you'll know what to do next time. I'm putting you in charge. I better do this first feed. She might have trouble getting used to the bottle. Watch me to see how it's done."

All eyes except Nell's watched as Cheryl put the teat into the baby's mouth. No response from the unanimated little face. Cheryl wiggled the teat up and down, then round and round. When she pushed it in fully, Alison made a gagging sound followed by a weak cough.

"These breastfed babies are a real nuisance," said Cheryl, reacting with irritation as if the baby had purposely defied her. "They get too attached to their mothers – that's their problem. I don't want to make the hole any bigger just in case we end up with another flood on our hands, but I'm not beat yet. I've got a few more tricks up me sleeve."

Cheryl asked Larry to bring over the honey jar and take off the lid. She dipped the teat into the honey and quickly put it into Alison's mouth before the honey had time to drip on the shawl. There was a wait of a few seconds before they all heard Alison make a swallowing sound. Jack cheered and his brothers told him to shut up. He started bawling and once again hid his face in Nell's lap. The baby's sucking action was weak but effective enough for it to eventually take in half of what Cheryl had prepared.

"That's a good start. You burp her, Larry. Hold her like this and rub her like this. That's it. I'll get going on the washing. I have to go home after that. When is Zita coming home?"

"In three weeks."

Cheryl's eyes widened. "That long? I thought she was due about now." She motioned for Dan to go outside where they could talk privately. "Nell's in a bad way. I think you should send for Zita now," she said in a dramatic whisper as soon as they were out of earshot.

"Take her out of school early? I don't know if I can do that. It's an important year for her, sitting her Inter Cert." He didn't tell Cheryl that Zita's main ambition in life was to win a scholarship and go to university. He didn't want to hear a sarcastic comment about young girls with fancy notions and big heads.

"It's only for a few weeks until Nell bucks up."

"I'm sure the boys and I can manage now that we know what to do."

"I don't think you can with the cows about to calve and all that.

The baby and Nell will be a full-time job until Nell gets over them baby blues."

"Is that what she's got?" Dan was glad it had a name. "Is it serious?"

"No. I had it meself with both of mine. It goes away by itself after a while but while you have it you're a bit of a basket case. I don't think you have much choice, Dan. The baby needs a lot of care and you can see Nell isn't in any fit condition to look after her. Zita is the girl for the job. You and the boys might be good farmers, but youse are useless housekeepers. If I didn't have me hands so full I could be more help, but I can only take time off in the middle of the day, and that's not every day."

"I appreciate that, and I appreciate what you've done this afternoon. I'll get on to the convent first thing in the morning."

CHAPTER 27

Fourteen-year-old Zita came home on the bus two days later and a red-faced Larry almost threw the crying, red-faced baby into her arms as soon as she put down her suitcase. He had taken Alison's crying to heart as she had started crying, from what he could judge, only after he had begun taking care of her. Before Zita could ask him any questions he took off out the door to join his brothers who had teased him and nicknamed him 'Mummy' during the two interminable days.

It was three weeks before the September holidays were due to begin, so Zita expected to be away from school for six weeks in total. The nuns assured her they would keep any important lesson notes for her so she wouldn't fall behind in her studies. They promised to pray for Nell's speedy recovery.

Dan thought that everything would be all right now that Zita was home.

Zita acknowledged, after she saw the state of her mother and Alison, that Dan's decision to take her out of school had been the correct one, though she had felt nothing but resentment towards her brothers when Reverend Mother had brought her into the parlour to tell her she was needed at home, and she realised her brothers would not be asked to make the same sacrifice.

"The Lord sees all things and knows all things, so He would have known since the beginning of time that this burden would be placed on you," said Reverend Mother. "Perhaps that's why you were born on the feast-day of St Zita and named after her. With the grace of God your mother's illness will last only a short time, and you will be back with us after the holidays. You have a wonderful academic career ahead of you."

Zita wished she had been born on the feast-day of St Luke, the patron saint of doctors, rather than on the feast-day of St Zita, the patron saint of unmarried housemaids.

The dairy was soon back in full production with the coming of spring. Dan and the boys were outside for long periods of time and Zita, knowing how hard they worked, lost the resentment she had initially felt at being called home. In the spirit of her patron saint, and following the example of the Virgin Mary, she undertook her tasks willingly and cheerfully. After all, it would only be for a short time, according to Cheryl, who popped in frequently to check on her.

"Fatten them up," was Cheryl's repeated advice to Zita.

Nell was making little attempt to feed herself or the baby, acting as if Alison had no connection to her, and wandering off if she was meant to be minding her, leaving her unattended.

Aunty Cat, up from Sydney to visit her sisters, who lived in nearby country towns, and her only brother, Dan, who lived on the old Hogan family farm, once again asked Dan if she could adopt Alison – "to lessen Nell's burden" as she put it. Cat had all the time in the world to rear a child. Her husband worked in his successful huckster's shop on an east Sydney beachfront sixteen hours a day, seven days a week, all year round, and that included Christmas Day. He never involved her in any way, which was just as well as she had grown to hate the sight of the place. Diversions such as embroidery, furniture restoration, pottery, quilting, art appreciation and wood carving had each in turn been used by her to fill the gap in her life caused by her childlessness, and each in turn had been abandoned.

Dan found it difficult to answer her with a civil tongue. "Can't you see it's the loss of one baby that has her the way she is? I'd hate to think what she'd be like if she lost two. It could tip her over the edge."

"I was only trying to be helpful," Aunty Cat said, wanting to point out that Nell had already gone over the edge from what she could see, but held back at the sight of Dan's outraged face. What did Nell have to get depressed about, anyway, Cat reasoned, with her eight healthy, bright, good-looking offspring when other unfortunate women like herself didn't have any children of any description?

"She should be over it by now," whispered another aunt to Cat later after Dan left the room. "All those weeks sitting around doing nothing – it's a bit self-indulgent if you ask me. It's time she pulled herself together."

"Nobody did ask you if I remember rightly," said a third aunt. "Apparently it's something you can't help. I heard of a woman who had it for a year and never snapped out of it. She ended up taking her own life."

"We can do without those kinds of stories, thank you very much, Lizzie," said Cat.

"We certainly can," said the other aunt. "It's not as if Nell would ever do a thing like that."

"Of course she wouldn't," said Cat. "She knows as well as we do that it's a mortal sin, even though she's only a convert."

Nell, lying on her bed, too tired to go into the kitchen to talk to Dan's sisters, heard through the open window her brother-in-law saying to his daughter, "Don't go in there. Wait out here for your mother. There's a madwoman running loose in that house."

CHAPTER 28

The Thompsons were wealthy graziers who lived eight miles west of the Hogan's farm on 20,000 acres of inherited land. They had intended keeping a perfectly good slow-combustion stove for one more year before replacing it with a newer, much larger model, but when they heard of Nell's plight they asked Wombat Churchill, a man who could turn his hand to anything, if he would dismantle it without delay and install it in the Hogans' kitchen. It would most definitely ease Nell's workload and raise her spirits. Doing it through Wombat, a friend of the Hogans and the town's Good Samaritan, took away the personal element and made it appear less like charity. Dan was a good builder but had no gift for plumbing, so there were no feelings of injured pride when Wombat turned up with the component parts without having consulted him.

Wombat had the stove in working order within a day. The family agreed that it was the most beautiful and useful thing the Hogans had ever owned, with its black and white enamel finish, shiny chrome fittings, two hotplates, two deep ovens, a drying rack and a copper cylinder attached to it that supplied the house with hot water. Everyone thought that Nell, after cooking over an open fire for so many years and having to boil a kettle or copper for hot water, would marvel at it and be thankful for it.

Nell didn't attempt to use it and treated it as if it were an obstacle that should be removed from the kitchen so she wouldn't keep bumping into it.

Alison was sleeping in the pram, Zita was blending ingredients in a mixing bowl with a wooden spoon and Nell was staring into space when Wombat came into the kitchen. He indicated he was waiting for Dan but it was Zita he wanted to see. He was hoping to be offered his usual choice of Zita's homemade biscuits.

Wombat had been a fixture in the Hogan household for a year, ever since he was the only young man in Redmundo who had not been signed up when he went along with his rugby league mates to enlist. 'Inability to speak' was the reason given for turning him away, rather than 'disfigured face' which he had been half expecting. The recruiting sergeant told Wombat he was already doing his bit for the war effort by working in the butter factory, but if he wanted to do more he could find a farmer and give him a hand at weekends. Primary producers were as important a factor in winning a war as soldiers were, the sergeant said.

The parish priest, Father Daly, put Wombat in contact with Dan Hogan, another parishioner, who lived on a dairy farm twenty miles out of town. Father Daly thought that Wombat, alone in the world since the death of his mother the previous year, could do with a substitute family, and that the Hogan couple, along with their seven children, would suit him down to the ground.

During that year Wombat gardened for Dr Carmody after work during the week, and on a Saturday and sometimes on Sunday as well, he drove out to the Hogans, initially to fulfil his patriotic duty, and later as a pleasure to meet up with people who had become good friends. He was particularly fond of Nell and was fascinated by her last baby, Alison, when it came along.

Wombat usually kept his distance from children as they were prone to say loudly to their mothers, "Why is that man's face all horrible? What happened to him?" and he would feel sorrier for the embarrassed mothers, whisking the children away, than he felt for himself.

At least babies couldn't speak and, as he had seen Alison every weekend since she was born, watching her flourish, fade and then flourish again, he felt comfortable in her presence.

He leaned over the pram to admire her recently regained plumpness. Alison squawked loudly. As a reflex action, he quickly turned away. Zita noticed his turning and the flush of mortification spreading across the back of his neck. She picked up the crying Alison, who had recently been fed, and put her into Wombat's arms, telling him to sit in the rocking chair and to hold the child against his shoulder for a minute. Alison was too young to be aware of Wombat's disfigured face, Zita knew, and the crying was likely to have been caused by pain from a residue of wind. Zita often didn't check if she had completed the procedure of winding, impatient as she was to get on to the next task on her long list.

"Pat her on the back like this," Zita said, taking Wombat's hand in hers and moving it for him in a rubbing, patting movement on the baby's back.

Wombat's flush turned a deeper red while she was guiding his hand and standing close, bending over him.

After a minute Alison emitted a loud burp and immediately stopped crying. Zita congratulated Wombat who managed to look pleased at the success of his technique.

Poor coot, she thought, echoing sentiments that she had often heard expressed by her parents. Obviously so fond of children and not likely ever to have any of his own. A cruel prospect for such a young, strong man to accept. His only hope was to meet up with a blind, deaf woman, one outspoken neighbour had been heard to observe, putting into words what other, more tactful people thought but didn't say aloud.

By the look of gratitude in Wombat's eyes when she first handed Alison over to him, Zita guessed that no mother would trust him enough to ask him to hold a baby. Nell would have trusted him, but it would not have occurred to her to hand over a baby for him to hold. She would believe it wasn't right to demean a man by giving him women's work to do.

Wombat, guided by Zita, changed Alison's position from his shoulder to the crook of his arm and looked down at her as if she were a holy infant. Alison gazed up at him and didn't look away like most people did when they saw him, but smiled at him instead. He became quietly tearful as he and the baby continued to stare into each other's eyes.

After the baking was completed, all the biscuits turned upside down on the cooling trays, the kitchen filled with the smells of home, Wombat motioned that he would like to keep Alison in his now confident arms while he, Zita, Nell and Dan, who had finally joined them, sat around the table to drink tea and eat a selection of biscuits. Wombat lined up four on his plate but refused the tea for fear of scalding the baby if his cup happened to tip over. Nell kept looking over at Wombat every now and again with a puzzled look on her face.

"You're a natural," said Dan, commenting on Wombat's handling of the baby. Wombat made a little snorting noise that signified pleasure. "Did you hear, Zita, that the Irish doctor's wife kissed Wombat before she left for being so good with babies?"

Nell perked up at the mention of the Irish doctor.

Wombat made hand and head movements as if to say, 'It was nothing'.

Zita hadn't heard as she had been away at school at the time. She was now keen to hear the details, as she thought she was the first person to have trusted Wombat with a baby. Dan told her how Charlotte Carmody, the doctor's wife, whom they had never seen, but who was the subject of much local interest, had kissed Wombat on the cheek and let him hold her baby just before she and her husband left a couple of months earlier to return to Ireland. The woman must be a saint to have kissed that face, Zita thought with a shudder. She could never imagine herself doing it. Who would have thought the woman, known for her standoffish ways and toffy accent, could do something so heroic? Many townspeople admired how gracious she had been, humouring him when he mouthed a word she took to be 'Wind', and right there and then going through the motions of winding the child to please him. She told him in her toffy accent that he had brought her good luck in the end. No one knew what she meant by that remark. Dan could only conclude, going on hearsay, that Charlotte Carmody, overjoyed at having given birth to a live child at last, had let her happiness spill over to someone so much less fortunate than herself. She had been carelessly unkind to Wombat when she first arrived in the district so, on the day she was leaving, had taken the opportunity to be extra kind to make up for it.

"What a dark horse you've turned out to be, Wombat. That was a lovely story," said Zita.

"Lovely," said Nell, smiling.

Zita picked up a bottle of milk that had been warming at the back of the stove. "I must be off," she said. "I'll take her now, Wombat. Thanks for your help. Would you credit it? She doesn't want to come to me, after all I've done for her, the little monkey. She's definitely taken a shine to you. Look at the way she keeps staring at you." She reached down and took Alison from Wombat, who was reluctant to hand her over.

Zita tucked Alison into the pram ready for the afternoon trip to the dairy and asked Wombat if he would keep an eye on Nell until he had to leave to go back to town. Wombat nodded that he would, but it was Alison he kept looking at with sorrowful eyes until she was wheeled out of his sight.

CHAPTER 29

Schools broke up for the September holidays. Kevin and Mick arrived home from their boarding school, bringing energy and fun into the home that had turned sombre since they were last there. They changed out of their uniforms and headed straight for the dairy, allowing Zita the luxury of not having to go for a change. Following Nell's example, Zita unpacked their cases and washed all their clothes. After everything was dried and ironed she put them back into the cases so they wouldn't get lost in the general chaos around the house and would be ready for their trip back to school.

Her own suitcase was packed, ready for her return to St Mary's after the holidays.

Her life's aim was to become a doctor, something she had never told anyone, not even her two best friends, for fear of being thought conceited or deluded. She also kept to herself the belief that she was bright enough to win a Commonwealth Scholarship that would be necessary if she were to achieve her ambition. She didn't have a minute's doubt that becoming a doctor was her true vocation.

The idea had first come to her when she heard her mother praising Dr Carmody, saying what a difference it made to have a warm and sympathetic medic looking after you when you were in labour or had a sick child. She was also influenced by the novels, and the films adapted from the novels, of AJ Cronin that depicted the lives of honourable, brave, compassionate, ethical doctors who improved the lives of the poor and deprived. She would like to be such a champion. She imagined a household waiting for her to arrive with her black bag full of instruments and medicines and her head full of knowledge to cure the sick mother of the family, and how each member would rejoice to hear her knock on the door, and say, "The doctor is here! Now everything will be all right." And she would enter, cure the patient and not charge anything if money was short, accepting the family's praise and gratitude as payment enough, and leave with a feeling of happiness at having done something so worthwhile.

"Please, dear God," she prayed every night after she finished the rosary, "let Mum get better. And please don't let it take too long."

Nell had taken to wandering and it became apparent that she was looking for her stillborn twin daughter, Dolores. Sometimes she left the house in a state of undress, sometimes wearing layers of inappropriate clothing. She sneaked down the dirt track to the mailbox, turned left or right along the main road and kept walking until somebody stopped to speak to her. Neighbours and strangers who came across her brought her back and pretended not to notice the look of embarrassment on the face of whichever family member came out to the gate to claim her. It was usually Zita.

More often than not it was Dan on horseback who went looking for her, always carrying an oilskin to cover her when he found her. It was a sad sight, the neighbours commented amongst themselves, watching Dan leading the horse back home, with Nell slumped in the saddle wearing the oilskin. Dan left the road as soon as he could after finding her, and followed the bridle tracks beside the fences to avoid being seen by the occasional passing traffic, though anyone looking out for them could catch glimpses of them passing behind the belt of trees lining the side of the road.

Neighbours called with casseroles and cakes and would like to have given more practical help but they had their own children to rear, dairies to run and paddocks to plough with no hired labour to give them any time off. Cheryl offered to take the baby home with her for a few hours on occasions to train her, but Zita said she could manage.

Cheryl said that Nell's baby blues were more extreme and lasting longer than hers had, so lent Dan their family car to drive Nell the twenty miles into Redmundo to see the doctor, in the hope that she would be given a remedy that would bring her back to her old self. Nell brightened up at the mention of the trip.

"A good tonic might be all she needs," said Cheryl, waving them off.

As soon as the doctor's receptionist, Marie Dawson, saw Nell coming into the waiting room, she left her cubicle and rushed over to greet her.

"It's lovely to see you, Nell," she said. "There's only one in front of you. Sit down there and take the weight off your feet. Did you leave the little one at home?"

"Yes," said Nell, looking past Marie. "Zita is looking after her."

The surgery door opened and some person Nell didn't know came out and went over to a chair to pick up his coat. An old man in a white coat called Nell's name from the surgery doorway.

"But that's not Dr Carmody," Nell said to Dan in dismay, pointing at the old man. "I thought we were coming in to see Dr Carmody. I want to go home."

Marie explained that Dr Carmody had left to go back to Ireland three months earlier. Dr Merton, who had taken his place, was every bit as efficient. Marie said that it might be a good idea if Dan went into the surgery with her.

"Did you see the doctor's baby?" Nell asked.

"Yes, of course."

"Was she a lovely baby?"

"She was indeed. I thought she had a look of a Hogan about her, to tell you the truth. Must be the Irish blood. But then I always thought Dan and Dr Carmody must have been related way back as they have such a similar bearing about them. Distant cousins, so to speak."

"Funny, I thought that, too. That's probably why I liked him so much." Nell smiled and followed Dan into the surgery.

Dr Merton checked out Nell and asked her a lot of questions. Dan told the doctor that Nell had suffered severe morning sickness throughout the last pregnancy, something she had not experienced with any of the earlier seven confinements. Dan then went on to answer most of the questions the doctor put to Nell, as she told the old man the first thing that came into her head, often on an unrelated topic, as if she wasn't even trying to concentrate.

After much murmuring and head-nodding, Dr Merton told Nell he was one-hundred-per-cent certain that she was suffering from a condition common in women who had recently given birth, with her condition no doubt exacerbated by the death of one of the twins, and that it would eventually pass and she was not to worry. She was a highly sensitive woman, so she might take a little longer than the average person to come out of this condition that didn't have a specific medical name. It was often confused with baby blues but it was more serious and longer lasting. He repeated that she most definitely would come out of it. All she had to do was be patient and trust to nature.

Dan thanked the doctor and stayed back, after Nell went out to finish her conversation with Marie, to ask him if he thought a visit to the grave might be a good idea. It had occurred to him that the sight of it might make Nell realise how futile it was to continue searching the roads for a child she could never hope to find. Nell had a fear of cemeteries and funerals and had not asked to see Dolores' grave after she had been discharged from the hospital fourteen days after the twins had been delivered and thirteen days after Dolores had been buried. This would be her first time for her to see the grave.

The doctor said it was worth a try and might even speed up her recovery.

Nell showed no response when she saw where Dan was taking her.

Dan didn't know what to expect as he led her to the little mound of earth with the words '*Dolores Hogan*' painted on a plywood cross marking the spot.

Nell looked down at the grave and read the words aloud. She appeared unmoved.

"We will order a headstone," said Dan. "You can design it and choose the wording."

"That would be nice," said Nell in her flat voice.

CHAPTER 30

The September holidays were over. Without saying a word, Kevin and Mick took their suitcases down to the roadside where they caught the bus to take them back to the nearest boys' senior secondary Catholic school a hundred miles away. Perhaps they had slipped off quietly so as not to upset Nell, but Zita thought it was more likely they didn't want to face her. By rights, she should be taking the same bus but by now she was so caught up with the responsibilities of Nell, the baby, the four other children still at home, the dairy and the vegetable garden, that she had come to accept that returning to school for the next term was an unrealistic ambition.

Dan did not talk to her about anything to do with her future. They both struggled on from hour to hour.

Reverend Mother wrote to ask if she was returning and hoped that Nell had regained her health. The nuns continued to remember her in their prayers. Zita wrote back explaining that her mother still had not recovered and that she herself was needed at home to look after the family for a little while longer. She presumed she would be able to return to school after the Christmas holidays for her fourth year. Nell should be better by then, and she expected that they, whoever they were, would not withdraw her State bursary after the circumstances of Nell's illness were explained to them.

Her friends wrote to say they missed her, that they weren't having as much fun without her, and that they couldn't wait for her to return.

Nell's wanderings became more frequent after she had visited the grave. She became more cunning about escaping from the house, and would set out at any hour. The first time she took off after dark Dan had noticed fairly soon afterwards that she was missing and had caught up with her before she had gone too far. He never knew if she would turn to the left or to the right at the mailbox, but this time he had guessed correctly. He felt a surge of anger when he saw in the distance a figure in a white nightdress heading down the hill, but by the time he caught up with her he was overcome with a rush of tenderness for his agitated wife and enclosed her in his arms before guiding her back home.

Zita remembered how, when she was younger, she used to watch her mother, in the middle of winter with the frost still on the ground, wrestling with double bed sheets, trying to hang them on the line in the teeth of a high wind and how a sheet would catch the wind and slap Nell across the face before tangling her in its icy folds.

Zita had dreaded the day she would become a grown-up and have to do that, as well as much worse. Scooping up the entrails of a dead rabbit from under the bed was one thing she would stay a child forever to avoid. She always knew the mess was there before it had time to putrefy as she could hear the cat, who chose the same spot under Zita's bed each time to deal with its victims, gnawing away during the night. Nearly as bad was cutting off the head of a hen with an axe, pulling out the innards and plucking it while blood oozed all over the place. Nell was a heroine the way she dealt with a disgusting job like that without batting an eyelid. Zita prayed that nothing bad would happen to her mother, causing all those stomach-churning jobs to fall to her.

Up until three months ago the prayers had worked but now Zita realised, with a rising sense of alarm, that the time for her to do all those nasty tasks might have arrived. She increased the intensity and duration of her prayers for Nell's recovery.

Wombat was by now helping Zita around the house more than he was helping Dan around the farm, occupying Nell and Alison and feeding them, and preparing lunch for all the family. Zita appreciated his assistance as well as his silence, which was calming to her nerves. She had already become so used to the burns on his face that she didn't notice them any longer, and often felt like kissing his cheek to show her appreciation after he had done something particularly thoughtful, which was often, but restrained herself for fear of appearing forward.

Nell answered questions when they were put to her but didn't initiate conversation, sitting for most of the day in an unfocused stillness when she wasn't wandering off. The only topics that animated her were stories about her original family in the old days, and about the Irish doctor and his wife and daughter. She showed little interest in the neighbours or even Dan and her own children.

CHAPTER 31

Dan, after the visit to the grave, disappointed that its significance had not registered with Nell, was in a bad way from worry and from lack of sleep. All the children were miserable with a severe dose of chicken pox. Jack, Stevie and Larry would have to stay off school for two weeks. It was clear that they did not want to stay at home during the day. The little bush school was only two hundred yards away from the perimeter fence of the farm and the boys could hear the shouts of the kids playing rounders at lunchtime and wished they could join them. They were annoying Zita who seemed to be in a permanent state of frustration, not helped by Nell's decision to give up feeding herself altogether.

Wombat wrestled with his conscience as he watched Nell's deterioration. He had in his possession information that, on the one hand might pull Nell out of her black pit or, on the other, might push her further down into it. He had no way of knowing beforehand what the consequences of giving her this information might be, but he judged that she had arrived at the stage where it would be more cruel to withhold it from her than it would be to impart it. Convinced that he was the only person who could tell her, as no one else in Australia knew what he knew, he felt the knowledge weighing heavily on his mind.

After a morning where he saw Zita crying with hopelessness and tiredness, he judged that the time had come.

He chose a quiet moment and handed Zita a note written in copybook copperplate that read, "*I have something very serious to tell you, and then Nell, but not Dan.*"

"Go on, then," said Zita, wondering what on earth he would come up with. He rarely resorted to writing notes as he usually relied on hand movements to get across his meaning. "I'm ready to hear it."

On a second sheet of paper he wrote, "*Alison and Dr Lochlann Carmody's baby are twins,*" and handed it to her.

Zita took the note. She read it quickly and spluttered with scorn when she took in its meaning. "Everyone knows that. Born in the same hospital on the same day. Of course they're 'twins'."

Wombat wrote: "*No, I mean real twins. Dolores is not dead. She is alive and is called Mary Anne Carmody.*"

"How come you think you know that?" Zita's voice was full of contempt.

"*I saw the Carmody baby on the day they were leaving. I had a really good look at her. She is identical to Alison.*"

"What a load of rubbish. Have you lost your marbles or what?"

Wombat wrote, "*It's true,*" and looked at her with pitying eyes.

"How do you make that out? You expect me to believe that the doctor stole one of Mum's babies? And palmed her off with his, which was dead? That's too horrible for words."

"*I didn't say it was deliberate.*"

"Why are you only saying it now? Why didn't you say it then?"

"*I tried to. They didn't understand me. They were in a rush to go.*"

"How can I take your word for anything? What do you know about babies? Haven't you heard that all newborn babies look alike? How come nobody else noticed?" Zita was spitting with temper. "Thank goodness you told me first. Don't you dare tell Mum your mad story. Do you want to stop her from getting better? And don't tell Dad. He'd run you off the place. What made you come up with that ridiculous story?"

Wombat wrote without hesitation, "*I'm positive it's true and I think it might help Nell get better if she knew.*"

"*You* think? When did you become an expert on Mum as well as babies? I think you're the one that needs to be told a thing or two." She stood up, snatched the notepad out of his hand, and grabbed his arm. "Why don't you go home? Why don't you bloody well talk? Everyone knows there's nothing wrong with your vocal chords. Why don't you make the bloody effort? Why don't you just bugger off and take your ridiculous idea back to town with you and stop upsetting this family?" She pushed him out the door. "And do us all a bloody big favour while you're at it and don't bloody well bother coming back."

She opened the door of the stove, poked Wombat's notes into the fire, and closed the door on them before following Wombat out to his vehicle and glaring at him until he drove away.

CHAPTER 32

Zita, her mind in a state of discord since her confrontation with Wombat, left Alison asleep in the kitchen and took her mother to her favourite seat under the walnut tree, from where they could both look out over the acres of sunlit pastures under a cerulean blue sky and listen to the parrots squabbling in the fruit trees. The place always had an animating effect on Nell.

"This is nice, isn't it, Mum?"

Nell said it was.

"Tell me, Mum. Did you ever see Mrs Carmody's baby before they left?"

"No," said Nell, her face brightening a little. She liked to talk about the Carmodys, a factor Zita was now relying on. "The doctor took her home straight after delivery. It made sense as Mrs Parker was on hand to look after them and the hospital was understaffed. I was sorry I didn't get to see her."

"Do you know what they called the baby?"

"Mary Anne. Two nice names." Nell took a long, quivering breath and spoke slowly with a dry mouth. "I was sorry to hear the doctor was leaving. Such a kind man. I got a shock when I saw the new doctor. I was expecting to see Dr Carmody. I forgot he had left.

The new one is too old." Nell sighed and lapsed back into silence.

Zita's harsh words kept Wombat away from the farm. He did not return the following weekend, as Zita half expected he would, to say that perhaps he had made a mistake and that he was sorry. Did he really believe that Alison's twin was not dead and that he was the only one in Australia who knew?

The only other person who could have known was Mrs Parker, the doctor's housekeeper, but she was not a friend of Nell's, so wouldn't have visited her and the baby during Nell's fortnight's stay in hospital, and had not seen her since, so would have had no way of comparing the two women's babies. Scottie Cunningham, the mailman, and Dr Merton, the only other two present at the departure of the Carmodys, had never seen Alison so there was no point in asking them anything.

No nurse in the hospital had seen Mary Anne Carmody. Sister Fullbright, with a dose of the flu, had arrived for work on the day but had been sent home by the doctor, and the doctor had taken his wife and daughter home before Sister Townsend arrived back in the evening for the night shift. The doctor had been on his own with the two women on the day the three babies had been born. All of this was common knowledge in the town.

Zita questioned Nell again later. "What was Mrs Carmody like?" she asked.

"I didn't get to meet her personally. Some people thought she was stuck up because she was the daughter of a lord, but I think she was nervy. She got worse after her first baby was stillborn. Stayed indoors to avoid strangers' germs, according to Mrs Parker who told Aunty Tess who told me. It wasn't that she was stuck up."

"I never knew that her first baby died."

"You must have been away at school. Everyone in the district felt sorry for her, even though they didn't know her. It was very sad. That was why I was so happy she had a live baby at last. Little Mary Anne."

That night, as she stood at the sink so she wouldn't have to make eye contact with her mother, Zita said, "Mum, did you see the twins straight after they were born?"

"No. I always had chloroform at the end."

"Oh? I didn't know that." Zita felt uncomfortable talking to her mother about anything to do with childbirth, but forced herself to continue. "Is that usual?"

"I don't know, really. I always asked for some. I couldn't face it otherwise."

"Did Mrs Carmody see the twins?"

"I don't know. I think she had chloroform as well. Poor Dr Carmody was run off his feet. I didn't want to take up his time asking questions."

"So you never saw Mary Anne?"

"No, unfortunately."

"And did Mrs Carmody ever see Alison or Dolores?"

"Not as far as I know."

Zita turned and saw that Nell was looking agitated. She didn't know if it was because of all the questions or because she had used the word 'Dolores', a word that Zita had yet to hear her mother say.

CHAPTER 33

A Sydneysider drove along a winding, unfamiliar road, suffering in sympathy with his new Jaguar whose beautifully engineered body was being shaken and rattled by the rough surface of the gravel road. He had been at a dinner party celebrating an old mate's fiftieth birthday and had decided to leave after it, rather than waiting until the following morning as his friends had urged him to do. He wanted to be home before the weekend and he would like to get a good few miles under his belt before taking a bed in a hotel for the night to break his journey. After leaving Clarence he had taken the wrong turn-off and blamed the error on his lack of concentration rather than on the effect of the number of drinks he had downed at the party.

It wasn't until the sealed bitumen surface gave way to unsealed gravel and dirt twenty miles outside of Clarence that he realised his mistake. By then he thought it wasn't worth his while turning back to take the correct turn onto the Pacific Highway, where he could glide along by the coast on the bitumen surface all the way to Sydney.

He and his car would have to suffer eighty miles on this godforsaken road, bouncing around countless bends on their way up the mountain range. Huge eucalyptus trees, towering on either side of the road, created areas of impenetrable blackness by blocking out the moonlight. He took swigs of whisky from a bottle by his side to take his mind off the indignities his Jaguar was experiencing. So far he hadn't seen another single vehicle going in either direction. He hoped he wouldn't fall asleep at the wheel before he reached Tamworth, his revised first stop. He had originally hoped to make it to Scone, but realised he wouldn't be able to stay awake that long. His eyelids were becoming more reluctant to open again after each increasingly lingering, sensuous blink.

A ghost appeared in front of him, waving its arms as if to flag him down. It was so close he had no option but to drive straight through it, expecting it to feel as if he were passing through smoke. It gave him a jolt to hear a loud thud. The car barely reacted to the impact and he drove on. Who would have thought a ghost would be composed of such solid matter? He hoped it hadn't dented his new fender.

It wasn't until a few miles further on he realised his front offside headlight wasn't working. That bloody ghost must have smashed it. Not a real ghost, of course. He was a rationalist who didn't believe in such things. But if he did believe in them, this road on this night would be the perfect setting for them to manifest themselves. The only thing that was missing was a howling wind. Most likely what he had actually hit was a grey wallaby. The waving arms bit he must have imagined as wallabies had such short little forearms. He should go back and check that the creature wasn't lying wounded by the side of the road. It would be the decent thing to do: to put it out of its misery if it was still there and hadn't managed to hop away. There were two problems with that aspiration – he didn't know how to put an animal out of its misery, and by now he had travelled so far away from the site of the impact that he didn't think he would be able to find it again in the dark if he went back to look for it. All the gloomy bends lined by gloomy trees looked alike.

With the offside light missing he was going to have to take care not to end up in a ditch. He took another sip of whisky and began to sing "You Are My Heart's Delight" to sharpen his concentration.

CHAPTER 34

Dan woke to find the covers on Nell's side of the bed thrown back, and the sheets cold to the touch. He turned up the wick of the kerosene lamp beside his bed so that he could see the face of his watch. It was half an hour past midnight.

He checked the rooms of the house with the aid of the lamp, and then the garden with the help of a half moon, all the while calling Nell's name softly so as not to wake the kids. Hearing no answer and finding no sign of her, he dressed and ran down the track as far as the mailbox. No white shape in the distance in either direction along the road. God knows how long ago it had been since she left or what direction she had taken.

He returned to the barn to fetch a bridle to catch Troubadour who turned out not to be in the yard where he should have been, ready for any emergency. The top slip rail was off. The horse must have knocked it off by pushing it up and out. Jumping over the remaining two lower ones would not have been a problem for him. The bugger was getting too clever for his own good. Dan grabbed a cob of corn and went into the paddock, calling, "Kip, kip, kip." He passed dark shapes of cows as he went forward, walking into nettles and thistles, tripping over tussocks, all the while calling "Kip, kip, kip".

The bastard never comes when he's called, he thought. Why would he come now when it's so vital? I'm wasting precious time. It's only in the movies that horses come up and nuzzle their masters, dropping their heads and almost putting on the bridle themselves. All the horses on this farm take off when they see a man with a bridle approaching. We have to bloody well corner them in the yard and keep our bloody arms out and they still push past, leaving us standing there like bloody idiot scarecrows.

Troubadour appeared from the side and made a snatch for the cob. Dan held on to it and reached out to put the reins around the animal's neck. Troubadour jerked up his head with a snort and cantered away into the darkness.

Dan's gut felt as if it would strangle itself with rage and frustration and swell into his neck. "You miserable bloody mongrel," he shouted after the stallion. "I'll teach you a lesson you'll never forget when I catch you, you bastard of an excuse for an animal." He stood, feeling helpless. "Nell, where are you now?" He turned in circles, trying to penetrate the darkness in which he stood, even though he knew she would not have come in this direction. There was no sound of distant hooves. "I'll blow your bloody brains out, you useless bloody bastard," he shouted, repeating a string of curses as he stumbled back to the barn and threw the bridle in through the door. With a rising sense of panic, exacerbated by the time he had lost, he untied his dog Cactus, glad of her company, hoping she would be of some use, and ran down the track to the roadside, where he stood undecided, not knowing which direction to choose.

"Please, God, let me make the right decision."

He chose to turn left, heading south, as that was the route Nell had marginally favoured up until now.

He ran for two miles uphill until his heartbeat boomed in his ears and his windpipe was scorched and he was forced to pull up to catch his breath. From the minute he began to run uphill he kept imagining Nell heading downhill in the opposite direction, resulting in their getting further apart with every step he took.

God damn Troubadour. Dan agonised that if that bastard hadn't got out of the yard or had come when he was called he would have travelled a lot further and faster than he had, and surely would have found Nell by now.

The conviction that Nell had gone in the opposite direction became so strong that Dan turned at the three-mile mark and retraced his steps. The downhill slant was a relief to his protesting muscles. When he reached his mailbox he didn't go up to the house to check if she had returned in the meantime, as no vehicle travelling in either direction had passed him on the road so he could only conclude that Nell had not been intercepted and rescued along the way.

In this darkness on this unsealed road it would be easy to trip on a protruding rock or take a false step into a pothole. He hoped that Nell had had some kind of minor accident and was at this minute sitting by the side of the road with nothing more seriously wrong with her than a sprained ankle.

Though he was confident that he knew every stone and dip in the road, he found himself confused in his orientation and at times mistaking the exact section of the road he was on. He jogged on for what he knew was five miles, as signalled by the roadside milestone that he knew so well, before having to stop to give the painful stitch in his side time to unknot.

By now he was convinced that Nell had turned south as he had originally guessed and if he hadn't changed his mind and come back prematurely at the three-mile mark he surely would have caught up with her by now.

He looked up the hill and saw the moonlight shining on the tin roof of the shack that belonged to his solitary bachelor neighbour, Bluey, who didn't encourage visitors. Dan was too far gone to care about encouragement. Bluey owned a Chev and that was something Dan could do with right now. He found the path to the house between blackberry bushes and banged on the front door, calling out until Bluey finally opened it. He was carrying a kerosene lamp and was fully dressed. There was no need to tell him what the matter was as he had been one of the people who had found Nell on one of her rambles and had brought her back home.

"Take the car, mate. The keys are in it, but the battery might be flat. Haven't been out in a while." The neighbours joked that Bluey's car had only five hundred miles on the clock after a four-year period. "Hold on till I come out and give you a push."

With Cactus in the boot, Dan drove south along the road, the direction he had initially taken when he had stopped at the three-mile stage. He drove eight miles from his mailbox this time, wishing the car was Troubadour. With the car he was afraid to stop at intervals to check the gullies for fear the engine might cut out and he wouldn't be able to start it again with the battery so low and the car going uphill. And he couldn't drive too near the edge for fear of skidding in the loose gravel and ending up in a ditch. If he were on Troubadour he could stay closer to the edges on either side, zig-zagging between them, to get a good look at the gullies in case Nell had slipped and fallen into one of them. Cactus, running along behind them instead of being stuck in the boot, would be quicker to sniff out Nell, quicker than he would be to spot her in the darkness.

He expected to see her resting on a milestone while she waited for her energy to return, ready for a further few miles of fruitless searching, but he didn't see her and he didn't see anyone else on foot, on horseback or in a vehicle. Not that he expected to at this time of night.

Back again at his mailbox, he continued and covered ten miles to the north and, starting at a crossroads three miles from the farm, five miles east on the road towards Redmundo.

He considered repeating the pattern, adding extra miles to each distance, but by now he was wondering if Nell had left the road at some juncture and was wandering along bridle tracks, or worse still had gone into the rough bush and become disorientated. He could imagine her stumbling around in circles in some wild part of the country, becoming entangled in the undergrowth and panicking at the realisation that she was lost.

He drove the car back to his neighbour's and left it outside the gate and walked home, praying that Nell would be there when he got there, returned only minutes earlier by an unknown traveller coming from the opposite direction.

There was no strange car coming down the track and no Nell in any part of the house.

He would wait for daybreak before searching again and this time would round up that bastard Troubadour and set out on him followed by Cactus. With that pair he couldn't fail to find her even if she had strayed far from the road.

At around five o'clock he fell asleep in the rocking chair beside the combustion stove.

At six he was woken by the sun shining in his eyes and by sound of horses' hooves.

She's here, he thought in a daze. Troubadour has brought her back.

He went to the front door. A sunburnt drover was at the gate, seated on one horse and holding the reins of another which had a swag draped over its saddle.

Bluey was with the drover. He told Dan later he hadn't been able to sleep after Dan's visit and had saddled up at daybreak and ridden off looking for Nell.

"I'm sorry, Dan. It's Nell," said Bluey, motioning towards the swag on the drover's packhorse. "This bloke found her. Hit by a car by the look of it."

The drover dismounted, removed his hat and opened the swag to reveal Nell in her white nightdress with her beautiful hair, usually caught up in a tidy bun, hanging down in wild, tangled loops.

The three men gently lifted her broken body from the saddle and took her inside and laid her on her side of the bed. As Dan crossed her arms over her breast he noticed that her flesh was still warm.

Still warm at six o'clock in the morning?

"Where was she?"

"Beside the culvert but not in the water."

Dan managed to choke down the taste of sickness in his mouth. He had driven past the culvert twice, once there, and once on the way back. It was four miles south. He had stopped one mile short of it when he was on foot the first time.

Still warm? How to bear it?

If he had been on Troubadour he would have been close enough to the edge of the road to look down into the culvert. Even if he had not been able to see Nell in the dark, the dog would have found her and alerted him, barking until Dan responded.

He could have saved her. To think he had chosen that direction initially but had turned back too soon.

The drover apologised for not being able to delay, but he had an inexperienced kid with him and the cattle he was in charge of would by now be all over the road, so he had to leave immediately and get the herd going in a controlled way before they caused an accident.

Dan wanted him to stay so he could question him further but, seeing he was intent on leaving, he asked him the hard question without any preamble. "Was she still alive when you found her?"

"No, mate. We weren't in time. I did a thorough check. Otherwise I wouldn't have moved her."

"Stay with Nell, Bluey, and don't let the kids in," Dan said after the drover left. "Zita will be getting up soon." He took the shotgun from the corner of the room and inserted two cartridges into the barrels.

"Don't do anything stupid," said Bluey, startled.

"I won't," said Dan as he left. "I just want to give the bastard a fright."

"I'll do your dairy. My lot can wait."

Dan was already heading down the paddock and was too far away to hear the offer.

"Kip, kip, kip," he called.

Zita dashed into the kitchen in her usual rush to get tea and toast ready for her little band of workers before they set off for the morning session at the dairy and stopped when she saw Bluey standing awkwardly at the stove.

"G'day," Bluey said, staring at the floor.

She was glad she had put on a dressing gown, even though her full-length flannelette nightie, like her mother's, couldn't be more modest with its high neck, long sleeves and thick fabric.

"Has Mum gone off again?" she asked, trying to hide the feeling of humiliation that she felt every time she thought of her mother's making a show of herself wandering around in public in her nightie. The fact that poor Nell didn't know what she was doing elicited pity but didn't make the shame any less painful.

"She's back," said the old bachelor, turning towards the stove, but not quickly enough to prevent Zita from seeing tears spilling down his cheeks.

At the sight of the tears, she felt an electric tremor shoot through her entire body, turning her bones to putty.

"Where is she?"

Bluey made a choking sound as he tried to answer but was unable to get the words out.

"Is she in the bedroom? Where's Dad?"

Bluey, still turned away, wiped his nose on his sleeve before answering with difficulty. "Dan said you can't go into the bedroom. He's gone down the paddock."

Zita, bent over with pain and weakness, stumbled out to the hall and into her parents' bedroom. Bluey followed, having no idea whether he should try to stop her or not – it was not in his nature to assert his will.

Zita saw the white-faced, motionless, bloodied figure of her mother on the bed.

"Don't let the kids in, Bluey. Oh, God, Mum, what happened to you? Keep the kids out, Bluey," she sobbed. "Mum, what are we going to do without you? What have you gone and done? Mum, I'm so sorry."

Zita experienced a sensation of tumbling out of control down a steep hill littered with loose stones, skidding and sliding, her flailing arms not able to help her keep her balance as she slipped head first into a black chasm where she could not find Nell and where she ended up crashing against a wall of rock and passing out.

Bluey did not know what to do in the face of the scene of grief in front of him. He backed out of the room and went back to the kitchen. He wondered if he had imagined it or had Zita actually said something that he thought was extremely strange: "Mum, why didn't I listen to Wombat?"

CHAPTER 35

Two priests from St John's drove Kevin and Mick over to the funeral at Redmundo. Cheryl made the decision that Alison, Hanna and Jack were too young to attend, and sacrificed her own attendance to look after them. Zita had no idea about the protocol of funerals and was willing to be advised by her. Dan left all the details to the undertaker and to Father Daly. Zita brought Larry and Stevie with her and sat with them, Mick, Kevin and Dan in the front pew. The aunts sat behind them.

The little wooden church could not accommodate the crowds of all denominations who came from all parts of the district, so many stood outside in the grounds in the sunshine, bowing their heads while the Requiem Mass in Latin was being said inside.

Wombat sat down the back, wishing he hadn't listened to Zita. She was only a kid. Why had he taken any notice of her? He should have given the note to Nell rather than to Zita. If he had, she might still be alive. She would have stopped looking for Dolores and wouldn't have been out wandering the road in the middle of the night, leaving herself open to disaster. She thought so much of Dr Carmody that she might have been happy to know that Dolores was in his care and that she had brought joy to his previously unhappy wife.

Zita could not forgive herself for not listening to Wombat. Had she believed deep down, like some of the people of Redmundo, that the fire he had fallen into at the age of four had damaged his brain as well as his face and that he was not in fact the full shilling? Her getting to know him, and seeing how well he could spell and write, should have convinced her otherwise, but the thought must have been there all the time, overriding her personal experience.

And even if Wombat were wrong, telling the lie could have made a difference to Nell if she believed it to be true. It could have saved her life.

Dan was thinking of the open gate and Troubadour down the paddock backing away from him when he approached with the bridle. He was convinced that he would have found Nell in the culvert if he had been on Troubadour.

Father Daly said in his homily that Nell was a virtuous woman and her price was above rubies. Dan thought that the priest had seriously undervalued her.

Zita wished she hadn't bombarded Nell with questions on the day that ended with the accident. Three times she had quizzed her, approaching the same topic from different directions and even saying the word 'Dolores' out loud. Who knew if all that prodding had been the catalyst that had sent her out searching in the middle of the night? The irony wasn't lost on her that, looking back, the answers Nell had given indicated that what Wombat had said was true.

Dan tried to console himself with the thought that Nell was now happy, reunited in heaven with her infant daughter Dolores. It was the only positive belief he could summon up to give himself any bit of solace.

Zita looked at her younger brother sitting beside her in his school blazer, and thought of her own blazer hanging in the girls' wardrobe, not likely to be worn again until it was Hanna's turn to go off to St Mary's in ten years' time. It would probably be half eaten by moths by then. She thought of the shining hospital environment she had hoped to inhabit during her internship and compared it to the cow bails covered in mud mixed with cow dung and wondered bitterly how she could bear to see her chances lost and how she would fill in the years on the farm until Alison was reared.

Wombat did not queue up with the rest of the congregation to file past the family to offer personal condolences, so Zita had to seek him out. She told him she was sorry for losing her temper with him, that she wished she had listened to him, and that she hoped he would continue to come out to the farm.

He looked relieved, and nodded that he would.

After the funeral lunch, supplied by the ladies in the CWA rooms, Kevin and Mick were the first to leave, driven off back to St John's by the two priests. Dan went down to the pub with a group of men, and Zita, Stevie and Larry took a lift home with a neighbour in time for the afternoon session at the dairy. Cheryl dropped the three youngest back and said that she had to give Jack a good slap as he wouldn't do as he was told, Hanna had whinged all the time and Alison had played up.

Zita felt hurt and embarrassed to hear that. "Alison doesn't normally play up," she said.

"You're spoiling her, feeding her every time she cries, that's the problem." Cheryl at last had a chance to say something she had been dying to say for years, and became slightly breathless with the impatience to get it said. "She needs discipline or she'll run rings around you. I didn't let her make a fool out of me today, I can tell you that. She gave in and cried herself to sleep. She learnt quick enough. You should feed her every four hours on the dot and nothing in between. She'll soon cop on."

Zita said she didn't know that that was what you were supposed to do. "Mum didn't like to hear a baby cry," she said to justify herself.

"Your mother was too soft-hearted by far, a slave to her kids. Small babies are full of cunning. I seen it time and time again." Cheryl's eyes were glowing with fervour, convinced that Zita was young enough and uncertain enough to be persuaded to follow the new ways. "Alison needs to be shown who's boss."

Zita, changed back into her work clothes, adjusted the flue-dials of the stove so that smoke wouldn't billow into the room while the door was open. She poked the embers with an iron bar and, so that the heat would be at the right level when she came back from the dairy to cook potatoes to go with the lamb casserole that a neighbour had left in earlier, she shoved in three pieces of split wood. They didn't fit.

She lifted her rubber boot to kick them in by force, but they didn't budge. She took out one piece, readjusted the other two and replaced the third. Larry came in and saw her in danger of overbalancing with the force of the impact she was making, kicking at the three pieces of wood jutting out from the fire box. The two little ones, waiting beside the pram in which Alison lay crying, backed away from her, staring at their big sister's rage with apprehension. Larry walked over in front of Zita, took out one piece of wood, fitted in the two pieces easily and closed the door, damped down the flue, and took outside the offending piece, hot at one end, and put it on the concrete path where it wouldn't set anything alight. Zita watched, tight-lipped and defeated, and gave the outside of the stove a series of whacks with the iron bar so that chips of enamel broke off, ruining its beautiful surface. It was the first piece of damage the stove had ever suffered.

Stevie had already started the diesel milking machine and had two cows hooked up by the time she arrived at the dairy with Larry and the little ones. Jack and Hanna were supposed to keep the flies off Alison in her pram, but they had a fight and stomped off in different directions. Zita felt too tired and dispirited to chase after them. She would sort them out tomorrow.

She pulled up a stool in the third bail, positioned a bucket between her knees, ready to coax Tulip to let down her milk before attaching the machine. She turned her face towards the cow's warm, comforting flank to hide from the others the tears of helplessness, temper and grief she could no longer hold back.

She felt surrounded by the cold absence of Nell who was now lost for all eternity. Today she was lost and tomorrow and every day after that she was lost. How to cope with the everlasting emptiness?

Zita would now be forced into becoming the substitute mother to all those children until Alison was old enough to fend for herself. Twelve years. The terror of the prospect had her pushing her face into the cow's side to muffle her heaving sobs.

She thought of Dr Carmody and how much her mother had thought of him and how much she loved to talk about him, and all Zita could feel for him was a savage hatred.

CHAPTER 36

Cat had never thought that Nell was good enough for Dan, brought up as she was in the sticks and leaving school at the age of twelve, though one would never guess that, judging by the way she spoke. As it turned out, she must have had brains as all the children were bright and that brightness couldn't have been inherited solely from Dan. Eventually Cat had to give credit where credit was due as Nell turned out to be a steadfast, hardworking, selfless wife and mother. In fact, the only bad turn she had ever done was to prevent Cat from adopting Alison.

Now that Nell was gone, Cat could see no reason why she shouldn't renew her request to Dan. He wouldn't have refused her the first time if Nell hadn't put her oar in. She would be doing the family a favour. A young girl like Zita would be pleased to get the baby off her hands.

"You have no reason to refuse me now," Cat said to Dan the morning after the funeral. "I could pack her up and be off in an hour and that would be one less person for you to worry about. You know I'll take good care of her."

Dan had been delivered home late the previous night by two neighbours who were proud to have been his guardians for the day.

In the condition he was in he was in no fit state to talk, but Cat couldn't contain her impatience until a later time.

He had never felt worse in his life. The hangover was a minor thing and would pass. His grief, guilt and outrage wouldn't. He wished Cat hadn't brought up that subject again.

"I never doubted you, Cat, but I already told you I can't let her go."

"But that was because of Nell. Now that she's gone . . ."

"Now that she's gone, how can I let Alison go? She has lost her mother and her twin. How can she lose her father and her seven brothers and sisters as well?"

"She won't lose them. She can still visit. It's not as if I'll keep you all a secret from her. I can give her everything. Zita will find it hard enough to cope with all those kids and the dairy and the garden without having to cope with a baby on top of all that."

Zita, sitting motionless at the treadle sewing machine behind the open door, on hearing that there was a possibility she might be relieved of Alison, felt as if she had been plugged into a battery that might activate a light that might dispel some of the fog of hopelessness that was clouding over her darkened brain. Was it really possible? She had resigned herself to the prospect of guiding Alison through the stages of growing up, but now that there was a chance she might escape all of that, she felt gratitude towards Cat.

If she had a sister around her age who could share the burden with her, she might not find the prospect of the next twelve years so daunting, but she was surrounded in the family by males and her only two sisters were still infants.

"She has managed up until now," Dan said in a voice that did not invite contradiction. "Nell trained her well and our neighbour Cheryl is a great help. Zita is a very capable girl."

"I can see that but the authorities might have something to say about a girl as young as that having to leave school and look after five young children."

"That won't happen. Zita is at the age when she can legally leave school, and she's very competent, so there will be no reason for anyone to be pointing the finger. It's a private family matter. Nothing to do with anyone else."

"There's a long, long road ahead," said Cat, making one last effort to get Dan to change his mind. "If Alison becomes legally mine, Zita will be free two years earlier, which at the age she will be then will be significant."

"That's not a good enough reason."

Not for you, perhaps, brother dear, but you're not a female. "Think of how Alison will benefit. Do it for her sake. She will inherit everything that Fritz has worn himself out for, working in that blasted shop all the hours God sends."

"That can't be a consideration for me."

Zita, getting up from the machine and emerging from behind the door, said before she had time to stop herself, "Let her go, Dad." She wanted to say, 'Let Hanna go as well,' but didn't dare. With the two youngest out of the way she thought she might have some chance of facing the future without giving in to despair.

Dan and Cat both turned sharply to look towards her. They had not realised she was there.

"It would be the best for everyone," Zita continued, surprising herself with her bravery in speaking up. "Aunty Cat would make a wonderful mother."

"Thank you, Zita. It's nice to hear you say that. I think I would as well, if only I could get the chance."

"I've said my last word on the matter," said Dan. "I don't want to hear another word on it from either of you."

He left the room and Cat, too upset to talk, also left but went in a different direction.

Zita went over to the cooling safe and took out a bottle of milk, lifted the sleeping Alison out of the pram, and rushed to follow her aunt who was heading for her car. Cat turned when she heard Zita behind her and asked her what she wanted.

"Take her," Zita said, handing her the baby.

Cat took her without thinking and looked lovingly at her through her tears.

"I can't," said Cat. "Not without your father's consent."

"Please," said Zita. "He doesn't understand."

"I know he doesn't."

"If you take off now you'll get a good head start and he won't be able to catch up with you."

"It wouldn't do any good. You don't know your father like I do.

He'd be on the next train to Sydney and he wouldn't come back without Alison. I'm really sorry, Zita," said Cat before handing back the baby. "I would love to have her more than you would like to get rid of her."

That isn't possible, thought Zita, as she stood with Alison in her arms, watching her aunt drive away.

CHAPTER 37

There were a number of war widows with one child or two – some itinerant workers, some local – who, during the following months, found their way out to the Hogan farm to offer to housekeep for Dan. They had been touched by the plight of a relatively young widower left to rear eight children, they said. The fact that Dan was a fine-looking man might have had something to do with their generous terms. Aware of his straitened circumstances they offered to work without payment, happy to accept the protection of his name and his home as payment enough. The number of Hogan children was not considered a deterrent. They could be handled.

Zita was not convinced by the generous offers. She reckoned that it was matrimony they were ultimately seeking. She was as horrified as Dan was to think any of these women, all worthy enough in their own ways, were deluded enough to think they could take Nell's place, even though by taking it they would set Zita free to go back to school and fulfil her ambitions. Dan was terrified of them and disappeared down the paddock as soon as he saw one driving up the track to apply for the job that had not been offered. He had every intention of staying loyal to Nell's memory by never marrying again and, knowing his strength of will, Zita could not see him changing his mind.

She had not forgotten how, in her despairing state, she had wanted to let Alison and Hanna go. She had not changed her mind, but it didn't matter what she thought if Dan wouldn't change his.

"One thing I would like to have," Dan said to Zita, "is a copy of those photos the Irish doctor took before he left."

Zita's head, bent over a sock she was darning, shot up. "Photos? I didn't know they actually existed. Mum mentioned something about them but I thought she was rambling."

Zita had already been lamenting the lack of images of her mother. The only ones she had seen were the few taken of Nell on her wedding day.

"He came out to see us a few days before he left and brought presents for the kids. Very generous. Insisted we pose for a family photo. Your mother was really happy then, I remember. That's why I'd love to have those photos. It was after that she began to go downhill."

"Is there any way you could contact him and ask for some copies?"

"He didn't leave an address. I wouldn't know how to go about finding him. Not that it turned out to be a family group anyway with three of you away at school at the time, but it's the closest we'll ever get to one now."

"Was Alison in them?"

"Yes. She was a month old at the time. The doctor said he wanted her centre stage on your mother's lap." Dan had not mentioned Nell by name since her death, just as he continued to avoid saying the name 'Dolores'. "In actual fact he took a close-up of her."

"Wasn't that a bit odd?"

"Not really. His child was the same age and he delivered them both, so he was bound to have had a soft spot for Alison."

"It was a pity he didn't leave an address."

"It was. I asked Marie Dawson if she had it but she didn't, and if she didn't, no one else would. I don't think we'll ever get to see those photos, unfortunately."

Zita tried to imagine what had happened on the day Alison's twin was stolen. Dr Carmody could have given his wife the wrong baby by mistake or he could have done it deliberately. Because he was alone Zita thought it would have been easy to make the switch without anyone's noticing. Or he could have handed his wife her stillborn child, and the wife could have swapped it for a live one, and he, knowing that, might have decided to keep his mouth shut to protect her. Either way, Zita was convinced that he knew.

To find out just how much he knew, she questioned Wombat in detail – she asking the questions and he writing down the answers. Wombat showed his relief that she believed him at last, though he felt it was all too late.

Yes, Mrs Carmody was relaxed on the morning they were leaving; Dr Carmody was agitated. Mrs Carmody handed him the baby, and kissed him, thanking him for bringing her luck. He didn't know what she meant by that. It was then he saw that the baby Mary Anne was an exact replica of Alison and had mouthed the word 'Twin'. Dr Carmody was the only one who knew what he was saying. He abruptly grabbed the baby out of Wombat's arms and herded him to the van like a sheepdog, talking nineteen to the dozen and acting nervy – not his usual calm self. Thanked him for doing the garden and repeating, "Good man, yourself" over and over, and opening the door for him and almost pushing him into the driver's seat. Couldn't get rid of him fast enough, whereas Mrs Carmody would have been happy to stand there all day long, proudly showing off Mary Anne to any passing townsperson, and thinking Wombat had said 'Wind' rather than 'Twin'. If it were she who had taken the baby she would not have kept her composure in the way she had.

At the end of the quizzing, Zita and Wombat looked at one another, both concluding that Dr Carmody was guilty, and that the mix-up had not been the result of an error committed in a moment of confusion.

Alison was given her immunisation shots by the bush nurse at Ober rather than by Dr Merton in Redmundo to make sure that anyone who had seen a lot of Mary Anne during her first month of life did not get to see Alison.

CHAPTER 38

Christmas and the six weeks' summer holidays came and went. Mick and Kevin took their suitcases down to the mailbox. Zita looked out the kitchen window to watch them catch the bus. She felt worse when she saw the bus pulling away than she had felt on the day of Nell's funeral.

She felt as if she might die of loneliness and envy during the following year.

At the dinner table each night Dan, listless and dull-eyed, might make a comment about rainfall or fencing, and Zita might mention the number of gallons sent to the creamery that week. Dan would ask after Alison, thank Zita for the nice meal, listen to the news and then go off to bed every night at seven thirty, taking the previous day's *Sydney Morning Herald* with him. The boys listened to the wireless if the battery wasn't flat until nine and then they went to bed, leaving Zita alone thinking of her friends at St Mary's, who were now beginning their fourth year, the year when you became special. A small class of fifteen was all that remained of the seventy who started in first year. The relationship with the nuns during fourth year became less formal and verged on the friendly.

She received a letter from Reverend Mother.

We were sorry to hear of your family's sad loss, and pray every day that God will vouchsafe you an acceptance of His Holy Will. All the Sisters are praying for the happy repose of the soul of your beloved mother. May her soul and all the souls of the faithful departed, through the mercy of God, rest in peace.

Your father has written to inform us that you will not be returning to St Mary's.

So it's final, then, thought Zita, who every now and then thought that her situation must be temporary, that it was all a bad dream and she would one day wake up with Nell alive and well, and her own case packed ready to go back to school.

You are a great loss to the school, but we all must bow to God's Holy Will, following the example of His Blessed Mother who said the inspiring words, "Thy will be done."

All of your teachers were confident that you would win a Commonwealth Scholarship that would lead you on to greater things, but God has other plans for you, and only He comprehends the reasons. Knowing your character as I do, I know you will rise to the challenge and not be found wanting.

We think Our Lord has chosen a heavy cross for you, while giving you the strength to bear it so that you will attain a higher place in heaven.

May God bless you. We will remember you and all the family in our daily prayers.

Yours in Christ,

Mother M Gabriel

Zita wrote to her two best friends and, to fill up a page, mentioned babies, laundry, school lunches, cows and crops. They wrote back. One of their classmates had got into trouble for smuggling an uncensored letter home with one of the day pupils and had been struck off the Honour Board; they were learning a new song in four parts, 'Australian Sunrise', written especially for their choir; they had a new maths teacher, Sister Ambrose; the movie they saw that week was *Knock on Any Door* and they all thought John Derek was gorgeous and some of them were in tears at the end; Caroline got maximum marks in the Intermediate Certificate and Lorraine was made captain of the netball team that included four seniors; a general science course would be introduced in the following year and a laboratory was being built in readiness.

Zita imagined writing to her friends and describing the scene in the kitchen the previous night, when she was preparing dinner for seven while the baby cried, Hanna grizzled, the pumpkin boiled dry, and there was no wood in the wood box when she went to take out a piece. Larry and Stevie were wrestling and they bumped into Jack who was carrying a kerosene lamp from the bench to the table. The glass globe toppled off the lamp and smashed on the floor. Jack looked stricken, knowing how precious the globes were. Larry and Stevie hung their heads, pretending to be sorry, but burst into periodic, uncontrollable explosions of laughter. Zita felt that because of her lack of authority all their lives were falling apart, and she was on the verge of demanding that Dan ring up Cat and ask her to come up and fetch Alison (and Hanna?), but the habit of respect for him was too deeply ingrained and his own suffering so great that she controlled herself, following the Virgin Mary's example of 'keeping everything to herself'.

Zita thought of the boarders, tired after a long day of lessons, sport, choir, friendship and fun, sleeping undisturbed in the spotless dormitories in St Mary's, recharging their batteries for an equally interesting day to follow.

She wrote back, asking questions and commenting on their news, making no mention of the irritations and worries of her life, aware that her letters must be boring to them, as they were boring even to her and it was her life she was writing about.

They answered with fewer details in a subsequent letter, and fewer again after that. Were they beginning to sense that she was now too far removed to catch the references or were they being tactful by not including any of the details about lessons or personalities that they must know she was so hungry to hear about? In the end, it was she who took the decision not to write any more. What could she possibly have to say that would interest them?

Zita tried to follow the example of the Virgin Mary even though their lives were too different to compare. Mary had only one child, and that child was the Son of God and presumably gave no trouble, helping His 'father' Joseph in the carpenter's shop for most of the time, staying out from under her feet. Mary did not have to labour outside the house, so presumably was not as exhausted as Zita was by the end of every day.

CHAPTER 39

1947

Seven years after he had first starting coming to the Hogans' farm and six years after the death of Nell, Wombat asked Zita to marry him. He wrote the proposal on a notepad and handed it to her, closely watching her face while she read it. She was twenty years of age by then and he was thirty-two.

Zita's face did not light up with pleasure after she registered the significance of the offer, but instead took on the expression of a tragic heroine.

"I can't marry you, Wombat," she said quickly, to take away that heart-breaking look of hope in his eyes. "Not because I don't love you, because I do, but because the family is still young. I have a long way to go. Alison has only just turned six."

Wombat extricated the notebook from Zita and wrote on it that Dan might marry again – there were a lot of women interested – or that he might employ a housekeeper, either way leaving Zita free to lead a life of her own.

"I know he won't marry again," said Zita. "He intends to stay faithful to Mum until the end. He can't afford a housekeeper and, even if he could, she wouldn't know how to handle the livestock or run the dairy. Dad and the kids would all hate an outsider coming in.

It's out of the question. I've accepted God's will that it's my responsibility. There's no one else. I'm doing this for Mum. I know she's looking down at me and giving me strength."

Wombat wrote that he would wait. Zita said she didn't want him to. Wombat said they could marry, and she could continue with her household duties and he could drive out from town to stay with her at the farm at weekends. Zita said she didn't think Dan would agree to that.

"*Are you just making excuses?*" Wombat wrote.

"No," said Zita. "I'm sorry, but I can't marry you or anyone else. I'd like us to continue just as we are."

Wombat, deflated, shook his head, collected his things, looked around sadly, nodded goodbye, and left with the dignity of a warrior chief going into exile.

Zita sensed that he would not come back. This time she wouldn't ask him to as she had nothing worthwhile to offer him. He had accurately read her attitude as love, and would believe that it was his burnt face and lack of speech that had led her to reject him. He might later reinterpret her actions and her words, not believing that she had ever loved him. He might become disillusioned when he looked back on the years they had worked as a team, thinking she had led him on solely because he was so useful around the place, and not because of any love she had for him.

Zita's real reason for refusing Wombat's proposal, plus any others that she might receive from anyone else in the future, was her determined resolve never, ever to have children of her own under any circumstances. The idea of childbirth was abhorrent to her, associating it as she did with danger, sorrow and death. Babies, if they did survive, were little parasites who sucked out the lifeblood of their mothers. She didn't think it fair to deprive a man of his chance to pass on his family name, but she also thought it would be unwise of her to explain her reasons for fear of being condemned as unnatural.

Alison missed Wombat, who had always been kind to her during her early years, in contrast to Zita, who hadn't, and asked why he had stopped coming to the farm.

Dan had already guessed what had happened between Wombat

175

and Zita, having noted the signs of mutual devotion over the years and then the abrupt departure, the subsequent non-appearance of Wombat, and Zita's unhappiness.

To save the scarlet-faced Zita from having to make up an excuse, he quickly answered for her. "He's helping out the nuns instead of us, now that the war effort is over," he said.

"The war was over two years ago," said Jack.

"I know, but people were starving after it ended, so primary produce was as important as ever."

"But he was always helping Zita," said Jack.

Dan gave him a look to silence him. "Not always. He was a great help to me. Anyway, the nuns need him more than we do as they aren't strong enough to do the heavy work around the convent grounds and they rely on volunteers."

That night Alison heard Zita crying quietly in the dark in the other bed in the girls' room. Hanna was asleep so Alison, who always took a long time to quieten her mind, was the only one who heard her.

The nightly crying went on for weeks.

Alison tried to stay out of Zita's way to avoid her sharp tongue which had become sharper since Wombat had stopped calling, and was directed specifically at her. She didn't think she behaved any worse than Hanna and Jack – in fact she tried to be perfect to defuse Zita's crabbiness – but it made no difference, and she couldn't wait to run off to school every morning to get out of Zita's way.

Santa Claus, with the help of Aunty Cat, brought the two young girls a china doll each, which was a change from the colouring books and pencils they usually received at Christmas time. Alison was the more delighted as she had repeatedly asked for a doll but, at the age of six, had given up hope that she would ever receive one. She lined a cardboard shoebox with one of her old baby shawls, placed the doll in it, read it a story and then rocked it to sleep. The doll's eyes were supposed to shut when it was placed in a horizontal position, but Priscilla's eyes stuck and had to be closed by hand.

Hanna didn't care about dolls. She grew tired of hers after a few hours and abandoned it out on the verandah. She liked boys' things like catapults and billy-carts.

There was a rush to get everyone ready for Mass on Christmas morning, with the usual search for head coverings for the girls. "A handkerchief will have to do," said Zita to Hanna, anxious about the time. Alison had already found a scarf and hung on to it.

While waiting for the others she looked out the back window and saw her two older brothers out at the wood heap lining up the two dolls on a wooden block. As they smashed the dolls' heads with an axe, they laughed in a loud, jeering way.

"Zita!" Alison shouted. "Stevie and Larry are smashing up our dolls."

"Don't bother me with that now. Come on, hurry up. We can't keep Dad waiting."

Squashed into the back seat of an old Wolseley that Dan had been given by his sister Cat, Alison once again raised her voice to complain.

"You'll have to be quiet back there," said Zita. "Dad has to concentrate on the road."

Dan drove as if he were riding a horse – leaning into bends, and ducking to avoid overhanging branches that scraped along the roof of the car.

After Mass Alison finally gained Zita's attention. "Stevie and Larry smashed our dolls," she said.

"It wasn't us," said the hovering Larry. "The draught horses trod on them. I saw them."

"Don't worry. I'll get you some other ones," said Zita who always said those consoling words whenever something was ruined or lost, but she never did replace anything as there wasn't any money in the house to pay for such things. The Children's Allowance was earmarked for groceries only. If it wasn't for Santa, they'd never get anything nice.

A neighbour came over to speak to Zita and she moved away.

"They're only girls' things, anyway," said Larry in a matter-of-fact tone to Alison, with no trace of malice in his voice. "They're no use for anything, so stop upsetting Zita about it."

CHAPTER 40

Alison and Hanna stood around watching the new neighbours unpacking furniture and boxes of belongings. There was smoke already coming from the chimney of the house. The smiling woman, surrounded by seven young blonde girls, asked if they would like to come inside to help unwrap the small items. The girls ran in before she could change her mind as they had never seen the interior of the pretty house before, with its brick chimney, three stone steps and painted weatherboard exterior, and always wondered what it was like. The previous neighbours had been elderly, childless and withdrawn.

"Here's the silver cutlery. Will you put each piece in the right drawers?" she asked, explaining her system. "I'll do the china dinner service and tea set. Wedding presents. Had them for years and never put them on the table – too precious to use." She looked at the underside of a plate and said proudly, "Staffordshire."

After Alison finished the cutlery, she put the books into a set of shelves, and then helped Hanna store the preserving and jam jars with their matching lids in the pantry cupboard.

The smiling woman, who was called Mrs Kendall, opened a tin containing a sponge cake she had brought with her, and made tea from the kettle boiling on the stove. Her husband, a returned soldier who stammered as a result of the torture he had suffered in a Japanese POW camp during the war, joined them and the seven girls for tea. The ordinary cups for everyday use were made of pottery rather than china, but they still came with matching saucers, and everyone – even the two-year-old – was given one.

"Start as you mean to go on," the woman said.

Hanna and Alison were ill at ease and looked to the woman to see how to balance a cup, saucer and slice of cake all at the one time. They had never handled anything so light and springy as the sponge, though they knew instinctively not to mention that when they went home to Zita, who would consider airy, fluffy sponges too insubstantial to offer to working men.

A week later the two girls watched as twenty dairy cows, a mixture of Jersey and Guernsey, were herded into the newly built bails. The woman and the two eldest girls milked them all by hand as the milking machine hadn't yet been installed. Mr Kendall didn't have the patience for such tedious work as milking as he suffered from his nerves.

The third girl in the family matched Hanna in age and the fourth, Helen, matched Alison and was in her class at school. Alison was as drawn to the mother as she was to Helen and hung around her after she followed Helen home from school. Hanna was now old enough to work in the dairy, so had to go home rather than visit the Kendalls.

"You're making a nuisance of yourself at Kendalls' place," Zita said to Alison after the visits had been going on for several weeks.

Alison felt the injustice of the rebuke. Mrs Kendall had told her often what a little treasure she was.

"No, I'm not a nuisance," said Alison. "I help with the little ones and don't get in the way."

"There's plenty for you to do around here. And don't give me any back answers, Miss Smarty Pants."

Mrs Kendall was never cranky with her kids and always spoke to them in a friendly tone. Alison wanted to be with her all the time, and felt sad when she had to finally go home before dark to confront a resentful Zita.

Zita made a few initial courtesy visits to the new neighbours, but then stopped calling altogether. The warmth of Mrs Kendall's personality reminded her too much of Nell's, causing painful memories to resurface, robbing her days of any small pleasures the Kendalls might offer.

Kevin, after finishing secondary school, had sat for the means-tested annual Hanratty Scholarship set up by a wealthy past pupil of St John's to benefit a bright boy who would otherwise miss out on tertiary education, and won it. He went to Sydney University, boarding in a college there, and studied engineering. When Mick's turn came to finish school, he won a Teachers' College Scholarship which paid for tuition and board in return for a bond to teach for five years and went to the University of New England in Armidale.

If anyone was aware that Zita was between her two brothers in age and should by now be in third level, no one mentioned it.

Alison listened one day while Dan told a visiting neighbour how well Kevin and Mick were doing. Zita was at the sink, washing the dishes and not taking any part in the conversation.

That night Alison heard Zita crying in the dark.

CHAPTER 41

1948

Where was everyone?

Seven-year-old Alison was alone, standing in the fading light listening to the wind moaning through the high, dark pines clumped at the edge of the convent grounds.

When had all the other boarders slipped off? She hadn't heard the bell for tea, but they must have heard it, and run from the grounds into the refectory while she was standing in a daze, fearing the strangeness of all these kids she hadn't seen until yesterday swirling around playing games whose rules she didn't know.

She wished she was at home, not here in the convent in Redmundo where she had to stay for three weeks to prepare for her First Confession and First Holy Communion. She knew some parents from the bush prepared their own children for the sacraments, but she didn't have a mother and Dan had too high a regard for the divine skills of the nuns and priests to think that anyone else but anointed ones could do the job properly. First Communion day was one of the most significant days in a child's life, the Hogans had been told from the time Kevin, the eldest, had spent his three weeks in this same place, not fearful like Alison, but joining in all the sports with exuberance, making friends and not taking the religious instructions

181

too seriously. Since his time her sisters and brothers had taken their turns in pairs. She was the first one since Kevin to be sent in on her own.

Why had all the boarders run off without her? She stood looking at the brown carpet of pine needles under the trees, so alien to her who could identify only cedar, eucalyptus and acacia. Where was the familiar warm smell of cows and horses? Here in the convent it was the perfume of pine and sweet peas and lilies that permeated the grounds and the nearby church.

She had been here one whole day. That meant she had to live through two more weeks and six more days before she could go home again and return to the little bush school with its twelve pupils, three of them Hogans.

She thought of Zita with Jack and Hanna making their way home from the dairy. Dan, after a day's mustering, would be taking the saddle and bridle off Harmony. Zita would go into the kitchen and light the lamp and pour the milk into jugs and open the door of the kerosene refrigerator and put the jugs inside, moving containers around to make them fit, sloshing some milk over the sides during the process, impatient as ever to get the dinner over and done with. Hanna might this very minute be asking Zita when was Alison coming home and Zita would answer, 'Not long. Now stay out of my way until I get the dinner.'

Twenty more days? Alison didn't think she could last that long. She hung her head to hide her tears even though there was no one around to see them, and tried to hold in the sound of her sobs but they escaped with a prolonged honk. She didn't think she could go into the refectory for tea to sit with all those boarders she didn't know but who knew each other. She couldn't think how she could stop her pain long enough to find her way back through the cold, falling mist but she knew she couldn't stay in this spot all night. Funnel-web and trapdoor spiders might climb up her legs, a snake might slither over her body, bats might fly into her hair and a rat might try to gnaw at the new socks and shoes that she loved so much. She wanted to be at home in the warm kitchen with her father and older brothers who would protect her from all those creatures and keep her safe.

A figure approached her from the direction of the vegetable

garden. It was Wombat, the man with the burnt face who was kind to her when she was little but who hadn't visited the farm for a long time. He had stopped coming out after the war effort had ended and had begun to help the nuns instead. She ran to him and he dropped his bag of implements and lifted her up and she strangled him with her homesick arms and dampened his collar with her tears. He carried her out from the falling darkness, high in the air, up to the convent building and along the verandah with its twin electric lights showing the way.

Sister Philomena came out and said, "There you are, Alison. We were just about to send out a search party for you. Thank you, Wombat. You'd be surprised at how often these bush children get lost when they come into town."

After the three-week course of learning prayers and parts of the catechism by heart, Alison made her First Confession and the next day her father, stiff in his old wedding suit, came into town for her big day, her First Holy Communion. She wore a beautiful white lace dress and veil that had been made by Nell's sister, even though she was not of the faith, and worn by Zita and Hanna before her. A lot of the mothers of the other communicants made a point of speaking to Alison and telling her how nice she looked. Alison thought all the other girls looked nicer than she did, as they all had long hair, and some even had ringlets. They looked like princesses, whereas she looked like an ordinary girl with hair like a bowl on top of her head.

She saw Wombat standing in the distance looking in her direction when they came out of the church and she waved to him. He waved back. She had seen a lot of him in the gardens since the night he found her desolate under the pines. Every afternoon after that incident she watched out for him. As soon as he drove up to the convent, where he helped out after his day's work at the butter factory and at weekends, she left the girls and their long, twirling skipping rope and ran to him. She took his hand and felt safe, in the same way she always felt safe with Dan. Early on he noticed how she didn't like the feel of dried earth under her nails, so he bought her a pair of children's gardening gloves to overcome the problem. She hadn't known such items existed. She loved them. They increased her pleasure in the digging and planting. When the bell rang at six thirty she took them off and left them with Wombat's things and ran into the refectory for tea.

Dan went over to Wombat to shake his hand and ask him how he was keeping, and said if he was ever out their way to call in for a whisky. Wombat's eyes flicked behind Dan to study the group filing out around him. Dan interpreted the searching look and said that Zita had stayed at home to look after Jack and Hanna. What he didn't say was that they were all due to come in, but Zita couldn't find any clothes good enough for the two young ones to wear, and no shoes that went anywhere near to fitting them, so made the decision to keep them at home to prevent them from being the objects of pity. Or, worse still, leaving the family open to someone's reporting it to the authorities for neglect.

After the ceremony the children stuffed themselves with cakes and cordial and ran around the grounds while the parents had tea and sandwiches, and then Alison followed Dan to the Wolesley.

There were a dozen sweet-pea plants wrapped in wet newspaper on the floor between the front and back seats. Beside the plants were her gardening gloves.

Dan, swerving and ducking, drove back to the farm, where Zita told her to take off the veil and change out of the dress at once before it got stained or ripped, to make sure their younger cousins would be able to wear it when their turns came.

Alison asked when Wombat was going to call again and Zita flushed and said she didn't know and to stop looking at herself in the mirror. Alison didn't dare contradict her by saying she wasn't – she was looking at the spider beside the mirror – as she knew that answering Zita back was one of the worst things she could do, and was liable to bring the full force of her temper down upon her head.

She put away her shoes and went barefoot again. The soles of her feet had softened after only three weeks of wearing shoes and socks. She wished she could wear them every day like town kids did, as they were so snug, and they protected her from thorns and nettles and barbed wire. She had overheard Dan telling visitors that the children didn't feel the cold on their hardened bare feet. Alison had run across the frosty grass in front of them, not letting on how miserable she was with the discomfort of the cold, for fear of showing her father to be mistaken.

Jack and Hanna were off-hand with her even after she changed into her ordinary clothes. They seemed to have formed a bond that excluded her because they knew about the two new calves that had been born while she was away for the three weeks and she didn't.

Wearing her gardening gloves, she planted the sweet peas along the wire-netting fence in the front yard and Hanna laughed at her in the gloves. Next morning she saw that all the plants had been eaten down to ground level. She presumed that rabbits had got into the yard which wouldn't be difficult for them as there were so many broken-down sections along the fence. She didn't say anything to anybody about it as no one cared about flowers. They only cared about crops and vegetables.

Alison's joy at being home wasn't as satisfying as she had thought it would be. She was having feelings of homesickness even though she was at home.

The next time Zita lined up the young ones to have their hair cut, Alison asked if she could be allowed to let hers grow long.

"No, you can't," Zita said sharply. "Haven't I enough to do without having to get knots out of your hair every morning before you go to school with you squawking away that I'm hurting you? Now put that towel around your shoulders and sit up here this minute. I haven't got all day."

Mr Kendall went into Redmundo to pick up bags of seed potatoes and some fertiliser. While he was in the store a local police constable approached him and said he had some bad news for him.

"There was no one hurt I have to say first of all, but I'm sorry to have to tell you that your house has burnt down," he said. "By the time the firemen got there it was too late, but at least there was no one in it when the blaze started. We can be grateful for that. Your family were out picking blackberries at the time. The house is gone. Nothing was saved. I'm sorry to be the bearer of such bad news," he concluded.

Mr Kendall could see that he really was sorry. "Is that all?" he later reported himself as saying to the policeman. "As long as the Missus and kids are safe, who cares about the house?"

Alison cared. There were seven girls, but only one pretty house with all its dazzling contents. Alison would rather have lost one of the smaller girls – who, judging from her own experience, were not of any use, especially since they weren't even boys – and still have the perfect house, filled with beds, wardrobes, clothes, toys, books, good china, hand-embroidered linen, photographs and food. Children were easy to come by. The smiling woman was about to give birth to her eighth but the house was gone forever. There would be no rebuilding. The insurance for wooden structures was high and Mr Kendall couldn't afford to pay it at the time, what with having to relocate and stock the new farm with dairy cows.

The family sold up and left the district, and Alison lost her first and only friend. The seat beside her at school remained empty after that.

The farm and stock were bought by a neighbour who already had a homestead, so no new family came to rebuild where only a brick chimney and three stone steps indicated that the pretty house had once stood there.

CHAPTER 42

Before and after school during the spring, summer and autumn months Zita, Jack, Hanna and Alison milked seventy cows that they knew by name and fed the seventy calves with the skimmed milk, separated by machine from the cream, which was collected twice a week for the butter factory in town where Wombat worked.

Because the farm was three thousand feet above sea level, the rains came regularly in the form of thunderstorms and heavy downpours, and were the envy of the drier, flatter parts of the country. The cattle grew fat, the milk yield rose, and Larry went off to Mungindi on the NSW/Queensland border to take a job as a jackeroo on one of the large sheep stations there.

It was expected that members of the family would leave home one by one and they did. Dan suspected that Jack might be the only one who would want to stay in this isolated place and eventually take over the farm if he could make money somewhere else first to give him the means to buy out the shares of all his siblings.

Alison liked the milking and feeding but hated watching the ear-marking, castrating, branding and butchering carried out by her father and brothers. She also hated the deep mud mixed with cow dung in the yard, and dreaded the swish across the face from a tail containing both if she didn't secure the cow's tail properly before sitting down to start the cow off before attaching the milking machines. What upset her most of all was the removal of young calves from their mothers and the subsequent bellowing and crying that went on between them for days. There always had to be a paddock between them. If they were in adjacent paddocks, both cow and calf would rip themselves on the barbed wire trying to reach each other.

Hanna called Alison 'Duchess' because she hated so much of farm life and wanted to learn ballet and the piano. With the nearest teachers of those subjects twenty miles away in Redmundo, Alison knew there was no chance and didn't even ask her father who would have been sad to have to refuse her, and she was sorry she had mentioned it to Hanna. She cut out magazine photos of the Royal Family and models and film stars and stuck them in a scrap book, decorating the edges of the pages with patterns, tinting them with coloured pencils. Hanna collected action shots of tennis players and went riding with Dan whenever she had the chance and was labelled a tomboy. She became more tomboyish after she heard herself described as such with such unqualified approval.

During the school holidays Dan took all the children with him to the cultivation paddock for the day to give Zita a break. Alison tired easily in the heat, and the flies annoyed her but she didn't complain as she realised the boys were doing the difficult and important tasks. Dan and the boys were experts at handling the two draught horses pulling a plough for the planting of either potatoes or corn. The synchronisation of the side-stepping and back-stepping of the two mighty beasts as they turned at the end of each furrow without tipping over the plough or tangling the reins and harness was a wonder to Alison who loved to watch. She never went up close to the draught horses as she was afraid one might tread on her foot and crush it with its enormous hoof.

Dan always said the best way to learn to balance properly on a horse was to ride bareback and Alison believed him as she believed everything her father told her connected with farm life. So it must have been her technique that was at fault, seeing she kept falling off all the time even though she squeezed her thighs and knees as tightly as she could to stay on. She had a feeling that with the help of a saddle and stirrups she might be better able to keep her balance and to brace herself on a bolting stock horse to give herself the strength to pull tightly on the reins and pull up the animal, rather than bouncing off and ending up on the ground yet again while Hanna watched and laughed. But Hanna had claimed the final available saddle, as was her right as she was next in line. After a few too many more tumbles Alison finally lost her nerve and gave up.

It was whispered amongst the aunts that Zita was the spitting image of Nell, that Hanna was Dan's right-hand man, and that Alison was the weak one because she was a twin and hadn't received enough nutrients before birth. At the time Nell probably wasn't eating enough for one, let alone three, as she had suffered terrible morning sickness during that pregnancy.

They also whispered, standing apart in judgment, that she was the beauty of the family. Aunty Cat in particular, on her annual visit up from Sydney, regretted how Alison's beauty was spoiled by greasy hair and bedraggled, second-hand clothing, and how her young life was limited by her lack of accomplishments. If Cat had been her mother, which by rights she should have been, Alison would by now be learning deportment, elocution, ballet, piano, calligraphy, tennis and perhaps even sailing. Milking cows and feeding calves was all very well if you married a farmer, but if you wanted any sort of a decent professional life, such skills weren't of any use.

Aunty Cat's latest interest was genealogy. She told Dan and her sisters that they should be grateful to her for doing all the research as it wasn't of lasting value to her, seeing she had no children to pass it on to, but that their children would appreciate it when they grew older. She would soon be coming to the end of what she could find out in Australia, and said she needed to go to Ireland to look up parish records if she were to go further back than 1845. Fritz wouldn't take time away from the shop to accompany her to Ireland and was too mean to fund her to go with a companion. She might have to abandon it and take up some other interest, though she couldn't think of any at the moment that would tempt her as she had already used up so many.

CHAPTER 43

When Alison was eight the rains stopped. The grass and crops didn't grow that summer or the summer after that. Where there used to be grass there was now cracked and dusty earth.

Water was supplied to the house and the animal troughs from a spring on the farm. Water from it was dammed so that a diesel engine could pump it a quarter of a mile uphill through pipes to the tanks beside the house.

Cows in the paddocks a distance from the house went to the dam to drink. The dam shrank in volume each day, leaving a width of deep mud around its edge. During the second year of the drought, in the course of one week, five of the cows became bogged in the mud up to their bellies before they could reach the water, and didn't have the strength to lift out their legs.

The children brought them buckets of water to drink. Dan tried to save them with the help of an improvised sling made from a tarpaulin, pulleys and ropes attached to the stronger draught horse, but only one could be pulled out and she died three days later. The other four who were further in and deeper in the mud died where they stood. Dan slit their throats to shorten their period of suffering as soon as he saw that their predicaments were hopeless.

Alison heard Zita crying in the dark with more abandon than usual. Dan must have heard her from his bedroom, as he came to stand at the doorway and listen.

"What's the matter?" he asked after a few seconds.

Zita took a while to answer. "The bills," she said. "The grocery bill isn't paid. What is going to happen to us?"

Alison kept breathing quietly, praying she wouldn't cough.

"Don't worry," said Dan in a troubled voice. "It has to rain soon." He stood there, a dark presence in a dark doorway, for a full minute before moving away.

A little later Zita stopped crying and must have fallen asleep. Alison stayed awake for a long time after that, worrying about the grocery bill.

"Zita was crying in the dark," Alison told her brother Stevie when he came home from boarding school for the holidays. "In bed. I heard her." She mentioned that Zita cried often, only never as loudly as this time and it made her feel frightened. She was conscious of a sense of importance that she had something so dramatic to tell Stevie. Normally she couldn't think of anything to say to any of her brothers as she was so much in awe of them. And if she did speak, she didn't seem to be able to break into any conversation among her siblings. No one listened to her voice which had no carrying power and ended up fading away in embarrassment.

"Dad told her it would rain soon and she stopped crying."

Stevie looked upset. "Don't worry. Dad's right. It will rain soon." It didn't.

All the denominations of churches said public prayers. Aborigines enacted special rain dances, and farmers looked up into the cloudless skies, some crying, some begging. All feeling angry and helpless.

Bills weren't paid. Everything necessary was bought on credit, with the understanding that all bills would be honoured after the rains came. Very few farmers could afford to import hay to feed their starving stock.

It was three years before the drought broke. The local butcher's shop and bakery had closed by then, while the grocery shop was still there, but noticeably under-stocked. Many farms and other businesses never recovered, and friends and neighbours left the locality. All of the Hogans' seventy cows known by name, as well as the two magnificent old draught horses, died, and their carcasses rotted unburied, dotted around the farm. The smell was disgusting and the children learnt to try to ride upwind to avoid it. The stock horses had survived as they were the only animals let into the yard around the house to eat the precious grass there, kept alive by Zita who collected all the domestic waste water and spread it around.

When the rain finally came Alison, Hanna and Jack ran whooping and cheering out into the garden, running around with faces upturned until their clothes were soaked through. The adults looked out the window at the rain and said prayers of thanksgiving.

Dan had no money to restock the farm so was forced to rent out eighty per cent of the land, accepting a much reduced rent because of the rundown state of the place with its broken fences, loose lengths of barbed wire amongst the nettles, and gates that didn't have two hinges and had to be dragged open and shut. Things had deteriorated quickly after Wombat had left.

At least Dan didn't have to sit around watching another man's cattle eating his grass or another man's potatoes growing in the cultivation paddocks. He and a neighbour secured a couple of the contracts for land clearance in preparation for the advent of electricity. They cut narrow gashes many miles long through eucalyptus forests to give access to the teams of workmen to erect the poles to carry the lines. After the lines were completed, they took on contracts to construct sheds, fences and stockyards for the new neighbours who had bought farms at reduced rates from the original farmers ruined by the drought.

There was no shortage of paid work available after electric power arrived. The rivers and cash were flowing again. Dan was chosen to fulfil contracts, despite the bad example of the collapsing state of his own farm, because of his reputation for hard work and honesty, and because people felt sorry for him as a widower with a large family to rear.

On the twenty per cent of land he didn't rent out he kept two stock horses, one house cow and two Hereford cows in calf. No more dairy cows. Like the shoemaker in the fairy story, he told Alison, he intended to build up his Hereford stock two by two, watching them grow fat on the now plentiful grass.

In the house the windows remained loose in their rotting frames, and newspapers were stuffed into the cracks to keep out the wind. Dan had little money when he bought the farm, so there had been no question of replacing the worn-out fences, let alone doing up the house, while the babies kept coming and growing up, needing to be educated. The money he made on contracts paid the bills that had accumulated during the drought.

"It's not the nest but the birds in it that count," Dan said to make light of their situation. Another one of his favourite sayings was, "Poverty is a great inconvenience but never a disgrace," and the children, some with more conviction than others, learned to quote it.

All the family, except for Alison, looked on the dilapidation around the farm as a badge of pride and made jokes about it, looking down their noses at neighbours who painted their fences and had new hinges on their smoothly opening gates. Alison secretly longed for that kind of order, but outwardly joked along with the others.

The place she liked best to be was at the bush school. The teacher, Clive Barnes, a returned naval officer, introduced his twelve pupils, three of them Hogans, to countries and customs that they loved to hear about but didn't really believe existed. Dead heroes such as Scott of the Antarctic, Burke and Wills, Edith Cavell, Marie Curie, Grace Darling, and, most revered of all, the young soldiers sacrificed at Gallipoli, convinced Alison that life in the outside world was meant to be extraordinary. She could not hope to be as brave as the heroes she was told about, but would like to do the next best thing: become a teacher as thrilling and as exuberant as Mr Barnes, and pass on his stories to another generation.

CHAPTER 44

Stevie, the fifth eldest Hogan, had left secondary boarding school at the age of fifteen, despite getting honours in his exams. He'd told Dan the two extra years leading to the Leaving Certificate would be wasted on him as all he wanted to do was work with timber and machinery, and he might as well start straight away. He was ambitious and hoped, through hard work and savings, to one day buy a house and a few acres of his own near town. Dairying was too boring and too reliant on the weather to have any appeal for him.

Stevie hadn't been telling the whole truth. He did want to work with timber and machinery, but his main concern was to help educate his three younger siblings while, at the same time, not being a burden on the family finances himself. Education was Dan's first priority for his offspring, so there was no question of their not going away after they had completed six years at the bush school. There was no senior secondary school within a sixty-mile radius of the farm, so boarding was their only option. If, unlike their older siblings, the three youngest failed to win bursaries, Dan would mortgage the farm rather than let them miss their chances. Stevie knew his help could be vital if such circumstances came to pass.

He had moved into Redmundo and rented a room in a boarding

house where the mailman's wife, Jean Cunningham, took in male lodgers to fill the gap left by her departed children. She didn't take in females who, according to her, were always blocking the plugholes with too much hair-washing, and leaving their laundered, dripping nylons dangling over the bathtub to dry.

The second room was already occupied by Wombat. Jean Cunningham had heard that he was not feeding himself properly after he had stopped calling out to the Hogan farm. The nuns constantly offered him food but he refused to accept it in case he was leaving them short. Jean had felt justified in using a bossy approach to make him come and board with her when he came over all weak in the street and a neighbour had to help him on to a public seat. The neighbour had gone into the café and brought him out a glass of milk and a sandwich which he drank and ate at speed while she looked away. It was common knowledge that he was too self-conscious about his face to enter the cafés or butcher shop or grocery store if there were customers inside them that he didn't know. As Redmundo was a gateway to the coast from the tablelands, there were often strangers in the shops. Jean's fear was that his hunger might make him come over all weak at the factory and he might find himself the victim of an accident or, worse still for him, cause one for someone else. She'd promised him a good breakfast every morning before sending him off to work with a packed lunch, followed by a three-course meal in the evening, after which he could join her and Scottie listening to the wireless together while eating homemade biscuits. He could rent out his own three-bedroom house and end up with a profit at the end of the week. He had agreed to Jean's proposal and had taken the second of the three rooms.

In the beginning Jean wondered how Wombat would get along with the fifteen-year-old Stevie Hogan, who was still only a kid in her eyes, but she needn't have worried.

The timber industry was the only industry on the mountain range not affected by the drought. The native trees survived this one as they had obviously survived others down through the centuries.

In the second year of the drought a South African called Bik Voeter had paid a bargain price in cash to a desperate farmer for a piece of land adjacent to the town, with the intention of building a timber mill on it. No one had objected to the change of function and the Council passed his application. Redmundo was grateful for the infusion of capital during those hard times, especially since the butter and bacon factories were on the verge of closing down and relocating to the coast.

Bik was a big, blond, confident man trailed by a timid little wife who looked as if she wouldn't say boo to a goose. While the mill was being built Bik did a lot of asking around. The first man he hired was Wombat. Bik had talked to the manager of the butter factory who knew better than anyone what a top-class worker Wombat was: intelligent, reliable and hard-working. He had come up with good ideas about streamlining production and would have been promoted to management if he could speak.

"People who don't know any of that take him too cheaply," the manager explained to Bik. "All that mouthing and hand-waving gives them the wrong impression. And the sad thing is there apparently isn't anything physically wrong with his voice box."

"Then why isn't he talking?"

"Shock originally, and then fear and habit after that, according to the local doctor at the time."

"What would any of those country quacks know? If any man can cure him, I can. I have experience making men who don't want to talk, talk. It's a special skill I have."

"Pleased to hear it," said the manager, laughing at what he presumed was a joke. "You'll have your work cut out. Good luck to you." He was grateful to Bik for taking on Wombat before the factory closed. Not that Wombat would stay unemployed for long, as he was so well thought of in the town, but mill work, with its emphasis on physical strength, would suit him more than most other jobs.

Bik took advantage of Wombat from the beginning, sending him around to his house after work and at weekends to enclose the property within a new high paling fence, to fit new kitchen cupboards and built-in wardrobes, to lay out a flower and vegetable garden that covered an acre and, last of all, to train an Alsatian dog as a watchdog, with specific orders not to turn him into a pet. Gretta, Bik's wife, and the two children were told to stay away from both Wombat and the dog.

Wombat was not happy to think he was deserting the nuns, but felt he had no option but to obey his new boss. Bik didn't care that the convent school received no government funding and the nuns no wages. If it weren't for the generosity of the parishioners, the nuns would go hungry. They relied on donations and voluntary work to supplement their frugal budget. The boarders, children from isolated farms, were charged the minimum amount, as none of them came from a wealthy background. Wombat's ambition had been to make the convent and school self-sufficient in vegetables and fruit and had gone a long way towards achieving it. He hoped some other volunteer would take over his work and not let the garden go to rack and ruin in the way the garden he designed for the Irish doctor had deteriorated after the Carmodys went back home and the elderly doctor took over.

Bik had specifically chosen Wombat to work around the house because he presumed no woman would give the disfigured man a second glance despite his impressive physique. The woman who passed as his wife was still a young woman – she was only fifteen when Bik first had her – and was still attractive enough to turn heads if only she carried herself with more confidence and wore more fashionable clothes. Bik would be able to stay in the pub with an easy mind after work, with Wombat at home as a kind of a guard, posing no threat to him.

Wombat trained the Alsatian, using finger clicks as signals, and became his master. Bik didn't notice, as the dog skulked out of the way when Bik approached, having received the toe of his boot in his ribs many times soon after his arrival.

Stevie Hogan had worked in a small mill for three years before he was offered a job in Bik Voerter's impressive mill. It didn't take long for Bik to realise he had a second treasure on his hands, but one that he wouldn't let within an ass's roar of the woman who passed for his wife on account of his good looks.

CHAPTER 45

Zita, from the age of seventeen, went to the dances in the local wooden hall, taking the children with her. Nearly everyone in the community attended. The children skidded around the slippery floor and sneaked into the supper room to have first choice of the homemade sponges and biscuits while no one was looking. The pensioners listened to the piano, fiddle and drums in between chats, while the young women lined the walls waiting for a male to walk across the floor to ask for a dance. The walk was not as agonising as it might have been as it was customary to accept anyone who asked you to dance unless he was too drunk to take up the dancing position.

Zita was never short of partners. Most of them were not near to her in age as so many young men of marriageable age had not returned from the war. The few who were around didn't consider her seriously as a romantic interest with Jack, Hanna and Alison trailing along behind her at the time, making her look like an old married woman with kids.

She was twenty-three before a man eventually took her seriously and began to monopolise her company. Richie Mitchell was a newcomer to the district, a teacher doing his country service in the hopes of eventually obtaining a posting to a school in Sydney. Zita had never met anyone like him before. He had studied drama and dance for ten years as a youngster and had at one time considered becoming a professional actor, but decided he wouldn't be good enough to make a success of it, so opted instead for teaching, which to his way of thinking was similar to being on the stage.

When he first heard from Zita the details of her circumstances, he had bowed as a mark of respect and admiration, rather than turning away from her.

He was thirty-four years of age, full of fun and had a wife who, it was presumed, would one day join him. In the meantime Zita could relax with him and look on him solely as a dancing partner.

"You're a natural," he told her. "If you learn to trust me enough to be led by me, you'll soon be able to master any dance. Even the tango."

It was such an exquisite feeling being held close to him, sometimes resting her chin on his shoulder. They were such a good fit. (Hadn't the nuns warned her about close dancing? Would she have to mention it in confession as an impure action? 'Alone or with others?' the priest would ask to clarify her situation in order to assess the leniency or severity of her penance.)

Richie was really nice to Jack, Hanna and Alison as if he genuinely liked kids and wasn't just pretending to in order to curry favour with Zita. Each time he saw them, which was only at the dances in the local hall, he slipped them a few shillings each when Zita wasn't looking.

He and Zita navigated the corners in the quick step without ever tripping over each other's feet, and Alison felt herself go all dreamy as she followed their smooth, wide-sweeping twirls in the waltz. Zita laughed a lot when she was with Richie, Alison noticed, and wished she laughed more when she was at home as it made her seem as if she were a nicer person. The pair attracted a lot of attention and comments which Alison was keen to hear but there was a lot of shushing whenever she walked past a group who were watching and, she presumed, admiring them.

Once at a dance Richie lifted up Alison and Zita took Hanna as a partner. To the music of a polka the four of them whirled, lunged, tapped and slid in circles until they all became dizzy and flopped laughing on the seats against the wall.

Zita noticed in her peripheral vision a familiar outline at the door and turned her head fully to see Wombat looking over at them. She felt a spasm of pain to match the pain she knew he must be feeling. He did not normally attend dances – Stevie must have persuaded him to come – so it was the first time she had seen him since she had said she couldn't marry him. The rare times she had gone into Redmundo since then, she had made a point of travelling during working hours so that there would be no chance of running into him. It was for his sake, not hers, that she avoided him, as she often longed to see him and spend time in his tender presence. She stood up to go over to speak to him, but saw that he was no longer there, and sat down again.

For days after a dance, apart from that one occasion when Wombat had turned up, Zita stayed in good humour, twirling her two young sisters around the kitchen in exaggerated dance moves while waiting for the potatoes to boil. Dan looked on, smiling.

Alison remembered those dancing moments as the happiest she had ever shared with Zita.

Dan did not attend any social functions after Nell died. He went to bed as usual at half past seven with the *Sydney Morning Herald*.

Aunty Cat, having heard that electricity was soon to be connected to the outlying parts of the plateau, arrived with a large electric wireless she had bought in the St Vincent de Paul shop. "It has a beautiful tone," said Cat, who did not want Alison growing up with no knowledge of music. "Make sure you listen to *Hospital Half Hour* every morning on the ABC at a quarter past eight. You'll hear some lovely pieces on that. And there's a play on once a week. Some of them have exciting endings you can't see coming."

Alison was now eleven, and Aunty Cat had given up hope of adopting her, but still felt she had some sort of a claim on her and took a special interest in her welfare.

The old wireless, which ran on a four-volt battery, was constantly going flat. Its precious energy was saved for the seven o'clock news and *The Bob Dyer Quiz Show* that Dan liked. The mailman, on his rounds, periodically took the battery to a garage in town to have it charged. Zita, imagining how inconvenient it was for him to do it, even though he did it cheerfully, tried not to ask him to do it too often.

The first thing Zita did after the workmen finished connecting the electricity to the house was plug in Cat's wireless. It took so long to warm up that she thought it might have rusted from the wait or been faulty to begin with, but at last a thrilling, rich, resonant sound poured out from it and she found herself dancing around the kitchen to the sounds of the Andrew Sisters. Dan walked in to see her with her eyes closed and her face alight with joy. She did a few more spins before clipping the leg of a chair and opening her eyes. She saw him watching her and stopped in embarrassment.

"I'll use it sparingly," she said quickly to Dan who would now have electricity bills to worry about on top of everything else.

"Don't," said Dan. "One thing I want you to do is not to stint on the electricity for the wireless. We have been silent for too long. Leave it on all day and all night if you want to. It will help you to carry your burden."

CHAPTER 46

It was Hanna's turn to go off to school, an occasion that Zita's recent good humour was not able to rise above. Alison wanted to make herself scarce but Zita insisted she be a witness when the old school case was pulled out from underneath the bed and opened. Zita expected moths to fly out, but the uniforms and blazer were in good condition, though a little musty.

After they had waved Hanna off on the bus, Zita turned to Alison and said, "If it wasn't for you, I could be leaving as well," and then added as if to herself, "Two more years. How am I going to stand two more years?"

Dan told his sisters and neighbours how Stephen had been head-hunted by the man who owned the largest timber mill on the plateau, almost doubling his wages when he was only eighteen. Larry was doing well at the sheep station at Mungindi on the NSW/Queensland border and was highly valued by his employer.

Zita listened to the praise and smiled in case a relative or neighbour looked over and saw jealousy written all over her face. She hummed a cheerful song to add credibility to her performance.

Cheryl called in to see Dan and spoke to him out in the shed. She told him there was talk that Zita was going out with a married man who was a teacher at the school. There wasn't a wife in sight but there was a rumour that he had one living in Sydney. He was a good dancer and that was the main attraction for Zita. Cheryl was sorry to be the one to tell him, but everyone else was hanging back and she thought he should know so that he could step in and do something about it before it went too far.

It was not in Dan's nature to speak to Zita about such a personal matter but he was disturbed by the information. He often said that no man or woman was worth the loss of anyone's eternal soul. Consorting with a married person was one sure way of putting oneself in danger of that unthinkable loss.

Zita came in from the garden with an armful of spinach and noticed a number of black ants stuck inside the honey jar on the table.

"Who left the lid off the honey?" she asked.

Dan looked up.

Alison backed away. Not putting the lid back on the honey jar was the fifth worst thing one could do. Leaving a gate open, a cow unmilked, meat uncovered or a tap running were the only things worse.

Dan smiled over at Alison and winked when Zita wasn't looking.

"It's all your bloody twin's fault," said Zita, her face contorted in an ugly shape as she ran crying out of the kitchen. "And why don't you stop biting your bloody nails? It's disgusting," she shouted back over her shoulder.

"Am I a twin?" asked Alison, hastily taking her finger out of her mouth. She was alarmed by Zita's reaction and the doom-laden sound of her words.

"Yes," said Dan, no longer smiling. "But she died."

"Why is it her fault?"

"It's not. How could it be? It's just that Zita's in a bad mood. I'd steer clear of her for a while if I were you."

Dan looked so upset Alison knew not to ask any more questions, even though she would have liked to know the name of her twin. She didn't know if he was upset because of the talk about the twin or because of the ants in the honey or because of Zita's outburst.

For weeks afterwards Alison thought of her twin whose name she found out from Stevie. If Dolores were still alive, she would be interested in dolls and ballet and flowers like she was. They would be friends, ganging up on Hanna and playing tricks on Zita. In the company of her twin she would not have been crippled by the loneliness that had been her constant companion ever since she could remember.

CHAPTER 47

Mr Barnes accepted a promotion to the position of deputy principal in a large primary school in Inverell, partly as a reward for having taught for five years in an isolated area. He was sorry he would not be around to prepare Alison for the State Bursary exam but was confident that she would pass without much effort, just as all her siblings before her had done. His place was taken by Mr Flagstone, a nineteen-year-old who had recently completed a two-year teacher-training course. He yawned a lot, picked his pimples and often dozed off in the afternoons. When the bursary winners' names were announced at the end of the year, Alison's name was not mentioned. She had not sat the exam. Mr Flagstone had omitted to register her name and apply for the papers. He called in to Dan to apologise, citing his personal life as an excuse: his girlfriend had broken off their relationship at the time and he was in such a state that the exam had slipped his mind.

Dan listened politely.

"I hope you're not thinking of letting Alison repeat sixth class," Zita said in an aggressive way after the young man had left.

"Spend another year with that drongo? Not likely," Dan answered.

Richie resigned from the Department of Education. The owner of the studio he had attended during his youth in Sydney had offered him a partnership in the business. The numbers of students wishing to study speech, drama and dance had rocketed with the prospect of the arrival of television in Australia. Rosalind, the owner, was keen to have a male instructor, and especially keen to have Richie as she had a great respect for his talent.

Richie asked Zita to come with him. The timing was perfect. Alison was about to leave home at last, so Zita had no reason to stay. It was meant to be, he said. He would give her a job in the studio and she could begin to experience the pleasures of life she had so far missed out on. He would enjoy being the one to introduce her to city ways.

Now that her escape to freedom was so close, Zita wished she had been nicer to Alison during her childhood years. It wasn't as if it was Alison's fault that their mother had lost her mind and died, though at the time it had felt that she was. The blame for that must lie solely with Dr Carmody for the wicked thing he had done. Alison's only crimes were being a surviving twin, being the youngest in the family by two years and not being adopted when she was a baby.

Zita packed one of Kevin's old cases with Hanna's castoffs. For Hanna the nuns had collected a set of uniforms from fifth-year students who were leaving and who had no younger sisters following on, so were able to present Hanna with a full set, and she was able to hand all hers, which had once been Zita's, on to Alison.

Stevie had offered to pay half the school fees. Kevin and Mick would help with the other half, even though both of them were engaged to be married.

The night before Alison was to leave for her first term in boarding school, Zita said softly to her in the dark, "You have a big day ahead of you tomorrow. I expect great things from you, so don't let me down. It's a pity about the bursary, but that can't be helped."

Alison felt guilty every time she heard the word 'bursary' as if the failing to win one had been her fault.

"We know you have the brains to get a scholarship to university," Zita continued, "so don't ruin your life by leaving St Mary's without one."

"I won't."

"Don't let anything distract you from that."

"I won't."

"You will love university. It's like heaven, with all those students – girls *and* boys from all over the state – hundreds of them around your age, all bursting with wit and ideas, and some of them will become your friends for life. You probably can't imagine it. It's a great privilege to go there and you won't be able to go if you don't win a scholarship. Promise me you'll work hard."

"I promise," said Alison, thinking how Kevin and Mick had talked constantly about their brilliant university years, and how it must have hurt Zita to have to listen to them.

"Then one day in the future you and I are going to go on a trip to Ireland."

"Ireland? What for?"

"To look up some people."

"You mean Dad's relations?"

"You could say that."

"What about Hanna and the boys?"

"No, they won't be coming. It will be just the two of us."

"Why only me?"

"Because you're the youngest and I've reared you since you were a baby. All I ask is that you say a prayer for me before you go to sleep every night from now on."

"I will," said Alison. She felt all shivery to hear her sister speak to her in such a gentle, serious tone, and stayed awake for a long time, waiting for Zita to stop crying in the dark before falling asleep.

Jack, Hanna and Alison caught the bus down on the road the next day. Jack was entering his Leaving Certificate year. For the first time since she had taken over Nell's duties twelve years earlier, Zita waved off the bus alone, and returned to an empty house.

Perhaps she had appeared mean-spirited by not commenting on the generosity of Stevie, Kevin and Mick, but any words of praise would have stuck in her throat. Weren't they lucky they were in a position to be able to help out? St Marys was not expensive, despite receiving no revenue from the government. If it were university fees they were paying for, it would be a different story. The nuns at St

Mary's, as in all parochial schools built on donated or long-held land, worked for the greater glory of God in heaven and received no wages on earth, so costs were kept down. The boarding section catered for girls from farms or small towns who, if they did not attend St Mary's, would have no access to a Catholic education, or to any secondary education at all. Any parents who wished to gain social advantage for their daughters sent them to expensive establishments in Sydney, not to St Mary's. So why all the carry-on from the relations? To hear them talk you would think the boys had handed over the bulk of their wages, leaving themselves in need. Weren't the older ones in a large family supposed to help the younger ones, anyway? Wasn't that accepted practice? Wouldn't she do the same as they had done if she were a qualified doctor with an income? As it was, all she had in the world was £23 that she had saved, shilling by shilling, out of the Children's Allowance during the last few years.

She stripped the beds, washed the sheets and hung them on the line. Her suitcase was already packed.

If Richie hadn't planned such a tempting future for her, Zita could imagine herself staying to housekeep for her father, who was now barely speaking to her, until tedium, loneliness and aimlessness poisoned her old age.

She asked the renting farmer if he would look after the hens until Dan came home from his latest trip, making sure to lock them up at night to save them from the foxes. The sole house cow had her calf returned to her so there was no need to milk her. The dog was with Dan. The cattle could look after themselves.

The renting farmer looked at her questioningly when they heard the distinctive sound of a Volkswagen Beetle being driven up the track.

Alison forgot about Zita as soon as the bus pulled away. There were some other girls on the bus in the St Mary's uniform. Hanna went over to sit with one of them she knew and left Alison sitting by herself. Jack squeezed into the back seat with a group of St John's boys that he knew.

When they arrived at St Mary's Hanna went off with her third-year friends, leaving Alison with all the new girls; it was a custom for the years not to mix with one another. Hanna was happy to go along with that, and Alison did not expect to be minded by her older sister.

The wealth of company the school had to offer dazzled Alison, who found herself in a year of seventy pupils. At the bush school there had been one other in her year after Helen left, and he was a male.

Some girls already knew one another and some were already stars, especially those who were up to eighth grade on the piano, having acquitted themselves well at the small convent feeder primary schools run by the Mercy nuns in towns around the diocese.

Alison was the only one in her year from a large family and the only one who had attended a bush school. All she knew about townies was what she'd heard from her cousins. Townies didn't do any work, but instead hung around cafés in their fashionable townie clothes drinking malted milkshakes while flirting with boys, and cycling their bikes to the swimming pool or to the beach every day during the summer holidays. She couldn't ride a bike or swim and she had never seen the sea, but didn't mind missing out on those things. What she would like to be able to do was flirt with boys. She was both fascinated and frightened by the thought of having anything to do with such exciting creatures. The fact that she had brothers was no help to her in working out how to talk to them, as she didn't know how to talk to her brothers either.

Alison wanted to tell her classmates about the farm and her amazing brothers and sisters, but she stayed quiet, knowing from experience she lacked the skills to enter a conversation and hold the interest of listeners. So many girls were brighter, prettier, more talented and more confident than she was that she didn't think she would ever break out of her silence.

Few references were made to home by any of the girls. Alison was glad of the reticence. She didn't want to have to mention Nell in case someone had heard that she went mad in the end and had been run over.

When Dan returned to the farm, the first thing he noticed when he came into the kitchen and went to put on the kettle, was that the combustion stove, continuously alight for twelve years, was cold to the touch. He looked around and saw cockroaches running around the floor, mouse droppings all over the counter tops and a letter from

Zita propped up on the top of the refrigerator.

In her letter Zita said that she was going away and would not be coming back, seeing she had fulfilled her responsibilities and wasn't needed any more, especially with his long and frequent absences. There was no mention of the teacher.

Looking around the farm later, Dan presumed the house cow with its calf must have found a break in the fence as neither was anywhere to be found. The hen house was empty. Dead hens and feathers lay littered on either side of the open door.

Four pairs of sheets and four pillowslips were all twisted around wooden pegs on the clothesline. A fifth pillowslip was found tangled up in a blackberry bush a fair distance away.

Cheryl came up to tell him that Richie had resigned from teaching and had gone back to Sydney, taking Zita with him.

Dan didn't know how he could face the people in the district now that there actually was a scandal and it had become public knowledge. He contacted Larry in Mungindi and asked him to ask around for any contracts or station work he could apply for out that way.

CHAPTER 48

"We'll marry as soon as we get all the documentation sorted out," Zita heard Richie saying and, for a second, wondered who he was talking about.

She had gone to put her case in the spare room and hang up her dresses and was about to re-enter the kitchen when she heard Richie in the middle of explaining his situation to his mother.

"Then we'll get a place of our own, so you won't have to put up with us for too long."

"You can stay as long as you like," she heard the mother answer. "It's not as if we don't have the room. I'm glad you're taking the plunge again. You're not getting any younger if you want to have kids. I ran into Adele a few months back in DJs with three lovely-looking kids. She didn't let the grass grow." The last observation was made with an unmistakable nastiness in the tone.

"She was never one to do that. Zita and I will soon catch up with her, don't worry. I can't wait to have kids, especially since I've finally met the right woman to have them with."

Kids? With me? The right woman?

He wasn't aware of the enormity of what he was saying.

How could he think she was the right woman when he knew, for a start, that her religion would not allow her to marry a divorced man? Apart from that, she would still rather die than have a child by anyone, even someone as nice as Richie, and she could never see herself changing her mind on that. She hadn't changed it for Wombat and she wouldn't change it for him. Then there was the matter of the promise she had made to herself and her dead mother: she wanted nothing to stand in the way of taking Alison to Ireland as soon as she had saved up enough money for two fares.

She had misread his intentions, thinking he was acting purely as a friend by giving her a lift to Sydney and using his contacts to find her a job and accommodation. After all that was accomplished, she presumed they would continue on as before, going to dances and perhaps watching movies together at the weekends.

During the long drive down he had told her the details of his marriage and divorce, but hadn't said anything about wanting to marry her. He was the innocent party in the divorce as his wife Adele had run off while he was away at the war, and he hadn't seen her since. They corresponded until their divorce was finalised. She married the man she had run off with, and that was the end of that, seeing there had been no children involved. The marriage had been so short-lived and had been contracted so long ago that he sometimes forgot it had ever happened.

Zita believed he had done nothing wrong but, innocent or not, she was forbidden to marry him. In her mind she could hear Dan's voice, ominous with fervour, intoning one of his often-repeated sayings, "No man or no woman is worth the loss of your eternal soul", and could not bear the thought of those words being addressed to her by him. No amount of persuasion by Richie could deflect her from wishing to avoid that kind of confrontation.

She tip-toed back to the spare room, fell onto the bed, faced the wall and covered her head with a pillow so she would not be able to hear any more of the mother-and-son conversation.

She had also told him on the trip that she had been a crabby and cranky substitute mother, impatient and sarcastic, telling the kids to shut up and to keep out of her way because she was too busy to be bothered with them.

"I can't imagine you being as bad as you make out," Richie had said. "It must have been overwhelming at the time. You're being too hard on yourself. I think you were heroic the way you coped. Especially at such a young age."

"Alison copped it the worst. She should have been given to Aunty Cat for adoption. I wanted to get rid of her all the time she was with me, and she knew it. Those last two years were a nightmare – the three of us at the kitchen table and nobody talking. Alison afraid to speak in case I bit the nose off her face. I probably took away her confidence. Mum sent me off to St Mary's full of bounce and I sent Alison off like a frightened rabbit."

"She's a bit shy, that's all. She'll grow out of that. Look on the positive side. If it weren't for you the family might have been split up and you'd all be strangers to one another."

"They were terrific kids and never shirked all the work they had to do. I didn't need to be so hard on them. Thank goodness Jack had his first five years with Mum or I might have broken his spirit."

"He turned out full of spirit, so you can stop fretting. They all turned out all right. Give yourself a big pat on the back for all the good you did. They had a lot of fun with us at the dances – don't forget that. I've admired you ever since I got to know you."

He only ever saw her at dances when she was in a good mood. If he'd known her better he would be able to see that she wasn't cut out to be a mother. That the responsibilities thrust on her by her mother's death had proved too heavy for her. Why did he keep dismissing every fault she confessed to as if it didn't matter?

She remembered telling him months earlier how relieved she would be when Alison went off to school and how she had no desire to ever have kids.

"It will be different when you have your own," he had answered, smiling confidently at her as if he knew what he was talking about. Had he already, at that time, assumed he would have a future with her and that it would include children?

She wondered if the townspeople had judged Richie to be an opportunistic cad with a smooth line taking advantage of an innocent country girl. What would they think now if they saw her lying chastely in a single bed in the spare room of his parents' house while he was in a different room talking about marriage?

Richie crept quietly into the room and whispered her name. She lay still and did not answer. He left and she lifted the pillow that was over her head and heard him telling his mother that it might be a good idea to leave her to sleep through until the next morning as she'd had such a long, emotional day.

The following day he took her to the studio to introduce her to his future business partner, Rosalind, and to see if there was any position Zita could be given in the expanding business. It was obvious to Zita that Rosalind was in love with Richie, though Richie seemed unaware of it. It was also obvious that Rosalind's grooming and style presented an image of a woman younger than she actually was, and that she did not welcome the presence of Zita.

"Zita is a natural," Richie explained with pride in his voice. "She would be a great asset to a place like this."

"Really?" Rosalind turned to Zita with a cold stare. "Can you type?" she asked.

"No," said Zita.

"Can you play the piano?"

"No," said Zita.

"What speech exams have you taken?"

"None."

"Dance?"

"A bit of ballroom."

"Professionally?"

"No. Just at the local dances."

Rosalind looked over at Richie and rolled her eyes.

"Perhaps she could answer the phone and do the bookings," he suggested.

"With an accent like that I don't think so. We don't want to put off our clients before they start. Just explain to me what exactly you are a natural at?" she asked, looking at Zita.

She hasn't even remembered my name, Zita thought, and doesn't care.

"No, on second thoughts, don't bother to answer that question. I can guess and I'd rather not hear about it, thank you very much."

Zita blushed at the inference and felt the injustice of it. Richie was making faces at Rosalind, showing his disapproval at what she was saying, but she continued.

"I am not running a charity to give employment to anyone's current

214

girlfriends. My two assistants have each done ten years of ballet, tap and ballroom, as well as speech and drama and shouldn't be expected to train in an aged beginner who would be neither supple nor toned to start with when they are already run off their feet with a full schedule of classes." She ended by saying something about reviewing Richie's position as a potential partner, as nothing had yet been finalised.

"That might be a good idea," said Richie. "Come on, Zita. We have plans to make."

After they left, he said, "Sorry about that. She's not normally so dismissive. I can't believe she was so nasty to you. Don't let what she said upset you."

"But it does because it was all true. I don't want you losing your chance of a partnership because of me. She was threatening you."

"Don't worry about Rosalind. I can deal with her later. She was completely out of order in there, but she gave me an idea. Why don't we get married soon? That would solve all our problems. Then you wouldn't need to bother looking for a job as you'd be bound to get pregnant straight away with the history of fertility in your family, and I would look after you."

He put his arm around her shoulder and drew her in close.

Later that afternoon when Richie was in town seeing his solicitor, Zita remained behind in the empty house. She wrote him a note – her second running-away letter in three days – and left the house in search of the nearest convent, as that was the only place she could think of in the city where she would feel safe. Except, of course, in Aunty Cat's house, but she wanted to avoid going there. She went to the train station, bought a map and asked the man who sold it to her where the nearest convent was. He didn't know, but passed her on to some other shop-owner who did, and who marked the place on the map and told her which trains to catch to get there. She found it and told the nun at the door her story, was given a bed in which she cried for hours at the loss of Richie.

The next day she was taken to a Catholic hospital where she accepted a job as a cleaner and settled down to living a frugal life, saving every penny, estimating that in nine years' time, by the time Alison turned twenty-one, she would have enough money saved for their fares to Ireland.

CHAPTER 49

Alison studied all her classmates and was drawn to the natural leaders, on whom she decided to model herself in the hope that she could bring herself up to their level of confidence. By the end of first term she had tried to change her personality three times but still hadn't managed to make an impression on herself, let alone anyone else. The hollowness she felt inside did not change with each outward transformation.

The nuns did their share of supervising, but an all-seeing God did a more thorough job, on duty twenty-four hours a day. Alison hadn't known before how powerful He was. She found herself entering His world, a world more extraordinary – more so because it was invisible – than the one Mr Barnes had introduced her to via his travel and historical tales.

Dan had never spoken about the finer points of theology to his children. He would not have considered himself qualified to do so.

Alison was told with unquestionable authority that a deprived and painful life was actually preferable to an easy one as it gave you a higher standing in the next. This was a revelation to her and, after she thought about it, found it very comforting, knowing that the poverty in which she was being reared and which she had considered a drawback, was actually an asset.

She wondered if Zita was still aware of that or if she had forgotten it during the intervening years. She would remind her about it first thing on her first day home for the holidays. They could try to calculate just how high up the scale Zita should go. Right up at the top in the company of the saints, Alison reckoned. It would make Zita feel a whole lot better and take away her simmering irritation, to know that all that domestic drudgery and farm work hadn't gone to waste and all the time was accruing credits in heaven.

To think she had spent the first twelve years of her life unaware of the world that could not be perceived by the senses, but which she believed through the gift of faith to be a more vital and dramatic one than the one she could see! It was similar in enchantment to the fairy stories she had read as a child about spells, witches, dragons, demons and good fairies who could grant three wishes. There was one major difference: the supernatural beings she was being told about in the Religious Knowledge class were real. She would have to remain alert so that she wouldn't be misled by Satan or else she would end up like all those characters in fairy tales who were granted three wishes but never got what they wanted, tricked into making a disastrous choice at the end. To think that if she had a great need and if she prayed hard enough, God, if He thought fit, would bend the laws of nature to help her! It was wonderful beyond belief.

"The greatest sacrifice your loving parents have made sending you away to school is missing your company," the Prefect of Studies told them.

Alison could not imagine Dan missing hers. He would miss her contribution to the house and the farm, but less so since the dairy closed. What else was there? Dan went to bed early every night and rose at daybreak and worked all day long. She couldn't remember any personal conversation with him and she couldn't remember being addressed by her name. He wrote every week to her and Hanna, with news of the farm and his latest work project, concluding each time with, "*Love, Dad*", but there was no mention of missing them.

In one letter he said he was sorry to tell them that Zita had left the house, and had not left an address so they would not be able to contact her.

After a thirteen-week first term there was a four-hour trip home on the bus, with a few stops along the way for motion sickness. The initial rush of pleasure at seeing the familiar setting soon turned to disappointment when Jack, Hanna and Alison found there was no one in the house to greet them. They had expected Dan to be there, and hoped that Zita might have returned. Dead blowflies littered the counter top, the stove was out, the fridge switched off with its door open, and a stale, smelly half pint of milk congealed in the bottom of a jug sat in the sink with a smelly dishcloth beside it.

They changed out of their uniforms and Alison wiped down the inside of the refrigerator before switching it on, emptied the overflowing tray of ash under the stove, brushed out the chimney, lit the fire and cleaned up the kitchen without waiting until the water cylinder had heated up. Jack split wood for the stove and filled up the wood box. Hanna went looking for the house cow. She ran into the renting farmer in the home paddock and asked him if he knew where the cow was and when was Zita due back.

"She's not coming back. I thought your father wrote and told you. She's gone off with Twinkletoes, that dancing teacher bloke, who's a married man, so they say, and the house cow's gone as well. Your father's blown a gasket."

For dinner that night they ate porridge made with water, and after that they went to bed. Alison felt as if enormous, black electric storm clouds were hanging low in the sky above them, enclosing the farm, ready to rock it with thunder and lightning at any minute.

Dan turned up four days later, tired and unsmiling. He said he was sorry he hadn't been there when they returned home. He didn't ask about school. Alison's head was full of her teachers, classmates and the choir, which she loved most of all, but she didn't mention them. She was at home and suffering from strong feelings of homesickness. No one mentioned Zita's name.

Alison now had two things she hoped her classmates would never find out about: Nell's madness and Zita's disgrace.

CHAPTER 50

Zita rang the studio a year after she left Richie, on an afternoon when she was feeling particularly lonely. She didn't want anything from him – she just wanted to hear his friendly voice and find out how he was getting on. A woman's familiar voice answered the phone. It was Rosalind. When Zita said she would like to speak to Ritchie, Rosalind said, "Hold the line for a minute, please, modom, and I'll dash off and fetch my *husband* for you."

She knows who I am, Zita thought. The way she stressed the word 'husband' and the mockery in her tone – she knows. Poor Richie, married to a woman who, Zita estimated, was almost definitely past childbearing age, though you wouldn't suspect that unless you looked closely through her make-up to her ageing skin beneath it.

She hung up.

Should she contact Aunty Cat to hear news of home? It was tempting but she didn't feel strong enough yet to face her aunt's questions and disapproval. Instead she sent a postal order for a five-year subscription to Redmundo's *Plateau Clarion*. Each weekly issue was to be sent to a post-office box she rented under a fictitious name so that no one would know it was she who had requested it. Now, at least, she would know each week who was in hospital, who had died, who had left the district and who had arrived or returned, along with the details of every social and sporting event that had taken place.

It was discovered early on that Alison possessed a clear, strong voice, so she was often asked to read aloud in class. This was a matter of pride to her, as it was the only thing she could do better than anyone else. Calling the horses, 'Kip, kip, kip,' and the cows, 'Cubbawd, cubbawd, cubbawd,' over long distances on the farm must have been what had developed the resonance in her voice.

Because of it, Sister Chanel thought she was the obvious choice to take the main part in the end-of-year play.

At the first rehearsal Alison stepped up on to the stage to speak the lines she had learnt by heart. Facing her in the assembly hall were seventy girls, all with serious expressions on their faces, some with heads cocked to the side, some with arms crossed, some with hands folded in their laps, all with their eyes fixed on her, looking straight at her alone on the stage.

They were not keeping their eyes down, following in their textbooks the words she was reading aloud from her desk at the back of classroom, as had happened up until now.

While she took a deep breath, preparing to speak, the faces of her classmates suddenly began to quiver and lose their definition as if they were being buffeted by the winds of a dust storm. The well-rehearsed words in her mind were blown away by the same wind. Her ears became blocked, and her voice, when she tried to speak, could not emerge from a mouth that was so dry it felt as if it had actually been filled with dust.

No sound emerged. She stood silent on the stage, lost in a frightening isolation.

"Alison, we'll have to get that throat of yours seen to," Sister Chanel called out loudly, leaving her chair on the front row to go quickly up to the edge of the stage. "There's a bad dose going around the convent at the moment and it takes a long time to clear up. Come on down. You can help me direct instead as you are always full of good ideas." She turned to face the silent group. "Mariella, you can take the part. Will you be able to learn the lines in time?"

All eyes now turned to a delighted Mariella, who said that she would do her best.

Alison left the stage while the girls were distracted. Sister Chanel waited for her and guided her to the seat beside her before handing her a sheaf of notes, not letting on that she saw tears smudged on Alison's red face.

How did I ever think I could stand up in public when I have been nothing but a shadow all my life? Alison asked herself, bending her head and pretending to concentrate on the notes so that the girls could not see her face.

What now for her dreams of becoming a teacher? Drying up in front of a class must surely be grounds for disqualification from that particular profession.

God must have other plans for her was the only conclusion she could come to. It was a pity He had to use such harsh methods to close off one desirable path before pointing her towards a different one.

The puzzle of her constant homesickness, whether at school or at home, was finally solved to her satisfaction when she read words of St Augustine who pronounced: *"Thou hast made us for thyself, O Lord, and our hearts are restless until they rest in Thee."* Alison felt a pang of recognition when she read that in her third year. At last her ever-present, underlying sadness was simply and perfectly explained. She would have to wait until after death to find her real home in heaven so there was no point in fretting until then about not belonging to one here on earth.

Each time she arrived home to dullness and despondency, especially after Jack had gone to work in Darwin and Hanna had left and she was often on her own with Dan away, she thought of those words to comfort herself. At certain times they didn't comfort her, no matter how hard she tried to believe them. She thought of her twin, Dolores. The promise of God's company in the next life was all very well, but that was a long time off, and until then her desolation was so immediate and so real she would give her eye teeth to have her twin with her in this life, and let God wait His turn.

CHAPTER 51

1956

Hanna was the only one of the three girls who wanted to live on the land. She turned down a scholarship after her Leaving Certificate and took a position as governess on a cattle station in west Queensland. The younger brother of the owner put his eye on her immediately he saw her. She was engaged within six months and married at the age of nineteen on the station a year later. Dan thought she was young to be getting married but she was quick to point out that Nell had been only seventeen when she had married him.

For five years Alison studied English, maths, Latin, French, ancient history and European history, all of which had such little bearing on her life that she came to believe that anything that did have a bearing on her life had no place in education.

Alison prepared fully for the final exams, leaving nothing to chance. She had done well in the trials, and her teachers had no doubts that she would win a scholarship to university so that she could qualify to teach English at secondary level. Not face-to-face in a classroom, unfortunately, but in the Correspondence School, which had been set up to cater for children living on sheep and cattle stations, hundreds of miles away from the nearest school.

Apart from achieving her ambitions, she wanted to do well to justify her brothers' investment in her education, to make Dan feel proud of her and alleviate a little of his sorrow at the shame Zita had brought on the family, and to honour the promise she had made to Zita nearly five years earlier.

In her second-last term, Alison received a letter full of misspellings, written in a childish hand.

It was from Cheryl, telling her that the Hogan homestead had burnt down, and that Dan had asked her to write as his hands had received second-degree burns in the fire trying to save the album containing the photos of Nell. The album was so hot it had burst into flames in his hands. All the photos were lost. It was the fourth house in the district to burn down during the last eight years. It had happened at one in the morning. Thank God Dan had woken up. He'd rung for the fire engine. It was lucky Sandra answered the exchange and put him through as sometimes she switched off after hours. The firemen from Redmundo didn't know where the farmhouse was and turned the wrong way at the T-junction. By the time they finally got to the house it was burnt to the ground. They should have got the mailman to come with them to show them the way.

The fire had been caused by a spark from the slow-combustion stove on the night of a high wind. Cheryl had noticed the flaking rust near the firebox where the hot-water pipe was attached to the side of the stove and had mentioned it to Dan a number of times, but he hadn't bothered to do anything about fixing it. The wind must have blown some sparks out into the wooden kitchen through a gap caused by the rust.

Dan sold the farm the next day to the man who was already renting, and went back to Mungindi to live in the workmen's quarters on the sheep station where he had been working. Alison was to stay at the convent during the next holidays, and after the exams she was to stay in the boarding house in Redmundo where Stevie lodged. It was all arranged. Jean Cunningham had agreed to temporarily lift her ban on female lodgers just this once, out of sympathy for the accumulation of Hogan misfortunes.

Cheryl thought Dan's decision to sell the farm had been too quick and he was probably already regretting it. The new owner was smiling from ear to ear – the nine good years since the drought had turned him into a wealthy man.

She enclosed a ten-pound note from Dan that he said should do her until school was over.

Dan was very cut up about the whole thing, Cheryl concluded.

CHAPTER 52

POPULAR RESIDENT LEAVES DISTRICT was a headline on the fourth page of the *Clarion*. The report following it said: *"A highly respected member of the community, Mr Malcolm Churchill, known to his many friends as 'Wombat' has left the plateau to travel to pastures new. Mr Churchill was Redmundo's Good Samaritan, ready to lend a hand to any of his fellow citizens in times of need, and will be sorely missed. His friends were pleased to note that 'Wombat' at last regained the use of his voice which had not functioned for many years as a result of the shock sustained when he was involved in an unfortunate accident during his tender years.*

We are certain that everyone in the district will join the editorial staff of the Clarion *in wishing 'Wombat' good luck in whatever endeavour to which he subsequently chooses to apply his many talents, and hope it will not be too long before he returns to his roots in Redmundo, where he was born and reared, as were his late parents and grandparents before him.*

The news was a week old by the time Zita read it, and it affected her with a power that surprised her. She thought she had got over Wombat, as her mind was usually so full of Richie, but she hadn't, and her loving memories of him had her trying to read between the lines to find out what powerful stimulus had activated his ability to speak again, and what circumstances had prompted him to leave Redmundo. She had often praised the *Clarion* for being so scrupulous about printing only the facts, and taking no notice of hearsay, but just this once she wished they had ignored their tradition and written down every bit of information that had come to them by word of mouth.

That night Zita cried herself to sleep in the dark.

The local people who read the short article found it difficult to believe that Wombat had gone away, as it was a well-known fact that he couldn't bear to be looked at by strangers. Some sensed a scandal, especially as his departure had been abrupt and secretive. No one could imagine what the particular scandal could be, seeing scandals usually involved either money or women. Wombat was honest with money and had never been known to have been with a woman, so it must be something else entirely. He hadn't given any notice at the mill or to his landlady, who was as much in the dark as everyone else. He had left behind in his room an extra month's rent in cash.

Mrs Trent, the Voerters' next-door neighbour had seen the 'whole thing', as she called it, through a knothole in one of the boards that made up the high paling fence that separated the two gardens. It was she who was able to tell a select few what had actually happened to make Wombat leave town.

She had taken to peering through the knothole after the Alsatian arrived. She loved dogs but her husband refused to have one even though their garden, which was as large as the Voerters', was crying out for one to her way of thinking. Perhaps she could talk her husband into getting one if the Alsatian next door did something dramatic like foiling a robbery. All a dream, of course, as house robberies didn't seem to happen in Redmundo.

Four o'clock on the dot Wombat arrived every weekday. Mrs Trent stopped her quiet weeding on the other side of the fence and watched how he trained the Alsatian, using bacon bits as rewards and finger clicks instead of spoken commands. Gretta, Bik Voerter's wife, was involved, using the same treats and signals. The dog came to obey her as promptly as it obeyed Wombat.

Mrs Trent ended up seeing more than she bargained for. While she watched the dog training and later the gardening, when Gretta and Wombat again worked side by side, she couldn't believe it at first but eventually had to admit that the two of them were falling in love with one another. The signs were all too plain. She felt a shiver of fear at the thought of it. Bik Voerter was not a man to be made a fool of.

The townspeople were used to seeing Gretta laden down with bags of groceries, her head bent to avoid speaking to anyone, making her way along the street looking like an old woman with a scarf covering her hair and a raincoat flapping around her ankles. They would not have recognised this laughing woman with loose thick blonde hair and shapely figure as the woman who snubbed them on the street and who was nicknamed 'Lady Muck' because she was married to the richest man in the town and made no effort to be friendly. Mrs Trent had called on her with a casserole when the Voerters first arrived in the town. She had been left standing on the doorstep and, as far as she knew, no one had ever been invited inside.

That Gretta and Wombat could fall in love was difficult for anyone to believe, but must have been particularly unthinkable for Bik who, everyone knew, had specifically chosen Wombat to work at his house because he thought no woman would look twice at him on account of his disfigured face.

Bik called into his house early one afternoon to pick up his cheque book on his way to the pub. He saw Gretta smiling lovingly up into Wombat's face while her hands held Wombat's wrists.

Bik let out a roar that made Mrs Trent jump back from the fence, fearing he had seen her, but realising that that wasn't possible, she quickly took up her position again.

"Bik was shouting shocking swear words," she later told her best friend. "He went for Gretta's throat. It was all I could do not to scream but even if I had they wouldn't have heard me with the dog barking like crazy. Then Wombat went for Bik and pulled him off Gretta and Bik went for Wombat and knocked him to the ground. Gretta clicked her fingers. You'd think the dog wouldn't touch Bik seeing he owned him, but Bik only ever kicked him and Wombat was really his master seeing he had trained him. The dog grabbed Bik's calf when Bik went for Gretta again and then Gretta clicked again and the dog dug his teeth in deeper and Bik roared and let go of her.

"It was then I heard this weird shout and I didn't realise at first that it was Wombat. Can you believe that? Wombat making a sound? You could have knocked me over with a feather. He then said, 'If you hurt Gretta I swear I will kill you,' in a rusty kind of voice and Bik said, 'If you don't leave town before midnight I'll kill Gretta and that's a promise. Now get this bloody mongrel off me, you bloody freak!' I don't think Bik should have called him that, do you? Bik tried to poke the dog in the eyes, but the dog kept twisting, still holding on to the leg. To cut a long story short . . ."

"Don't. Don't shorten it. I want to hear every little detail."

"The dog kept a hold of Bik while Wombat and Gretta went to the gate, and Gretta told him in a clear voice so that Bik could hear that he was not to worry as the Alsatian would look after her. After a bit she came back and clicked for the dog to let go. Bik raised his arm as if to hit Gretta, but the dog growled and Bik didn't do anything and went inside. He came back out with a rifle and shot the dog right in front of Gretta. The dog's blood splattered all over her dress. 'You'll be next if you ever put your face outside this house again – get inside, woman,' he shouted in a scary voice. She looked terrified after that. He went back inside with her and I didn't see any more. I was that upset. Don't know if he went to the doctor or not with the bite marks on his leg. He thinks all doctors are sissies, sitting around all day listening to old women whining, so he probably didn't."

"Let's hope he doesn't go and that he gets tetanus. That would be the best thing that could happen to him, the bastard."

"My thoughts exactly, though I wouldn't use that word," said Mrs Trent who didn't think she'd ever get over what she had seen. "At least one good thing came out of it. Wombat is able to talk again."

Mrs Trent's account passed from one person to another until it reached Cheryl who wrote to Dan in Mungindi to tell him all about it. He would want to know, seeing Wombat had been part of the Hogan family for so long.

CHAPTER 53

The small bus pulled up outside the convent gates where fifteen girls waited to be driven two miles to the Public High School to sit the state Leaving Certificate exam. Sister Paschal, the cook, handed each of them a packed lunch, proud of the extra treats she had put in for them. She would be fasting for the week to make up for her extravagance. The nun who taught English, Sister Chanel, waved them off and wished them good luck.

Alison had made sure she stuffed herself with porridge, scrambled egg and extra bread at breakfast – the nuns liked to indulge the Leaving Certificate girls – so that her stomach wouldn't rumble in front of all the strangers during the quietness of these supremely important exams. She could imagine the Public High School kids lifting their heads to look at her if her weakness made itself heard, the girls with irritation and the boys with derision, while she sat there, unable to do anything about it and wishing she could become invisible.

The Public High School students, allowed to wear their ordinary clothes during the exams, looked over at the girls in their navy serge tunics, white blouses, school ties, black stockings and lace-up shoes and wondered how they were able to cope with the heat in all that garb. Huddled together under the shade of a tree, some of the convent girls read through their notes, while others looked over at the sight of a number of boys their own age, and marvelled how the girls, casually mixing with them, were able to concentrate with those exotic creatures in the classroom. There were a few nods between the two separate groups from under their two separate trees, but no one spoke. A pair of male twins who came from up the river and had been taught at home by their parents with the help of the Department's Correspondence Course, arrived a few minutes after the bus, and stayed on their own, looking at their notes. Alison felt sorry for them not having a group to attach themselves to and thought their note-studying could be a guise to hide their awkwardness.

Alison would like to have found out where the washrooms were but was too shy to ask with all those boys standing around the place. She knew she would be able to hold on for three hours, and after that she would watch to see where the public school girls headed.

The assembly hall had been fitted out with single tables far enough apart from each other to make it difficult for students to look at each other's work or pass notes without being seen. There were two supervisors at the front and one at the back. One of the overhead fans was making a loud, rasping noise. The head supervisor made the decision to turn it off and opened the back door to create a draught and compensate for the lack of a fan. Neither the fan nor the draught made much impression on the damp, energy-sapping heat. A large clock on the front wall showed there were ten more minutes to go before starting time. The atmosphere was similar to the one in a church just before a solemn procession was about to begin.

The head supervisor, pink from the heat as well as from the awareness of the drama of her action, broke open the seal on the envelope. She slid out the English Language papers, tucked them in the crook of her left arm, then walked up and down the aisles, lifting off a single paper at each desk, pausing and checking before placing one face down in front of each student.

Alison made sure again that her fountain pen and ink bottle hadn't leaked. She had a moment of panic before the signal to commence was given, fearing that when she looked at the paper it would contain passages so dense and topics so difficult that she wouldn't be able to answer them, but when she turned it over, there it was, looking like all the past papers they had studied in preparation for this day. There were the usual essay topics, a comprehension passage that was so familiar she presumed she had recently read it in a novel, and everything else exactly as expected.

Three hours later the convent girls grouped under the one tree to eat their packed lunches. Even though hers was tasty and filling, Alison added to it a chicken drumstick that she had saved from dinner the previous night and ate it on top of all the rest. The overeating had successfully prevented stomach rumbles in the morning, and she hoped it would work again during the English Literature paper that afternoon.

The chicken was warm. She had placed her bag in the wrong place on the verandah and it had been in direct sunlight for at least an hour. Her friends noticed her unwrapping the saved chicken and made no comment. One of them offered her half a cheese and chutney sandwich and another half an egg sandwich, but she declined both and noticed they ate them rather than putting them back into their bags.

Alison turned over the exam paper. She would do the Shakespeare first. **"Compare and contrast the speeches of Brutus and Mark Antony . . ."** She started writing before she finished reading the question as she had answered an almost identical question in the trials. Nicely rounded off in three pages and only half an hour used up.

Next: **"Comment on the device of using Nellie Dean as the narrator of *Wuthering Heights*."** Another question she could answer without too much trouble.

She had only half a page written when she experienced the onset of cramps and felt, rather than heard, a rumbling sensation in her insides. She pressed her hand against the spot to try to compress it, but the action made her feel worse and produced a quiver of nausea.

Please, God, don't let this happen. Make it go away. Please, God. I will live the life of a saint if You will make this go away.

She stayed still and tried to relax. The sensation of nausea expanded.

Please, God, let it be nerves or the result of eating too fast this morning or too much at lunchtime. Please, God. Don't let it be anything worse. It's such a small thing for me to ask and for You to grant.

There was an unmistakable urgency in the signals she was now receiving. She pushed back her chair and tried to walk sedately out of the room. All supervisors looked in her direction and the man at the back made a move towards her, but she couldn't wait. She was glad the door was open so she didn't have to exert any physical pressure on its handle to open it. After she crossed the verandah she ran towards the washrooms, thanking goodness she had found out where they were during the lunch break. She pushed open the door of the washroom and saw the blessed, beautiful cubicle nearest the door right in front of her.

She was in time.

After three waves of sickness had passed she felt so empty she was confident there would be no more eruptions, but stayed sitting on the concrete floor with her head hanging over the bowl, waiting a little longer to make sure. She didn't know how much time had passed as she didn't possess a wristwatch.

When she went back into the examination hall, she thought, she would have to write some of her answers in note form if she found herself running short of time. That was one of the exam tips that had been passed down by older students to the present applicants – even if you only sign your name on the page, hand it in. The markers want to give you points. If you are foolish enough to spend too much time on one question and leave yourself short on the last, don't waste your time writing a few perfect sentences, but use headings to let the examiners know that you know your stuff. Put it all down, and then if you have time at the end, write your sentences and paragraphs.

Alison assembled the facts in her head and ran through quotes from Shelley and Keats to ensure they were word perfect so that she wouldn't waste a moment when she returned to her desk.

She stood up and felt a little weak but all discomfort was gone and she was confident that her body had expelled all infection from her system.

The thought of entering the hall was so daunting she nearly couldn't bring herself to do it. Everyone would look up to see who it was coming in, some showing annoyance at being distracted in the middle of a carefully constructed argument, the boys assessing her and deciding whether or not she was a good sort.

After crossing the glaring quadrangle in the pulsing sunlight, the verandah was dark and she knew the hall would be darker. She paused at the door which had been open when she left but was now closed. Before turning the handle she closed her eyes to give her pupils a chance to dilate so that when she entered the exam room she would be able to locate her empty desk quickly to make sure she wouldn't go down the wrong aisle.

Turn the handle. Push the door. Step in.

"Excuse me," someone whispered out of the darkness.

She started.

It was the male supervisor.

"Excuse me," he repeated in a slightly louder whisper, enunciating clearly. "I'm afraid you can't go in." He motioned for her to step back onto the verandah.

"What's the matter?" she asked when they were both outside.

He took her arm and led her further away from the door where he was able to speak in a louder voice. "You left the room."

"I was sick."

"You should have asked for a supervisor to accompany you."

"I didn't know."

"You should have been told. It's a rule to prevent cheating. You have been gone for half an hour – that's a long time. You could have been looking at some notes."

"I wasn't. I was sick all the time. I couldn't wait. I was going to vomit. I didn't want to disturb anyone. I didn't know. I would never cheat. It wouldn't cross my mind." She could feel herself ready to cry and tried to restrain herself.

"I'm sure it wouldn't but I have to follow procedure. I can't let you write another word or your paper will be disqualified. This way at least what you've written will still count."

She thought of her measly one and a half questions answered and couldn't hold in the tears in any longer.

"I'm sorry," he said. "I must get back in. It will be less disruptive if you stay out here. Your paper has already been collected. I'm sorry I can't do anything to help you. I will give a warning to all the others at the conclusion of the exam, so that it won't happen again. I am deeply sorry. "

He slid back in and closed the door behind him.

Alison crossed the quadrangle to the washrooms, where she locked herself into a cubicle different to the one she had been in earlier, put the lid down over the bowl, sat on it and contemplated her future which looked a lot less bright than it had looked earlier on in the day. What would she do if she failed English, a compulsory subject required for entry into any section of tertiary education? How could she face her brothers? What would she say to Zita if she ever saw her again? Was there anyone in contact with her who would write and tell her what a mess her youngest sister had made of her chances? And what about poor Dan? Her troubles were insignificant compared to his, but he would be disappointed on her behalf when he found out.

Five girls squashed in around Alison on the bus on the way home to hear what had happened. They were the ones who had planned to go on to tertiary level and who had applied to attend the same university as she had. They counted Alison as part of their group even though she was not the best friend of any of them. After trying out many personalities Alison had settled on being a studious, religious, shy loner and had been accepted as such. The five were unable to believe that she might have lost her chance of a scholarship when she was the most likely of all of them to win one.

"Perhaps not," said Barbara, one of the five. "You could still scrape through. You'll get your usual 90% for the first paper. That translates to 45% when the two papers are combined. How many questions did you do on the second?"

"Only one and a half. At least I did the Shakespeare."

"So that would be 30% at the most. Say 20%, which is really 10%. That brings you up to 55% so you could still pass."

"There's no way I would get 90% on the Language paper. Sister Chanel is an easy marker. The Department ones would be miles tougher."

"You don't know that."

"Perhaps if you get really high marks in your other subjects that will pull you through."

"I don't think it works like that."

"What's Sister Chanel going to say?"

"Don't tell her," Alison said. "She'll be upset. She'll find out soon enough when the results come out. At least I won't be around then to see her face."

Alison had to lean heavily on her faith to cope with the disappointment of her failure. She already knew that when God didn't answer your prayers, He had already answered them, so all she had to do was accept His Holy Will – it wouldn't be easy – and stay on the alert for the next directive. He was a hard taskmaster.

Kevin, Mick and Stevie were disbelieving about Alison's misfortune, but were not sympathetic. She should have had more sense than to eat a leg of chicken that had been left in the sun. Let her settle for an ordinary job and get on with life like the majority of the rest of the population had to do. As far as they were concerned, she had been given a chance and she had not utilised it, but compared to Zita's disgrace, the house burning down and Dan's selling the farm, Alison's bad luck was hardly worth talking about.

CHAPTER 54

Fritz, Aunty Cat's husband, had been standing at the counter of his shop one minute, and the next minute had keeled over with a stroke. He was to stay in hospital for weeks before being moved to a rehabilitation centre where he would be prepared for his return home. Cat dreaded having him in the house all day, attending to his needs year after year while he sat in a chair, immobile, helplessly fretting about the shop and the assistant she had got in to run it, some stranger they didn't yet know who would be robbing them blind, year after year, according to Fritz, while he was sitting there unable to do anything about it. Typical of him, thought Cat, spending his life earning lots of money that would be used up paying for nurses to help her care for him.

But Fitz turned out to be more accommodating than usual and a month later suffered a second stroke, this time a major one, and died.

It was the way he would have wanted to go, said Cat.

The first thing she did after the funeral was buy a television set. Fritz had said he wouldn't have one of those new-fangled things in the house. Time-waster, he called it. Happiness, the new widow called it. She would need something to distract her from memories of Fritz, she told her friends. She sat in front of it every night with her feet up, watching and enjoying every programme to make up for the months she had missed.

It was a surprise when she found out that she had been left an extremely wealthy woman, and after she sold the shop, wealthy beyond her imaginings. Who would have thought a little huckster shop could be worth so much? She went into town to pay the death duties and while she was there she picked up brochures from the P&O office and took them home to study them and make plans about her trip back to the old country to further her research.

As soon as she heard that Alison had failed her exams, she telephoned Dan in Mungindi to ask him where she was. She had just the thing to take Alison's mind off her bad luck.

"A trip to Ireland," she said. "Just the thing. Remember I told you my genealogy had ground to a standstill and that I can't do any more from here and need to look at local parish records?" Cat guessed that he probably hadn't heard her in the first place, as it was around the time of Nell's death she had first spoken of it. "I am offering Alison the position of my paid assistant. Can't wait to spend Fritz's money and think of him spinning in his grave while I'm doing it. If he does, it will the first bit of exercise he's ever taken."

You had to hand it to her for tenacity, Dan thought. After seventeen years she still hadn't given up on Alison, and it was just as well, really, seeing the poor girl is now homeless and without prospects. He remembered how difficult it had been the first time he had to tell her that Alison was not available for adoption, and how easy it had been the second time when Nell was ill, and the final time after Nell died.

"With this dicky heart of mine I can't risk travelling on my own," Cat went on to explain. "None of our sisters or my friends can afford the fare and I'm not forking out for someone as old and decrepit as I am. I need someone young and energetic."

And attractive and bright, thought Dan.

"It's a great opportunity for Alison, you have to admit. I don't want to end up like Fritz, falling off the perch before I get a chance to travel the world."

Dan told Cat to ring Jean Cunningham's boarding house as that was where Alison was staying.

Cat took the lift to the third floor of the hospital where Fritz had been treated. She was on her way to the office to discuss details about making a donation to the Stroke Wing in memory of Fritz. As she stepped out of the lift she thought she would suffer a stroke herself when she found herself looking straight into the face of Nell reincarnated.

The woman standing in front of her turned out not to be Nell, of course. It was Zita. The likeness between daughter and mother was more pronounced now that Zita was older. Zita put down the mop and bucket she was carrying and made an involuntary movement as if she were about to run away. Cat caught her by the arm and Zita stood in front of her with her head bowed as if she were overcome with shame.

Cat rang Alison that night.

"I have someone here who is dying to see you," said Cat.

"Who is it?"

"Can't you guess?"

Alison did a quick run through her cousins but, seeing she hardly knew any of them, couldn't imagine that any of them would be dying to see her.

"No. I can't guess."

"I could keep you in suspense but I won't. Who else could it be but Zita?"

"Zita?" Alison looked quickly towards Stevie, sitting beside the window reading the paper, and wished she hadn't said the name aloud. It would sound so dreadful to him, like hearing the worst swear word in existence shouted out in anger – two syllables that hadn't been said aloud in the family for five years.

Stevie lifted up the paper to hide his face from Alison's line of vision.

Thinking of how angry and disappointed Zita would be about the Leaving Certificate debacle, after the promises she had made to her, she could barely get out the words, "Is she all right?"

"She's in good health. I only found her today. It's a long story. I'll fill you in when you come down. Just get yourself packed. I'll mail you up the fare."

"Thank you, Aunty."

"We'll go on a spending spree for clothes when you get here. Send me a telegram to let me know when you'll be arriving. Get Stevie to put you on the train at Raleigh. I'll meet you at Central Station. We can't have you getting lost on your first visit to the Big Smoke. And wait until you see how wonderful television is. You'll never want to go back to the bush again after that."

"Three minutes. Are you extending?" asked the telephonist.

"No, thank you. See you soon, Alison."

Alison placed the receiver back on its cradle.

"Has Cat made contact with your sister?" Stevie asked from behind the paper.

"Yes."

"Is she all right?"

"Yes."

"That's good," said Stevie.

Alison noticed the paper was shaking.

CHAPTER 55

Aunty Cat felt that her day had come at last as she stood on the platform at Central Station waiting for the North Coast mail train that would bring Alison to Sydney for the first time. Nell would be looking down from heaven at the meeting, no doubt listening to every word, and Cat intended to show her sister-in-law a thing or two about how to do the right thing by a seventeen-year-old. Nell's death had not diminished Cat's desire to outshine her.

As Alison emerged from the train, looking satisfyingly unconfident and dishevelled, though not at a level to detract from her good looks, Cat felt a rush of happiness and claimed her with a sophisticated air kiss.

"I've left the car at Gordon Station. We have to go down a level to catch another train to get us there. Follow me and don't get lost in the crowd. You're not in the bush now, you know," she couldn't help adding. "We'll talk when we get on the train."

Alison tried to keep Cat's feathery bonnet in sight while alternating between staring at the vaulted ceiling of Central Station, and trying not to bump into people who were all striding out in different directions as if they knew where they were heading.

"Zita is nervous about meeting you," Cat said after they had settled on the train to the North Shore suburbs. "I want to fill you in first while she's not around. Just make sure you don't let on that I told you anything."

Alison was seated in the corner, with Cat beside her, leaning in towards her ear so that the other passengers would not be able to listen in. Alison didn't like the sensation of sitting so close to her, but preferred it to the alternative of sitting opposite and having to make eye contact. As it was, she looked at the floor for the whole time Cat was telling the bits she knew of Zita's story. Alison wasn't sure if she wanted to know any details; she felt all discomforted inside at the thought of the awful things she might be forced to hear about her disgraced sister, but it would not have occurred to her to interrupt her aunt's flow, or object to being forced to listen.

"She hasn't tried to be reconciled with your father. I told her he was so cut up about her running off with a married man that he sold the farm and moved away for that reason. It wasn't the burning down of the house that made him do it. He couldn't bear the thought of all the gossip. You know what the Bible says about great punishments that will be visited on those who give scandal."

Alison wondered how she would be able to look Zita in the eye when she met her.

"All she has to do is write to him and tell him nothing happened with the married man and that she left him after a day, but she won't do it. If there was any sin involved it was in thoughts and desires, not actions, so there's really nothing to gossip about. It's as if she wants to punish him in some way. She's very sour on him. She won't tell you this but she's been living a life of hardship, saving up every penny, not smoking or drinking, never going out. A bit extreme if you ask me, but she said she promised you on the night before you left home that she would take you to Ireland, and that's what she's working towards. You have to admire her for her dedication of purpose, all the same. With that low wage Zita's being paid she'd be middle-aged before she had enough for two fares, so that's where I've stepped in and come to the rescue. She has enough for one and I'll pay for you as my employee. The three of us will go together."

Alison was glad she wouldn't be travelling alone with Cat. "That's good of you, Aunt," she said.

"It's nothing. I can afford it. You will need to know what topics to avoid when you're talking to her. Dancing is the main one, of course. I can't imagine her ever wanting to dance again. Cleaning is another, and marriage and children the touchiest subjects of them all. Now, here we are. My car is parked just over there. Don't let on I told you anything. That's a very light suitcase. That won't get you very far. We'll soon have that bursting with fashionable clothes."

Zita stayed in the kitchen when Cat's car pulled up and waited, standing behind a chair, holding on to the back of it.

Alison entered and stared at Zita who looked as if she had just completed a walk of hundreds of miles and used up all her energy.

Neither made a move.

"It's been a long time," said Zita. "You've grown your hair, I see."

As soon as Alison heard the familiar voice she felt a wave of something she could not describe as love – as she did not know what love was, convinced she had never experienced it – but felt it must be something resembling that emotion. It was like a gravitational pull towards something familiar and desirable.

"Yes. It took me four years to get it to this length," she said in reply, and then after a pause added, "I'm sorry about not winning the scholarship."

"So you should be." Zita's expression was cold. "That on top of the bursary. It seems like more than bad luck. It looks like some kind of a curse. It was the one thing I asked you to do, and you couldn't even do that much for me, you with all your opportunities handed to you on a plate."

"You've nothing to be sorry about," Cat chimed in hastily when she saw Alison's face redden with mortification. "It was pure bad luck. We've other more important things to think about now, anyway. We'll be in Ireland for your eighteenth birthday."

"So we will," said Zita. "It promises to be a memorable occasion."

"It certainly does," said Cat. "Here, girls, take a seat and I'll put on the kettle. I'm dying to hear all the latest news."

"I'm surprised you don't wear your hair loose," said Zita.

"I had to have either a plait or a ponytail at school. No loose hair touching the collars. That was the rule."

"I remember it well," said Zita.

"I got used to wearing it this way."

"I think your plait looks nice and tidy, Alison. Tell me, how is everyone in Redmundo?" asked Aunty Cat. "Any scandals?"

"How is Wombat?" Zita asked at the same moment, seating herself opposite Alison.

"Wombat has left the district. Everyone's talking about it," Alison told her.

"I read that in the *Clarion*," said Aunty Cat, who also had the paper posted to her every week. "What's the story behind that startling piece of information?"

"I'm sure Cheryl found out all the details and rang Dad to tell him all about it," said Zita, her voice loaded with disapproval. "You don't need the *Clarion* when she's around."

"She's been a bit preoccupied lately as it so happens," said Alison. "Her son got a three-month sentence for causing grievous bodily harm to some poor innocent bloke in a café who looked at him sideways. But the whole town knows about Wombat. The story spread like wildfire. Bik ran him out of town. It was completely unexpected. The long and short of it is that Wombat is in love with Bik's wife Gretta."

"What? Are you joking?" Zita reacted as if she had just heard that the sky was falling down.

"No, it's true. I wouldn't joke about a thing like that. Are you all right, Zita?"

"Yes, yes. Go on."

"The next-door neighbour saw it all through a hole in the fence. Just as well or no one would have known what happened otherwise. Bik came home unexpectedly and caught them holding hands in the garden. He went for Wombat, and the Alsatian went for him – the Alsatian Wombat had trained for Bik – and Bik went for Gretta, and Wombat got his voice back and threatened Bik. At least some good came out of the mess with Wombat speaking again, not that we'll ever hear him as he can't come back to town because Bik said he would kill Gretta if he ever did."

"Perhaps she'll try to make a bolt for it. Wombat could organise it," said Cat.

"Her neighbour said she's under house arrest and the kids have been warned."

"Well, I never!" said Aunty Cat. "That sounds more like a film than real life. Look at the time. You'll have to leave telling us the details till later. Come on, girls. Into the lounge we go. Quickly – *Six O'Clock Rock* is about to start. Hurry up, Alison, I don't want you to miss it. I envy you seeing television for the first time. I'll never forget the experience. It changed my life. You sit there, Zita. You sit here beside me, Alison. Now, no talking while this is on. It's one of my favourite programmes even though I'm supposed to be miles too old for it."

Zita stared at the screen. Alison looked over at her. Zita, aware of the look, turned with a smile to make up for the harsh words she had said earlier but Alison looked away before she saw it.

"Wasn't that wonderful?" enthused Aunty Cat after the programme was over.

Alison did not need to fake her excitement at seeing singers performing. Previously she had heard their voices only on the radio and wondered what they looked like and what movements they were making while they were singing. "It was even better than I imagined," she said.

"I knew it would be. And to think poor Fritz wouldn't allow it in the house. What a lot of pleasure he denied himself. We aren't going to make the same mistake which leads me on to the next thing. I think being a dogsbody in a TV studio where you could meet all those famous people visiting from overseas would be much more exciting than a career in teaching. Who's going to see you there? Who will you talk to? With your good looks, Alison, you shouldn't even contemplate hiding yourself away. A job as a researcher on television would be the best. I have contacts in high places. All you need is an introduction and you would win the place after that on your looks alone, though it wouldn't hurt to take some deportment and elocution lessons just to be sure – they'll do wonders for you. Everyone wants to work in television these days if you ask me, and who could blame them? If it had been around it my day I would have gone for it like a shot."

Alison wanted to contradict Cat, telling her how influential teachers had been in her life and how she felt that it was her vocation to become one, but she didn't have the skill or the confidence to contradict Cat's assumptions.

Zita shook her head at Alison while Cat wasn't looking to show that she didn't agree with what Cat was saying.

"Now let's talk about our trip. We can confirm our bookings now that we know Alison is definitely coming."

"What about Hanna?" asked Alison.

"What about her?" said Cat.

"Won't she feel left out? She's the only girl in the family not going."

"As if she would care. Isn't she on the pig's back?" Zita answered with acid in her voice. "All smugly married to a man on the land and probably a baby on the way by now. What could be more perfect for her? There'll be no scandals coming from her direction. Anyway, I never promised her the trip, and I doubt if she'd want to go."

"You can say that again," said Cat. "Once a girl marries her loyalties shift, and after the kids arrive you're lucky if you get a look in, with their eyes swivelling around following their kids' every movement, boasting about them non-stop and boring people half to death with stories about how clever their offspring are, God preserve me. And I should know. I've been left out in the cold by my sisters ever since they started their own families. They're not the slightest bit interested in my life, treating me like some kind of pariah. There was no way I'd invite any of them to come to Ireland with me even though their tongues are hanging out for it now that their kids are reared and I've come into money. Sod them, I say." Cat's voice had begun to falter by the time she finished speaking, so she changed the subject, turning to Zita to persuade her to stay the night.

Zita agreed and Aunty Cat put the two girls into a room with twin beds.

That night Alison heard Zita crying in the dark, in the way she used to do when they were younger. At that time Alison never let on she heard, but now she felt compelled to ask, despite expecting another rebuke, "What's the matter?"

Zita took a while to answer. "It's Wombat," she said. "It's wonderful that he can speak but I'm sorry things didn't turn out well for him after he found someone who loved him."

245

CHAPTER 56

The three women boarded a liner to take them from Sydney to Southampton, calling in to South Africa and the Canary Islands on the way. From England they would make their own way across the Irish Sea to Dublin.

On board, Alison seemed too frightened to speak to the other passengers, and avoided contact with the stewards and staff.

Cat had been saddened to see that Alison had been afraid of shop assistants, waitresses, hairdressers and ticket collectors while they were shopping in preparation for the trip, and it had been left up to her to do the talking and make the choices.

Alison, gnawing away at her fingernails until they bled, tended to walk behind Cat or Zita and relied on them to speak for her if anyone asked a question. Zita's commands to her to stop the disgusting habit of biting her nails made no impression.

"One thing you must do before we arrive is learn how to smoke," Cat said to Alison, taking her aside for a quiet word. "It's very sophisticated if you do it properly and it will give you confidence."

"What about Zita?"

"She plans to take it up after the trip. I was working on her to start, but she kept going on about the cost of them, which is ridiculous. Less than two shillings a packet! That's nothing when you

246

think of the amount of pleasure you get out of them and how they make you look like a film star. You'll be easily able to afford them with what I'm paying you. Here, take this cigarette and don't inhale at first or you'll cough. Hold it like this. Lean over and I'll light it for you. There. It suits you. Relax. You'll get used to it in no time and you'll be able to do a full inhalation and a slow exhalation. It's a good skill to have. Then you'll have to grow your fingernails and paint them as they'll be on display all the time." Cat was determined to succeed over the nail-biting issue where Zita had failed. She hoped Nell was looking down from heaven, admiring her clever bit of psychology. "You never know, when Zita sees how like Joan Crawford you look, she might change her mind and take it up straight away. Just make sure you don't blow smoke out your nose as that is not considered to be ladylike. We don't want to put off all those men who keep looking over at you. As soon as you get practised enough to smoke in public, they'll all be rushing over to light your cigarette and then introduce themselves. It gives them an excuse to approach you. If we achieve nothing on this trip except you learning to smoke, the trip hasn't been wasted."

So Cat has got her hands on Alison at last, thought Zita as she watched the smoking lesson from a distance. After I did all the hard work in the beginning she comes along at the end to claim her and set about reshaping her life with all her money and her contacts and her grandiose plans for the future. There'll be no mops or buckets in Alison's life, that's for certain.

Zita did not begrudge Cat her triumph, seeing she had been unfairly deprived of Alison for so long. She was welcome to mould her in any form she saw fit. Just as long as Zita could have her for the few minutes that would be needed to demonstrate that Mary Anne was not the natural child of Dr and Mrs Carmody. A few minutes that would result, with luck, in the ruination of the lives of all the members of that particular family.

She would not contemplate her own bleak future until after this trip was over.

PART 3

MARY ANNE AND ALISON

IRELAND, 1959

CHAPTER 57

Mary Anne was luminous with happiness, and her friends were giddy with excitement when they called in to ask Lady Edwina if they might look through the period clothes stored in various rooms throughout the townhouse, to choose something to wear to the birthday banquet.

"If it's a special gown you are looking for, Mary Anne," said Edwina, "I have just the thing. I would be frightfully pleased if you would wear it as a particular favour to me."

"Of course I will, Weena. I will be delighted to as long as it fits me."

"It may need to be taken in a little but, apart from that, it will look as if it were made for you. It has never been worn."

The dress was the one Edwina had intended to wear forty years earlier to the Tyringham Park Hunt Ball. Its high neckline was designed specifically to show off the Blackshaw diamonds which, she discovered on the morning of the hunt, had been stolen. As it turned out, she wouldn't have got to wear the diamonds, anyway, as that was the day she had suffered her accident. The diamonds were never found and the dress was never worn.

One of the girls in the group, waiting for Edwina to finish talking to Mary Anne, whispered the word "engagement" and was immediately silenced by the others.

Edwina heard the word but pretended she didn't, having already judged by the girls' demeanours that they were preparing for something a lot more momentous than a mere banquet. An engagement? Of course. What else would have them simmering with such joy?

An engagement!

It had come a few years earlier than expected, but was no less welcome for that.

This will be one in the eye for Mary Anne's republican stepmother, Edwina gloated. Despite the best efforts of that woman with the ridiculously-spelt Irish name to derail Mary Anne's true destiny of becoming a Blackshaw by marrying William, blood has won out in the end.

"Are you nervous?" asked Niamh, as she cleared the table after the evening meal.

Mary Anne was about to return to the townhouse, this time alone, to speak to Edwina.

"A bit. I know Weena will be disappointed that I won't be marrying William, but when she gets to know Toby I am sure she will like him."

"Of course she will."

"If only she would make the effort. She never addressed one word to him when he was at the Park and she has never enquired after him in the five years since he left to join the guards."

"Perhaps she has softened during those years. She'll have to talk to him now and she's sure to get to like him as soon as she does, wonderful young man that he is."

"I hope she does."

"You would imagine her ladyship would be impressed by his horsemanship, if nothing else."

"That upsets her more than anything else. He's better than all of us cousins put together."

"Oh, dear."

Lochlann, entering the discussion for the first time, said with confidence, "I don't think you have anything to worry about. Edwina has always had your best interests at heart. Once she knows your happiness depends on marrying Toby, she will give her blessing and finally welcome him into the family."

"I hope you're right."

"Do you want us to come with you for moral support?"

"No, I'd better do it on my own. She won't think I'm mature enough to get engaged if I need you to back me up. Thanks for the offer all the same. Wish me luck."

"You're such an innocent," Niamh said after Mary Anne had left.

Me an innocent, thought Lochlann. The man with the blackest soul in the whole of Ireland? How little she knows. How could I ever be considered an innocent? "Why do you say that?"

"How could you think that Edwina will accept Toby when she has never even accepted you? She won't. Never in a million years. She will be repelled. If you think that the old she-wolf has Mary Anne's best interests at heart, you must have been wearing blinkers and earplugs for the last couple of decades."

Edwina had requested that she be lifted out of her wheelchair and placed on a two-seater couch beside Mary Anne so she could sit close beside her while hearing her good news.

After the manservant left, Mary Anne said, "I've something to tell you, Weena."

"I was wondering when I would be let in on the secret. You're in love."

"I am. How did you guess?"

"One doesn't reach my age without being able to read the signs," said Edwina. Especially if in one's youth one had experienced that state of delirium oneself.

"And here was I thinking I wasn't giving away any clues."

"You've made me a very happy woman. It's what I wished for you. Tyringham Park will be restored to its former grandeur. I knew it would happen in the end."

Mary Anne looked uncomfortable. "I think there's a misunderstanding, Weena. It's not William I have agreed to marry. It's Toby Prendergast."

Edwina, with a discipline she attributed to centuries of breeding, choked back her horror at the sound of that name and said in a controlled voice, "Does your father know of this?"

"Yes, of course. He was the first person I told. Niamh was the second."

"Has your father given you his consent?"

"Yes, he was delighted. He thinks the world of Toby. As does Niamh."

"A view shared by many, apparently. I wonder your father didn't object on the grounds of your different religions."

"He thinks love is more important than religion, and so do I. We will have plenty of time to work out what compromises need to be made. There will be a four-year-long engagement, so we're not exactly rushing into anything. We'd like our families to get to know one another better."

Four years? That should give me more than enough time to get rid of this Toby person, thought Edwina, and show William how to select the right cards and how to play them correctly if he wants to win his cousin. He was probably about to make his move when that cuckoo in the nest swooped in there in front of him.

"I am looking forward to getting to know him and doing something for him," said Edwina after a long pause. "With my contacts I should be able to find him a posting that will do him justice."

"Thank you for the thought, Weena," said Mary Anne, relieved that her grandmother was taking the news so well.

A posting in the British Army would do nicely, thought Edwina. One that would send him to some colony, as far away as possible from Mary Anne who, at such a young age, would soon forget him and turn to William, with whom she has so much more in common. It is a pity India is no longer a member of the Empire as it would have been the perfect place to send him to get rid of him.

"You don't have to do anything for Toby," Mary Anne said, "though it's kind of you to think of him, Weena. He is happy where he is, making his own way in the Garda Síochána."

"Please don't use that unpronounceable foreign language in my presence. 'Royal Constabulary' did well enough for years and, if they had to change it, what is wrong with 'Police Force'? It's clear and to the point. Has he so little ambition?"

"He has wanted to become a detective since he was eight years of age, so it's not a passing whim. With his personality and talents it's only a matter of time before he is chosen to train for that division."

"I can't think that anyone would choose to be a member of the Irish Police Force rather than an officer in the British Army."

Mary Anne could see lots of reasons but, as usual in matters of cultural differences, she did not bother disagreeing and murmured something noncommittal instead.

"So I can't be of any use to him? Never mind. I presume he will be presented to me at the banquet?"

"Before that if you wish. He has a day off on Friday week. His mother is coming up to Dublin to buy an outfit for the banquet so you would be able to meet her as well."

"I think I shall be able to contain my curiosity until the banquet, if it's all the same with you." Ridiculing the mother's speech, dress sense or demeanour would be much more satisfying done in public than in private. It shouldn't be difficult to single out some fault fairly quickly.

"As you prefer, Weena. She remembers seeing you around the Park when she was a little girl and remembers how much she looked up to you."

"I can't say I have any memory of her."

"She is the same age as my mother, but they never spoke to one another."

"That's how things were done in those days." And it's a pity they still aren't and then I wouldn't have to deal with Toby Prendergast.

"It's lucky for me things have changed for the better. I must say you have been wonderful about this, Weena. Wanting to help Toby and all that."

Edwina did her best to smile in response to Mary Anne's gratitude, though the resulting shape of her mouth looked more like a grimace.

"I would dearly love to have the wedding in Tyringham Park when the time comes, if everyone agrees," Mary Anne said as she was leaving. "Then I can place my bouquet on my mother's grave after the ceremony."

Edwina once again tried to smile, making the grimace look even more ghastly.

CHAPTER 58

It was all so easy. Zita looked up a telephone directory, a copy of which covered the entire twenty-six counties of the Republic of Ireland, thanking goodness that Lochlann wasn't a Murphy with its hundreds of entries. It took her less than a minute to check the twelve entries listed under the name of Carmody, spelt in the way she assumed it would be. Only one was designated as 'Dr' and only one had the initial 'L' and they referred to the same person. How could she have known on the other side of the world how easy it would be to find him? She wrote down the address and phone number and later bought a map of Dublin to locate the square on which he lived. It was within walking distance of the city centre, she was relieved to see, as she didn't want to have to study bus routes and timetables in addition to all the other planning that was crowding out her mind.

She had a childhood memory of the doctor that was not clear enough to pick him out in a crowd, but would be adequate, she assumed, to identify him emerging from his own front door.

"Are you sure you won't change your mind and come with us, Zita?" Aunty Cat asked, as they stood in the foyer of the hotel waiting for the taxi that was to take Alison and her to the station.

Alison left Cat and Zita talking and went outside to have a last look at the magnificent old buildings lining the street.

The first thing that attracted her attention was not a building, but a young man in a hurry weaving his way down along the crowded pavement. She felt a charge of attraction at the sight of him. He was a floppy-haired, slender, artistic-looking type, with an animated expression that became even more animated after he spotted her.

Perhaps he's a little too brazen, she thought, even verging on the arrogant, but then she didn't yet know the social customs of this country and perhaps his open appraisal was considered to be acceptable behaviour here. He looked as if he knew her, but how could he when she was a stranger in the city? Usually when men stared at her in so interested a fashion, which was often, she would look away, but this time she didn't, wanting to imprint his image on her memory because she fancied the look of him so much and didn't expect to catch sight of him ever again. A chance sighting in a crowded street in a foreign country. That was all it was, and she was lucky to have experienced it.

He looked at her, blinked, then looked again and kept walking straight towards her.

"Hullo there, cuz," he said, not stopping. "Didn't recognise you there for a minute. What have you done to your hair? Sorry, can't stop. Late for Bennett. See you Wednesday." The last bit was said over his shoulder as he crossed the street, before running up some stone steps and disappearing behind pillars and doors into an impressive building she had admired earlier, wondering how anyone, especially a girl like her from the bush, would ever have the courage to enter it.

The posh accent. That disconcerted her. She had only heard that kind of accent before in the movies, and it would have turned her off him instantly if his looks and bearing hadn't already made such a favourable impression on her before he had opened his mouth. To look at him, with his worn clothing and dishevelled hair, she would never have guessed he would have an accent like that. And he called her 'cuz' in such an affectionate tone. Was it short for some posh name or for 'cousin'? Little point in wondering, really, seeing she was never likely to find out. The warmth in his tone had affected her as she was not used to being spoken to in that way and it made her feel weepy.

She went back inside the hotel foyer, where Cat and Zita were still talking, and took a deep breath to give herself the courage to ask the beautifully groomed receptionist if she knew the name of the building directly opposite.

"I do. It's the Kildare Street Club," she said. "Very well known. A landmark." When Alison reacted with a blank look, she added, smiling, "It's exclusive. For the gentry. And for men only, so I don't think we'll bother applying for membership any time soon."

That explained the accent. "Thank you." Alison smiled back before turning away, deflated, to join Cat and Zita standing at the door. She decided not to tell them about the man she had just seen as they would ask too many questions and laugh at her if she blushed, which was what she was likely to do.

"Are you *sure* you won't change your mind and come with us?" Cat was repeating to Zita.

"Positive. I have a great desire to just walk around Dublin, to look at old buildings and talk to people." To look at one old building in particular and talk to one specific person, to be precise, she thought. Where's that taxicab? I wish this pair would hurry up and leave so I can get started. "I'll arrive with a *big surprise* for your birthday, Alison, to make up for my late start."

Alison was staring out the doors at the building opposite and didn't answer.

"What's the matter with you? You look like a sick calf."

"Nothing. I was just admiring the stonework." And feeling like a sick calf.

She wished Zita was coming with them. Her feelings of homesickness had returned at the thought of parting from her big sister again after so recently being reunited with her. Abrasive and cutting though she was, at least she was familiar in a way Aunty Cat could never be. What if looking up parish records, the job for which Cat was paying her, turned out to be too boring to be borne?

And more urgently, she wished the man who had disappeared across the way would come back out so that she could see him once again before she left, and perhaps even force herself to talk to him and find out why he had called her 'cuz'.

Cat had sent Dan the address of the hotel in Cork in which they would be staying for the initial month, in case he needed to get in contact with his daughters. Now she wrote it on an envelope and handed it to Zita, along with a roll of ten-pound notes, whispering as she did so, "This is so you can stay here in comfort. Don't go to that hostel dormitory. It's my treat, so you don't have to feel guilty." Aloud she said, "We'll definitely see you for the birthday, then. In the meantime make sure you don't fall in love with a tall, dark and handsome Irishman." She had nearly said 'run off with' instead of 'fall in love with', but checked herself in time. "We don't want to go home without you."

"As if anybody would care if you did," Zita mumbled quietly.

Her aunt and sister heard what she said, and their high spirits took a dip, before rising again at the arrival of the taxicab that was to take them to Heuston Station where they would catch a train to Cork city.

CHAPTER 59

Zita, already prepared with her coat on and the map in her bag, waved goodbye to the travellers and set off to find the house belonging to Dr Carmody.

She had a fair idea what Cat would be saying about her once the train was on its way. 'She's a bitter pill, that sister of yours," would be her opening remark. 'I know life has dealt her a bad hand, and nobody has more sympathy for her than I do, but she shouldn't have let it turn her into a bitter pill. It is beginning to show on her face. A woman of that age can't afford to let that happen."

Alison would say nothing in her defence. Why should she after the way she had been treated?

Zita soon found the square with its tall redbrick houses grouped around a park which was enclosed by iron railings. Inside the railings was a dense, dark-green hedge. Having no experience of terraces, she at first could not work out where one house finished and another one began, and wondered why they were even called 'houses', all joined up as they were in an unbroken line along the length of a street. They were four storeys high, with tall windows, and stone steps leading up to impressive entrance doors with pillars on each side and an ornate fanlight above them.

She checked the address she had written down and found No. 42

which was in the middle of the terrace. How best to keep her eye on its front door to find out who went in and who came out and what they looked like? At the moment there were only two other pedestrians on this side of the square, so walking up and down, merging into crowds, which was what she had envisaged she would be doing, would not be an option. Standing in the park looking through the hedge might be the best way to obtain a good view, while at the same time avoiding drawing any attention to herself.

The best time? Obviously not at two thirty in the afternoon, the time it was now, with nobody about. Rush hour the next morning would be a better time, with adults going to work, students to college and children to school.

So here was the house and here was she standing outside it. To think Dr Lochlann Carmody actually lived here – a man of flesh and blood, and not the malignant spirit she had held in her mind for nearly eighteen years.

She remembered one particularly lonely Sunday in Sydney when she had threaded her way through happy, laughing crowds to stand at the water's edge, and how she had felt the urge to continue walking until she was out of her depth. The prospect of sinking to the bottom of the harbour, and staying there, had been particularly tempting to her depressed mind at the time. The only thing that prevented her from going in was the certainty that every single person on the shoreline possessed a lifesaving certificate, and at least one of them would spot her and jump in and drag her out before she had time to take in even one mouthful of water. And there she would be, very much alive, looking bedraggled and foolish, while her rescuer would be surrounded by admiring friends slapping him on the back, and she would have to make her way home alone in her wet clothes with passengers on the train staring at her as if she were some kind of foreign misfit.

Looking back, it felt strange to her that during that episode she hadn't once thought of her hatred for Dr Carmody as a reason for not going into the water. Now she could think of nothing but her hatred for him. How glad she was that she had not drowned herself in Sydney Harbour on that particular day and that she was here now.

How would she cope if the beautifully painted glossy black door with its brass plate and brass adornments opened and he came out while she was standing there, staring at it and imagining him? She didn't think her brain would be capable of comprehending it, and she would probably pass out from her reaction to the reality of his presence.

In her peripheral vision she saw the head of a scarf-wearing old woman popping up to street level from behind the front railings of the house, and a few seconds later the rest of her person came into view.

Where had she come from? Zita, unaware of the existence of such things as below-ground-level basements in houses, had been caught gawping up at the façade of the house by the scarf-wearing old woman.

To cover her embarrassment, she was about to pull out her map and pretend to study it when the old woman said, "The doctor's at the hospital at the moment, dear. If you want to see him in his rooms, you'll have to come back at four."

She must be the grandmother, was Zita's immediate assumption. Attracted by the friendly grandmotherly face, she answered, "Thank you. I'll wait. I've nothing else to do."

"Is that an Australian accent I hear, by any chance?"

Zita didn't think she had any accent, but answered that it was. "I've only just arrived."

"Have you really? That's very exciting. I have a daughter in Perth, that's how I know. Her children talk like you. I hope you see a bit of sunshine while you're here." The old lady stood as if she were in no hurry to move on.

"I didn't come for the sunshine. I can get plenty of that at home."

"That's just as well. You'll be lucky to catch sight of it here, though I hear we're in for a good summer this year." Her eyes filled up. "I'll probably never see my daughter again, but she's happy settled there with a family, so that's the main thing. Says she could never come back to all our grey skies." The old woman wiped away the tears. "I can't begrudge her a new life, though I do miss her something dreadful. We talk on the phone once a month. I have to make do with that."

Was this daughter in Perth a sister of Lochlann Carmody's? No one had heard anything about his having a sister in Perth, a fact that would surely have been mentioned. Perhaps she was younger and had gone out after Lochlann had returned from Redmundo.

"You've an hour and a half to wait, dear. Can I treat you to a cup of tea and a scone to fill in the time, and you can tell me all about Australia? You don't come from anywhere near Perth by any chance, do you?"

"No, from the other side, but I hear it's a lovely city to live in."

"So my daughter keeps telling me. I'm glad for her sake. There's a nice tearoom between here and O'Connell Street where I catch my bus. It's not often I get the chance to talk to a real Australian. You're only the second one I've met. I want to hear more about what it's like to live there." The old woman adjusted her scarf, buttoned her coat and motioned to Zita to come with her. "Funny, the doctor was out there for a few years but no one can get him to talk about it. Strange, that."

Not strange at all if you knew the reason why, Zita thought, unable to believe her luck. The grandmother was in the mood for talking and she was in the mood for listening and for asking strategic questions. It could save her hours of loitering behind hedges.

"It sounds as if your son didn't like it while he was there."

The old woman made an odd sound in her throat and then laughed. "You've made a mistake, dear," she said, wiping her eyes again. "The doctor is not my son. If only he was, wonderful man that he is. No, I'm the cleaner and have been working for the family for ten years. I'm Mrs Kaye, though the daughter does call me 'Granny', probably because of my white hair. The doctor told her not to be cheeky but I told him I liked the name and it stuck. Sorry for being so rude as to laugh. You're the first person to ask me that and it took me by surprise. Any Irish person would know from my accent that I wouldn't be his mother." She kept smiling at intervals until they reached the tearoom.

Zita didn't wish to appear too eager to find out information in case the old lady became suspicious and clammed up, so fulfilled what she considered to be her side of the bargain by describing for her companion the good points about Australian life with its sunshine, beaches, space, career opportunities, tropical fruit and a climate conducive to playing sport all year round. Mrs Kaye was pleased to hear all that praise from a "fair dinkum Aussie", as she proudly used the term to describe Zita, and in turn, prompted by

Zita, talked about the Carmody family, ending with a description of the daughter's upcoming eighteenth-birthday celebrations.

"I've only seen Tyringham Park once so far myself and I'll never forget it. Like a castle out of a fairy story. Mary Anne – that's the daughter's name – is organising an exhibition of her mother's paintings on the last weekend in May – that's what she requested for her birthday, which is actually . . ."

On Monday, June the first, Zita wanted to say aloud, but controlled herself.

"On Monday, the first of June," Mrs Kaye continued. "She's very friendly with her relations down there in County Cork. There's talk of an engagement announcement to the eldest of them on the Saturday night which will be a grand occasion. A banquet. Her grandmother has asked her to wear a special dress that once belonged to her, so that will be nice."

"That's all fascinating. What's the dress like? Have you seen it? Talking about fashionable clothes is one of my favourite things."

"I've only this morning ironed it. It's black taffeta. Lovely to the touch."

"What style is it? Short or long or ballet length? Straight or full skirt?"

"Full length with a fitted waist, a very full gathered skirt, three-quarter-length sleeves and a high neck that's great for showing off diamonds – though she won't be wearing any."

A stab of jealousy. "Sounds glamorous. What else has she planned?"

"On the following morning, after Mary Anne and her father put flowers on her mother's grave, they –"

"Her mother is dead?" Zita choked on the words.

"Yes, dear, she is. I'm sorry the news upsets you. It was a long time ago and Mary Anne doesn't remember her, so don't be upset."

"Sorry." Zita blew her nose, annoyed at herself for snivelling. "Silly of me when I didn't know the woman. I feel sorry for any motherless children even when I don't know them." She didn't want to elaborate on that observation, afraid she would be asked about her own mother, so hurried on with the next question. "Did the doctor marry again?"

"He did. That was a piece of good fortune if ever there was one.

She is adored by everyone who knows her. Especially by the doctor and Mary Anne. It was a great sadness for her that she wasn't able to have a child of her own, but she dotes on Mary Anne, so that is a great comfort to her."

"I'm sure it is. You were saying that after they put flowers on the grave . . ."

"The house and grounds will be open to the public. I'd say the estate will be packed. Loads of people are dying to see the Park even if they're not interested in the paintings. It will probably be in all the papers."

Zita couldn't believe her luck. A gathering in County Cork. Not that it would have made any difference in which county it was to be held – she and Alison would be there, with Alison in a black dress with a high neck, three-quarter-length sleeves, fitted waist and full, gathered skirt.

A grand occasion. Perhaps even an engagement to her cousin? That was all too perfect! If what Wombat had said was true, she and Alison would not only be Mary Anne's closest relations at the celebrations, but the only ones connected to her by blood. And the only ones attending without an invitation. The whole event, even if she had organised it herself, could not have supplied a more dramatic backdrop to her planned unveiling of Alison.

"It's a lot of work for Mary Anne. Just as well she sat the Leaving Cert last year or she'd be up to her eyes in books at this time of year. There was talk of holding her back as she was the youngest in the class but as it turned out it was no bother to her as she's so bright, according to her teachers, though you'd never know it to talk to her. She never shows off and is so down to earth."

I think I'm going to be sick, Zita thought.

"She's going for medicine like her father."

On hearing that, Zita experienced a sting of envy so sharp that she felt her face contort in response to the pain of it. She put her hands across the bottom half of her face to cover the ugly physical contortions reflecting her ugly thoughts, until she felt the spasm had passed and her face felt as if it had reverted to its normal shape. When she was sure she was in command of herself again she asked Mrs Kaye if she would be attending the party.

"No, dear, I won't. They invited me but I'd feel like a fish out of water in the middle of all those grand people. I made up an excuse why I can't go so they wouldn't talk me into it – but I hope it goes well for Mary Anne as she's such a great girl."

"I'm sure there's no reason why it shouldn't."

Mrs Kaye handed over a printed card belonging to her daughter and made Zita promise that, if she ever travelled to Perth, she would look her up. "And when you come back from your touring, you must call in and have tea with me again. Maybe next time we will have it in No.42."

"That would be nice. Thank you. I will look forward to that."

The two talked on, and half an hour later left the tearoom, reluctant to part. Zita said she had changed her mind about visiting the doctor in his surgery as the pain she had felt earlier had completely disappeared for some strange reason.

Zita returned to the hotel to lie on her bed for the rest of the afternoon. During her life, which had been full of tiring days, she had never felt as contentedly tired as she felt at this moment. All that information extracted in one hour, and she didn't even have to disclose her name. She didn't want the doctor alerted. It was a satisfying feeling being on the right track, edging closer. The quest was nearly over. She lay motionless on the bed and experienced a sensation of lightness and freedom at the thought of finally passing her burden over to the person to whom it rightfully belonged.

How glad she was that she had resisted the urge to drown herself in Sydney Harbour that time. To think that, if she had, she might have missed this wonderful day!

"Zita used to be such a sunny kid. Always full of fun," Cat said to Alison as the train was passing through Limerick Junction. "I imagine you would find that hard to believe."

"Yes, I would."

"It was before you were born, of course. Before everything fell to pieces. I'm hoping that after this trip she will get her old cheerful self back again, and there's something I'm going to do for her that might speed up the process." Cat leaned in as if she didn't want their fellow passengers to hear what she was saying. Alison automatically backed away, and Cat leaned in further. "Keep this to yourself and I'll tell her on the way home. Presuming she doesn't meet a nice man and settle down, which isn't very likely seeing she's nearly past it by now, I'm going to put her through university to study medicine and I won't take no for an answer. I know it's her one ambition. With all the money Fritz left me it's only a drop in the ocean, so there's no need for her to feel grateful. She'll have to do a cramming year first to get her Leaving Cert but that should be no trouble for a bright girl like her. You could repeat at the same time if you liked, just for you own satisfaction. I have it all worked out for Zita. She's thirty-two now, so she'll be thirty-eight when she's finished. Some people would consider her too old to waste money on, but in my experience doctors don't ever retire so she should be able to practise until she's over eighty. There's no way you could call that a waste of an investment in education."

Alison felt a rush of affection for her aunt for thinking of such a perfect plan for Zita's future and she hoped she would be in Zita's company to share her delight when she heard Cat make the offer.

CHAPTER 60

Zita, with renewed energy, checked out of the hotel the following morning and, after refusing the porter's offer of ringing for a taxi for her, dragged her suitcase to a hostel in a less desirable part of Dublin. The luxury of the hotel with its deep-pile carpet, tapestry-upholstered chairs and heavy velvet drapes had made her feel uneasy, and it was painful for her to waste money on something that was basically only somewhere to sleep. One week in the hotel would cost the same as eight weeks in the hostel. Staying in a wooden-floored dormitory containing twelve people would not bother her. In fact, it would remind her of her happy days in St Mary's and make her feel secure.

After she was settled in at the hostel she filled in the afternoon buying two inexpensive black dresses, made of cotton rather than taffeta, that were full length and had round necks and long sleeves. She would cut off the sleeves at three-quarter length and leave the raw edges. No one would notice. A momentary effect was all they were meant to supply. Before she forgot, she bought two large squares of black lace, a straw hat with a wide floppy brim, and some pale foundation cream and face powder that would be needed to tone down Alison's tan so that it wouldn't stand out against the fair complexions of the Irish.

Next morning she was in the park by seven and took up a position behind the hedge that gave her a clear view of No. 42's front door.

At seven thirty she saw Mrs Kaye arrive for work and use the basement entrance.

First to leave the Carmody house was an elegant woman who must be the second Mrs Carmody, Mary Anne's stepmother. She carried a Gladstone bag to a car parked at the front of the house and a few minutes later drove off.

There were a lot of people on the street, most heading towards the city centre. Walking in the opposite direction to the hurrying workers were two mature-looking girls, taking their time. One waited on the pavement to light up a cigarette while the other went up the stone steps to ring the bell of No. 42.

A girl came out of the house. She was putting on a jacket as she ran down the steps to join her friends.

Even though Zita had been expecting a shock, she didn't reckon on the effect of its being so electrifying when she saw the girl who must surely be Alison leaving the house by the front door. That is, the girl would have been Alison if Zita didn't know for certain that Alison was nowhere near the square, but was definitely staying in Cork city.

So this was Mary Anne Carmody right there in full view.

Mary Anne had a more erect posture and a more confident aura than Alison, Zita noticed, but the height, shape and features were the same. She was so like Alison, apart from the effect of her short hair which contrasted with Alison's long plait, that it continued to be difficult to believe that it was not actually Alison.

That is my stolen sister coming towards me. Zita was hardly able to believe the truth of the words even as she thought them.

It was a relief to see her. There had always been a possibility that Wombat might have been mistaken. At last she could accept wholeheartedly that he was right, without the slightest trace of doubt. She could now go ahead and ruin the doctor's presumably perfect life without any misgivings. Bringing him to account for the damage he had caused would be some kind of antidote to the poison that had stunted her life, stultified her brain and frozen her affections.

She refused to label her bitterness self-pity and she would not repent. If anyone was culpable, it was God and the doctor. She would punish God by losing her soul – let Him pine for the single lost lamb. As the Good Shepherd, He should have looked after His lamb more conscientiously than He had. The doctor she would deal with directly.

The three girls talked and gesticulated as they crossed the street and entered the park through a gate. When Zita saw they were heading in her direction, she moved quickly to sit at one end of a bench that was already occupied by three old men who shuffled along to make room for her. She rummaged through her bag and took out an old letter, which she opened and pretended to read, holding it a distance away from her eyes as if she were in need of reading glasses. By focusing on the top of the page, she was able to shift her gaze slightly without having to raise her head, and was able to study Mary Anne without fear of being noticed.

If she looked over at me now, would she experience a flicker of recognition for an unknown sister, Zita wondered. Would she pause and try to work out why my face was so interesting to her? Probably not, as I am supposed to be the dead spit of Mum, whereas Alison (and therefore Mary Anne as well) takes after Dad.

Zita was sitting less than twenty feet away from the girls, who were talking about what it felt like to be in love and what they would wear to the Tyringham Park banquet. The one who had lit a cigarette earlier lit up another one and said she envied Mary Anne who knew what it was like to experience love – to be secretly engaged, no less – and whose decision about what to wear had already been made.

Zita couldn't stop staring at Mary Anne. How happy she is in the company of her friends, thought Zita. As I would have been at that age if I'd ever had any.

"Ah, don't light up another one, Patricia," said the third girl a few minutes later. "We're going to be late."

"Just a few puffs," said Patricia. She took a few long drags on her second cigarette before stubbing it out on the path.

The three girls moved towards the gate, still talking.

Zita, shoving the letter back into her bag and taking out a handkerchief, ran after them.

"Excuse me," she called out.

The three girls stopped and turned around to face her.

"Did you drop this?" Zita asked, holding out the handkerchief to Mary Anne.

Mary Anne looked at the handkerchief and then at Zita and smiled. "No, I didn't," she said. "In fact, I forgot to bring one today."

Zita kept her unblinking focus on her sister. She *must* feel a connection, she thought, continuing to stare, wishing she could think of something to say that would hold Mary Anne back when it was obvious she was in a hurry to be on her way.

As if on a signal, the three girls looked at one another and then at their watches before murmuring their goodbyes and saying they were running late.

"Thank you for checking, all the same," Mary Anne said, smiling. "Goodbye."

Zita watched them walk away. She felt high on emotion. I took a bit of a risk there. What if she had spotted a family resemblance? It was on the tip of my tongue to tell her who I was just to see her look of incredulity. Thank goodness I held back. I need to be more careful. I shouldn't have approached her but I couldn't resist the temptation to see her up close and to speak to her. How lovely she is. How charming. Her face so open and mobile, so unlike Alison's closed and watchful one. But then, of course, if Dr Carmody had stolen Alison instead of Mary Anne, Alison's face would be open and mobile, and Mary Anne's would be closed and watchful.

On her way back to the hostel, Zita bought a sharp pair of scissors. She would need to cut Alison's hair to a length that would match Mary Anne's if the twins were to look the mirror image of each other.

CHAPTER 61

"I want to ask you, as a *special* favour, Mary Anne, if you would delay announcing your engagement to the public until the New Year."

"But that's six months away!"

Edwina saw the look of suspicion that flicked across her granddaughter's face. "There is no rush when you can choose any other date during the next four years," she said.

A girl with a broken engagement behind her would inevitably be classed as second-hand goods, and that would not reflect well on William when he finally claimed Mary Anne, so it made sense to Edwina to prevent the engagement from taking place in the first instance. The thought of an official engagement notice appearing in the *Times* was too repugnant to contemplate. A postponement would give Edwina time to come up with a plan to get rid of Toby altogether and to leave Mary Anne's reputation free from any whispers about dubious associations in her past.

"I'll tell you why I'm making the request," Edwina said sweetly. "I know you'll see my point of view and wonder why you didn't think of it yourself. It's nothing negative about your young man, so don't worry. I think that the focus during that weekend should be on your mother's exhibition, seeing it's the first and last one she will ever have, whereas you have any number of choices of days after that. It's also the first time the Park will be open to the public, so Giles and Georgina will be preoccupied. Then there's that award your father is to receive shortly after the birthday. It wouldn't do to deflect attention away from that important honour. Besides, with all that going on, your engagement won't hold centre stage as it deserves. If you delay it until January when all this fuss is over, we will be able to give it our full attention."

Mary Anne put her arms around Edwina's neck and said tearfully, "Of course I will postpone it. We'll keep the news strictly between family and close friends until then. How selfish of me not to have thought of all that in the first place. I feel so ashamed."

"Don't. Your mother wouldn't want me to chastise you. Now we can all concentrate our energies on making Charlotte's exhibition a great success. She was such a wonderful woman that her reputation should be known to the world."

"Thank you, Weena. It's lovely to hear you say that."

"I wouldn't say it if it weren't true."

CHAPTER 62

Two girls in the hostel, Maria from County Offaly and Evelyn from County Tipperary, noticed that Zita was alone and asked her if she would like to go set dancing with them. Zita said she didn't know what sort of dancing that was. They said it was Irish dancing but she didn't need to know anything about it – she would soon get the hang of it. Learning it was half the fun. Zita thought to herself that at least it wasn't ballroom dancing, so it wouldn't bring back painful memories of Richie and Wombat. Buoyed up by the success of her spying and unable to resist the thought of dancing again in a place where no one knew her, she agreed to go with them.

When she first walked into the room, she was reminded of home. All ages and all shapes and sizes of people were on the floor, but instead of doing waltzes and quick steps they were executing the complicated routines of jigs and reels. The band sounded like one she'd heard on her grandparents' wind-up gramophone.

The three girls stood watching. The set looked so intricate that Zita thought she would make a fool of herself if she tried to join in and she wished she hadn't come. But her foot was tapping despite herself and she found it difficult to stand still and not launch herself into the crowd, making up steps as she went along.

The music stopped, the dancers clapped and moved off the floor.

Some went over to a table where soft drinks were being sold.

There was an announcement in a language Zita guessed was Gaelic. Two young men came over to claim Maria and Evelyn. The girls introduced Zita as their new Australian friend, and one of the men went off to bring back a partner for her.

A shy, smiling young man called Tadhg then appeared beside her. "I don't know any of the steps," she said.

"Don't worry. You will soon," said Tadhg, leading her off.

A lot of the couples looked serious, even though their moves were joyful. Zita kept turning in the wrong direction and tripping over herself. When it got to the spinning-around bits she was hesitant at first, not trusting Tadhg to hold on, but she gained confidence in him and soon whirled so exuberantly that, if he had let her go, she would have flown across the floor and crashed into the opposite wall, knocking over other dancers in her path. She was laughing. Carried along by the exuberance of the music, she gave up caring if she was making a fool of herself or not, and set about making a deliberate fool of herself by improvising steps. Tadhg was enjoying her enjoyment. Maria and Evelyn kept looking over with approval. Her quick eye and quick feet helped her make a fair approximation of the actual steps, so that when it came time to change partners in a complicated number of moves, she was able to do it without putting anybody out.

"Can I buy you a lemonade?" Tadhg asked after three dances. "I'm parched."

Zita said she would like one. He and the two boys went off.

"He fancies you," said Maria.

"That's a feather in your cap," added Evelyn. "He's very choosey."

Zita was short of breath, but managed to say, "I think he's having a good laugh at how hopeless I am."

"I think it's more than that. And you're really good. It's hard to believe you've never done it before."

"Are they your boyfriends you're with?" asked Zita.

"Not yet, but we're hoping," Evelyn said, laughing.

"Tadhg would like to emigrate to your country," said Maria, "but he has family ties and can't leave."

Zita felt a slight chill. "Is he married?"

"Tadhg? Married?" Evelyn laughed before turning serious. "Nothing like that. His father had a stroke six years ago, so he's tied down as the breadwinner of the family."

Later all six agreed to meet again the following night and Zita felt a sensation of happiness in the centre of her shrivelled heart.

CHAPTER 63

Now that Mary Anne was so close to coming into her own fortune, Lochlann felt the need, stronger than ever, to divest himself of the one Charlotte had willed to him. Mary Anne, with her own fortune, would never want for anything, even after she married Toby who would work all his life for a modest wage.

He was trying to think of a way of transferring a large portion of the inheritance to the Hogans in such a manner that they could never guess where it had come from. It was a form of compensation for stealing Mary Anne from them. He presumed Dan and Nell had ended up with at least ten children at the rate they were going. Perhaps illness had struck the family. One of the later children might have been born with a handicap. One might have had an accident on the farm and might need expensive treatment. Perhaps there had been a string of bad seasons and Dan might have had to mortgage the farm. One of the girls might have married a hopeless case and need financial help. The list could go on but the conclusion was always the same. Lochlann would not feel happy until he had transferred most of Charlotte's fortune to the Hogans. No point in thinking it was crass to equate Mary Anne with money. History could not be reversed, and money was the only thing he had that he could offer.

* * *

William was relieved that Edwina had been told that he and Mary Anne were not in love with one another. As if he could fancy his cousin who was like a sister to him. It wouldn't seem right.

After all that was out of the way, he could break the news to his parents that, despite their efforts to influence him, he had no intention of devoting his life to the upkeep of a Big House after he inherited the Park. Some of his friends considered it an honour to be the custodian of tradition, but it did not appeal to him. Only a small fraction of the original Tyringham Park estate remained, the government having facilitated the sale of land to the tenants. Even if William ran a stud on the remaining acres himself to save paying wages, he could not meet the costs of keeping the house in good repair. Most of his neighbours who hadn't been burnt out in the twenties had sold up and moved to England. The old days, during which time his class had owned most of Ireland's land, were lost forever. Taking on the responsibility of the estate would be for him a form of slow suffocation. Even if he did marry Mary Anne for her money, he would not want to continue living there. If it were legally possible, he would agree to give up his inheritance in favour of his younger brother in exchange for freedom. Nigel loved the house and would be prepared to sacrifice his life to it.

William, now aged twenty-three, knew that in earlier times he would have been expected to help control a colony or become an explorer, but in this year of 1959, with the Empire lost and all the exciting places on the planet already discovered, he'd had to look elsewhere for a diversion and he'd found one that thrilled and absorbed him. He would find it difficult to bring himself to say the name of his chosen profession to his hunting friends. He could imagine their hoots of derision and shouts of disbelief when he confessed to them that he was determined to become an actor on the stage.

He had played Antonio and Rosencrantz in two productions put on by the university's Dramatic Society and was soon heading off to live in London to be on hand for auditions to appear on the professional stage. He had one thing in his favour that might put him ahead of other aspirants, and that was his authentic high-class accent.

Not too many years from now, after he had mastered some of the classic roles, he could picture himself taking curtain calls in the theatres in the West End of London or in Stratford, or in the Abbey or the Gaiety or the Gate in Dublin, bowing low, with his hands pressed against his heart after a particularly emotional interpretation of the character of Hamlet, acknowledging the standing ovation of an appreciative audience. High on adrenaline despite the mental and physical exhaustion that followed the playing of a lead role, he would think for a minute how the heady life of a thespian compared to that of a Big House custodian, walking through freezing, stately rooms checking on rotting window frames and bulging plaster, wondering when he would be able to afford to hire the craftsmen needed to make the repairs.

CHAPTER 64

"What was the name of that Irish doctor your mother was so fond of?" Aunty Cat asked, looking up from the local Cork newspaper.

Alison concentrated on coordinating the bacon, egg, white pudding, black pudding and sausage on her plate so that her forkful contained equal amounts of all the separate components. The best part of the genealogy research was staying in this Cork city hotel with its daily offering of a full Irish breakfast. Aunty Cat was forbidden to eat fried food because of her dicky heart, so settled for porridge followed by dry toast and black tea, but wouldn't hear of Alison's forgoing her feast in sympathy, asserting that she enjoyed watching her eat it.

"Dr Carmichael or Carmoding or something like that," said Alison, heaping butter on a slice of toast before soaking up the fatty juices with it. She felt as if she were in heaven.

"Could it have been Carmody? Was his first name Lochlann?"

"That sounds familiar. He was the one who delivered me."

"That's what I thought, but with all these Irish names popping up I was beginning to think I was imagining things. Listen to this. A notice in the *Social and Personal* column. '*Mary Anne Carmody, daughter of Dr Lochlann Carmody, is holding an exhibition of paintings in the ballroom of Tyringham Park to celebrate the work of her late mother, the Honourable Charlotte Carmody (née*

Blackshaw), who was tragically drowned on the estate while attempting the heroic rescue of her former nanny. Tea and scones will be served and one selected painting will be raffled on behalf of the Irish Red Cross. All welcome. Admission free. The exhibition will be opened on Saturday May 30th.' Well, what do you think of that? Do you think that could be the doctor?"

"Has to be."

"No 'has to be' about it. Have you seen the number of Seán Murphys and Séamus O'Briens in the phone book? The trouble with being in Ireland is that nearly everyone has an Irish name and there seems to be a limited amount of them. No wonder we're having so much trouble with your paternal grandmother. 'Hanley' or 'Handley'? What chance have we got when even the official documents can't agree on the spelling?"

"It doubles the work all right."

"Let's hope we have better luck when we get to Galway and hopefully have only one spelling of 'Hogan' and of 'Fahey' to contend with. Until then we'll just have to soldier on. As I say every day: 'This could be the day'."

Cat mentioned the exhibition to the owner of the hotel before setting out to spend a day in Mallow looking through parish records there.

"Tyringham Park? That's only up the road a mile or two from the village of Ballybrian. I have an aunt living on the outskirts so I know it well. You could get a bus from there that would drop you outside the gates and you could walk up the avenue to the house. You should try to fit it in. Well worth a look. It's a rare chance as it's not usually open to the public. The whole county will be there on Sunday. The place is steeped in history, and not always happy. Some say the place is cursed with all those drownings in the Dark Waterhole in the river but I don't go along with those superstitions. Still, eleven in the last eighty years makes you wonder. Some even say there is a creature living in the Waterhole who grabs you by the leg if he gets a chance, and drags you down."

"Imagine that!" exclaimed Cat, turning to wink at Alison.

"A more probable explanation is that people go there with the express intention of drowning themselves. It's the only really deep section of the river. If they weigh themselves down with stones, they are bound to succeed in what they set out to do."

CHAPTER 65

Zita was having such a good time with Tadhg, as well as with Evelyn and Maria and their boyfriends, that she delayed taking the train to Cork until the day before the banquet. She reassured her new friends she would return to stay in the hostel as soon as the weekend was over. Because she and Tadhg both knew there was no future in their relationship, she was relaxed and affectionate with him.

Cat and Alison noted the change in Zita as soon as they saw her. Alison had never seen her sister in such a good mood, even during the times she had been out dancing with Richie.

"Are you in love?" Cat asked in disbelief.

"No. Nothing as ordinary as that, though I have made five new friends and have been out dancing most nights. Great fun." Zita was vibrating with delight. "Better than that. I found out where Dr Carmody lives and went to meet him. Such a nice man. He remembered taking the photos of our family but said he put them away so carefully he can't remember where they are, but he's going to concentrate on finding them before tomorrow. Won't Dad be pleased?"

"He certainly will," said Cat. "He could do with some good fortune."

"As well as that, I met his daughter, and guess what?"

"How could we possibly guess?"

"She's having a banquet at Tyringham Park tomorrow night and she's invited Alison and me along. Sorry, Aunt, it's only for young people."

"Why would she want us to come when she doesn't even know us?" asked Alison in a sulky voice.

"Lots of reasons. She was so excited to hear you were with me. Born in the same hospital on the same day, delivered by her father. She's dying for him to meet you. He never talks about his time in Redmundo, so she wants to hear as much as she can from us."

"Well, I don't particularly want to meet her. She left Australia when she was a month old. What could we possibly have in common?"

"You'd be surprised. Anyway, I told her we would be there and I bought our outfits, so all we have to do now is turn up and have a good time."

"It will suit me fine to have an early night," said Aunty Cat. "We were reading in the local paper about open day at the Park the day after, so I'll conserve my energy until then."

I did well, Zita later thought to herself with satisfaction. I lied so convincingly about the Carmodys I almost convinced myself.

There was a letter for Alison tucked into the board at the back of the reception desk on the morning Zita arrived. It was the first correspondence any of them had received since they'd left Australia.

Alison turned over the airmail envelope and read the name and address on the back. "It's from Stevie," she said.

"I hope nothing else has happened to Dan," was Cat's immediate response.

"His hands should be healed by now," said Alison.

The three went straight up to the bedroom so that Alison could read the letter in private and pass on the news without having to lower her voice.

Zita felt a pang. As the elder of the sisters by fourteen years, if all else had been equal the letter should have been addressed to her. She was now forced into a position where she had to wait, like a younger sibling, until Alison opened the letter and read the contents first.

"What is it?" asked Cat when she saw the disturbed look on Alison's face.

"Bik Voerter is dead," said Alison, reading ahead as she spoke. "An accident at the mill."

"Show me that," said Zita, snatching the letter and reading for herself Stevie's account of the accident. Her face turned pale before she finished. "So it looks as if Wombat will be getting married."

"What are you talking about?" asked Cat.

"Now that Bik is dead Wombat will come back after a respectable lapse of time and marry Gretta."

"Are you serious?" asked Cat.

"Yes. You heard she was in love with him."

"I thought that was a rumour made up by an overexcited, nosy neighbour. I didn't take it seriously for a minute. We are talking about the same person, aren't we? The mute with the burnt face?"

"Yes, we are. There would hardly be two people with that nickname," said Alison.

"You have picked his two least important characteristics, Aunt," said Zita. "Anyway, have you forgotten Alison said he is talking again? If you knew him well you wouldn't even notice his burns. Take it from me, Gretta Voerter is a very lucky woman."

CHAPTER 66

That night Zita stayed awake crying in the dark for a long time. Around one o'clock she gently lifted Alison's single plait, moved the scissors up along its length and cut off the greater part of it.

The next morning when Alison woke and saw the cut-off section of her hair lying the low locker between the two beds she let out a single scream so loud that Aunty Cat came rushing in from the adjoining room to find out what the matter was. She saw Alison sitting up in bed, clutching herself in a tight hug, rocking backwards and forwards, and whimpering, and on the locker she saw the plait. Zita, lying in the second bed, looking unconcerned and paying no attention to Alison, told Cat what she had done.

"Why did you do that? It's such a nasty thing, I can't believe you did it," said Cat, horrified. "You know Alison waited for years to grow her hair. What you have done is not the conduct one would expect from a person who wants to be a doctor."

"'Wanted', not 'wants', Aunt," said Zita. "Past tense, if you don't mind. Those days are gone."

"Doctors are kind and compassionate people."

"Is that a fact? I'd like to hear you repeat that to me tomorrow morning. I will remind you of it."

"I don't know what's got into you, Zita, doing such a mean thing and then talking in riddles instead of explaining yourself. Look at this!" Cat lifted up a section of Alison's hair. "Do you expect her to go to the party tonight looking as if a rat has been chewing at the ends? Come on, Alison, get up and get dressed and I'll take you to the best hairdresser in the city to repair the damage, even if I have to buy the salon to make sure you get an appointment." She added in a loud whisper to Alison, "She's jealous because you are younger and prettier than she is. That's why she did it."

Was there ever anyone as lucky as she was?

Mary Anne surveyed the decorated ballroom that in a few hours' time would be filled with people who had enriched her life. She would have to put Toby at the top of that list, followed by her father, stepmother, grandparents, aunt, uncles, cousins, girls from school, particularly Patricia and Jo, who had been her best friends since she was four years of age, colleagues and friends of Lochlann's and Niamh's, neighbours from Dublin and all the local landed gentry from County Cork and many from other counties, Manus and his wife Sinéad and family of four, and Toby's grandfather, parents and young sister.

She thought of the people now dead whose names she knew well and whose lives had impacted directly and indirectly on hers even though she didn't know many of them personally: Waldron, Victoria, Harcourt, Charles, Harriet, Beatrice, Bertie, Verity, Sid, Dr Finn, Nurse Dixon, and most importantly of all, her mother Charlotte who had loved her dearly, and whose presence was felt more strongly here at the Park than it was in the townhouse.

She thought of her wonderful father whose melancholy, which he tried so hard to conceal, was becoming more and more evident as the years went by. She hoped he would be up to the large celebration she had organised. He was not as sociable as he used to be and would turn down the award he was to receive shortly if it weren't so important to the charity. For her birthday celebrations she knew he would make the effort for her sake. He had loved two women equally, he told her, when she first mentioned putting on the exhibition. She found that difficult to believe, as she couldn't imagine his loving anyone more than he loved Niamh. It was nice to think, though, that he had really loved Charlotte.

Three extraordinary women had reared her: Charlotte, Iseult and Niamh. Her life could have gone so badly wrong, she believed, but because of them and because of her father she had ended up the happiest girl in the world. She hoped that God would give Charlotte a first-class view from her place in heaven so that she could feel part of the celebrations and rejoice along with her daughter.

Edwina, wheeled into the ballroom by her manservant a few seconds later, watched Mary Anne with arms outstretched, her smiling face uplifted to view her mother's paintings as she twirled with joy around and around the vast expanse of the ballroom floor.

"Put this on," said Zita, producing the broad-brimmed hat and smoothing it out. "We'll be in Ballybrian in a minute."

Alison, who had not said a word during the bus trip from Cork city, ignored her.

"Go on, put it on."

"What for? To cover my hair?"

"No. Your hair looks perfect. The hairdresser did a good job. Just do it because I tell you to."

"I'm not a kid any more to be bossed around," Alison muttered.

"What did you say?" Zita's voice had the tone to it that Alison remembered used to frighten her as a child, and still had the power to do so.

"Nothing."

"Don't come over all sullen with me at this late stage, young lady. Just do as I say."

Zita didn't mean to sound so waspish, but the injustice of Cat's accusation of jealousy had upset her greatly.

Only one more day and everything will be revealed, she thought, and I will be vindicated at last and all my actions will make sense and Aunty Cat will cringe thinking how wrong she was. All I have to do between now and then is stick to my plan and make sure that Alison plays her part without being aware that she is doing so.

Alison, cowed, took the hat and put it on her head.

Now here's the tricky bit, thought Zita, as the bus pulled up in the main street of Ballybrian. Getting from the bus to the hotel to our room without anyone seeing Alison's face. There's bound to be people here who know Mary Anne Carmody, especially the shopkeepers and people invited to the banquet.

"Keep the hat pulled down at the front and let me do all the talking," she said. "Here, I'll take the bag. Follow me. God, the streets are packed. Everyone looks happy. What a crowd! They must all be here for the opening. This is supposed to be a quiet village. Keep your head down for God's sake."

Zita led the way to Doughertys' Hotel where she had been lucky to book the last available room which, they had been warned, was hardly bigger than a linen cupboard. She was tempted to sign the register with false names, but was afraid they might be asked for their passports so put in their real ones. The Carmodys were hardly likely to come into a hotel when they had a place as large as Tyringham Park to stay in, so she should be safe enough, she reassured herself. Alison waited at the bottom of the stairs with her head averted.

When the two girls reached the room, Alison took off the hat and threw it on the bed which was only three-quarters the size of an ordinary double. Even at that size it was too big for the room and had one side jammed up against the wall.

"Now I'm going back down to find out about booking a taxi to take us up to Tyringham Park later," said Zita. "You stay here and don't leave the room. I'll order some sandwiches so we can eat here and won't have to go downstairs again."

Zita was confident that she and Alison could gatecrash the banquet without arousing anyone's suspicions. Five years working in a hospital had taught her one thing at least that was now going to come in useful. It seemed to her that every performer arriving in Sydney, from the worlds of theatre, dance, music hall and especially the circus, felt duty bound to offer their services free of charge to entertain the long-term patients. The artists turned up in a variety of gear, sometimes in a blast of orchestrated publicity and sometimes unannounced, and no one thought to question their right to be there. All they ever had to say, even if it wasn't self-evident, was, "We are the entertainment", to be assured of a wholehearted welcome. Zita had no doubt but that the same formula would work at the Park as it had done at the hospital if anyone stopped and questioned them.

No need to explain any of that to Alison. Any mention of standing in front of a crowd and being looked at would have her digging in her heels and refusing to budge to go anywhere. She couldn't risk that. Better to continue with the bullying without attempting to explain. It had worked so far.

CHAPTER 67

Saturday was Manus's last day as head trainer at Tyringham Park. The two people he would miss most from his time working there were Charlotte and Victoria and they were both dead. He intended, while he had the chance, to keep a vigil by the river after the banquet was over, to honour their memory.

With the legacy Charlotte had left him, he had invested in two yearlings to train on his twenty acres. Three of his children had emigrated to England to find work, but one son had stayed in Ireland and had worked with horses in the Curragh for years before returning to Ballybrian, declaring that his father's methods were as good as the best of them. Father and son had bets on that they would win the Irish Derby before Giles Blackshaw managed to do so. The son said Manus had better get a move on as he wasn't getting any younger.

Manus's main focus during the banquet, which Mary Anne insisted he attend for her sake, was to avoid Edwina in case he was tempted to say something hostile to her because of her disdainful attitude to Toby. After this night he would make sure never to see her again and he was not sorry, despite what they had once shared.

Most of the invited guests were in the ballroom of the Park by six thirty for an informal viewing of the paintings – the official opening was due to take place at midday on the following day – and they all made a special point of complimenting Mary Anne on her mother's wondrous talent. Most asked if she had inherited Charlotte's gift and she replied that sadly she had not.

Edwina saw a broad-shouldered, well-dressed, vibrantly masculine young man she didn't know talking to Mary Anne just inside the door and presumed that he must be one of the Carmody cousins. Between the pair was a small woman standing with her back to Edwina.

Please don't bring that man over to be introduced, Mary Anne, impressive though he may be, Edwina pleaded in her mind. The thought of having to make polite conversation with Toby and his mother in a few minutes' time, if they turn out to have punctual habits, is bad enough without lumbering me with another one of your common connections. There's only so much tedium one can put up with for your sake, Mary Anne. Please send that one off before you come over.

Edwina straightened the rug across her lap and turned around to face away from the door so that she would not be forced to make eye contact with anyone she did not wish to acknowledge.

She heard footsteps approaching and Mary Anne saying with pride in her voice, "You remember Toby, don't you, Weena?"

Mary Anne gently pushed back the wheelchair to make room for Toby to greet her.

"Your Ladyship," said Toby, inclining his head by the number of degrees necessary to denote respect but not enough to indicate deference.

Edwina did remember Toby, but only as a slim, wild-haired, badly dressed young boy who had no right, looking the way he did, to have such an elegant seat on a horse. That young boy bore no resemblance to the impressive man whom she had taken to be a Carmody cousin. It was five years since Toby had left Tyringham Park to go off to join the Irish police force. She had hoped at the time that she would never have to inflict her eyes with the sight of him again.

"Your Ladyship, may I introduce my mother, Mrs Prendergast?" said Toby, stepping aside to reveal his nervous mother who had been trying to hide behind him. "Mother, Lady Edwina Blackshaw."

Edwina saw the diamonds first and didn't bother looking at the woman who was wearing them. "How do you do?" she said automatically.

"Very well, thank you, Your Ladyship," Daisy answered. She had been practising a curtsy, but Toby held her arm in a tight grip which prevented her from bending her knee.

"I cannot help admiring the design of the necklace you are wearing, Mrs Prendergast."

"This old jumble of beads?" Daisy stuttered, fingering the central large fan shape. "Yes, I do like it, even though it is only made of glass."

"Might I be so bold as to enquire how you came by it?" Edwina asked.

Toby noticed the necklace for the first time and was jolted by the sight of it. He hadn't thought about it for years. If he had known his mother had intended wearing it, he would certainly have prevented her from doing so.

"Toby gave it to me when he was a boy."

Mary Anne raised her eyebrows at Toby in disbelief. With her cultivated taste she had thought when she first saw the necklace that it was a superior piece.

"Did he really? And where did he obtain it?"

"He bought it at a charity stall with money that Manus gave him."

"What would we do without charity stalls and jumble sales, I wonder? You had good taste even at a young age, Mr Prendergast."

Toby presumed the comment was not a compliment, so only nodded to acknowledge he had heard it.

"Toby was always a good boy. He could have spent the money on sweets, but instead he bought a gift for me."

"How admirable. Most touching. I have to say, though, that I'm surprised that the person running the stall sold it for a few pence, when it has the look of quality about it. That's a problem, manning those stalls with people who have no idea of the real value of things. Are you sure that's where you obtained it?"

"Does it matter?" Mary Anne remonstrated. She didn't like the tone of Edwina's voice.

Toby wished he hadn't complicated matters back then with the story of the stall. Why hadn't he said he had picked the necklace up off the ground beside the avenue where it had been dropped? What choice did he have now but to repeat the lie? He couldn't very well tell the truth, saying he took it from where it lay beside a woman lying dead at the bottom of the stairs in the nursery wing, on the same day he had seen Manus pulling Mary Anne's mother out of the river.

"It was a long time ago," said Toby. "I can't say for certain as my memory of it is so vague."

"Vagueness would not be a desirable attribute for a policeman, I would imagine," said Edwina. "Do you have any distinct or even a vague recollection of a sapphire necklace on the stall beside the diamonds?"

"No, Your Ladyship," answered Tony truthfully. Not on the stall, but he did remember seeing them in a pouch. He felt no obligation to elaborate.

"A pity. Now, Mary Anne, would you please wheel me to the study where I can use the telephone in private? I'm sure the Prendergasts will excuse us."

Mary Anne did as she was asked, telling the mother and son she would rejoin them shortly. In the study she handed down the telephone to Edwina and asked if she could dial the number for her.

"No need, dear. I will go through the exchange. Now could you leave me in private for five minutes before you send in one of the servants to take me back? There is no need for you to make the journey a second time. Go on, off you go and join your guests."

After making sure that Mary Anne was out of earshot, Edwina asked to be put through to the Serious Crime Section in Cork city, and ordered that four policemen be dispatched immediately to arrest two thieves who were in the process of stealing a priceless diamond Blackshaw heirloom at Tyringham Park and she didn't want them to make their escape before the policemen turned up. "The younger thief is under the illusion that he is a Dublin policeman," she concluded, "but take no notice of him when he tells you that."

On re-entering the ballroom, Edwina saw Toby talking to Mary Anne. They looked so delighted to be in each other's company. William went over to join them and they moved apart to include him and they joked with one another as if they were equals. It made Edwina furious to see Toby acting as if he were every bit as good as they were. She was glad she had done what she had done.

CHAPTER 68

"Tonight will be the last time I will ask you to do things that seem to make no sense," said Zita as she covered Alison's head and face with one of the large squares of lace, having already applied the pale foundation cream and powder. "After tonight you will have no need to question me, I promise you that."

Zita sounded so pleased when she spoke that Alison could have been moved if she didn't hate her so much for cutting her hair.

"There. You look perfect."

"Why do the sleeves have raw edges? You should have complained at the shop."

"I cut them myself to make them look more fashionable. Now, no more questions."

The taxi driver arrived at exactly eight fifteen as he had said he would.

"You're part of a select crowd," he told the two sisters as he drove into the estate. "From what I hear there's going to be an engagement announced tonight. You should be in time for it even though you're a bit on the late side. The heir, Master William. I've known him since he was in short trousers. To his Dublin cousin, so I've heard. She's the daughter of a doctor."

"I thought tomorrow was going to be the big day," said Zita who had sat in the passenger seat to talk to the driver, to save Alison from having to do so.

"So it is. For the public. Don't talk to me! I've so many bookings to pick up people at the station that I might have to get my sons and sons-in-law and my cousins and their cousins to help. It looks as if the whole country's coming to have a gawk and who would blame them? First time to have open house, and first time for the paintings to be on show."

The car crossed the bridge and turned left along the avenue.

The driver crossed himself. "There's something that might interest you as a tourist – a waterhole that's haunted. There it is over there," he said, pointing upriver. "Sucks people down, so it does. My great-uncle was one of them. A strong swimmer, so he was, who went in to rescue two children in trouble. All three perished, so they did. The families never got over it. Same spot where the body of Lady Charlotte Blackshaw was found. She was the wife of the doctor and the mother of the girl getting engaged tonight. Very sad."

Alison, huddled in the back seat with her face hidden behind the square of lace, shivered.

"It looks pretty tame to me," said Zita.

"It's deceptive. It looks harmless from here, but it's so deep it goes down as far as subterranean caves, so they say. I haven't heard that any potholers have ever attempted to explore it. Hope no one has too much to drink tonight and falls in or jumps in for a dare."

Alison shivered again at the thought of the cold and the claustrophobia that a potholer might experience.

The windows in the front of the house were shining in the late evening sun. The size of the building almost daunted Zita who had made a resolution not to be impressed or intimidated by anything she might see on this side of the world, and especially not anything connected with Mary Anne Carmody.

The driver pulled up at the entrance. "Here you are then, ladies. No extra charge for the guided tour."

"Thank you. It was most informative and enjoyable." Zita paid him and added a generous tip.

"Do you want me to come back later to pick you up?"

"No, thanks all the same for the offer, but we don't know yet how long we'll be staying. Goodnight."

Zita took in a long, triumphant breath before turning to check that the square of lace covering Alison's head and neck was sitting correctly. She wore her own square over her shoulders like a shawl.

"The driver must have thought I had something wrong with my face," said Alison. "I feel stupid wearing this thing. Why do I have to keep covering my face?"

"Remember I said no more questions? Don't worry. You won't have to cover it for much longer."

Zita had planned to make things easy for Alison, to lessen the chances of her refusing to enter the room or, worse still, make a bolt for an exit at the last minute. She wouldn't have to say a single word. Just stand there. They would walk into the centre of the room. That would be difficult for Alison, but having her face covered should make it bearable enough for her to be able to endure it.

Zita would call for silence once they were in position and, without wasting a second after that, in case Dr Carmody recognised her straight away and was quick to intervene and send some young men rushing over to bundle them out of the room, she would say in the loud, clear voice that she used to call home the cattle on the farm, "I have travelled twelve thousand miles to claim back my sister who was stolen by Dr Lochlann Carmody from my mother who later died of grief because of it." One sentence. She should be able get that out in time. She would then pull off the black lace square covering Alison's face and look directly at Dr Carmody while she was doing so, watching for his reaction. Perhaps he would keel over with a heart attack at the sight. Perhaps, instead, he might cry out with remorse, or perhaps, perversely, weep with relief at being found out at last.

Inside the front door was a cavernous vestibule. Alison, peering through the black lace, was awestruck by the double staircase ahead, the enormous fireplace at the sides, and the portraits and mounted antlers on the walls. She felt as if she weren't significant enough to be in such a place and didn't want to venture any further.

An old servant standing to attention asked if he might take their coats even though they weren't wearing any.

"No, thank you," said Zita, pulling Alison by the hand, walking straight ahead without pausing, following the noise of conversation in the distance until it became louder as they came closer to the banqueting hall.

No one approached them, so Zita did not have to use her prepared explanation about being a surprise entertainment act. That was a relief, as such information might frighten Alison so much that she would cease to listen to Zita's orders.

Zita propelled Alison behind one of the large open doors, which opened outwards from the entrance into the hall, and squeezed her up against the wall.

"Why are we hiding when we're invited?" asked Alison.

"I want to wait until after the speeches," Zita whispered back. "I have my reasons."

Alison rolled her eyes in irritation before peering through the crack between the door and the wall. Her view was limited to about a thirty-degree angle on the right-hand side of the room. She was dazzled by the lights from the large crystal chandeliers hanging from an elaborately decorated ceiling. Along the panelled walls were lights alternating with gilt-framed shiny portraits. Filling the floor space were long tables covered with white cloths, porcelain, silver, crystal, centrepieces, candelabras and flowers. Seated around the tables were cheerful, glamorous people who seemed at home in their splendid surroundings. How would she ever have the courage to enter such a place? And she was seeing only a section of the hall. How big must it be?

"Get away from there and let me look," Zita said in her bossy voice.

As Alison was about to step back, her focus shifted a little to the left and she spotted a familiar face in the background. It was the floppy-haired student-type she had seen on Kildare Street, she was sure of it, even from this distance. The man who had called her 'cuz'. She couldn't see who he was talking to – not that it mattered as she wouldn't know anyone else in the crowd anyway.

"Move away, I said," Zita commanded, pulling at her arm. "I want to find out where the doctor and Mary Anne are seated so I'll know which way to face when we go in."

Alison was not unrealistic enough to think that a girl from the bush had any hope of winning a man like the floppy-haired youth, but shouldn't the fact that she had seen him twice in two different locations in a foreign country signify something? What were the chances of that happening? Was her guardian angel working overtime on a special mission on her behalf?

"Blast. I can't see at this angle," said Zita.

There was a clink of a knife on a glass and then a gradual lowering of the noise level. Lochlann stood up. He looked around at the assembly and, while he waited for silence, said something to Mary Anne who was seated beside him.

The waiters ceased clearing up and stood against the wall, white cloths draped over their left forearms. The guests with their backs to Lochlann either turned their chairs around or sat still, while those facing him looked directly at him.

"Family and friends," he said. "You are all very welcome here tonight. Can you hear me down the back?" He raised his voice. "Is that better?"

The Hogan sisters could hear clearly, now that all the guests had stopped talking.

"It is very humbling to be in the midst of so many wonderful friends. Some of you have travelled long distances to be here for the preview of the exhibition which will be formally opened tomorrow, and will show to the country Charlotte's inspired body of work."

Applause.

"We are assembled for a double celebration. We will talk more of the exhibition tomorrow. Tonight I would like to concentrate particularly on the generosity of the women who have been instrumental in shaping Mary Anne – you'll have to excuse a father's indulgence – into the warm, charming, thoughtful, light-hearted, admirable young woman that she has turned out to be on her eighteenth birthday."

There was clapping, a smattering of "Hear, hear" from the older generation, and whooping from the younger crowd.

Alison, listening behind the door, was sad to think that no one would ever say those things about her as she was such a ghost of a nobody with no personality – always lonely, homesick and timid.

Zita put her forefinger in her mouth and acted as if she were about to vomit. "What a spoilt Daddy's girl," she commented in a whisper to Alison.

"The first woman I want to mention is Charlotte, whose courage throughout her life was demonstrated so unequivocally in her final tragic end. She is a true heroine but tonight I would like to single out for attention her loving care of Mary Anne which was an inspiration to those close enough to her who witnessed it while, unfortunately, I was forced to be absent."

Zita put the square of lace over her head, slipped out to stand in the open door so that she could identify the doctor and register where he was located in the room, and then slid back behind the door and rearranged the lace over her shoulders. No one had taken any notice of her as everyone was concentrating on the speech. These squares were a great idea of mine, she congratulated herself. One can see clearly through them, but no one can see in.

Lochlann continued, "Next are my mother Grace and my sister Iseult who guided Mary Anne through the sorrowful aftermath of Charlotte's death, keeping her secure and unafraid. And what can I say about my wonderful wife, Niamh, whose generosity of spirit could single-handedly turn the pejorative term of stepmother to one of praise and blessing? She is a pearl beyond price."

He paused.

"There is one other I must honour . . ."

Edwina perked up, expecting her name to be the next one mentioned.

". . . who will mean nothing to anyone in this room, but it's a name I want to put on record. One day Mary Anne might appreciate knowing it, preferably after my death."

"Don't talk like that," Mary Anne said, touching his arm.

He remained serious as he acknowledged her gesture, then continued: "The woman's name is Nell Hogan."

Alison and Zita were both startled to hear their mother's name and looked at each other in disbelief.

"She lives in Australia," Lochlann continued, "and that is why no one here knows who she is. I became indebted to her when I was living there. It is so great a debt it can never be repaid. The nature of the debt remains private, but I want to acknowledge it in public so that Mary Anne will remember in years to come that I did."

"What could he possibly be referring to?" Alison whispered.

"Shhh," said Zita.

"Mary Anne has never given all those outstanding women or myself one moment of trouble during her exemplary life," Lochlann continued. "She has enriched our lives with her sense of fun and her generosity, the virtue she inherited from all those exceptional women. She is a daughter any parent would be proud of. Now would you all be upstanding and raise your glasses to Mary Anne."

Everyone except Edwina and Mary Anne stood up, repeated the toast, "To Mary Anne", and sat down again with a loud scraping of chairs.

Lochlann lifted his glass a second time, in a private toast to Mary Anne, before kissing her on the forehead and taking his seat again beside her.

"Come on, this won't take long," said Zita, grabbing Alison's wrist and pulling her out from behind the door. "Before the next person gets up to speak. Quickly."

People were talking again and the noise level was rising.

Alison hung back when they went through the door but Zita turned to snap at her, pulling her by the wrist, and she followed her dutifully into the hall. No one took any notice of them. Alison turned her attention to the right, looking for the young man.

The top table was directly ahead of them. Zita saw Mary Anne at the table listening to the doctor. She had thought she might not recognise him when she saw him again after a gap of eighteen years, but she did. He was still a remarkably handsome man.

Mary Anne laughed and then bent her head to listen to what the doctor was saying, leaning her forehead on the heel of her hand.

Good, thought Zita. Alison can't see her face properly with her hand up like that.

Zita took a few more steps before gauging she was in the centre of the room.

"*Silence!*" she shouted out loudly, without giving any warning. "*Silence!*"

Alison jumped with fright at the unexpectedness of the shout and tried to retrieve her wrist, but Zita held on tightly.

People at nearby tables stopped talking and turned towards Zita's commanding voice.

There was a lot of shushing but the guests around the edges of the hall, including those seated at the top table, did not hear and continued with their own conversations.

"*Silence!*" Zita called out more stridently, and this time the whole room quietened.

Zita was looking at Lochlann, who was filling the wineglass of the woman on his right-hand side, and did not look back. Mary Anne took her elbow off the table and searched for the source of the noise, her face now in full view, but Alison, resigned to being restrained, was still scanning the room to locate one particular face.

Zita took a deep breath. She began her single rehearsed sentence. "I have travelled twelve thousand miles . . ."

"Look! Look there! Who's that?" Alison shrieked, interrupting Zita's pronouncement.

Lochlann put down the wine bottle without filling his own glass and glanced up to locate the source of the disturbance.

Zita told Alison to be quiet.

Lochlann squinted, shook his head, took a pair of glasses out of his breast pocket and put them on. "Nell Hogan," he said with incredulity.

"Look! That girl straight ahead." Alison's voice was shrill and frantic in tone.

"What did you say?" Mary Anne asked Lochlann.

"Shut up," Zita hissed at Alison before continuing in her penetrating voice. "I have travelled twelve thousand miles to claim back my –"

"I won't shut up. What are you shouting about, making a show of yourself? That girl is the dead spit of me."

Lochlann pushed back his chair and stood up. He bent and whispered something to Mary Anne.

"To claim back my sister," Zita continued in her raised voice.

"*She looks like my twin!*"

"That's because she is," Zita said to Alison. "Now shut up, for God's sake, and let me finish."

Lochlann found himself hemmed in on both sides. After the meal was over the guests along one side of the top table had pushed their chairs against the back wall in order to get a better view of him during his speech, and to stretch their legs at the same time. One by one, Lochlann had to alert each person along the half row that he wished to pass. Perhaps if he had gone the other way – he had been positioned in the middle – it might have been quicker, but it was too late to change now. All the guests in the row were either talking with animation or listening with interest. He thought he might explode from frustration as he interrupted each conversation and waited for each guest to ascertain what he wanted, and then each one seemed to feel the need to congratulate him on his daughter and on his speech, and to ask who the mysterious Australian woman he had referred to was, before apologising and pulling in chairs to allow room for him to pass.

"But my twin is dead," said Alison.

"She obviously isn't."

"Excuse me," said a man's voice, just as Zita felt a dart of pain on her right shin.

She turned to see a woman in a wheelchair right up against her.

"Excuse me," repeated the manservant in charge. "Make way."

Zita instinctively dropped Alison's wrist and stepped back to avoid another clip from the wheelchair's footplate. The woman in the chair took in Alison's veiled figure on one side of her and turned to glare at Zita on the other.

"We are the entertainment," Zita said.

Lochlann was breathing through his mouth in shallow gasps by the time he finally extricated himself from the top table and headed down the space between the other tables.

The elderly woman and her manservant glided between the Hogan sisters in the direction of the doors.

The guests were talking amongst themselves.

A man caught Lochlann's sleeve as he was passing. If the man had been young, and if he hadn't been weeping, he might not have stopped, but his instinctive courtesy towards the aged and the distressed made him pause and bend down to hear what the man had to say.

"You act as if you knew all about her," Alison, keeping her distance, said to Zita in an accusatory tone.

"*Silence!*" Zita shouted again, but this time no one took any notice of her, having dismissed her as a cracked stranger with an accent, accompanied by an odd figure covered by a veil.

Zita's behaviour now made sense to Alison. The veil, the haircut, the hat, the cut-off sleeves, the fear that a local person would see her face, the gate-crashing . . . the promise made years ago: 'You and I will travel to Ireland. Just the two of us.'

"How long have you known?"

"A long time."

"*And you didn't tell me?* I'm the one who should have known. Who else knows?"

"No one in the family."

The room quietened.

Zita prepared to speak again, thinking the guests had stopped talking to listen to her, but they were not looking her way – they were turned to face the entrance doors, where four policemen in uniform were talking to the woman in the wheelchair.

Lady Edwina pointed to the table at which Toby and his mother were seated, and then told a detailed story about the Blackshaw jewels and their history. The four men, in deference to her age and disability, and aware that the crime they had come to sort out was minor, listened patiently.

"No one's listening to you," Alison said with satisfaction.

"Even if they don't listen they can still see."

Zita reached across to pull off Alison's veil but Alison, alert with suspicion, ducked out of her way and held on to it tightly.

Lochlann appeared beside Zita.

"You have no right to do this." Alison, not registering the presence of the doctor because she was by now beside herself with rage, fixed Zita with a contemptuous glare. "No wonder you're a bitter old maid and no one likes you. I hate you for depriving me of my twin. I hate you for planning all this. You're nothing but a jealous old bully."

The four policemen fanned out across the room and approached Toby and his mother's table from different directions.

Zita made a second grab for Alison's veil. Alison sidestepped her and then gave Zita an almighty push that caught her off balance, and sent her flying towards the nearest table.

Zita's head hit the corner of the table with such force that she fell senseless to the floor, her head spouting blood.

Lochlann immediately knelt beside her, took his handkerchief out of his pocket, folded it into a square and pressed it against Zita's wound.

There was a roar of disapproval from the guests. Lochlann looked up but couldn't see what it was that had antagonised them. It couldn't be the fight between the sisters as only a few people nearby had noticed it. If he stood up to check he would have to release the pressure on Zita's wound and, seeing he couldn't very well do that, he did not see the policemen officially arrest the Prendergasts.

Toby, outraged when he realised that the policemen had come to arrest him and his mother, tried to convince them that they had made a mistake as no robbery had been committed that night. Even telling them he was one of them made no impression on them. In the end he decided to leave quietly so as not to prolong the public spectacle which must be causing Mary Anne so much embarrassment. He could not bear to look in her direction.

Lochlann asked one of the guests at the table to send a servant to fetch his Gladstone bag from the room he was staying in.

"Excuse me, Doctor," a voice said a few seconds later. "Just hold on until we squeeze past."

Lochlann did not need to move as the three people walking abreast changed into a single-file formation. He looked up to see a furious Toby, handcuffed between two policemen, followed by his white-faced mother, also handcuffed between policemen. He instinctively stood up to protest, but blood poured from Zita's head and he had to kneel back down immediately to reapply pressure.

"But he is a guard himself," was the observation repeated over and over by guests to the arresting officers as they went past. "This won't do his career any good."

Lochlann longed to be with Mary Anne, who must be in a state of shock, but he knew it was more imperative that he deal first with Zita Hogan's presence at this location. He asked two of the young male guests if they would carry her to the study where he could attend to her in private.

He motioned to the veiled girl to follow the small procession to the study.

Mary Anne appeared at his side as he walked along beside Zita and the two men. "They have arrested Toby and Daisy," she said frantically. "Did you see? Weena is making out that the necklace Daisy is wearing is hers and was stolen here tonight."

"I'm sorry I can't help, Mary Anne. The error will be sorted out in no time. I must look after this woman."

"But there are at least twenty doctors here tonight. Let one of them look after her."

"I can't. It's personal."

"Who is she anyway? She looks familiar. What was she shouting about and who's that one trailing along with the veil on her head? What is she supposed to represent?"

"I can't tell you right now. As I say, it's personal. I have to take care of this woman."

"They weren't invited here tonight. Where did they come from? Why are they wearing copies of my dress? Who do they belong to? Why are they monopolising your time?"

Lochlann hastily kissed his daughter. "Go back to Niamh, love," he said. "She will straighten out your grandmother if anyone can."

The look Mary Anne gave him as she left was one of disbelief and disappointment and cut him deeply.

Mary Anne, supported by Niamh, pleaded with Edwina to call back the policemen and tell them the whole episode was a mistake. Edwina did not react and her look of self-satisfaction did not alter. She was confident that one day Mary Anne would thank her for preventing her from marrying Toby and making the biggest mistake of her life.

Lochlann sat beside the prone Zita, and continued to apply pressure. After the servant dropped in his bag he was able to make a bigger, thicker wad of cloth and secure it in place with a bandage, before proceeding to check all Zita's vital functions.

"You are Alison, aren't you?" Lochlann asked the figure huddling in the corner as he worked. "I recognised Zita immediately as she bears such a marked resemblance to your mother. She would be the same age now as your mother was when I knew her. From what I heard you say earlier, I presume she brought you along to unveil you in front of your twin here tonight."

"Yes," said Alison in a small voice.

"And she so nearly succeeded. I didn't think this moment would ever happen, though in the back of my mind I have feared it for years. I'm glad for Mary Anne's sake that the public unveiling failed. I would rather explain it all to her in private."

Zita opened her eyes and stared at Lochlann as if he were a poisonous spider. "Tell her lies, you mean. Make out it was a mix-up and that you didn't do it deliberately."

Lochlann took her hands in his. "No, I won't say that. It was deliberate, God help me, and I can't offer any excuse. I have regretted it every day since, but rejoiced in the presence of Mary Anne at the same time. Now no more talking about that until you are fully recovered. Thank goodness there was no great harm done, but you have suffered concussion and will have to be kept under observation for twenty-four hours just in case. Where are you staying?"

"In the hotel in Ballybrian," Alison answered. "Our aunt is coming to join us there at eleven in the morning."

"Well, I will take you there and stay with you until she arrives. You can tell me all about Nell and Dan and how they're getting on while we're waiting. I'll just write a note to Mary Anne to explain."

He went over to a side table with a desk lamp and sat down to write.

Zita motioned for Alison to come close. "Don't tell him anything about Mum," she whispered. "He has no right to know."

"I won't," said Alison.

"He's taking us back to the hotel to get us out of the way and keep an eye on us so that no one will see you."

Lochlan stood up from the table. "Yes, I think that's the safest thing to do. Now I'll go and get my car and bring it around the side of the house. Alison, keep a close eye, and please, I beg you, do not show yourself to anyone here."

"He seems nice," said Alison after he left the room. "Why didn't you tell him Mum was dead?"

"I'm saving that for another time."

"Did Mum know about my twin?"

"No."

"Did you find out before she died?"

"Yes."

"How did you find out?"

"That's a story for another day."

"What gave you the right to keep it to yourself?"

"I didn't want to spoil this day."

"It's spoilt anyway."

"I don't need you to tell me that." Zita pushed herself up into a sitting position. "I definitely don't have concussion. I didn't work in a hospital for five years without picking up some knowledge. I didn't black out. The doctor is using it as an excuse to stick with us, to keep us away from your twin. Will you take off your veil and come into the hall with me now? It's not what I had planned but I'm not left with many options."

"No, I won't. Mary Anne has too much on her plate to cope with as it is. It would be cruel to add to her troubles."

"So you think more of her than you think of me?"

Alison hung her head and didn't answer.

"Don't worry. I didn't expect you to, after what you said to me in there. Anyway, right now I need to go to the ladies'."

Alison stepped forward. "I'll help you," she said.

"Don't bother. I can manage on my own." Zita stood up and walked a few steps. "I feel quite steady and my head feels clear apart from the throbbing."

"I hope it won't take you too long to find the ladies'. If the doctor gets back before you, I won't know what to talk to him about."

Zita folded the lace square into a triangle and placed it in such a way over her head that it covered most of her bandage. "You can ask him about the photos he took of you – Dad would like some copies – but don't tell him anything about our family. Let him talk to you instead about how wonderful Mary Anne is. That should keep you going for a couple of hours at least."

CHAPTER 69

Zita left the study and walked with confidence through the house to the front door, from where she set off down the avenue.

Reaching a large building, apparently a stables, she followed a path along the side of it which led to the river. There, it was so overgrown and secluded that it would be a good place to hide until darkness fell. Pushing through some foliage, she found a grassy spot right beside the river. With a long exhalation of breath, she sank down on the bank, and closed her eyes.

A knife between her ribs would have been less painful than hearing Alison say that she was a jealous old maid and that no one liked her, and that she hated her and thought she was a bully.

When she opened her eyes and gazed at the river, she realised she was looking at the Dark Waterhole. Up this close it wasn't as deceptive as it had seemed from the avenue. She could see where the lighter shade of the shallower, fast-flowing water gave way to unrelieved blackness.

So this was where Mary Anne's 'mother' had died. A heroine, trying to save the life of another. How different to Nell's death – hit by a car that didn't stop, leaving her mangled to die by the side of the road like a dog or a wallaby.

She could imagine, not too far in the future, when Lochlan would finally admit to his past, Alison's becoming absorbed into the Carmody family, soaking up their unearned approval. She would call Dr Carmody 'Lochlann' or even 'Daddy' and ask him to adopt her so she could count herself a member of his devoted family, living in his big house with his wife and 'daughter'. That is, if Aunty Cat with all her wealth didn't jump in and grab her first. The twins might delight in playing identical-twin pranks. Who knew, Alison might marry William, seeing Mary Anne was engaged to Toby, and end up one day as Lady Blackshaw of Tyringham Park. Stranger things had happened. What a sensation that would cause back home. It would give Dan another member of the family to boast about. She would end up as the only member of the family good for nothing.

Zita stared into the water which was catching the fading pink light along the top of the ripples.

Her hopes for the future were very different from Alison's.

She hadn't made any plans. She hadn't thought past this night which had turned out to be a failure after all her plotting.

What was there to look forward to? Back to Sydney, knowing Richie was there and was out of reach; that in Redmundo Wombat would soon be out of reach when he married Gretta; Dan out of reach, making no effort to contact her; the home farm gone; Aunty Cat, at last, with an adopted 'daughter'; Hanna living life on the land and producing lots of little wranglers and cattle kings; the boys all with careers and most with families of their own by now; and, bleaching the life out of anything that was left, the absence of Nell. The thought of returning to that life filled her with weariness and abhorrence.

Tadgh, Evelyn and Maria would be expecting her back in Dublin on Tuesday. Her suitcase was there in the locker beside the bed she had reserved for the next three weeks. The two girls were soon to move out, having secured positions in a hotel that provided staff accommodation. Poor Tadgh, with his desire to emigrate, would remain at home to care for his father. It was so like her own situation had been that she could feel his frustration. In his predicament, though, there was no end in sight as his father could live for years and Tadgh was the only one in the house strong enough to lift him.

She thought of Nell and could not bring an image of her face to mind.

Why didn't you stay inside the house for a few more months, Mum, until you got better, she raged in her mind. Why did you go looking for the missing one when you had eight at home who needed you? It doesn't make sense. Dad should have locked you in, even if you were crying to get out. He didn't know what to do. He was out of his depth. He didn't believe you weren't in your right mind.

What a relief it would be to stop my mind from going over and over things. To give up trying to make sense of my destiny. To give up apportioning blame. To give up wishing the past was different.

She stared at the waterhole that now had no light reflected on its surface.

Mum, you must have some words of thanks to say to me now that I have found your lost baby. Mary Anne is charming and confident, but of course why wouldn't she be? Living in luxury, never having to do a hand's turn, loaded with money, studying medicine and all her family and her boyfriend adoring her? It's easy to be nice when everything goes your way.

Perhaps you wouldn't have gone mad if you had known that the doctor had taken charge of her and was sure to provide her with a happy life. Mum, are you disappointed in me that I don't want to meet her or get to know her? All the Hogan that was in her at birth must have been bred out of her by now, so why would I want to? What would a rich medical student have in common with a poor skivvy like me?

Were you ever angry with me at home? Is Alison right? Did I do a bad job? Did it upset you to watch me make a mess of things? Dad didn't have to sell the farm. You must have reacted badly when you saw that happening. He thought I had disgraced him. He should have stood by me even if I did wrong. Not sold up and moved to Mungindi.

I am very tired at the moment. I don't have the energy to move. I'm wrung out. My mind is tired. My bones are tired. My memory is tired. My will is tired.

I'll lie down here and stop thinking for a while in the hope that God will allow you to tell me what to do for the best. Mum, I can't wait to hear your voice again.

The room quietened after the drama of the Prendergasts' arrest. Very few had noticed the Hogans and those who had were only mildly curious about them.

Manus noticed that Edwina, rather than acting ashamed of what she had done, was actually gloating and calling people over to her to tell them about the stolen diamonds and how she had personally informed the authorities of the identity of the thieves.

A little while later she was talking to the top racehorse trainer in Ireland and sent word to Manus to come over to be introduced to him. Manus's right hand was already sore from all the handshakes he had received during the night, with guests congratulating him on his career and wishing him the best for his retirement. Quite a few trainers had tried to entice him with generous offers to oversee their operations in an advisory capacity, but he had declined, thinking of his own twenty acres and his great plans. He did not wish to speak to the most successful of them all, especially in the presence of Edwina who was bound to try to belittle Manus's talent in comparison to her own as a way of spiting him for his obvious favouring of Toby over William.

"Please tell Her Ladyship I have an appointment and am leaving to keep it," he said to a servant, and left the banquet earlier than he had intended to, specifically to avoid her.

Manus made his way to a tree near the stables that provided good coverage and that overlooked the river. Probably just as well he had left when he did, as he had been in danger of eating and drinking too much, and that would have hampered his plans to keep a vigil through the night in honour of Victoria and Charlotte.

He sat down on the ground, leaned against the trunk of the tree and lit his pipe, thinking how splendid the river looked as it reflected the fading light, and how glad he was to have escaped the banquet which he had attended solely to support Mary Anne and Toby, and which had turned into such a debacle. Sinéad, who had said she wouldn't be seen dead attending it, would still be eager to hear all the news about it the following morning.

CHAPTER 70

Nothing to say to me, Mum? Have you deserted me as well? Has God refused you permission to talk to me because He thinks I should leave your lovely doctor alone? Or did you make the decision for the same reason and not even ask Him?

How restful it would be to slip into that deep water, to sink to the bottom, to drift into subterranean caves then rise again and let the river take my weight and float me down to the sea without my having to move a muscle to guide myself.

No more struggling. My mind could break free from my underused brain at last, and fly unhindered throughout the universe.

I feel dizzy. Mum, how I wish you were here to hold a cold cloth against my forehead like you used to when I was a kid and had a temperature.

Life should not always be so difficult, should it? I do not have to keep pushing a boulder up a steep hill. There is nothing to stop me from standing aside and letting it roll down the hill. Letting it crash into whatever is in its path on the way down.

I need to see you again, Mum. You are the only person who can console me.

If you don't come to me, all I have to do is go over to the Dark Waterhole and I will see you again at last. We have such a lot to talk about, Mum. Please come as soon as you can.

Manus looked towards the river and saw a dark shape rising from a sitting to a standing position on the edge of the riverbank.

Dear God in heaven, it's not happening again, is it?

He pulled himself up from the ground and ran as quietly as he could, half crouching, in the direction of Zita's swaying figure. He reached her just as she was about to take a step forward into the water, encircling her with his arms without touching her so as not to frighten her.

When she became aware of his presence she looked intently into his face in the final light of the day.

"Who sent you?" she asked.

"I'm not sure, but somebody did."

"It must have been my mother. You have the look of Michael the Archangel. I was just going over to the Dark Waterhole to talk to her."

"Don't go yet," said Manus. He let his hands rest gently on her shoulders. "I would like to talk to you first about your mother."

"Are you to be my guide?"

"Yes. I have been given that honour."

"I'm glad. I feel safe in your presence." She leaned in towards him.

"Come with me," he said, turning her away from the river. "I'll make you a warm drink in the stable's office and you can tell me all about your mother. She must have been an exceptional woman."

Zita smiled gratefully. "She was. I would love to tell you about her. She lived a humble life and died young, so not many people know about how wonderful she was."

"I have a really comfortable chair for you to rest in while you tell me all about her. Now let's go and get you settled." And as soon as I can I'll send up for Dr Carmody to come down to the stables to check that wound on your head.

After a lapse of a couple of hours Edwina contacted the Serious Crimes Unit and withdrew the charges against the Prendergasts. She was told it was just as well as a Special Branch detective by the name of Quirke had been on to the Cork Station to say that Lady Edwina

Blackshaw, despite her age, could be charged with wasting police time by making frivolous accusations.

Edwina felt that even if she had been accused it would have been worth it. She had achieved what she had set out to do. She was confident that the public arrest had done enough damage to Toby's reputation to ruin it for life. 'Where there's smoke there's fire' was such a comforting truism that it had inspired her before and would inspire her again if Toby did not release Mary Anne from their engagement. She would initiate damning rumours if he didn't. It was so easy, especially from her exalted position, to take away a man's good name.

She had to admit that Toby possessed an unobtrusive charm that put her in mind of Manus in his younger days. Toby had probably modelled himself on the older man. Not that it would do him any good as he didn't possess any of the precise requirements she valued in a future partner for Mary Anne. Only William Blackshaw had those.

What of the real story behind the necklace?

Edwina had always believed that a servant, Teresa Kelly, had stolen the necklace and taken it with her to Australia, and here she was confronted with the evidence that the necklace had never left the county.

It was so famous it could not be sold on the open market without its being recognised. It had been hand-crafted centuries earlier and its existence was well documented. Its design, and that of its matching tiara and bracelet, was unique.

She would summon Toby the following day and ask him where he had actually found the necklace and if there had been a bracelet with it, and ask him again if he had noticed any sapphires. She didn't believe the charity-shop story. The theft had mystified her for years and she would be grateful if he could help solve the forty-year-old puzzle before she died. His secret would be safe with her, she would tell him. In return, she would write a reference to his superiors, retracting her charge in writing and vouching for his good character.

CHAPTER 71

As arranged, Aunty Cat arrived at Doughertys' Hotel at eleven o'clock the following morning to find the little room crowded, with the two girls lying back to back in the bed and Dr Carmody sleeping in the solitary chair.

"So we meet at last," Aunty Cat said after he woke up. "My sister-in-law Nell was always singing your praises."

"Wholly undeserved," said Lochlann. "I will now leave you in charge. Zita hit her head and suffered slight concussion, but she is in no danger. I have written a list of things to look out for, though, just in case. We have had a quiet night and morning. The girls are not speaking to each other or to me, so I took the opportunity to catch up on some sleep. I will see myself out. Goodbye, ladies. I hope to meet up with you again under different circumstances."

Lochlann picked up his bag and left the room.

"Now, Zita, what has you looking like a wounded soldier?"

"I tripped and hit my head on the corner of a table. Clumsy of me. Nobody's fault. Sorry to upset your plans to view the house and gardens at the Park."

"She didn't trip," said Alison. "I pushed her and I'm not sorry. She's known all along that I have a twin and she kept it to herself."

"But Dolores died," said Aunty Cat, startled.

"No, she didn't," said Alison. "She is alive and well and goes under the name of Mary Anne Carmody. I saw her with my own two eyes last night. According to Zita, Dr Carmody stole her deliberately and substituted his own dead baby."

"Is this true, Zita?"

"Yes. He stole Mum's baby."

"Stole the other twin? My heart. Dear God in heaven. My tablets. Quickly, Alison, pass me up my bag. Your poor mother . . . Alison, run and get me a glass of water from the bathroom."

"I'll be as quick as I can," said Alison, flying out the door. "Sit there quietly, Aunt, and don't move."

"As if I could even if I wanted to. I'm frozen with shock."

"Breathe deeply, Aunt," said Zita from the bed. "We don't want you passing out and have to call for a doctor."

"This is no time for jokes. Are you a hundred-per-cent sure about this?"

"Yes, Dr Carmody confessed to us last night, and even admitted that it was deliberate. He didn't have to do that. There were no witnesses."

"How did you find out? Does Dan know? When did you tell Alison? So many questions. Imagine – the doctor did this wicked thing to your mother who thought he was a saint."

Alison came back in with the water and stayed standing while Cat took a tablet.

"It's hard to credit, all right," said Zita. "I'll tell you the whole story when we're on our own, Aunt. I don't want a running commentary from Alison while I'm talking."

"Now, Zita, that's not a nice thing to say. What did you think when you saw your twin, Alison?"

"I nearly died of fright. She's exactly like me to look at, right down to the short hair. You wouldn't believe it unless you saw it yourself. I couldn't take in the weirdness of it. But she's a much better person than I am. You should have heard all the praise heaped on her by the doctor in his speech. I bet he's relieved he picked Mary Anne instead of me after all the complimentary things he said about her. I would have been a big disappointment to him."

"Don't be so stupid, Alison," said Zita. "If he had taken you instead of her, you would have been Mary Anne and she would have been you."

"How do you know that? Go on, Zita, you go ahead and tell Aunty Cat the whole story seeing you know everything and nobody else does." Alison flopped down on her side of the bed, turned her face into her pillow and sobbed. "If you had told Mum my twin was alive and was being well cared for she might still be alive today."

Zita's face turned bright red. "You don't know that for sure. What's the point of talking about what might have happened? Who knows? I am going back to Dublin, Aunt, and I don't want to see Alison again until we take the boat back home in August, and I won't be talking to her then, either. After all I did for her, and she wouldn't do one thing I asked of her. All those broken nights' sleep I suffered when she was a baby and then having to get up at six and bring in the cows for milking. And living through a drought where all our cows died and we hardly had enough to feed ourselves."

"None of that was my fault," Alison said in a defiant voice.

"I didn't say it was. But I think it's time you heard my side of the story. I had to watch you all waltz off to boarding school without a thought for me left behind when I should have been going there myself. And Dad taking it all for granted without a word of thanks, and none from you lot either. The humiliation of going to town in worn-out clothes and the kids looking like orphans which they nearly were. Avoided by the few young men that were around because I looked like an old married woman with kids dragging out of me. I was loved by two good men I could have married but I didn't because of all you kids. I ended up with no friends. I gave up on my St Mary's friends because we had nothing in common any more after they flew ahead and I stayed behind with my brain rotting. I had a good brain and never got to use it. I was supposed to get excited about a line full of nappies flapping in the wind, and they weren't even white. Everything got stained by the red earth and I couldn't get the stains out. I had to listen to Dad telling everyone how bright Kevin and Mick were, and how successful Stevie was and what a great horseman and manager Larry was. It was like having acid dropped into my ears, hearing all that praise for them and none for me."

"None of that was my fault," said Alison in a less defiant tone of voice.

"I didn't say it was, did I? Then working as a cleaner in a hospital because I had no money, no back-up and no qualifications and no time to train for anything better. By rights I should have been a doctor in that hospital, not a cleaner watching a new batch of nurses come in every year, and seeing all the fun they had together and all they learned, and flirting with the doctors, living in the nurses' quarters, becoming friends. I had no friends there either. The other cleaners in the hospital were all older and married and rushed home after every shift. I spent my days off on my own, wandering about the city watching little groups talking and laughing together. And thinking it would be a good idea if I didn't have to look at them any more and no one would miss me if I went ahead and drowned myself in the harbour. I didn't know where to meet people in the city. Everyone seemed to be connected. Dad not talking to me. I didn't do anything wrong. All I did was dance with a married man who was a wonderful dancer and I loved dancing and it was the only enjoyment available to me, but Dad thought the worst and froze me out without even asking me anything. I think he would have been relieved if I did drown myself."

"But you could have told him the truth," Alison said in a small voice.

"He should have trusted me. He was too quick to listen to Cheryl. Then at the end finding out that you hate me. I don't think any of you like me. I didn't know what I was doing half the time. I was muddling on from day to day with Cheryl in my ear telling me to slap you, to be hard on you, to take no nonsense. I shouldn't have listened to her. If I had my time to do all over again I would do it differently. I would do it better like our mother and Mrs Kendall did. And then you finding me, Aunty Cat, and ignoring me because you like Alison better because she's the pretty one and she's still young and you can enrol her into expensive classes so that you can show her off to all your city friends, while I'm too old at thirty-two to be good for anything. All of this is not self-pity. It's the truth. What have I to look forward to when I go back except taking up smoking and drinking to fill in my time?"

"That's not true," said Alison, near to tears. "I didn't mean what I said earlier. You're not too old to do something better. Aunty Cat, say something. You must tell her now, Aunt."

"Tell me what?"

"My plans for you and I only wish I had told you sooner. My poor, dear Zita."

CHAPTER 72

Lochlann called back to the hotel at six to check on Zita, to find she had already left and taken a train to Dublin.

It was a relief that Aunty Cat had gone out for a walk, as Alison feared what she might say to the doctor if she were in his company.

"Was she feeling all right?" asked Lochlann.

"She said she wasn't suffering from any ill-effects."

"Thank heavens for that. I'll catch up with her during the week. I have a serious proposition to put to her."

"She refused to tell us which hostel she was staying in. She still hasn't cooled down."

"I'll find her," said Lochlann. "It's not as if the city is overrun with hostels or Australians."

"How's Mary Anne?" asked Alison. "I would love to meet her."

"I'm sure you would, but now is not a good time. She is still unaware of your existence, thank goodness. She is in a bad enough state without having to cope with that. The exhibition and open day were a huge success, apparently. She was such a stoic to get through the day when the whole village was buzzing about the arrest of her fiancé. I will tell Mary Anne about you, I promise. I just need to judge when the time is right. And then we will arrange a meeting."

"Thank you. I look forward to that."

Alison had visions of Mary Anne's wishing to come out to Australia as soon as she found out about her real family. Alison, not Zita, would be in charge of her, seeing she was her twin. She would be so proud introducing her impressive brothers and pretty Hanna to her. Mary Anne would win them all over in no time, even Dan, and Alison wouldn't feel a hint of jealousy, only pride. And she would feel happier than she had ever felt, with her old demon of loneliness no longer able to torment her.

"What can I do to make it up to Zita?" asked Alison, ill in bed.

"Give it time," said Cat. "It's only a week. She'll realise eventually that you didn't mean what you said."

But I did. I just should have kept it to myself. "What if she never speaks to me again?"

"Then that will be her choice and there won't be anything you can do about it."

"Zita had planned that night for years and sacrificed everything to it."

"Once again, that was her choice. Now stop fretting or you'll make yourself worse."

"Do you think we can move on to Galway, and give up on Cork for the time being? At least I could go to see a doctor there without any risk of being recognised, and I could be prescribed something to make me sleep. I feel dizzy all the time from the lack of it." Alison's eyeballs felt as if they had been scratched and her stomach was in a constant state of tension.

"That's a good idea," said Cat. "You'll soon be back to normal once you get your sleep pattern sorted out."

As if she could ever get back to normal with Zita cutting her out of her life.

If only I hadn't said those things, she thought. Why didn't I once thank her or tell her that I admired her?

And why am I constantly thinking of Mary Anne and William and wishing I could see them? Dr Carmody said everyone thought they would marry each other, but Mary Anne chose someone else. William is unattached.

"And let's not leave a forwarding address," she said. "We can ring back at a later time to see if there are any letters or messages for us."

"If that's what you want." Cat sat down on the side of the bed. "I've been thinking. Wondering. Do you know what I've been wondering? I've been churning it over and over in my mind. What I'd like to know is why didn't the doctor say that his wife had given birth to twins rather than that Nell had? You know your mother didn't know she was carrying twins, and if the doctor's wife had been she mightn't have known either. It wouldn't be the first or last time a doctor didn't know there were twins on the way. Nell would have gone home happy with one live baby and would not have been killed looking for Dolores. Mrs Carmody was obviously happy with a live child at last. Do you not think that would have been a kinder thing for the doctor to do?"

"I don't know what to think. My brain is scrambled."

"I'm not surprised after all you've been through. I mean, he had done something so wicked that what difference would an untruth make to his conscience? To lie about which mother had the twins would have been a great kindness, to my way of thinking, that's all I can say."

Back in Dublin, a week after the banquet, Lochlann confessed to Mary Anne. She said, from her point of view, that stealing her was the best thing he had ever done. She secretly presumed, however, that some nurse had been guilty of a mix-up at the hospital, and that Lochlann had taken the blame. Next he told Niamh, who had misinterpreted his melancholy withdrawals throughout their married life and was relieved to hear the real cause of them. She secretly thought that it was Charlotte who stole the baby – she was good at appropriating people who didn't belong to her – and that Lochlann was taking the blame to shield her. Mary Anne told Toby, to whom she was now engaged, with a ring and a notice in the *Times* to make it official, and they both told William, who had remained puzzled about his meeting in Kildare Street with a girl he took to be Mary Anne but in some way felt she wasn't.

As a group, the five decided not to tell anyone else unless Alison turned up in person and they were forced to acknowledge her.

Lochlann tried to organise a meeting between Mary Anne and the Hogans. He contacted the Ballybrian Hotel only to be told that the

Hogans had moved out and had not left any forwarding address. After many phone calls he located the hostel in which Zita had stayed, to be told she also had moved out and had left no forwarding address.

Lochlann secretly hoped that the sisters had returned to Australia and, if there were to be a meeting of the twins, it would take place there.

"Could you not say the mix-up was accidental if you were questioned?" Niamh asked, worried about the effects of a full revelation.

"I have no desire to. I felt a sense of relief when I told the Hogans. It was as if a large burden had been lifted off my shoulders. But let's not think about that until we have to, and hope it never comes to that."

CHAPTER 73

A solitary journalist sat yawning in the Oak Room of the Mansion House. He had drawn the short straw in his paper's newsroom, sent to report on Dr Lochlann Carmody's being awarded the Freedom of the City of Dublin. He was hardly going to get his first big scoop here covering this mundane event.

He looked through the list of previous recipients, noting the names of Charles Stewart Parnell, George Bernard Shaw, John McCormack and Hugh Lane, and compared their fame to the lack of fame of this ordinary man, who did good works in a foreign country, but was hardly worthy of being included in their company.

His editor had told him there was a chance he could be lucky. Both major political parties wanted Dr Carmody to stand under their banner in the next local elections with an eye to the general election after that, and they might send along some of their more senior ministers and, if they did, the journalist should be on the alert for some verbal sparring.

He read the doctor's profile:

First hospital appointment in Australia at the beginning of the war. Returned to serve in North Africa, and then took part in the D-Day landings in Normandy. Now working in a major hospital in

Dublin as a Consultant Physician. One daughter, Mary Anne, a medical student. The first wife drowned in the notorious Dark Waterhole on Tyringham Park estate in County Cork.

The journalist thought that one day he might research and write an article about the superstitions surrounding the Waterhole's drowned victims, and publish it around Halloween – it should create a lot of interest.

Married a second time. No children from the second union.

An old woman in a wheelchair, with a nurse in attendance, was brought in and positioned in the aisle near the front. The journalist enquired who she was, to find she was Lady Edwina Blackshaw, the mother-in-law of Dr Carmody.

The dignitaries entered in procession. After them came the Carmodys who all walked past the woman in the wheelchair and ignored her, even though she seemed to be keen to speak to them. The family took its place on the dais.

The daughter was a beauty. He could look at her all evening and consider his time well spent.

He counted four senior politicians in the crowd and wrote down their names – not that he was likely to forget them, but training was training.

The first person to speak after everyone was introduced was a medical volunteer. He praised Lochlann Carmody for organising the team of medics and dentists who gave up their annual leave to offer their services to the mission hospitals in Africa free of charge. The stories he told of the children who were released from pain, infections, blindness and speechlessness had members of the crowd applauding the work and smiling at the joy of it.

"Privileged as we are to live in a country where everyone has access to care, it is difficult for us to see such deprivation and not rage at the injustice of it."

Lochlann spoke next. The journalist noted his modest demeanour and thought to himself that here was a man not puffed up with his own importance. Funny how one could tell that just by studying someone for a few seconds. Perhaps his journalistic sensibilities made his observations more acute than those of an ordinary person.

It was a scandal that services such as those offered by the team were given on a charitable basis, Lochlann said, when they should be available as a right. European countries had enslaved the African people and plundered their natural wealth to create powerful empires, leaving the Africans with fractured societies and some roads that had been built to cart away their resources. Neither he nor any of the volunteers deserved recognition but he was accepting the award on behalf of the African people who had been so badly served by the developed world, and in the hope of pressurising the government into giving more aid to build and staff hospitals there.

He ended by saying, "Ireland is considered to be a poor country, but from what we have seen elsewhere it is wealthy beyond the dreams of many, and we can afford to be generous," and took his seat.

Two Fianna Fáil politicians spoke to each other with animation during the applause which was not as robust as it would have been had Lochlann told more heartrending and heart-warming stories rather than concentrating on the evils of colonialism, which everyone in the room knew about, having suffered under its yoke themselves, but didn't want to hear about at a social event.

The journalist was writing notes when he heard a loud communal gasp from the crowd. He looked up to see the doctor's daughter standing in front of the microphone on the spot that had been vacated by her father. Why was the crowd reacting? Why wouldn't a daughter wish to speak in favour of her father? Unusual for a female to do such a thing, of course, but hardly revolutionary enough to cause such a rumbling from the crowd. He glanced across at the doctor to gauge his reaction to his daughter's public display of support to see, not a proud paternal smile but a facial contortion of pain as if he had just been stabbed in the chest. Sitting beside him was his daughter – not up at the microphone? – with a similar look of horror on her face.

He looked back at the girl at the microphone and his journalist's antenna signalled a scoop at last.

The girl's hand shook so violently as she spread out a single sheet of paper on the lectern in front of her that he doubted if she would be able to read a word. Two grim-faced young men, one slender with floppy hair and the other broad-shouldered and darkly threatening, stood up from the front row and approached the podium.

They are going to bundle her off. Her presence here is obviously unexpected and unwanted and we'll soon hear why if they let her speak – if she can manage to speak in her agitated state.

The doctor motioned for the two young men to go back and sit down, and spoke urgently to the daughter sitting beside him and held her hand.

His gaze, fixed on the girl about to speak, had turned from horrified to resigned, the journalist noticed. That's odd, he thought, when the others are so antagonistic. The wife reached out to touch her husband's hand and squeeze it momentarily. What could that possibly signify?

The girl waited until the two young men had resumed their seats. The floppy-haired one lifted his clasped hands in a pleading gesture. The girl saw it and shook her head to signal a refusal of his request and, by the look of her, took no pleasure in doing so.

The doctor's daughter sprang out of her chair and went to beg the girl at the microphone not to speak.

"I'm doing this for Zita," was her reply.

The doctor came up to claim his daughter and gently led her back to her seat.

Some members of the crowd were silent, trying to hear above the noise the rest were making.

An official loomed up, but Lochlann lifted up his hand in a gesture that indicated he should not interfere.

"Go on, Alison," he said finally to the twin at the microphone. "Say what you came here to say."

Lochlann wondered in a detached way whether, if he had picked up Alison instead of Mary Anne that night at the hospital, Mary Anne would be now standing in front of the microphone ready to say the damning words that were about to ruin his life, and would it be Alison sitting beside him?

CHAPTER 74

As part of her routine, Zita read selected items from the daily paper to Tadhg's dying father to divert him. She had offered to help out after the father had suffered a second stroke, at least until the following month when she was due to catch the boat back home to Australia, by which time the father was expected to be dead. She'd had no contact with Cat or Alison since she left Doughertys' Hotel, and didn't expect to see or hear from them until they met on the boat. After that, she wondered if she and Alison would ever become reconciled. She couldn't imagine that they would after the harsh things Alison had said to her. As far as Mary Anne was concerned, she still had no inclination to get in touch with her, even though she often passed by her door.

She had a lot of thinking to do as her options, which had once seemed so limited, had expanded at an exhilarating rate.

Aunty Cat had offered, not only to fund her medical training, but to give her an allowance generous enough to free her from having to work during the holidays to make money to live on. ("You have worked long enough and hard enough to earn a break from all that," Cat had said.) And on top of all that, Zita would not be expected to live with Cat to cut down on expenses, but was to live in a college on campus so that she could fully participate in university life.

327

And then there was Tadhg, soon to be released from his family responsibilities and still eager to emigrate to Australia. He and she had grown very close to each other since she had moved in to help with nursing the father after the stroke.

And then there was Dr Carmody's wish to put a 'serious proposition' to her, as he had told her during the night he had kept watch over her and Alison. She had not questioned him at the time as she could not bring herself to speak to him. Could he possibly be thinking of making some kind of recompense to the Hogans for the loss of Mary Anne?

She nearly missed the small article on the ninth page, but the word 'Australian' caught her eye.

Doctor Commits Almost Perfect Crime. Exposed by Australian Twin, was the heading, followed by:

A doctor preparing to be given the honour of Freeman of the City of Dublin was exposed as a child thief and, as a result, the honour was not bestowed.

The popular humanitarian Dr Lochlann Carmody was tipped to win a seat in the next Parliamentary elections, but after these revelations is not expected to stand. He was struck off the Medical Register, and will be replaced as the co-ordinator of charity work abroad. He is quoted as saying he has no ill will against Alison Hogan, the identical twin of his stolen daughter, who exposed him in a most dramatic fashion at the ceremony in front of family and dignitaries, who were unaware of the twin's existence. There were attempts to remove the young woman, but it was Dr Carmody himself who insisted that she complete her testimony.

One irate alderman interrupted Miss Hogan, asking her what relevance Dr Carmody's private life had to do with his humanitarian work. The alderman was ruled out of order and asked to return to his place. He left the room in protest.

An elderly woman, who turned out to be the doctor's mother-in-law, was taken ill in her wheelchair and received medical attention on the premises before being taken off to hospital by ambulance.

At the conclusion of the speech, Mary Anne Carmody turned her back on her twin and on her father. It was Dr Carmody, who had wept when he heard of the death of the twins' mother, who approached Alison Hogan, and enclosed her in an embrace that she appeared to welcome and to accept with gratitude.

If you enjoyed
Return to Tyringham Park by Rosemary McLoughlin,
why not try the first two chapters of a previous title
Tyringham Park
also published by Poolbeg.

TYRINGHAM
PARK

ROSEMARY MCLOUGHLIN

PART ONE: THE COUNTRY

CHAPTER 1

Tyringham Park, 1917

The mother wasn't seen to lose her composure and the father didn't return from London when Victoria Blackshaw, the pretty one, went missing at the age of twenty-two months.

The first person to notice that the baby carriage was empty was the mother, Edwina Blackshaw, and the second was Manus, the horse-trainer.

Edwina, disbelieving, snatched up the tartan quilt and the feather mattress, shook them, and let them drop from her hand to the ground. She felt around the dark interior of the carriage for Victoria's red-headed doll or anything that might provide a clue to the child's absence, but the only things her hands touched were a crumbling biscuit and a teething ring.

Manus noted with relief that all the stalls and the gate leading into the paddock were closed, but was sickened to see that one of the double doors of the stables entrance was unsecured and standing slightly open. He wrenched the door fully open and raced to check the avenue in front of the stables, and the banks of the flooded river behind it, then the weir and the bridge with its view downstream, before running around the perimeters of the outbuildings, expecting to see a little figure in white every time he turned a corner.

Edwina tested the latches of the seven occupied stalls first, rattling the lower half-doors to see if they were fastened and not merely closed over. The instinct of a horse, no matter how docile, to lash out if grabbed by the back leg without warning was what she feared; a little body smashed up against a wall was what she dreaded to find.

In a state of heightened expectation Manus ran back into the courtyard in the hope that Edwina had found Victoria in his absence, a hope so strong he thought for one second he saw the child's outline, but the image quickly dissolved. With uncharacteristic roughness he pulled Mandrake out from his stall and, despite the gelding's sidestepping in reaction to the panic in the atmosphere, had him bridled and saddled in a minute.

"I'll follow the river in case she went in," he said, mounting.

"Get help first in the hope that she didn't." Edwina was standing in the middle of the yard, swaying slightly. "We need to widen the search immediately."

By now he presumed the child had fallen into the river and been carried away but he didn't want to take away her hope by disobeying her order. Silently cursing the minutes he would lose by riding up to the house, he did as she commanded.

Edwina found herself turning in circles as one indecision followed another. She knew so little about her daughter. Was she two yet? Having falsified the date of birth on official records, she could never remember which was Victoria's real birth date and which was her registered one. Surely the child must be two by now? Were two-year-olds capable of clambering out of carriages unaided, or would someone have to lift them? Could Victoria climb? Walk a distance? Make her way back to the house?

If Edwina knew the answers to these questions and if she had any idea how long the child had been missing she might have had some inkling of what to do next.

Later she explained to the policemen that she had positioned the baby carriage on the shady side of the courtyard, confident that Victoria would sleep for an hour (information supplied by the nanny, though she didn't mention that to them) while she helped Manus change the dressings on the shin of a nervous filly. The wound exposed the bone and a flap of skin and flesh was dangling, she elaborated to add realism to her account. Manus couldn't have managed on his own without causing distress to the animal. Of course he could have waited until the stable lads returned but, seeing she was there, it would have been foolish not to make use of her expertise. So Victoria was unattended for about twenty minutes (it was actually forty but Edwina affected vagueness so she wouldn't have to admit to that) and the child could have disappeared any time during that period.

When they asked her if she had felt the mattress before lifting it out, to see if it was still warm, she had to admit that in her distracted state she hadn't thought of it, and when they asked if the double doors had been open or closed at the time she went to attend to the filly, she said that they certainly were closed – she would have shut them behind her out of habit after she'd wheeled Victoria into the courtyard.

And what was Victoria's date of birth? The inspector turned the page of his notebook and, pen poised, waited for the answer.

Edwina's mind went blank.

"Excuse me a moment," she said, rising from her chair and leaving the room, feeling no obligation to give any reason for her departure to the two policemen.

The housekeeper Miss East never forgot how Manus appeared on horseback like a messenger from the Apocalypse to bring the bad news up the hill to the house.

His shouting brought her flying out through the front door.

"Victoria has gone missing. Round up everyone!" he called across to her, making no attempt to prevent the swerving, stamping Mandrake from damaging the lawn with deep gouges and hoofprints.

Despite her fear of horseflesh Miss East ran onto the grass right in front of the animal to find out more details. Mandrake high-stepped backwards at her approach and Manus didn't check him.

"I'm searching the river. I fear she's drowned," were his only responses to her outpouring of questions. He turned with a snap of the reins and Mandrake, reacting, accelerated with such speed that Manus barely had time to shout over his shoulder, "The stables!" before he was gone, leaving Miss East's person splattered with clods of earth.

Fired by an awful dread, she rushed around the house to the

walled garden adjoining the kitchens. With relief she saw quite a number of the servants in the enclosure, all making the most of the sun: some sleeping, some talking or playing cards and one poking at a line of ants with a stick.

"Listen! Everyone listen!" she thought she shouted, and then clapped her hands when no one moved. She called out in a stronger voice. "Victoria is missing! Come quickly!" This time they heard and stumbled upright, dazed and sluggish from the sun, exclaiming and cursing. "Stables," she pointed, then flapped her hands as if herding geese. "Immediately. Go quickly. Run!"

They were already moving off.

She followed them through the garden gate, and called to the youngest boy, "Ned! Your legs are younger than mine," and had to pause to catch her breath before adding, "Run as fast as you can. Tell Sid and then the steward. Tell them to go to the stables. There's a good lad."

The boy looked pleased to be singled out. He promptly changed direction and headed for the coachman's little cottage behind the rowan trees, some distance from the house.

Miss East felt her agitation quieten a little. The servants would be able to cover a lot of ground in a short time, and the steward and Sid would take charge and know what to do.

I wouldn't want to be in Nurse Dixon's shoes, she thought to herself, not for all the tea in China. With all her faults, and God knows she has plenty of them, she's never managed to lose a child before now.

As she ran after the others, two maids, mindful of the limitations of middle age, turned back to check that she was all right but she waved them on, saying she was fine, she would only hold them back, and to keep going. When they rounded the corner of the house her legs weakened and she sank to the ground on her knees. Dear God, she prayed, let the precious little one already be found. Please, Lord, have pity and don't let her come to any harm.

CHAPTER 2

With her back to the window and a hand mirror held to reflect light on her face, Nurse Dixon searched for laughter lines around her eyes and was relieved to see there weren't any. Look at her friend Teresa Kelly, run out of options, gone with her wrinkly old face to the other side of the earth at the age of forty to marry a sixty-year-old stranger because she was desperate to have a child and a home of her own before it was too late.

There's no way I'd let that happen to me, Nurse Dixon told herself with feeling. Not that it ever could, not with my youth and looks, and the divine Manus about to propose at any moment.

Tilting the cheval mirror, she noted her waist and ankles were still slender, and, angling the hand mirror, checked her back and side views – good posture, good tilt of the head. She must remember that pose – it was particularly flattering. She would try it out next time she saw Manus.

The clock on the nursery wall chimed three. Teresa Kelly would be leaving Ballybrian about now, Lady Blackshaw would be bringing Victoria back soon, and then the long dreary evening would begin.

With the once-placid Victoria, the pretty one, beginning to show signs of alarming wilfulness, Dixon was glad that someone else would be wasting years of effort trying to straighten her out, only in the end to find her turning out like Charlotte, the plain one. How wonderful to leave the Park and marry Manus at last, escaping the bone-aching tedium of rearing two rich brats. Her own children when she had them would be hard-working and sensible and a credit to her. And, of course, bonny. How could they escape being bonny with herself and Manus as parents?

She sat down to rub lemon juice into her hands, and let her mind turn, as it often did, to the injustices in life. If fate had been more kind to her and less kind to Lady Blackshaw, they could be sisters: both light-brown-haired and attractive, both tall and strong, both young. She wouldn't mind the gulf between them so much if Her Ladyship made the most of her position by indulging in a life of luxury and fashion, but she went around all day with her untidy hair piled on the top of her head with a single comb that couldn't cope with the straggly bits, and worse, wore men's riding breeches stained with saddle oil and horse sweat and didn't even dress for dinner while the master was away, which was most of the time. Dixon remembered the day she saw Lady Blackshaw in the full riding habit – top hat, veil, fitted jacket, silk stock, tailored skirt and fine leather gloves and boots – and how she had almost swooned at the elegance of it, and how she couldn't believe it when she heard it was the last time her mistress would dress like that as she intended to switch from the side-saddle to riding astride, as she had done as a girl, so that she could fulfil her ambition of riding like a man. "If it was good enough for Joan of Arc and Marie Antoinette to ride like that, it's good enough for me," she was reported to have told a conservative old neighbour who admonished her for adopting such an immodest and unladylike style. "And look what happened to them," the old woman responded with relish. "And served them right."

As the wait for the servants to arrive lengthened, Edwina, after retracing the route around the stables that Manus had already followed, took the steps up to check the first-storey quarters where the stable lads lived. If Victoria could climb, the steps up to it might have caught her eye. Only one door was open – it revealed a small kitchen – and it took only a moment to see that there was no one in it. The three men had gone to a shebeen in the village as they did every Friday afternoon. She already knew of their routine and hadn't expected to find anyone in their quarters.

Standing on the balcony, looking down on the enclosed courtyard, she sensed that the baby carriage and tartan quilt were accusing her from the opposite wall.

She would not allow herself to think of the child and the river and the open door in a single image.

What Manus had told her earlier came back to puzzle her like a half-forgotten refrain. Teresa Kelly, he'd said, was so devoted to Victoria he couldn't believe she would let herself be parted from her, and right up to the last minute he had thought she would change her mind and, for the sake of the child, not leave the Park. But he'd been mistaken. She had left. She was already gone.

It was the word 'gone' that resonated with Edwina and the fact that Manus, a man not given to idle conversation, had thought the woman's leaving worth mentioning in the first place.

Twenty minutes after he'd told her about Teresa Kelly, Victoria was gone as well.

She wished he hadn't ridden off so abruptly before she'd had time to question him further. It was a seven-mile stretch of river from the Park to the sea. If he had to ride the full distance it would be hours before she saw him again.

It was only when the gravel dug into the soles of her feet that Miss East realised she was wearing her indoor shoes, now wet and looking two sizes larger with all the mud clinging to them. Under ordinary circumstances Lady Blackshaw would be cross if she saw her housekeeper inappropriately shod, with soil stuck to her usually spotless clothing, but at a time like this she would surely hardly notice such things. Was that Sid driving off in a pony and trap along the avenue towards the gate lodge? How had he harnessed up so quickly? Had she miscalculated the time she'd spent in that blackout of anguish after the servants had left her?

Ignoring her tears and her status, she ran the rest of the way to the stables.